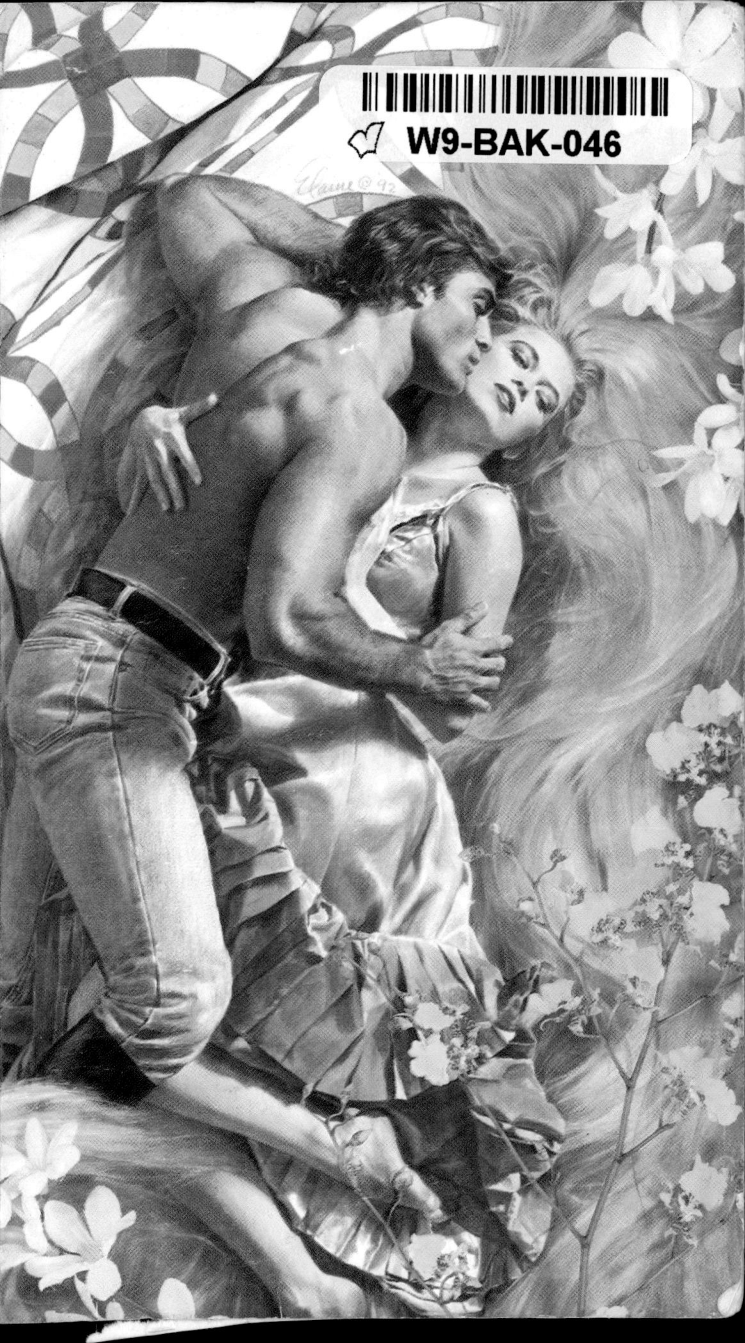

There was a grander design at work—a design that was altering the fabric of Madeleine's inner being. With the innocence of a child, she stepped into the water and waded in to her waist. It was cool, rushing around her, startlingly pleasurable against her bare legs.

Fresh and invigorating, the waterfall cascaded over her arm, then her shoulder, and finally, as she stepped forward, Maddie's entire body. It was glorious. She rubbed the bar of soap over her skin and watched the froth rinse away in the next instant. When she stretched up her arms to wash her hair, the sensation of water streaming down her exposed breasts, belly, and thighs was sheer ecstasy. Through the blurry curtain of water, Maddie saw the china blue sky, the shallow curve of the stream bank, a hawk gliding in the distance . . . and Fox standing high above her on the rim of the gulch, shirtless, staring.

FIREBLOSSOM

Cynthia Wright

BALLANTINE BOOKS • NEW YORK

Copyright © 1992 by Cynthia Wright Hunt

All rights reserved under International and Pan-American Copyright Conventions. Published in the United States of America by Ballantine Books, a division of Random House, Inc., New York, and simultaneously in Canada by Random House of Canada Limited, Toronto.

Library of Congress Catalog Card Number: 92-90622

ISBN 0-345-36782-0

Manufactured in the United States of America

First Edition: November 1992

This book is dedicated to the two men in my life—Gene Challed, my colorful father, who took me to Little Bighorn when I was a little girl, and Jim Hunt, my husband, who turns research trips (and everyday life!) into romantic adventures. You both are wonderful and I am very lucky!

PROLOGUE

June 24–25, 1876
Little Bighorn River country, Montana Territory

"Our nation is melting away like the snow on the sides of the hills where the sun is warm, while your people are like the blades of grass in the spring when the summer is coming."
—Red Cloud of the Oglala Sioux

"It is a good day to fight! Strong hearts, brave hearts to the front!"
—Crazy Horse, June 25, 1876

I<small>T WAS THE SAME DREAM AGAIN</small>.

Dan Matthews jolted awake shortly before eleven P.M. Next to him in the bivouac, Capt. Myles Keogh snored lustily. All around him lay more than six hundred soldiers sleeping on makeshift pallets. Enlisted men—officers, and scouts in Lt. Col. George Custer's Seventh Cavalry. Most were unashamedly exhausted after the two days of thirty-mile marches up a dust-choked Rosebud Creek. They were "huntin' Indians," tracking them as if they were antelope or buffalo.

Dan was so tired, he was numb. Still, the dream—a haunting blend of his father's colorful stories and his own, more recent experiences—would not leave him alone.

In it he found himself in a spacious Lakota Sioux tipi, lying on buffalo robes and munching cherries. The air was rich with life smells and a sense of peace that was overwhelming. The Lakota men, finished with the day's work, were lying in their tipis and around campfires, telling stories and playing with their children. Women puttered around the village, watching over their men and children, making jerky or tending to other chores while chatting among themselves. A lethargy stole over Dan, too, like a blanket of peace. His Indian brethren smiled at him, calling him Fox-With-Blue-Eyes. The differences between them were many, but therein lay the lessons. Had God, who made all races, intended one to rule over others?

3

Dan's father had taught him much about the native people of the plains, whom he saw as appealingly human and fascinatingly, proudly different from whites. Zachary Matthews had been a fur trader with the American Fur Company and had lived for months at a time among the Sioux and other tribes. After journeying East to Washington, D.C., in 1843, he'd married a schoolteacher named Annie Sunday, and one year later Daniel was born. As time passed, Zach returned less and less to the West and his old, free life. But he'd relived the best of his past with his sturdy, blue-eyed son. Spellbound, Dan would listen for hours to tales of villages that covered acres of rough prairie and cottonwood valleys, buffalo herds that blackened the Great Plains and inspired hunts that took days and proved the stamina of Indian warriors, and a philosophy of life and nature that was a far cry from that of the white world. Zachary had learned to enjoy the present during the seasons he'd spent among these happy, prosperous, relaxed people who appeared to have been born completely free of avarice.

The lessons Dan had learned from Zachary—of humility, honor, and respect—would stand him in good stead through the years. While serving in the Union Army during the Civil War, he was rewarded with a commission for his fearless, intelligent leadership of volunteers—but the cause had been clear and just: Daniel Matthews had killed to end slavery and reunify the nation.

After the war he'd left the army, studying in Europe and then retracing his father's routes in the Dakota Territory. There Dan lived among the Oglala and Miniconjou tribes of the Lakota Sioux, who named him Fox, or Fox-With-Blue-Eyes. The experience both exhilarated and disturbed him. As he became painfully aware of the wave of events that was slowly destroying the Indians' way of life, his confidence in the government he had so valiantly defended just years before was undermined. After Zachary's death in 1874, Dan returned to Washington to be with Annie Sunday Matthews. Old friends, whose careers had flourished following the Civil

War, now urged him to come back to the army: officers of quality were badly needed on the frontier.

Dan had flatly refused any involvement in the Indian Wars until President Grant invited him to the White House for a drink this past April. Grant was furious with Lt. Col. George Armstrong Custer, who had recently come to Washington to testify before Congress about frontier fraud and had said all the wrong things. Although the president didn't even want to send Custer back to take part in the campaign to drive the Sioux out of the unceded territory between the Great Sioux Reservation and the Bighorn Mountains of Wyoming, the other officers involved felt that Custer was an important asset.

"I want you to keep an eye on that hothead for me," President Grant said vaguely. "If you'll resume your commission, I'll make you a captain. What do you say? I know you're fond of the plains and you know that world out there. Also, you're acquainted with Custer, aren't you?"

"We knew each other. I served under him briefly soon after he was made a brigadier general," Dan had replied, weighing each word as he met Grant's sharp eyes. "You know far better than I, sir, that the war poured glory over the heads of some very young men. In my opinion, Custer may have been bright and daring, but he was never careful. When threatened, he knew only one course of action: charge the enemy at any cost. We didn't get along; he wasn't one to consider his options by calculating the loss of lives, and I wasn't able to take orders from him in good conscience."

The president waved his hand, drained his glass, and said, "Oh, I know all about Custer—and even though my approach to winning that cursed war was not unlike the one you've just described, that doesn't mean he and I are alike. I did what had to be done to end the bloody business; Custer was caught up in the romance of the charge." Lighting a cigar, he closed his eyes for a moment as if overwhelmed by the past. "Well, it wasn't pleasant, but we had to win, and I know that you will agree with me on that score, Matthews. Now then, back to the matter at hand. You're a man of principle. What I'm asking you to do is not a task that will earn you pleasure or prestige or the sort of glory you mentioned before. All I can tell you is that I have serious concerns about sending Custer back to the Indian Wars; it's a feeling in my gut. I would sleep better if I knew that someone I could trust was there—''

''Mr. President, with all due respect, I sympathize with your concerns about Lieutenant Colonel Custer, but I must tell you that I am morally opposed to this war that we are waging against the Indians. If there were some other way I could help—''

''But there is! It's a simple enough matter, Matthews. You needn't resume your commission if that's what's bothering you. I'll send you West to join the Seventh Cavalry as a 'special adviser.' Wouldn't you like to go West? Feel free to stay on after this business is over. Wonderful time of year to be outdoors!'' Pleased with this new scheme, Grant rubbed his hands together, his cigar trapped between his weathered fingers. ''You have the credentials, having spent time living with the Indians, to be qualified as an adviser, but what I really want is for you to stick close to that vain lieutenant colonel. Thank the good Lord he stopped being a general when the war ended! Anyway, if you can just keep an eye on him and try to see to it that he doesn't do anything crazy, I'll be grateful. You know, he's been badgering me all week for an interview so that he can wrap up his business in Washington and get back to his regiment. I've put him off, saying I have a cold, while I've tried to come up with a plan. I couldn't find you for three days and had to refuse Custer permission to leave the city!'' The president chuckled, then fixed the handsome young man with a keen stare. ''I want you to be on the train to Chicago with him; I expect he'll manage to escape by the first of May. You'll go with papers from me . . . like a thorn I've pushed into his side that he can't remove. Are we in accord?''

A sense of duty and a spirit of adventure compelled Dan to agree, though he had strong misgivings. Everything he knew about the wave of change that held all of America's Indians in its grip repulsed him. He didn't want to contribute to the forced destruction of their culture. But he'd wondered if his silence and lack of participation might not prove equally destructive. So Dan had agreed to serve—as an adviser—and now found himself in the midst of a nightmare, attached to Company C of the Seventh Cavalry.

The sounds of Keogh's lusty snores mingled with those of other men and with the nighttime rustling of animals in the brush. But as Dan lay there listening, he heard something else as well—something unexpected but unmistakable: others were awake. He sat up and donned his boots, then stepped out of the bivouac to stand in a spill of moonlight.

Maj. Marcus A. Reno, sent to rouse Matthews as well as other assorted officers for a premidnight meeting with Custer, paused momentarily as he rounded a tent and caught sight of the younger man. The swarthy, unappealing Reno could not suppress a pang of jealousy at the sight of Dan standing tall and unself-conscious in the starlight, buttoning his shirt with lean fingers. He was handsome, but wore his looks easily, without conceit. At better than six feet tall, he possessed the bronzed, hard-muscled physique of a seasoned trooper; his chiseled face was clean-shaven, his chestnut hair cut too short to curl as it preferred to do. Dan's eyes, a clean, piercing blue that made them unforgettable, were honest. He didn't often voice his opinions, but his eyes betrayed him. Custer sensed his disapproval, and it was no secret that the flamboyant commander put up with Matthews only because President Grant wished it. Right now, sorely aware that he was in Grant's bad graces, Custer would have tolerated much to regain the favor of his commander in chief.

"Lieutenant Colonel Custer wants to see the officers in his tent," Reno said as he approached Matthews. "You're invited too, I guess."

Dan, scraping a match that flared as he lit a cheroot, merely nodded. Should he be surprised that Custer was rousting the men from their exhausted slumber? On the contrary, he had come to expect that which made the least sense. To his mind, the most insane thing was their presence in the area at all.

Two days after splitting from General Terry's forces, the Seventh Cavalry had headed up Rosebud Creek with instructions to track the Sioux and Cheyenne. The plan called for Custer to join with Colonel Gibbon and the other companies that remained with Terry, then together entrap the recalcitrant Indians with a pincer movement. Earlier that morning, however, Custer's men had come upon the site of a recently held Sun Dance, complete with ominous drawings in the sand that had made the Indian scouts highly uneasy. Apparently Sitting Bull, a highly honored Hunkpapa Sioux medicine man who was thought to be leading the renegade Indians, had had a vision as a result of the Sun Dance, a vision that foretold an attack on their village by white soldiers. According to the drawings, all would be killed by the Sioux and Cheyenne warriors.

Although Custer and his officers had scoffed at such nonsense, the scouts had looked worried. This was evidence of powerful medicine—left in the wake of a trail that was much fresher than anyone had imagined. The valley was covered with the scratches of trailing lodge poles, and the grass was close-cropped for miles around, indicating the recent presence of a huge pony herd. In the end Custer had sent his Crow scouts ahead to figure out what the new signs meant.

Now, following Reno back toward Custer's bivouac, Dan recalled a conversation he'd had that very afternoon in the sweltering Montana sunshine.

"Do you ever question what you're doing here?" he'd asked a trooper named Jeb Campbell as they'd lingered over an unappetizing, salty lunch.

"What I'm doin' here?" Campbell had repeated, swig-

ging whiskey from a beaten tin flask. His stained front tooth
was broken in half and he sucked on it as if to hide it. "Well,
sir, I'm here to kill Injins. Everybody knows that they'll run
if they see us comin', so we hafta be careful to keep 'em
from escaping."

"Why do we have to kill them?" Dan asked carefully.

Campbell gave him a darting, uncertain look. Although
this man had been with the Seventh for only half a dozen
weeks and he didn't wear a uniform, he acted like an officer
and was treated like an officer. But what soldier talked like
this? "Well, uh, we hafta kill 'em 'cause they won't stand
aside and let us whites make progress. They murder our set-
tlers and try to stop the railroad. Christ, everyone knows that
the Injins is ignorant scum, and pagan savages to boot! Sir—
what's yer name?"

"Matthews." Dan considered for a moment, then said
what was easiest and what he and President Grant had agreed
upon. Even an adviser ought to have a title. "I'm Captain
Matthews, Private Campbell."

The scrawny trooper squinted, then shrugged. "Huh?
Well, Cap'n, it seems to me that the only answer is to get rid
of every damn one of them redskins!"

"But . . . did it ever occur to you that they were here first?
What gives us the right to push them off land where they have
lived for hundreds, maybe thousands, of years?"

"Whose side you on, Captain?" Jeb demanded, narrowing his eyes and sucking agitatedly on his broken
tooth. "Fact is, they ain't human like us. We're Christian; God's for *us*."

Since the Civil War, Dan knew better than to engage in
arguments regarding God's opinion on such matters. "What
about the Laramie Treaty? We promised the Indians they
could continue to live and hunt here—this *is* unceded territory, after all. It's been only eight years. Is it right for our
government to make promises and then change the rules?"
Dan's blue eyes had grown darker as he spoke, though his
tone remained calm.

"Look here," Jeb Campbell hissed, "why pretend? Everyone knows that this is all about the Black Hills . . . and the piles of gold waitin' there. Why couldn't they of just forgot about that durned treaty, give us back the Hills, and spared us all a lot of trouble and bloodshed? Ever since gold was found there in '74, we knew we'd hafta get the Hills back from them heathens. They don't even have the sense to dig the gold out themselves! Maybe you didn't know this, bein' from the East, but the Injins think the Black Hills is sacred, and they only go up there in the fall to cut *lodge poles*! There's gold everywhere and they don't even *care*! Well, let me tell you, Cap'n, white folks care about gold!" He laughed harshly. "We ain't fools like those red savages!"

"You're right, Campbell," Dan agreed, with a dry smile, "you and the Sioux have nothing in common."

They'd marched and ridden on after that lengthy lunch near the site of the Indian Sun Dance, finally making camp. The Crow scouts still had not rejoined the regiment at dusk. Hours later, while Dan was trying to sleep, Goes Ahead, Curly, Hairy Moccasin, and White-Man-Runs-Him rode wearily into the camp and reported their findings to Custer.

Now other officers were scrambling into the moonlit night, rubbing their eyes, buttoning trousers, and appearing generally disoriented. Lt. Col. George Armstrong Custer sat at a folding table inside his white tent. The light from a guttering candle played over his sunburned, aquiline features, drooping mustache, and pale brows. Although famous for his long, curling "yellow hair," Custer now wore his locks cut short. Slicked down with cinnamon oil, his hair and beard were unromantically brown.

When Dan entered the commanding officer's bivouac, he received the most cursory of glances. It obviously galled Custer to be polite to this "adviser" in order to mend fences with President Grant.

The officers, including Custer's brother Tom and his brother-in-law James Calhoun, crowded into the bivouac around Daniel Matthews. Never had Dan witnessed so much internal conflict within a regiment as he had these past weeks with the Seventh Cavalry. Although several officers backed their commander, others barely concealed their contempt for their leader. Custer's two senior subordinates, Reno and Benteen, were the most glaring examples.

"I've had to make a decision," Custer announced. The candle flame danced fitfully over his face and his scarlet cravat. "The scouts tell me that General Terry's intelligence was in error. The Indians are not on the Rosebud. Their trail goes west just ahead of us, then climbs the divide between the Rosebud and the Little Bighorn rivers. The freshness of this trail makes it clear that the Indians must be on the lower Little Bighorn."

A tense hush fell over the men while Custer drank from a cup. "We await your decision, sir," Lt. William Cooke said.

"Well, we're going to march, of course," their commander said in cavalier tones. "Now. Tonight. We'll alter our course and march through the night across the divide, rest tomorrow and establish the location of the hostiles' camp—and then surprise them with a dawn attack the morning of the twenty-sixth." He drew his brows together grimly. "Of course, you'll all agree that we can waste no time. If the Indians suspect that we are coming, they will scatter across the prairie rather than fight."

Dan's mind whirled. He knew that this theory about the Sioux being cowards was nonsense and realized that all these weeks he had refused to seriously consider the possibility that Custer might be shrewd enough to track them down and engage in an actual battle. There were other, more immediate concerns as well.

"Sir, the men are extremely tired after the past two days," Dan suggested quietly. "Perhaps it would be better to let them sleep tonight—"

Custer's eyes blazed. "No. These are the experiences that make men of boys and heroes of men! We're going *immediately*!" He jumped to his feet, emanating a manic energy that sent chills down Dan's back. Looking around at his stunned officers, Lieutenant Colonel Custer took great gulps of air to calm himself, then added, "Allow me to remind you that the element of surprise is crucial. No man must stray from his column or raise his voice. Trumpet calls are forbidden." He set his chin jauntily. "Now then, I'm counting on all of you. Rouse the troops and tell them that the adventure is about to commence in earnest!"

The Seventh Cavalry seemed to grope its way through the night, marching clumsily up the harsh, rocky valley of a small stream. It was slow going, but Custer managed to coax six more miles out of his men before allowing them to make camp again, short of the summit. While they rested and made coffee, the Indian scouts and their leader, Lt. Charles Varnum, rode on ahead to locate the enemy.

Some of the men dozed on haversack pillows, but Dan's growing sense of unease would not grant him peace. After pouring himself a cup of coffee, which proved virtually undrinkable because of the alkaline water, he went to stand beside George Armstrong Custer.

"Matthews," Custer muttered in greeting, staring out into the rose-and-tangerine sunrise that stained the eastern sky.

Dan tried to read his face, which was partially shaded by a wide-brimmed white hat. "General," Dan murmured, using Custer's Civil War rank as a sign of courtesy, "why not let it go?"

His head seemed to snap back. "What are you talking about?" he inquired coldly.

"The battle you hope to fight. These Indians have done nothing to warrant this treatment—"

"President Grant issued the order for them to get off this unceded territory and back to their reservation. You know that. They had a deadline of January thirty-first, and when that date came and went without a response, they were certified as hostile. Are you saying that the president has changed his mind? If so, I wish he would have told me when I was in Washington." Custer spoke with icy finality.

Sensing that Custer was about to walk away, Dan said, "Sir, I am aware of the deadline that Sitting Bull and Crazy Horse ignored, but we could argue for hours about broken treaties and where blame lies on both sides. The truth, in human terms, is that the Indians should be commended for finding a way for so many different tribes, both Sioux and Cheyenne, to live together in peaceful cooperation. They only want to continue the traditions that were handed down for centuries before white men even knew this continent existed." He paused for effect, then finished, "Our government has made and broken an embarrassing number of promises to various Indian tribes. Is the Laramie Treaty to be tossed away as well?"

"Has the president sent you out here to *advise* me to call off the army's actions against the Indians?" Custer shot back in acid tones. "No? I thought not. I know what my job is; do you? I am here to follow orders, and those orders haven't been rescinded. Besides, the Indians have broken plenty of promises themselves." Satisfied with his handling of this annoying argument, Custer gave him a thin smile and turned away.

Dan had known it was useless, but he'd had to make the effort. The scouts were riding back into camp now, and he took a few steps backward, watching the scene unfold.

The scouts had gone up to Crow's Nest, which overlooked the Little Bighorn River fifteen miles away. Bluffs had obscured their view, but what they *could* see was a valley hazy with the smoke from campfires and, on the flats beyond the river's west bank, a moving smudge that denoted a huge pony herd. All signs pointed to a massive mobilization, far more Indians than any of them had supposed. Popular theory held that any Indian village could contain no more than a few hundred members, otherwise there would not be enough food for everyone or enough grass and water to support the warriors' ponies. Moreover, the Sioux were too feisty and uncivilized to maintain order in large numbers. Custer clung to those theories, shrugging off the scouts' fears and warnings.

Clad in a blue-gray flannel shirt, buckskin trousers tucked into boots, and a regular army hat, Custer now mounted his horse bareback and rode around camp in a fever, shouting orders to his thirty-two officers. At the cookfire of the Arikara scouts, he listened impatiently to the admonitions of Bloody Knife, a half-Sioux scout he had known for years.

"There are more Sioux ahead than you ever guessed, more Sioux than we have bullets," Bloody Knife warned. "If you attack without waiting for the other troops, it will take two or three days to finish fighting."

Custer smiled. "I guess we can finish them in a day. Besides, we cannot afford to wait for reinforcements. If we linger so near for very long, we risk discovery, in which case the entire village will be gone before we can mount an attack."

Listening, Daniel Matthews knew a sense of sickening doom. Custer had been handed an excuse to postpone his invasion and still he persisted, apparently caring as little for the lives of his own men as for those of the Sioux. Dan wished he could turn away, wished he'd never come. The insanity and injustice of the situation rose from his heart and gut, threatening to choke him.

As the columns began to move, Custer rode up to Crow's Nest for a look, and Varnum, Matthews, and a few other officers accompanied him. However, by the time they arrived the Little Bighorn was shrouded in a mist and no sign of the village was visible in the distant valley.

Dan followed Custer back to the main column of soldiers. "There's no need to rush, sir," he said as he brought his roan beside Custer's white-stockinged sorrel, Vic. "To attack, I mean. My sense is that we should listen to the scouts and exercise caution."

"Is Bloody Knife in charge here?" Custer shot back. "Bloody Knife talks as if there are *thousands* of Indians in that valley. Such harmony and cooperation among that race is unheard of, Matthews.'' He reined in Vic and stared into Dan's eyes for a moment. ''I think that these tales of 'the largest Indian camp in the world' are exaggerations, to put it kindly, and based more on the superstitious, fearful readings of those drawings in the sand than on actual sightings of the camp itself. In any case, you may relax your vigilance for the moment. As I said before, we shall spend today resting and taking stock of the situation.''

Lieutenant Colonel Custer urged the sorrel onward then, galloping down the grassy, dusty hillside toward the columns of troopers. Some had removed their blue coats in deference to the heat, rolling up their sleeves and donning straw hats. As Dan himself drew closer to the men, he read the panic and uncertainty in their expressions. Custer was conferring animatedly with Benteen and Reno, and suddenly it seemed very hot, as if the sun had intensified within seconds. Capt. Myles Keogh walked his horse, a clayback gelding called Comanche, over to Dan. Keogh sighed.

''What's happened?'' Dan drew off his gray slouch hat and raked a hand through his hair.

''We were still packing when one of the men spotted a couple Sioux warriors not far from camp. Then we saw another party a little while ago. The worry now is that they've already warned the village and it may be scattering as we speak.'' Keogh stroked his thick mustache. ''It would be a damned shame, wouldn't it? If we've come all this way, tracking the biggest village of all time, and they may escape before we can attack . . .''

Dan's head had begun to pound. How could these soldiers, many of whom had risked their lives to ensure that Negro slaves could enjoy the freedoms all Americans deserved, now care so little about the lives and rights of the Indians? Were gold and land more important than justice?

Custer was yelling, his face alight. ''We cannot wait or we shall lose them. We have no choice but to strike now. My adjutant, Lieutenant Cooke, will form the regiment into three battalions so that we may efficiently surround the hostiles and prevent their escape. Major Reno will command one battalion, Captain Benteen will lead the second, and I shall take the third and largest.'' George Armstrong Custer waved his hat in the air and declared, ''We'll win, boys! I could whip all the Indians on the continent with the Seventh Cavalry!''

Jeb Campbell, standing a few yards from Dan, could not contain his glee. With a grin that displayed his broken front tooth, he whooped, ''It's one helluva day to kill us some Injins!''

The scene on the hillside was charged with the thrill of impending conflict as Cooke began separating the men into battalions. Dan wheeled his roan around and went back to Custer. He found the commanding officer flushed, his eyes sparkling, fingers reflexively clenching Vic's reins.

''If you're determined to give me more advice, don't waste your breath,'' Custer said.

Dan's mind cautioned that he exercise calm and reason, but some other part of him was in charge. ''You can't do this! It's *mad*, don't you see that? I know the Sioux, and I can tell you that what the scouts saw this morning was *real*—not some vision to be scoffed at!''

''I really don't have time for this. I have been patient with you, Matthews, given the burden of my task here, but I've had enough. I wouldn't have thought you a coward, in light of your record as an officer in the Union Army, but perhaps I misjudged—''

Blue eyes blazing, Dan cut in, ''You are *wrong*! Even though I hate everything that this military exercise stands for, I am prepared to ride into battle with the Seventh if I cannot persuade you to listen to reason. In the meantime, I will do whatever it takes to stop this, though. Don't you see that this is *insane*? The Indians are *not* cowards; they won't run away if you wait for the other troops to arrive, but if you insist on attacking blindly, it won't be glory that you find.''

A vein stood out on Custer's brow as he leaned toward Dan and ground out, ''You could be court-martialed for insulting me this way, but you've kept yourself safe by coming out here as an 'adviser.' Well, Matthews, keep your advice and your insults to yourself. As for your offer to assist us when we ride into battle—I *decline*! I don't want any man near me today who isn't loyal to our cause. I want you to get out of here—not back to camp, but *gone*! You can go back to Washington and tell President Grant that if he wants me to have a keeper, he'll have to do the job *himself*!'' Custer was trembling with rage as he added, ''I am in command here, I am the *general*!''

Dan's head throbbed and sweat dripped down his neck as he turned and started to leave. This was the damnedest day of his life, worse than the bloodiest battle in the Civil War, because today he was torn apart, unable to steer events in what he knew was the right direction. If Custer held only his own fate in the balance, it wouldn't matter, but—

''Hey, Matthews! Where are you going?''

He glanced back to see Captain Keogh shading his eyes in the blinding sunlight, his expression quizzical. Rage burned like poison in Dan's gut. ''I'm getting the hell out of here!'' he shouted back.

At the top of the hill, he paused for a last look back. The troopers were divided into three battalions now, restless and eager for battle. Some were looking up the hill at him, no doubt wondering why he was leaving at such a moment. How unreal it all seemed, Dan thought . . . especially the Indians. Those young soldiers reminded him of boys playing war, certain only that they would emerge victorious and unbloodied.

Although Dan knew that he'd had no choice, that the policy behind this battle was corrupt, and that Custer had ordered him to leave, he felt oddly chilled; tainted somehow, like a deserter. All his life, he'd easily separated right from wrong, but now it was as if he'd reached a blind corner. His heart felt torn in two.

Wiping his tanned face with a kerchief, Dan watched the columns of mounted troopers start off across the parched ground toward the Little Bighorn. He shut his eyes, whispered a prayer for them, and then set off alone toward an unexpectedly muddied future.

PART ONE

"An Eden in the clouds—how shall I describe it! As well try to paint the flavor of a peach or the odor of a rose."
—Samuel Barrows—reporter and member of Black Hills Expedition of 1874.

Chapter One

THE LONG JOURNEY FROM PHILADELPHIA TO Deadwood had sorely tried Madeleine Avery's sense of decorum, but now she, her brother, and her grandmother were nearly to their new home. Their wagon jounced through the mud, up a precipitous road carved out of the mountains, and everyone in the wagon train said that Deadwood lay on the other side. Out West, people spoke the word *Deadwood* in the same tone reserved for *Paradise*. Everyone Maddie and her family had met during their days aboard trains, steamboat, and finally prairie schooner had been envious when the Averys had revealed their destination.

"Remember that man in Sioux City, Maddie?" Benjamin Avery, wide-eyed and grimy at nine years of age, scrambled back into the wagon to stare first at his sister and then at his grandmother. "He said that there's so much gold in Deadwood, the streets are covered with it! I'll bet that when we reach the top of this mountain and look down, we'll be able to see the town shining in the trees!"

"Well, it's a lovely thought, Benjamin, but I rather doubt that will be the case," Maddie replied, with a weary smile.

The Black Hills themselves were incredibly beautiful, although they had entered only a few miles on the northern side. What she had seen so far was a wooded wonderland, lush with wildflowers and washed by cool streams. The sunspangled air was pungent with the scent of pine. It wasn't difficult to imagine the Black Hills's most famous town boasting streets of gold. Summoning a bright tone for Ben-

21

jamin's sake, Maddie continued, "I'll own that I'm excited to arrive, too. I can hardly wait to see the house Father has built for us. These past months have been so difficult . . ." She paused, tears welling in her eyes as she looked to her grandmother. "I dearly long to fix up our new home, to plant a garden and take care of everyone."

Susan Hampshire O'Hara gave her granddaughter a tender smile. She, too, was still grieving the recent death of her daughter, Colleen, Maddie's mother. "Darling girl, have you not noticed? This isn't Philadelphia. Unless I miss my guess, Deadwood will be even more uncivilized than the towns we've passed through on the plains. Gold towns create an atmosphere that is hardly conducive to gentle pastimes like raising flowers and baking cream puffs."

Her brow furrowing slightly, Madeleine braced herself as the wagon dropped suddenly into a deep rut. Her gaze traveled back to one of the several trunks she'd brought—in spite of letters from her father admonishing her to pack lightly. It had been much too difficult to abandon her favorite books, many of which bore the faint inscription "Colleen O'Hara Avery." They would comfort her in strange surroundings, as would the various keepsakes she had cushioned from their home. But the Avery furnishings had been left behind, gone into storage at Gramma Susan's house against the day Stephen Avery or his children might want the pieces chosen by Colleen with such impeccable taste and care.

Of course, the most astonishing adjunct to the Avery entourage had been added at the last minute: Susan O'Hara herself. The eighty-three-year-old matron would never have believed that she could leave Philadelphia, where she had been born and lived most of her life, to come to a godforsaken place like Deadwood. However, she'd always been impetuous, and when it came time to bid Maddie and Benjamin good-bye, she'd been unable to remain behind. It was as if she could hear her darling daughter's voice, speaking to her from heaven. Colleen had loved Stephen Avery, almost to a fault, but she had played both parents' roles much of the time while he chased around the country in search of wealth and adventure, usually in the form of speculation during gold or silver booms. Although Colleen's frail health had kept him by her side in Philadelphia during her last years, Madeleine had increasingly assumed her mother's duties, taking care of Stephen as well as little Benjamin. There was no telling what kind of father or homelife awaited the Avery children in Deadwood. At the last moment, Susan had felt compelled to go with them.

How very peculiar life was, Susan decided as she observed her beautiful granddaughter. Like Colleen, who had comported herself as a lady nearly from infancy, well-mannered Madeleine seemed bound and determined to enjoy fine things and cultivate a gentlewoman's sensibilities—generally at the expense of whatever fun life had to offer.

Susan O'Hara had her doubts about how deep Madeleine's refined streak really ran. After all, the child was the image of Patrick, her dear departed, rollicking rogue of a husband. At twenty Maddie was achieving a woman's beauty, with long, luxuriant hair the color of marmalade, big, sparkling emerald eyes, a mouth both wide and rosily sensuous, and milky skin with dustings of freckles across her nose, bosom, and over her thighs. Maddie tried to tone down her looks by twisting her mass of waves into a prim chignon and disguising her remarkable body with high necks, long sleeves, and restrictive corsets. It was an image that Colleen had encouraged, but Susan liked to think that there were smoldering embers deep within Maddie that would one day ignite and match the blaze of her beauty. She hoped she'd live to see it.

"Look!" shouted Benjamin, breaking into Susan's reverie as their wagon heaved over the crest of the hill. "There's Deadwood!"

Madeleine helped her grandmother come forward so that they could share this first view of their new home. The sight that met their eyes caused them both to gasp involuntarily. "Perhaps," murmured Susan, "there's been some mistake. That couldn't possibly be—"

"That's Deadwood, ma'am," interrupted their driver, Hugo. He spit out a stream of tobacco juice. "It's too late to turn back now!"

Below them, tucked into a twisting gulch crowned by cliffs of white rock and studded with burned stumps, lay a muddy, makeshift town. Deadwood seemed to consist almost entirely of half-built frame buildings, log cabins, and hundreds of tents. Maddie could hear the shouts and laughter of men echoing up the mountainside, men who appeared to be moving over every inch of the town and the barren sides of the gulch. Miners.

"Goodness," Madeleine whispered.

"Doesn't it look tremendous?" Benjamin demanded, looking from Maddie to his grandmother.

"Quite," Susan agreed wryly. She ran a soft, wrinkled hand over his unruly curls. "Just the sort of place a little boy dreams of living."

"Do you suppose there are any other women there?" Maddie asked.

"Oh, sure," Hugo assured her, winking. "Where there's gold, there's always plenty of women . . . if you know what I mean."

"How delightful," Susan said as they started down the rocky, rutted road. Her granddaughter sat down and gave her a rueful smile. "This promises to be *quite* an adventure!"

Stephen Avery, tall and erect in a stiff-bosomed white shirt, plaid vest, and slim, dove gray trousers, stood outside the new frame building that housed Peter Gushurst's grocery store. The day was growing warmer by the minute; the stench of waste rose from the bog that was Main Street.

Watching the handful of rickety wagons creak down the side of Deadwood Gulch, Stephen tried not to worry what Madeleine would think of him for bringing her and Benjamin here. She was so much like her mother. He'd never have dreamed of uprooting Colleen from her beloved Philadelphia and the tranquil, refined life she had there. What had possessed him to do so to Madeleine?

A thin rivulet of sweat trickled out from under the band of Stephen's bowler. He removed it, smoothed down his wavy black hair, and leaned forward to peer at the wagons as they approached Deadwood's Chinatown. The north end of the gulch was wide enough only for Main Street and Whitewood Creek, and the exotic-looking shop facades always startled people who were seeing their first Chinatown. The strong scent of incense pervaded the air. Stephen was watching anxiously when he saw first Benjamin, then Maddie climb out from under their wagon's soiled cover to sit beside the driver. Their innocent faces looked this way and that, taking in the ramshackle Chinese grocery, laundries, joss house, and restaurants. Even more startling, however, was the area of town that came next—the "badlands," a virtual hotbed of vice and corruption. Filthy miners, painted whores, and rowdy gamblers lounged in doorways and on the occasional balcony, laughing, shooting guns into the air, and drinking as they watched the newest crop of pilgrims roll into Deadwood.

Again, Stephen silently expressed his gratitude that Colleen could not comment on his decision to bring their children to this bawdy, smelly, uncivilized town. Of course, he wasn't glad that she was dead, but he never did feel that she quite approved of him after the rosy glow of new love had left her eyes more than twenty years ago. Even now he often imagined that he could hear her chastising him for this latest episode of "ill-considered" behavior. Colleen was known to murmur things like, "Will you never grow up, Stephen? I am losing hope . . . but as long as you don't try to take us with you into the wilderness, I shall try to be patient. I can only hope that one day you will tire of arduous journeys into the unknown and long for the pleasures of a family, a beautiful home, and a city of culture like our own Philadelphia."

Colleen would have wanted her children to remain in their home, even if it meant that Benjamin would be raised by female relatives rather than his own father. Now, as the covered wagon bearing his offspring drew closer, he earnestly—and uncharacteristically—prayed that they would be happy in Deadwood. Were they not his children, too? Perhaps they might even thrive on the contrasts between this new life and the past. . . .

Pulled by a team of tired mules, its wheels clotted with mud, the Avery wagon groaned to a halt.

"Hello, Father."

Stephen's heart hurt, as it always did after a separation, when he saw Madeleine. She seemed to grow more exquisite with each passing season, although physically she resembled neither of her parents. Even after weeks of travel, Maddie appeared fresh, glowing, and ladylike from the roots of her shining hair to the tips of her kid leather-shod toes. "My dearest daughter, how happy and relieved I am to see you both safely arrived!"

The driver had no qualms about climbing down into the stinking mire, which oozed halfway up his boots. "Ma'am, unless you want to step in this muck, you'll have to let me hand you over to the grocery steps."

With a game smile that masked her exhaustion and horror, Madeleine glanced down to make certain the lawn tucker that shielded her bosom was securely in place, then lifted her skirts and allowed Hugo to catch her in his arms. She liked him well enough from a distance, but at close proximity he smelled like something that had not met soap and water for many weeks. Somehow she kept smiling until she was set beside her father on the brand-new pine steps. It was a great relief to have the journey at an end, but she had a premonition that Deadwood might be worse than any place they had passed through to get here.

"Father, how did you know we would be coming today?" she asked as they embraced.

"Nearly everyone in town has known you were coming, my dear," Stephen replied, reaching out to swing Benjamin over to join them. "One of the men who just arrived by horseback told a saloonkeeper about the wagon he'd seen coming into the Hills from Pierre. Tippie sent someone to fetch me, and I questioned the fellow. As soon as I mentioned your extraordinary hair he remembered you—and Benjamin, of course. Now, then, about your things . . ."

"Did the fellow remember *me*?" called a female voice from the depths of the wagon.

Stephen's head snapped back slightly while expressions of shock, then disbelief, passed over his craggy face. "You'll laugh, children, but for a moment I thought that sounded like—"

"It is, Father," Madeleine confirmed as Susan Hampshire O'Hara's wizened face peeped out. "Gramma Susan came with us."

"Impossible!" he cried.

"But true," his mother-in-law declared, arranging her blue calico skirts before surrendering bravely to Hugo's waiting embrace. When Stephen set her before him, she favored him with a winsome smile. "You needn't worry that I shall ruin your fun. In fact, I think you'll find me helpful. My world travels with Patrick acclimated me to all sorts of conditions, so I may be able to encourage darling Maddie." Turning pensive, she reached up to smooth back his side-whiskers. "You are going gray, dear boy. I hadn't noticed before."

He swallowed audibly. "Colleen began to count them just before—"

"Stephen," Susan said as her grandchildren politely looked elsewhere, "it's been a hard year for me, too. Colleen was my only daughter . . . and I found that I couldn't bear to let the children go so far away. I will try to do all I can to help, not hinder, in your new life."

He knew her too well not to be aware that there was much more to her decision than that. Twenty-five years ago Susan had begun protecting Colleen, and then Madeleine and Benjamin, from the carelessness born of his wanderlust. "I don't know why I didn't expect you all along, Mrs. O'Hara," he said.

"Gramma Susan was wonderful during our long journey West," Maddie offered. "I can't imagine how we should have managed alone. I could never have answered Benjamin's questions . . . or calmed my own fears. Gramma Susan did both."

"Then I am deeply grateful to you, madame," Stephen

said, bowing lightly before the diminutive old woman. Even in her bonnet with its dauntless plume, she was scarcely as tall as her granddaughter. "Now, unless there is something that one of you needs, I propose that we go immediately to our new home." He snapped his fingers and a Chinese man scurried out of the grocery, carrying a bag. "Meet Wang Chee, my cook and helper. Having him with me has been a godsend. He's seen to it that I have at least one hot meal a day and a semblance of clean clothes and linens. I'll venture that you are all famished, but Chee will soon take care of that!"

Even as Madeleine gave Wang Chee her most gracious smile, her heart sank. It had never occurred to her to wonder how her father had been coping thus far, whether he could cook or wash his own shirts or keep house. Such questions hadn't entered her mind, particularly since they had had a staff of servants in Philadelphia. Colleen, and later on her daughter, had had enough to do to manage such a household, overseeing meals, parties, and a host of personal daily details. That wouldn't be the case in Deadwood, though, Maddie knew. Somehow, as they'd traveled West, the romance of a bare, new little house had excited her imagination. Daydreams had filled the long hours, making her happier than ever she'd felt since her mother's death.

Now it seemed that she would be no more than an honored "guest" in Wang Chee's scrubbed little house. Tears pricked her eyes.

An open wagon was being filled with the trunks and crates from Hugo's prairie schooner. Eyes bright, Maddie beamed at her father as she accepted his assistance up to the seat beside him. Susan sat on the outside, and Benjamin and Wang Chee found places in back.

"I know, I know," Stephen Avery said in tones of apology as his mules struggled to pull the wagon forward through the mud, "you're wondering why I've brought you to such a godforsaken town, but I hope that you'll be patient and reserve judgment for a bit. Mrs. O'Hara, I don't expect you to fall in love with Deadwood, but I suspect that my children may have a bit more of my blood flowing through their veins than any of us have heretofore suspected.''

"Mama told me towns like this were only in books!'' Benjamin exclaimed, unable to repress his enthusiasm a moment longer. "I bet if she'd known a place as tremendous as Deadwood could be real, she'd've come, too! Right, Papa?''

"Well, Benjamin,'' his father began, aware of Susan's warning glance, "as it happens, Deadwood was not *real* until this past spring, so your dear mama was quite right. However, I have a notion that she might not have liked such a town as much as we men do. I can only pray that Madeleine will be more broadminded.''

Although she couldn't imagine her father resorting to prayer, Maddie was unwilling to dash his hopes. She put on her bravest smile. "I must own that the town is beginning to look a trifle more respectable,'' she murmured, gazing around at more tents and cabins, which appeared to be occupied by relatively normal-looking people. At least here there were no more half-naked women watching from windows, or gamblers and rowdies cursing loudly between swigs of whiskey.

With a nervous chuckle, Stephen said, "How remiss of me . . . I should have explained that the part of town you saw when you entered is known as the 'badlands.' The West is different from Philadelphia, but I believe that each person can make his own world out here. Deadwood's like a baby— it needs influences of all kinds to grow up healthy. Part of the reason I bought the land I did was so you children wouldn't have to be near the badlands.'' They crossed a rutted lane crudely labeled WALL STREET, and Stephen pointed right, to the hill above Main Street. "People are trying to keep the badlands on the north side of Wall Street, and proper houses are being built up there, on the hillsides. There will be steps leading up to them, and I was advised that that would be the ideal spot for our house. But I decided the view wouldn't be the best for my children. I want to shelter you, as much as possible, from Deadwood's seedier side.''

"Oh, Stephen, you always were the most conscientious

father," Susan said, with just enough irony to secure his attention.

Madeleine, meanwhile, was beset by waves of despair. She had seen no young women her own age—at least none who were fully clothed—and there was no sign at all of younger men who might be deemed appropriate for her acquaintance. Was her house far from town, a shack surrounded by a wide moat of mud? Where would she shop, and what could she buy? Half of the "stores" were tents with barrels stuck out in front to display the owner's wares. If not for the responsibility she felt toward her little brother, Maddie might regret coming to Deadwood already.

"There it is." They had turned on Deadwood Street, which cut across to connect with Sherman Street, the one other main artery following the gulch. Stephen was pointing toward the gently sloping hillsides above Sherman Street, but all his family could see were more miners, burned logs, mud, and tents.

Even Benjamin wasn't enthusiastic enough about the West to camp in a tent. "Papa. . . ?"

"I own five claims, three hundred feet each, on that hillside. Those men work for me. On good days, my claims pay one thousand dollars." He couldn't resist glancing at Susan to see if she appeared impressed.

"Stephen," she said carefully, as if he were slow-witted, "I cannot describe how tired I am. Have your claims paid enough to yield a house with a bed or two in it?"

The wagon had rolled farther south and now turned up a lane that slanted sideways up the hill. Looking carefully, Madeleine made out the shape of a house behind a stand of pine trees. She sat up a little straighter, and Stephen caught her eye, smiling. When they reached the top of the drive, he guided the mules past the trees and brought them to a standstill in front of the new house.

"Golly!" cried Benjamin. "It's the finest house in Deadwood!"

"A singular honor," Susan murmured dryly as she climbed down from the wagon unassisted.

Madeleine let her father lift her to the ground. The house had a tired-looking dirt yard, but at least it wasn't as muddy as the streets below. Pine boards had been laid out end to end from the door, forming a makeshift walkway.

The house itself was grand indeed, for Deadwood. "I would have built it with bricks," Stephen explained, "but we haven't a kiln here yet. No hardwoods, either, so it had to be pine. I did my best under the circumstances."

A little porch extended in front of the two-story white-washed dwelling. Stephen said that as soon as the paint he had ordered arrived, Madeleine could choose proper colors. Inside, she discovered that the house had a little parlor first, with a plain drop-leaf table, some battered chairs, and a settee against one wall. Stephen walked across the raw pine floor and proudly touched the back of the settee, which was on old rococo revival piece trimmed in scarred mahogany. The original maroon velvet upholstery peeped out from under a cover of flowered Chinese silk.

"You've no idea how difficult it still is to obtain real furniture here," he said proudly. "The army and the Indians make it hard for any transportation company to get supplies into the Hills, but that will change soon. In the meantime, I've been begging and bribing to furnish the house for you and Benjamin, Madeleine. Soon we'll have a nice stove to heat the parlor. I know it's nothing compared to what you're used to, but I'm counting on you to transform this shell into a proper home."

Susan tottered over and sat down on the hideous sofa, raising a cloud of dust. "You've outdone yourself this time, Stephen," she said, and sneezed.

Maddie touched her father's arm, feeling sorry for him. "I can see that you've worked very hard, Father, and nothing would please me more than to keep house for us—that is, unless Wang Chee would feel that I was interfering. . . ."

"Good Lord, no! He's been hoping daily that you'd arrive so that he can go to work on the claim I've given him to manage. Once they get a claim, usually someone else's left-overs, the Chinese miners are extremely patient and successful.'' Nestling his daughter's hand in the crook of his arm, Stephen led her back into the kitchen. ''Chee will be happy to assist you in any way he can, however. He's suggested that we send our washing to his wife. They operate a small laundry in Chinatown.''

Madeleine was pleased that the house was hers to manage; it was her nest to feather, just as she'd wished. Yet looking around at the large, rather frightening wood-burning stove and the meager assortment of crude cooking implements and iron skillets, she felt hopelessly out of her element. Nothing in her background had prepared her for such conditions. The sparse kitchen boasted three tiers of unpainted shelves for storage, one level of which was lined with heavy white crockery and tin cups. Three wooden planks stretched across two carpenter's horses passed for a table, while an assortment of crates and camp stools served as chairs.

Seeing her dismay, Stephen sighed. ''If I could have gotten anything better, I would have, my dear. And I give you my word that as soon as new shipments arrive, you may choose whatever strikes your fancy.''

''At least . . . we are all together,'' Maddie whispered. ''That's what matters.''

Benjamin bounded through the house while Maddie made a quieter tour. There was a bedroom downstairs, opening off the other side of the stairway. In it was a water-stained bureau and a high full-size bed with one leg missing, now replaced by a stack of yellowed copies of *Harper's Weekly*.

Upstairs, under the eaves, a rough woolen blanket had been hung to divide the two sleeping areas. The narrow beds were nearly identical, each with its own dressing table, which consisted of a packing box turned on its side with shelves nailed inside. A kerosene lamp, tin pitcher, basin, and cracked mirror completed the supplied necessities. Maddie knew which bed was meant for her and which for Benjamin: a little toy soldier wearing a chipped Union uniform was propped on her brother's muslin-sheathed pillow; on her own rested a little china doll with golden curls of real hair. Slowly Madeleine picked up the long-forgotten toy, given to her father when he'd come home from Nevada to fight in the Civil War. Although she'd only been six at the time, Maddie remembered now what she had said in her earnest little presentation speech:

"Papa, you should take my dolly with you because she's the prettiest one I have. She has hair like Mama's . . . though it's not as pretty as hers. But I thought she might remind you of Mama a little bit while you are away again, and then maybe you'll come home sooner."

It never would have occurred to Maddie to give her father a doll that looked like *her*.

"I've convinced your father to let me sleep upstairs with you, darling," Gramma Susan said from the doorway. Though slow-moving, she remained agile enough on steps. Now she crossed to slip an arm around her taller granddaughter. "Ah, there's your doll. Do you know that I gave you that for your sixth birthday? I wanted to buy you a little doll with red hair and freckles, but you'd have no part of *that*."

"I thought she looked like Mama," Madeleine whispered.

"I know, love. Your mother was beautiful, but certainly no more than you."

Maddie laughed. "Oh, Gramma Susan, you needn't try to make me believe such fairy stories. Everyone knows that Mama was perfect."

"Nonsense!" Glimpsing the tears that gleamed in Maddie's emerald eyes, Susan embraced her fully. "Colleen had her share of problems. She was quite human."

"I miss her—" Maddie's voice broke on a sob. It was comforting to press her cheek against her grandmother's white hair, freed now of its bonnet. Gramma Susan always smelled faintly of violets; it was a scent that reminded Madeleine, sharply, pleasantly, of her childhood.

"I know you miss her, darling. We all do."

Lifting her head, Maddie looked out the narrow window that brought light in under the pitch of the roof. Deadwood's Main Street was dimly visible from their hillside home, and she could hear the curses and laughter of the miners from the other side of the pine trees. Her father's men. "Mama would be horrified by this place," she murmured at last, relieved to say the words aloud. "Every detail of our new life would repulse her . . . even this house."

"Madeleine, your mother isn't with us any longer, and you are free to form your own opinions." Susan's blue eyes gleamed behind her spectacles. "What's important, I think, is that all of us who loved Colleen, and miss her, are here together, endeavoring to begin anew. There are challenges ahead, and I believe they constitute a better use of time than sitting in a darkened room in Philadelphia, mourning uselessly."

"I'm so *glad* that you came, too, Gramma Susan. I fear that I should be curled up on my bed, consumed with self-pity, if not for you."

"I rather doubt that your father shares your gratitude, but I shall do my best to help all three of you." Susan sank onto her granddaughter's bed, unbuttoned her shoes, and slipped them off with a grateful sigh. "I hate to admit it, but I *am* getting old. I'm glad we're finally here."

Although still melancholy, Maddie felt a little stronger. She stepped to the window, surveying the muddy, ramshackle, vice-ridden town below with a rueful smile. "In a way, I should be happy. I ought to be safe from people's expectations here. Everyone in Philadelphia pressed me about becoming active in society . . . and marrying, of course." Glancing back over her shoulder, Maddie laughed with uncustomary mischief. "I shan't have to suffer any attempts at wooing me here! There would appear to be sufficient numbers of . . . women to attend to the needs of the sort of men swarming through Deadwood. I have yet to glimpse one of them, save Father, who looks as if he's bathed since Easter! *I'm* certainly not their type, and I couldn't be more pleased. . . ."

Chapter Two

DANIEL MATTHEWS RODE INTO DEADWOOD FROM the south, downhill into the crazy zigzagging gulch. It was hot and the town stank, revealing its character before he could take a visual inventory.

The Black Hills themselves, one hundred miles long and sixty miles wide, were still nearly as enchanting as they had been when he'd first visited them with Lakota people half a dozen years ago. A lush, forested, game-rich island rising miraculously out of an endless sea of grass, the Hills possessed a unique beauty that far surpassed any grander mountains he'd ever seen. They'd been virtually untouched then, revered by the native people as sacred. Even now, though the white man was doing his best to cut a greedy, destructive swath through the Hills, the land was still breathtakingly beautiful . . . until Deadwood's assault on the eyes.

Most of Main Street was blocked by two newly arrived bull trains. The oxen, mooing plaintively, were slumped in the mud in front of supply wagons now being unloaded by surging crowds of men. People were everywhere, scurrying in and out of tents, shouting at one another in the street, leaning out of windows in various states of undress. The town was pure, unbridled chaos.

Matthews pushed back his brown slouch hat and slowed his roan, whom he'd christened Watson during one particularly endless day in Wyoming. It made him feel sad and frustrated to see what his own people had done to this pristine haven. On the other hand, Deadwood was exactly the kind

35

of town he needed. Disreputable characters of every sort wandered in and out of gold towns virtually unnoticed; scoundrels, outlaws, and others running from something or someone were the rule rather than the exception. Right now, Dan welcomed the prospect of blending in among them, unnoticed and unknown. He was grateful to have planned for an extended stay in the West; he had brought plenty of money.

His emotions had been intense following the final scene with Custer and his departure from the Seventh Cavalry. Now, however, Dan mainly felt fed up. He'd considered returning immediately to Washington, but Grant *had* encouraged him to linger and enjoy his time out West—and, besides, he didn't much feel like facing the president. Custer had been right on one count—Grant was the person responsible for setting in motion the chain of events that led to the insanity at Little Bighorn. Plus, Dan knew that his reception at the White House would not be warm. Perhaps Custer had written to the president regarding Dan's conduct? In any case, he hadn't had much luck carrying out his assignment. The knowledge that he had been morally right afforded Dan some peace, but what good had it done?

Lying awake these past nights under the starry Wyoming sky, Dan had gone over the scenes between Custer and himself. He felt faintly sick about the whole business, since it was clear that his arguments had only incited Custer further. Perhaps if he had taken a different tack, less true to his own beliefs but tailored to appeal to Custer, he might have had more success.

The hell with it, Dan thought now, *I'm sick of brooding*. Deadwood looked good to him, and he looked forward to just lying low for a while and waiting for the dust he'd raised with Custer to settle. There would be plenty in this rowdy town to take his mind off his real life.

Smiling grimly, Dan reflected that he'd be a mite difficult to recognize these days. He was bearded and much leaner, having barely eaten during much of his ride through the unceded territory, where there were no forts or white settlements. He'd bought some of his clothes off friendly Cheyenne near the border of Wyoming Territory. Snug buckskin trousers were stuffed into well-worn boots, and he wore a shirt of faded blue chambray with a brick red kerchief knotted loosely around his neck to soak up excess sweat. A holster and a Smith & Wesson Schofield .45 single-action revolver completed the picture. It wasn't showy, just extremely effective.

When it became nearly impossible to guide Watson through the dense crowds, Dan tied up the horse in front of a false-fronted building bearing a sign that read PIONEER PRINTING OFFICE. As he dismounted he was met by a man wearing a paper collar and a worn brown suit.

"New here, aren't you?" he said, thrusting a newspaper into Dan's hands. "Permit me to introduce myself, pilgrim. I'm C. V. Gardner, previously a captain in the Union Army during the War between the States, and a lawyer, but currently the publisher of the *Black Hills Pioneer*, first newspaper in these parts! We've only been printing a month. Always looking for readers, and I thought you might like a copy."

Gardner was dark-haired and wore a medium-long beard. His deep-set eyes made Dan think of a mournful hound, but when he smiled, his face was transformed. Smiling in return, Dan shook his hand. "Pleased to meet you, Gardner. My name's Fox, and I've just ridden in from the southern Hills. Before that, Cheyenne. I appreciate the newspaper." Glancing down at the front page, Dan saw that it was devoted to stories on Deadwood's celebration of the centennial Fourth of July. "Where can I get a bed and a decent meal?"

Gardner winked almost imperceptibly. "Depends on what sort of bed you had in mind, Fox. North of Wall Street, you can get yourself plenty of whiskey, a warm little chippie, and probably a bed, too. Try the Gem Theatre first, if you're interested."

Sensing that his eyebrows were about to fly up at this information, Dan nodded soberly and went on his way. He'd encountered his share of hard drinkers and soiled doves over the years, particularly during the war, but such pastimes were indulged in with a measure of discretion. Clearly Deadwood was a different sort of place.

The prospect of a bed warmed by a willing woman was tempting, but first he needed food. Salvation appeared in the form of the Grand Central Hotel, which, with just one story constructed thus far, served only meals. Crossing Lee Street, Dan spotted the sign, went in, and consumed huge quantities of mutton, beans, mashed potatoes, and apple dumplings with cream, all for fifty cents. While he ate, he read most of the *Black Hills Pioneer* and drank three mugs of coffee. Finally, his hunger appeased and many of his questions about Deadwood answered, he found himself dreaming of a whiskey or two, some leisurely conversation at a bar, and then the companionship of a pretty, affectionate woman.

He swung into the saddle again, bound for the makeshift livery stable down Main Street. It went against his better judgment to leave Watson in such a place, but Dan's mood was reckless. For nearly a fortnight he'd been on the move, eating little besides dried beef and sleeping outdoors in a bedroll. Conflict over his departure from the Seventh Cavalry tormented him. But now, forgetfulness through sinful pleasure awaited him just north of Wall Street. . . .

They called this part of Deadwood the "badlands," he'd read in the *Pioneer* and it was wilder than any place Dan Matthews had ever seen. The freight wagons were nearly unloaded now, and bullwhackers cracked their long whips as they moved the protesting oxen down Main Street. Crates containing everything from store fixtures to caskets were stacked in front of buildings and tents while merchants attempted to deal with the influx of goods. Now that the excitement was dying down, the gamblers and serious drinkers were wandering back into the saloons.

The Gem Theatre had a balcony that was currently crowded with fancy ladies, rouged and scantily clad. They'd come out to investigate the latest shipments of goods, calling out questions about lace, silk, pearls, perfume, and other hoped-for finery. Now, the sight of Dan riding slowly in their direction caused the girls to linger.

"Hey, handsome!" called one. Short and blessed with long black curls, she wore a flowered silk wrapper sliding off her plump shoulders. Even from the street, Dan could see the curves of her breasts bursting forth from her camisole. "Come on in! Tell Al you want Victoria!"

"No!" countered a slimmer blonde, laughing. "Tell him Bessie! What's *your* name?"

"Fox." It was a pleasure to be in a town where surnames and past histories were cumbersome details easier left unspoken.

Now they all began giggling and calling to him at once, leaning over the balcony railing to display their charms. Pushing back his hat, he flashed a grin up at the eager group on the balcony and felt the twinges in his loins warm and spread.

"I just have to stable my horse," he told the girls. "Pour me a whiskey and I'll be straight up."

"I'll just bet you will!" one of them answered in a naughtily suggestive tone, then they all scurried back inside, giggling.

Dan looked around, suddenly aware of the strong smell of incense that wafted south from Chinatown. Across the street he saw the livery stable, and there was a bathhouse, too. He yearned to scrub himself clean, but other needs took precedence. Drawing on the reins, he began to guide Watson across the still-crowded thoroughfare, heading toward the livery. Then he saw the boy.

He couldn't have been more than nine or ten, with brown eyes the size of saucers. First he crept around the corner of the Green Front and paused in the narrow alleyway flanking the theater. Since all the rooms weren't finished upstairs and some of the new girls were still being tried out, there were a couple of curtained booths that opened off the alley. It was supposed to be a convenience; men in a hurry could have a girl standing up, without going upstairs or even bothering to remove their trousers.

Dan was a grown man who had seen a great deal, but this shocked him. Then, the sight of a little boy leaning forward to peek around the edge of the curtain was more than he could tolerate. In an instant he was at the entrance to the alleyway.

"Come over here." Dan spoke from the saddle, high above the child. "I won't hurt you."

The boy's clothes were soiled, but of good quality. He wore brown pants held up by suspenders, a plaid shirt, and muddy boots that looked as if they'd been custom-made for his small feet. His sandy hair stuck up in cowlicks, accentuating the size of his brown eyes. "My pa says I shouldn't talk to strangers," he piped.

"What's your name, son?"

"Benjamin."

"Well, Benjamin," Dan drawled, with a slow smile, "I have a suspicion that your pa doesn't want you running loose in the badlands, either. There are a lot worse folks than me around here, so why don't you come on up and let me take you home." He couldn't believe he was saying it himself, considering the other pressing appointments on his schedule, but he didn't see that he had a choice.

Benjamin retreated, nearly backing right into the curtained booth. However, before he could make matters worse, Dan brought Watson forward until the boy was within reach. He scooped up the struggling youngster as if he were a sack of feathers and let the roan prance daintily back into Main Street.

"Now then," Dan said firmly, "I'd be obliged if you'd direct me to your house, or tent, or wherever it is you live."

"I don't want you to take me home, mister!"

"I can assure you that I am not delivering you back into your parents' care because I *want* to do so, either. So stop wasting my time and show me the quickest route. There are other extremely pressing matters I must attend to once I'm rid of you."

"Yeah, I can guess what they are! I heard you talking to the girls on the Gem balcony," Benjamin dared to blurt, then pointed south. "This way."

"Little hellion," Dan muttered between clenched teeth. "Your parents ought to keep you on a chain!"

"Gramma Susan, where did Benjamin say he was going? I can't see him from the windows, even upstairs."

Madeleine came into the kitchen, where her grandmother had begun hanging the blue calico curtains they'd sewn. The bolts of silk and satin that Maddie had brought from Philadelphia would be used to make draperies for the parlor and gowns for her and Gramma Susan. Now, pausing to appraise the results of the first kitchen pair framing a window, Madeleine smiled with what she hoped would pass for genuine admiration.

"How charming they look!" she exclaimed. Actually she would never have chosen the calico if there had *been* a choice, but that was true of the entire house. Madeleine felt as if she were spending every waking hour endeavoring to make a silk purse out of a sow's ear.

"When you smile like that, you are the image of your mother," Susan remarked wryly.

"Shall I take that as a compliment?"

"Mmm . . . frankly, no. The world could never live up to Colleen's standards, and that's not a quality I'd wish for you, darling." Susan stood beside her granddaughter to admire the curtains. "You'll never be content here if you can't manage to lower your own standards, you know. As for Benjamin, I thought he said he was going down the hill to play with the Gordon boy on Pine Street."

"I've asked him to stay in sight." Worriedly Maddie peered out the window that overlooked Sherman Street. "There's far too much mischief for a boy his age to get into in a town like this. I do *not* intend to lower my standards for Benjamin, Gramma!" Glancing down at her pretty peach-and-cream-striped taffeta walking dress, Maddie thought stubbornly that she would not lower her personal standards, either, no matter what anyone said. She had been raised a lady and would remain one, even in rollicking, sinful Deadwood.

"It's a shame there are so many flies," Susan was saying as she fanned herself. "Isn't it hot? I'd open a window or two, but I fear we'd be overtaken by insects. Let's not use the stove tonight. We can make a cold meal."

"That's not very nourishing, is it?" Worry about Benjamin joined with the oppressive late afternoon heat to fray Maddie's temper. "I think I'll go outside and call him. I mean, really Gramma, almost anything could happen to such a little boy. If Father were home more, I'm sure Benjamin wouldn't be so quick to misbehave!"

Susan sighed as she watched her granddaughter hurry out of the kitchen, skirts raised against the very thought of dust, every modest curl pinned neatly in place. Madeleine was certainly right about Stephen. Ever since they'd arrived, he'd been away more and more. Two days ago he'd announced that he had to leave Deadwood for a "short journey," muttering about mining supplies. Who knew when he'd return? The situation outraged Susan. What if she hadn't come with the children? And even so, this was not the sort of town where an old woman, a beautiful girl, and a scamp of a boy ought to be left all alone to fend for themselves.

It was cooler outside and there was a faint scent of pine up here above the town. As she trod the warped pine boards that made a path across their property, Madeleine thought briefly that there probably wouldn't be flies if people would stop throwing their waste into the streets. Gazing down the path, she saw no sign of Benjamin and knew a sharp pang of worry. She called his name in a high voice that sounded foolishly inadequate. Her face felt warm.

Then came the sound of hoofbeats against packed mud. Someone was coming up their slanting drive, but she couldn't see who until the horse gained the top of the hill and rounded the stand of pine trees that separated their residence from the miners working Stephen's claims. Please, she thought earnestly, let it be someone with news of Benjamin.

Maddie made out the roan first, then the familiar sight of Benjamin's pale, freckled face and spiky hair. Then she looked at the big man who held her brother captive in the saddle, and immediately she felt a tightness in her breast.

Never had she seen a more appealingly, overwhelmingly masculine man in her life.

The details were blurred: he was tall, lean but brawny, deeply tanned with an approachable white smile. Bearded, yet possessed of a ruggedly chiseled face. His eyes were piercingly blue. His hands were large, strong, long-fingered.

"What are you doing with my brother?" Maddie demanded rudely as he drew near. Something about the man rankled her. "I must insist that you identify yourself! What do you want?"

Dan laughed. "For God's sake, lady, I'm doing you a favor!"

When Benjamin fought to scramble down from the saddle, Dan let him go, and the boy nearly landed face first in the mud. "Maddie, he practically kidnapped me! He just grabbed me up on his horse! Isn't that against the law? He could've sold me to the Injins or something!"

The man found Benjamin's last bit of business extremely amusing. When at last he stopped laughing and looked down, he found himself meeting the flashing green eyes of the most exquisitely beautiful woman he'd seen west of Washington, D.C. "My young friend has a flair for melodrama," he said, "honed perhaps during visits to the Green Front. . . ."

"The . . . Green Front?" Maddie repeated, wrinkling her brow. "What is that?"

"Well, it appears to call itself a theater, ma'am."

Thoroughly confused and alarmed, Madeleine looked down to find that Benjamin had scurried behind her. "But, surely you don't mean to imply that my brother was in . . . that part of town!"

"We've reached the point where I ought to speak to the

boy's father.'' Dan swung down from Watson's back and stood towering over Maddie. ''This really isn't a matter for your delicate sensibilities.''

''I've no doubt that you are correct, sir—''

''Call me Fox . . . Maddie.'' He felt like Fox now, comfortable in the name.

''You may address me as Miss Avery,'' she replied primly, then glanced down at the cowering Benjamin. ''Go into the house and wait for me, young man.'' When the front door had slammed behind him, Maddie lifted her chin and met Fox's clean gaze. ''My father is away and I must deal with Benjamin in his absence. I will be honest with you . . . Mr. Fox. We are new to Deadwood, recently arrived from Philadelphia. I am quite out of my element.''

Cocking an eyebrow, he said laconically, ''You're a city girl? I never would have guessed, ma'am.''

''Of course you are teasing me, but such amusements are quite inappropriate at this moment. I don't know who you are, sir, or why you took it upon yourself to bring my brother home, but I am grateful. Now you must tell me exactly what it was that he was doing in that . . . area of town.''

''I couldn't possibly speak of it to a lady, Miss Avery.''

Fox had removed his hat and held it in sun-roughened hands. Madeleine noticed now that his hair, a unique shade of rich chestnut, curled luxuriously over his collar. All in all, he was so intensely male—and so self-assured—that she took an involuntary step backward, confused and momentarily intimidated. The young men she had known socially in Philadelphia, intellectuals with proper manners and clean fingernails, had been nothing like this.

''I appreciate your consideration, Mr. Fox, but—''

''Just Fox will do, ma'am.''

After a moment's hesitation Madeleine sighed and continued, ''I understand . . . Fox, that there are many aspects of life here in Deadwood that may shock me deeply, but circumstances dictate that I become aware of them if I am going to protect my brother. I must insist that you enlighten me accordingly.'' Was she phrasing her thoughts too formally for this earthy man? Smiling politely, she added, ''Do you understand what I've said?''

''Just because I'm not wearing a paper collar and a Prince Albert frock coat doesn't mean I'm slow-witted,'' Fox replied, with a harsh laugh. He rubbed his eyes then, suddenly aware of the exhaustion that was seeping into his bones. ''You know, I've just arrived in Deadwood after a long journey myself, and—''

''I would certainly invite you in, sir, were it not imperative that we speak in private. I must shield my grandmother as much as possible.''

''Of course.'' Never in his wildest dreams would he have imagined finding such an incongruous female in the Black Hills. One side of his mouth quirked slightly as questions surged up in him and he pushed them back down. ''I appreciate that pretty speech, Miss Avery, but we both know that I'm hardly the sort of person you'd invite in for tea. Come to think of it, it may be a while before you find anyone worthy in these parts. But, that's another matter. You wanted to know about the Green Front, and Benjamin . . .''

''Yes, please.'' Flushing, Maddie looked down and fussed with the peach taffeta ruching that encircled her left wrist.

Fox took a breath. Part of him was enjoying this scene. ''Are you familiar with the mating rites of men and women, Miss Avery?''

''I beg your pardon!'' she cried, gasping.

''You insisted that I be forthright. Shall I repeat the question?''

''No!'' Her face burned. ''I cannot imagine how this— this indecent subject could possibly have any bearing on— Oh, for heaven's sake! Naturally, as an unmarried woman, I am not *personally* familiar with the act you named. However, I am educated . . . if you take my meaning.''

''I admire your delicacy, ma'am.'' His eyes, bluer than the sky, were dancing. ''I assume, then, that you're aware that all unmarried women are not chaste like yourself. And, as it happens, a whole lot of those fallen women are right here in Deadwood. In fact, this town is bursting with sin.''

Maddie's heart was pounding. ''What on earth could that possibly have to do with Benjamin?''

''He's just curious, which is natural, but when I saw him in the badlands I thought he might be learning a little more than he needed to at— How old is he?''

''Nine,'' she said faintly.

Fox shook his head. ''Well, it may be too late, but let's hope he still has a little innocence left. You see, the Green Front, along with most every establishment in the badlands as far as I can tell, has—uh . . . ladies of the evening . . .''

''I am familiar with the term, but I hardly think that Benjamin would know what such women do if he happened to pass one on the street, or whatever it is you're saying.''

''I'm afraid there's more to it.'' He was losing patience with this careful, circuitous conversation. ''In one of the alleys, there are a couple of curtained booths built into the Green Front's outside wall . . . for men who don't want to bother with . . . the usual formalities. Your brother was sneaking around next to one of those curtains, listening to the noises inside, trying to get close enough to peek around the—''

''No!'' The blood drained from Maddie's face; even her lips were pale. ''You're lying!''

''The hell I am. Listen, lady, I've been as polite as I know how to be about this! I was only trying to help, but if you're going to insult me, I'm more than happy to go. There are a dozen places I'd rather be than here.''

''All in the badlands, I surmise!'' she shot back, infuriated, numb with shock.

''Not that it's any of your damned business, but yes! I'm thirty-two, not *nine*, and if I want to indulge in a few pleasures of the flesh, that's my choice. So, if you're done calling me names . . .''

Madeleine felt as if she were drowning in a sea of unreality. Her mother . . . dear Lord, what would her mother say or think if she knew how her darling little son was passing his time? How could Maddie hope to control him in this wicked town, short of locking him in the house? A sense of powerlessness surged through her, taking with it the last vestiges of her strength. She felt cold in the July sunshine, then dizzy and weak.

Fox noticed the beautiful burnished lights of Maddie's hair when she tipped her head down, and then he heard the rustle of her taffeta gown as her knees gave way. Startled, he realized that she was fainting—and managed to catch her just before she tumbled into the mud.

Cradling her slim yet satisfyingly curved body against his broad chest, Fox couldn't suppress a wry smile. It looked like he was going inside her clean and proper house after all. . . .

Chapter Three

"GRAMMA SUSAN, COME QUICK!" BENJAMIN shouted as he clattered down the stairs. "That man—that awful man is carrying Maddie! Maybe she's dead! Maybe he killed her!"

Susan came into the parlor, calmly wiping her hands on her long, snowy apron. "Benjamin Franklin Avery, have you been spying out of windows again?"

"Well, *you* wouldn't watch, and someone had to make sure that Maddie didn't get hurt!" The little boy's hands and face were newly scrubbed, but his hair still stuck up in cowlicks. "Gramma, *hurry!*"

"Were you watching . . . or listening?" Unperturbed, Susan opened the door just as Fox reached it, his arms filled with Madeleine's still body. "My goodness! What's become of our Maddie?"

"She seems to have fainted," Fox replied. "Where would you like me to put her?"

Susan led the way into the downstairs bedroom and gestured to the big bed Stephen now shared with his son. Gently Fox laid Maddie on the blue-and-white quilt, then stepped backward to admire the beauty of her features in repose.

"What's wrong with her?" Benjamin demanded loudly.

Madeleine stirred slightly as her grandmother pressed a damp cloth to her brow. Fox, meanwhile, gave the boy a dangerous look. "Actually, I believe that *you* are the cause of your sister's distress."

48

"How could I be? I wasn't even there! You probably did something to her, just like you pulled me up on your horse when I told you to leave me alone! I think—"

"Benjamin, be silent!" Susan said sharply. Leaning down, she gazed into his petulant little face. "I won't allow such rudeness, especially toward your elders."

"Gramma . . ." Maddie breathed, opening her eyes with an effort.

"Darling, you're all worn out." The old woman gave her a loving smile and kissed her cheek. "Just rest for a few minutes, then I'll bring you some soup and we'll talk."

When Madeleine obeyed, closing her eyes, Susan ushered Fox and Benjamin out of the bedroom. She shut the door, then turned first to her grandson.

"Young man, I want you to go upstairs and lie down on my bed. Keep your eyes and ears to yourself until I call you."

Benjamin gave Fox a narrow look, but he obeyed, mounting the steps loudly and slowly, as if he were en route to the gallows. When he was out of sight and the upper floor fell silent, Susan sighed and turned to the tall, roughly attractive stranger.

"I don't believe we've been formally introduced, sir. My name is Susan Hampshire O'Hara."

He took her tiny, withered hand and smiled. "It's an honor, Mrs. O'Hara. I'm Fox—Fox Daniel, actually, but I rarely bother with a surname out here. It's simpler."

"Is it?" She bit her lower lip and fixed him with a perceptive stare. "That's interesting."

He quickly changed the subject. "Miss Avery mentioned that you all had just arrived from Philadelphia. You wouldn't by any chance be related to Senator Lion Hampshire from Philadelphia?"

Now Susan was *really* intrigued. It was highly unlikely that many Deadwood reprobates, running from unsavory pasts, would be familiar with a Pennsylvania senator whose career had reached its zenith half a century ago. "I'm proud to say that Lion Hampshire was my father, and the finest man I ever knew—except, of course, for my darling husband, Patrick. How do you happen to know of Papa?''

Fox silently cursed his quick tongue. ''Now that you mention it, I can't recall! Must've learned about him in school— or maybe from my mother. She was a schoolteacher and made me read even when I didn't want to. I know I always liked that name, Lion.''

''Just as you like the name Fox?'' she inquired, with a benign smile. ''Never mind. I'm teasing you, and I shouldn't. Instead, I must offer you an apology for the behavior of my grandchildren. I heard Madeleine raising her voice to you outside, which shocked me. Usually she is most ladylike, especially with new acquaintances. And Benjamin—goodness, he was absolutely horrid! His mother died recently, which has doubtless taken more of a toll on him than he'll admit. She was my daughter, also, so we've all been grieving. We came West to join the children's father, but Stephen is too busy and away too much to give Benjamin the discipline that he needs.''

Fox found himself charmed by Susan O'Hara's candor. Her proud face revealed a character rich with wisdom and humor, reminding him not a little of his mother. ''Well, I appreciate the apology, but it's not necessary. The truth is, I like Miss Avery. If she sounded upset with me, it may be that I was doing a little teasing of my own.'' Fox started toward the front door, and Susan walked with him, listening intently. ''As for your grandson . . . I agree with you. He's badly in need of a firm hand, preferably male. It's clear that he respects you, Mrs. O'Hara, but he knows that you aren't going to ride up behind him on a horse, grab him off the street, and carry him home to be punished.''

''You may as well tell me everything,'' she said in tones of surrender as they stood on the pine-board footpath outside. ''I doubt whether I'll faint, but perhaps you ought to be prepared.''

He threw back his head and laughed out loud at that. Then,

more quietly, he told her as much as she needed to know, omitting the lurid details about the convenience booth. It was enough, he decided, that she be aware that Benjamin was sneaking around the badlands rather than playing innocently with other little boys. She knew enough of the world to infer the rest.

"Well, that's hardly worth fainting over, but Maddie does endeavor to take after her mother." Susan tapped her foot for a minute, thinking. "Something will have to be done, though. . . . Fox, how would you like to join us for supper evening after next? I like you, and I think that it would be beneficial for Benjamin. Perhaps the two of you may be able to deal together more congenially over a home-cooked meal." She paused, watching the play of thoughts in his blue eyes. "That is . . . unless you are just passing through Deadwood. There's no point in forming attachments if you're not going to be here next week."

He stroked his short, sun-bleached beard and gave her an appealing grin. "No, ma'am, I plan to stay put for the time being. And I'd like to come back here for supper. I thank you for the invitation." He swung onto Watson's back, then leaned down to speak. "Are you certain you shouldn't consult with your other relatives about this? I doubt whether either of them will be happy to see me."

"*Phsssh!*" Susan waved a hand in the air dismissingly. "Come at six o'clock and leave the rest to me!"

By the time Fox got back to the badlands and left Watson at the livery barn, a lot of the pleasure seemed to have gone out of his plans for a juicily wicked evening. However, he hoisted his bedroll and saddlebags over one broad shoulder and walked through the mud to the Gem Theatre.

There were already a few dozen barrooms and many billiard and card halls in Deadwood, but the "theaters of ill repute" were best known: Gem, Bella Union, Melodeon, and Green Front.

Most of the saloons looked as if they'd been thrown up

overnight, and some of them were little more than tents. Their roofs leaked and the walls tended to come down during drunken fights or storms. Fox liked the sturdier look of the Gem, and of course, it had real rooms upstairs for privacy. The badlands was so crowded now that he began to wonder if he could get a bed without paying for a girl to go with it.

Inside the Gem, exhausted and dirty miners were drinking, while the card tables were filling up with dishonest-looking types ready for a night of gambling. Fox approached the bar and stood next to a heavyset man who was pungently malodorous. He wondered if he smelled anything like that, then decided that Madeleine Avery would have given some sign of it, like delicately wrinkling her nose in revulsion. Annie Sunday had raised her son to perceive such hints.

After a long wait for the bartender's attention, Fox ordered a double whiskey and downed it without delay. Perhaps it would banish the memory of the past few weeks and all the conflicting emotions that had been churning inside him ever since his final confrontation with Custer.

"Want another, pard?" asked the bartender, a frail, bald man with a black mustache.

Fox nodded. He took the second a little slower, but instead of erasing his thoughts, the liquor seemed only to intensify them. He'd always tried to conduct his life honorably, allowing for lapses into harmless sorts of masculine vice. He wasn't a saint, but he believed in the rights and freedoms upon which America was founded.

Why, then, did his experience in Montana leave him with the taste of cowardice in his mouth? He'd offered to ride into battle, and he would have insisted on it if he'd felt the cause was just. Emotionally he continued to feel torn between his sense of duty as an American male and his sympathy for the plight of the Indians. Which side was right?

What the hell, Fox thought. It was a bigger problem than one person could unravel, so what did it matter what he thought or did?

"I declare, I thought you'd forgotten me," a soft voice purred at his shoulder.

Fox glanced down through burning eyes to discover the little raven-haired girl who had flirted with him from the balcony. Now she wore a dress of worn pink sateen, specially altered to reveal half her breasts. The fabric poufed over a bustle set high in back, then trailed down across the sawdust-covered floor. She smelled of toilet water and had a thin blue ribbon tied around her neck. Fox liked that.

"No, I didn't forget." He touched a tanned finger to her cheek. "What's your name, sweetheart?"

"Victoria." She couldn't believe that he was as attractive up close as he'd looked from a distance, but it was true. His eyes were incredibly blue, he had even teeth and a full head of chestnut hair, and his trim beard framed a strong face. He looked like he could pick her up with one hand and lift her overhead. "My mama named me for the queen of England."

Fox arched a brow, appreciative of this irony. "That was a fine gesture of faith on her part."

"Folks say I'm prettier than Queen Victoria," she remarked.

"Well, I'd have to agree with that."

Victoria asked for gin and bitters from the bartender, and Fox paid for it, extending his own glass for a refill at the same time. He was beginning to feel the way he'd hoped to feel—kind of numb and extremely distant from the real world. It was almost possible to pretend that he had no problems, no guilt, no past, no future. All that the moment demanded of him was that he smile and enjoy himself.

"You look like you've wore yourself out getting to Deadwood," Victoria decided, leaning against his broad chest so that her breasts brushed against him. "Was it worth it?"

Before he could answer, someone shouted for quiet and an odd-looking trio appeared on the Gem's small stage, which was located at the far end of the barroom. There was a woman wearing a fancy gown of crimson velvet that looked too hot for the season, a man with a fiddle, and a youth carrying what appeared to be a trumpet. The man who'd been shouting stood in front of the stage. He waved his hands in the air.

"Now, folks," he cried, "I gotta ask you to give us your attention. You all are in for a *rare* feast for the senses, an opportunity to witness a performance by the one and only Queen of Song. Yes, pards, I am indeed referring to the world-famous Miss Viola de Montmorency, who is here in Deadwood on the eve of her departure for the great capitals of Europe, where she will sing before kings and queens and emperors and such!"

As Miss de Montmorency began her first ballad, accompanied by the two game musicians, it occurred to Fox that she looked a bit worn around the edges for this songbird role. Victoria seemed to read his mind.

"You look like you're in the mood for a little repose. Want to come upstairs where it's quiet? I can take off your boots and rub your neck. . . ."

It was a funny thing, the instincts a man had for a woman. Fox didn't care for her scent, yet it worked on him; and he didn't find her particularly attractive, but his body responded anyway to her warm curves pushing at him and the suggestive invitation in her voice. Annie Sunday used to say that a true man rose above his primitive impulses and would never sleep with a woman he didn't love, let alone barely knew. Too bad the world couldn't live up to Annie Sunday's standards. It kept tempting Fox, and sometimes he felt reckless. Maybe it was really weakness, but "reckless" sounded more manly.

"That sounds like an invitation I'd be a fool to refuse, Victoria. I'll bring the bottle, just in case we get thirsty." He gathered his other possessions and followed Victoria up the stairway, which was already beginning to warp. It smelled like freshly cut pine and cheap perfume and men who needed baths. Fox watched the way Victoria's bustle twitched as she mounted the stairs above him. Bemused by life and his own baser instincts, he smiled.

Upstairs, there were more curtained doorways, with girls' names written above them in chalk. Fox was relieved to discover that Victoria's room had a real door; it seemed a favorable portent. When she turned the knob and stood aside, she glanced at him under her lashes with coy shyness, and he almost believed that it was genuine. Inside the narrow bedroom, with one window overlooking Main Street, Fox set down his belongings, doffed his hat, and let out a harsh sigh.

"Sit right down there on the bed and make yourself comfortable," she instructed, while lighting an oil lamp on the bureau. "Here, lie back. I'll take off your boots."

Sheer exhaustion, coupled with the wallop of the whiskey, struck Fox with astonishing force as soon as he put his head back on the pillow with its perfumed-lace covering. Victoria was a blur above him, tugging at his boots.

"I don't know," he managed to mutter, "if that's a good idea. I should've had a bath. . . ."

Victoria poured him another whiskey and held it to his lips, cooing, "Now, now, don't you fret. You think I'm used to a clean man in *this* town?" She laughed, hugely amused by that notion. "I know you're tired, and I know what you need for a good night's sleep. Just lie still. I'll undress you."

God, tired was a weak description for the way he felt. The bed, with its lumps and broken springs, was like a gift from the angels, and Fox seemed to sink into it. He let his mind drift. He saw Custer, with his curls shorn, sitting astride Vic in the dawn light. And then he dreamed about a rattlesnake stalking him as he slept under the Wyoming moonlight. Madeleine Avery was making tea and serving it in her best china cups, but she said that Fox couldn't come into her house and drink his portion until he'd had a bath and donned clean, pressed clothes. "You must wear a paper collar," she said, backing away from him as if repulsed, "and a Prince Albert frock coat, and I will not permit cursing. . . ."

Victoria found that it was rather a chore to undress such a

big man, particularly since he appeared to be completely unconscious. Still, she enjoyed every moment, each glimpse of lean, tanned flesh. The more she saw, the more she prayed that he'd revive enough to do what they'd come upstairs for. Fox was the best-looking man she'd seen since coming to Deadwood. His hair, burnished in the lamplight, curled just so over his collar and across one temple. There was a crinkled pattern of laugh lines framing his eyes, which had thick lashes. His face was strong, weather-beaten, and bearded, but there was something about his cheekbones and the line of his nose and the shape of his mouth that reminded her of a man of breeding . . . the kind of man she'd seen pictures of but had never actually met.

Biting her lip, she unfastened his buckskin trousers and slowly worked them down over his hips and long, well-muscled legs. Her heart beat fast when she stood back then and drank in the sight of him, for Fox wore no drawers. He was a big man: tall, yet lean-hipped, and chiseled like a statue. Even his private parts were well shaped and looked highly promising to her now experienced eye. When she tried to get his blue shirt off, Fox woke up a little. He smiled at her, as if she were a nurse, and lifted his arms obediently.

"Mercy," Victoria breathed, tilting her head to one side as she stared at his naked body. His face was turned on the pillow and he'd slipped back into his dreams, one arm curved above his head. Victoria decided that in her opinion, this was the ideal male body. His sun-darkened chest was broad, hard, and covered with the perfect amount of crisp hair, just like his legs and forearms. Although she didn't care for men with smooth chests, an overabundance of hair was almost worse, especially when it grew up their backs and over their shoulders. Some fellows also had big white bellies, and those she longed to charge double.

Her inventory of Fox ended, there seemed little for Victoria to do but have another drink, get undressed, and join him in bed. It was awfully early for her to be in bed with the intent to sleep, but it would probably do her complexion good.

Besides, she mused as she sipped her whiskey and wrestled with the fastenings on her gown, if she snuggled against him naked and touched him just so, there was no telling what might happen in the middle of the night. . . .

Chapter Four

July 9, 1876

"YOU TRULY GOT YOURSELF A BED?" ASKED OLD Frenchy Cachlin, wide-eyed under the frayed brim of his stovepipe hat. "That was real lucky."

"I know, and I'm grateful." Fox, who had paid ten cents extra for the clean water Frenchy'd carried in buckets from Whitewood Creek, recognized immediately that the proprietor of the bathhouse was dull-witted. Still, he liked the fellow. After soaping his head and dunking it under the water, Fox surfaced and gave him a smile. "Yesterday I went back to the Grand Central Hotel for another of their very tasty meals. While I was eating, Wagner, the owner, let me know that there was space now in the upstairs. I was glad, particularly because the food's so good there."

Old Frenchy nodded with enthusiasm. "I know! Aunt Lou Marchbanks is the cook. She's a colored lady, you know. Real dark."

"A woman of rare talent." Fox rinsed his hair again, rubbed the droplets of water from his beard, then stood up and shivered. Frenchy, who was also known as the "bottle fiend" because of his huge and unusual collection of glass receptacles, rushed to hand him his biggest, thickest towel.

"I like you, Fox."

"I like you, too." He gave Frenchy a grin, then began to rub his head vigorously. Part of the reason that Old Frenchy was so happy to see him, Fox knew, was because few of

58

Deadwood's residents ever came near the bathhouse. As much as they hated lice, they seemed to hate soap and water more.

The bathhouse was actually owned by Dr. O. E. Sick, which was why Fox had passed Frenchy an extra dime after his first bath yesterday. This morning he was inclined to make it fifteen cents. When at last he was dressed in clean clothes fresh from a Chinese laundry, he gathered up his toilet kit and turned to Old Frenchy.

"Now, there's fifteen cents for the clean water, ten cents more for hot, and this last fifteen cents is for *you*. Don't you go giving it to Dr. Sick."

"Much obliged!" His face lit up with innocent joy. "Y'know what I'd like? I'd like you to come to my cabin sometime and see my bottles. There are *thousands*, I bet."

"I'd be honored." Fox shook his hand, then headed out the door into the July sunlight.

Standing on a crate that was half sunk in the swamp where Wall Street turned onto Main was a thin, black-haired, bearded man with the fire of God in his eyes. "Repent!" he shouted into the badlands. "Do not stray from the laws of God and you shall find salvation!"

Fox dropped a coin into the hat that the minister had propped before him. There were a few pinches of gold there already, but nothing else. This was a place sorely in need of the word of God, and Fox knew Annie Sunday would want him to offer the fellow encouragement.

"Bless you." The minister paused for a moment, bending over to clasp Fox's hand. "The name's Henry Smith, but folks in the Black Hills just call me Preacher Smith. I see all kinds come and go in this town every single day, but you're different. A good man, I think. It's something in the eyes I've learned to recognize."

"Well . . ." Fox bit his lip, thinking of the coy, knowing smiles he got from Victoria every time she saw him. He wished *he* knew what they meant. "I s'pose I'm a sinner just like everyone else who's drawn to a town like this, but I do like to think that in spite of my mistakes, God cares for me

. . . and maybe He thinks I have"—Fox flashed a grin—"potential."

Preacher Smith didn't smile much, but it was hard to resist this strong, tanned fellow with the look of a renegade. "God won't give up on you, son, and neither will I." Gazing heavenward, he shouted, "Dear Lord, look kindly on this town! The folks here need your love and your forgiveness, too. . . ."

Continuing on his way, Fox felt that familiar, prickly mixture of conflicting emotions, made worse by the reminder that God knew all the secrets he was trying to keep from everyone else in Deadwood. Fortunately he had a supper engagement and welcomed the distraction of preparations. Madeleine and Benjamin Avery were guaranteed to take his mind off his troubles.

"I agree that we should fix a special meal in honor of Father's homecoming," Maddie remarked to her grandmother, "but do you really imagine that he expects such extravagance?" She looked around at the bounty that seemed to spread throughout the kitchen. "I had no idea you were buying such things. Why didn't you take me with you?"

Susan O'Hara turned to face her granddaughter, her pretty gown of violet silk covered by a long blue-checked apron that was dusted with flour. "I had a mind to do a bit of exploring on my own, to tell you the truth. Wang Chee was kind enough to take me while you were outside in your new garden. I made the acquaintance of young Peter Gushurst, who has the store where Chee's been buying our supplies. Mr. Gushurst had other treasures that he hadn't put on the shelves, and he told me about one or two other shopkeepers in town who are selling produce and jam and baked goods and such." She swept a blue-veined hand from left to right, indicating all her purchases.

Maddie followed her gesture with a puzzled frown. There was a bowl of succulent, fragrant strawberries, which Gramma Susan had announced would be wedded with the fresh buttermilk biscuits she'd just baked to make strawberry shortcake, topped with rich cream. She'd gotten hold of some game birds, now plucked and cleaned and difficult to identify with certainty. They were waiting in a pan to roast in the wood-fired oven. There was a basket of string beans and carrots, and several young cucumbers formed a pyramid on the table.

"I bought some rice, which I thought would taste good with gravy," Susan was saying as she began snapping the ends off the beans. "They eat differently out here than we did in Philadelphia, but that's to be expected. Certainly we can't buy the same variety of foods, yet I was surprised to find canned goods, like tomatoes, and fresh herbs, and soda crackers. I bought some lovely-looking brandied peaches, and a fine bottle of sparkling catawba wine to accompany our meal."

"Gramma Susan, are you simply in a cooking mood, or is there more to this?" Madeleine had spent the past two hours working among the seedlings in her carefully planned flower garden, determined that it would be beautiful and graceful. Dreams for the garden had occupied her thoughts all morning, but now she let them go. Her indefatigable grandmother was up to something.

"Perhaps I have a surprise for you all," Susan said, with a secret smile, as she slowly turned her head and gazed out the window. "Indulge me, my darling."

"What *kind* of surprise could you possibly have in this godforsaken town? Sugar for our coffee? Did you find a gold nugget that you are going to unveil during tonight's celebratory meal?" Madeleine's voice rose, betraying her impatience. "Oh, Gramma, how can you be so—so *high-spirited*? The only source of excitement in my life at this moment is the prospect of my seedlings flourishing during the next fortnight! I confess, I begin to wish I had never come here. Benjamin is always off running wild with that other little boy, and I don't know how to stop that—"

"Maddie, dear, he's a little boy himself! It's summer. What would you have him do besides play in the sunshine? Sit indoors and read *Gulliver's Travels*?"

Madeleine's green eyes were beginning to flash. "Now that you mention it, that's an excellent idea! And what about Father? We came out here to be with him, yet he seems to make appearances in his own house just to be polite! I thought that he *needed* me. . . ." She stared at the strawberries, then defiantly popped one into her mouth. Good breeding demanded that she chew and swallow before continuing, which gave Susan the opening she sought.

"Madeleine Hampshire Avery, what sort of attitude have you slid down into? Why, I thought that you were stronger than that—stronger and more resourceful. You're nearly a grown woman now . . . and certainly bright enough to know that you can't look to a person or a town to make you happy!"

Maddie seized on one phrase, ignoring the rest. "You're right—and I would be willing to give this *town*, and our new life, a fair chance, if Deadwood were inhabited by civilized human beings rather than—than barbarians! Honestly, Gramma, every time I have ventured down the hill, I've been leered at and—and *worse* by the most repulsive men I've ever seen! Even the placer miners Father pays stare at me and call out to me and—" She turned away, upset by her own loss of composure.

Susan O'Hara came around the worktable to stroke Maddie's shining hair. In hushed tones she soothed, "Don't despair, my darling. Wait a bit; give Deadwood a chance. It's nothing like Philadelphia, I'll admit that, but I believe in adventure." She kissed Madeleine's flushed cheek. "Now then, I'll give you a hint regarding my surprise, just to lift your spirits. Everyone in Deadwood isn't immoral or lice-ridden or crazed with lust. I've invited someone to join us for supper tonight, someone I think your father will like and we'll all enjoy entertaining."

" 'Entertaining'?" Maddie echoed faintly. "*Here*? Why, there's still so much to be done before the house is fit for guests! I don't see how we can possibly—"

"*Phsssht!*" Gramma interrupted with a wave of her hand. "The meal I have planned and the company of all of us should be more than enough to please the most discerning caller. However, if you're that concerned about the appearance of our home, you might want to continue unpacking that trunk filled with Colleen's things. There's plenty of time to hang a picture or two, to spread your mother's lace cloth over the table, to arrange her needlepoint pillows on the settee . . . and don't forget the silver service and Colleen's good china." Susan nodded briskly. "Well, you are far more accomplished at such niceties than I, darling, and hardly need *my* advice. I'll leave you to it."

"But I'll need a bath—and my hair—and what shall I wear?" Maddie exclaimed in a rush, staring down in horror at her dust-covered calico dress.

"No need to fret, dear. We've hours to prepare." The picture of serenity, Susan returned to her string beans. "Everything will be just fine."

It was exciting beyond words to anticipate a real dinner party, with a real guest, in this hideously vulgar town. Perhaps there really was society here after all, and her dear Gramma had discovered one of its members! Maddie was in a near panic, mentally making lists and wondering how she could ever do all that was necessary in a few short hours. The trunk; that would come first! Her heart began to pound with anticipation as she hurried off to find it. So great was her pleasure that she forgot to ask or even to wonder about the identity of the mystery guest.

"You!"

When Madeleine opened the front door, pink-cheeked with excitement, she couldn't suppress an exclamation of shock at the sight of Fox. Ever since their first meeting, she had tried to block the memory of him from her mind. Now he had returned just when their first dinner guest was due, tainting her pleasure and perhaps ruining everything.

"My dear Miss Avery," Fox said, sweeping off his hat as he bowed before her, "may I say that your beauty does this humble town great honor?"

"No, you may not!" she snapped, blocking the doorway.

"Mr.—Fox, or whatever your name is, I must tell you that we are expecting a very important dinner guest, and—"

"Fox!" Susan O'Hara emerged from the kitchen, having removed her apron. She looked exhilarated and ageless as she extended her hands to her guest. "How handsome you look! Goodness, you are altogether devastating!"

A wry smile crept over his mouth as he glanced down at the Prince Albert frock coat, starched white collar, pressed gray trousers, and expertly knotted black silk tie he had donned for the occasion. The clothes, he knew, emphasized his broad shoulders and powerful physique. "It's kind of you to say so, Mrs. O'Hara, but it seems that my efforts were in vain. I had hoped to change your granddaughter's opinion of me, to convince her that I am not the oaf she believes. However . . ."

"I am astute enough to know, sir, that a lot of fancy decoration is worthless if it's covering up something—or *someone*—that is low and crude and—"

"Madeleine!" Gramma Susan broke in, horrified. "Never in my life have I heard you display such a shocking lack of manners. What would your mother say if she could hear you?"

Angry and confused, Maddie felt as if her cheeks were on fire. "Gramma, you don't understand. Why do we have to see this man? Especially now, when we are expecting your dinner guest. How *hungry* I am for a few hours of civilized conversation, for the company of a person of quality, not this . . . this brute!"

Fox, discovering that he was enjoying himself immensely, turned to his elderly hostess and cocked an eyebrow. "I believe I did try to warn you. . . ."

Susan shook her head. "Imagine my dismay! It seems that I must apologize once again for my granddaughter, who has been, until now, the most rigidly decorous young lady I have ever known." She turned to Maddie, longing to shake her. "My dear, your faux pas intensifies with each word you utter. Don't you see. . . ? *Fox* is the surprise guest I have invited to join us for supper!"

For an instant, Maddie's horror was such that she feared she might faint again. But then the door to her father's bedroom opened and he and Benjamin appeared. Benjamin looked grumpy but impeccably groomed in his little blue suit and the shoes he'd worn to church in Philadelphia. They were pinching him now, and his pants were too small, but his hair was neatly parted in the middle and slicked down, and he even wore a paper collar. The instant he recognized Fox, the boy's freckles seemed to become twice as prominent against his suddenly white face.

"What are *you* doing here?" he cried.

"Mr. Daniel is our guest for supper tonight, and I trust that you'll remember your manners," Gramma Susan said, with a brief, threatening glance. She turned toward her son-in-law. "Stephen I would like you to meet Fox Daniel. Fox, this is my son-in-law, Stephen Avery."

As the two men shook hands and exchanged pleasantries, Fox said quickly, "Please, everyone just call me Fox. I'd rather forget I have a surname. I like my life as simple as possible these days."

Susan and Maddie had converted a corner of the parlor into a dining area, daring to raise the leaves on the creaking drop-leaf table. Covered with Colleen's lace cloth, the table was made even more charming by a Tucker porcelain vase filled with wild daisies, orange wood lilies, and delicate blue harebells. Earlier, Madeleine had unpacked the china and set each place with loving care. Her mother had cherished beautiful things, and many of the treasures Maddie had grown up with had been acquired by her great-grandfather Lion during his days as a sea captain during the China trade. So tonight the table was set with green-and-white Cantonese dishes, silver flatware, and fresh linen napkins. Long white tapers flickered in carved silver candlesticks. The effect was so lovely that Maddie might have been able to pretend that they were not in Deadwood at all, just for these few hours—if their dinner guest had been anyone else.

"Ah," Stephen murmured in bemusement as they approached the table, "I see that my darling daughter has been toiling diligently this afternoon. I had no idea that you had brought so many of your mother's things, Madeleine. Apparently my instructions about packing sparingly were ignored.''

Maddie flushed. Her father didn't know the half of it. There were still books, quilts, and other assorted knickknacks that she had yet to unpack. Fortunately her father seemed to be so absentminded these days that he hadn't noticed the framed botanical prints and landscapes that now graced the walls, or the embroidered pillows, or any of the other additions to their humble parlor.

''Don't spoil the few pleasures left to Maddie, Stephen,'' Susan O'Hara said in a quiet, firm tone. ''She's Colleen's daughter through and through, and you couldn't expect her to change into some sort of female bullwhacker just because she's moved West.''

''God forbid,'' Stephen replied, laughing. ''No, we certainly couldn't have that!''

They took their chairs, with Fox seated between Stephen and Susan, across from the two Avery offspring. As Wang Chee appeared to pour wine and serve a cold julienne soup, Fox stole a leisurely sidelong gaze at Madeleine Avery. She was worked up, despite the disappointment of his presence— worked up by the excitement of an *occasion*. When she looked at the table, which she had created with unerring good taste, her emerald eyes were agleam with pride and pleasure.

Fox took a sip of wine and decided that the table and the appealing food could not compare to Madeleine's own radiant loveliness. It was jarring to encounter such a woman in a town like Deadwood, saturated as it was with the worst sort of men on the loose, men who chose to live raucously, without the gentler influence of women. Fox understood how Stephen Avery had come to bring his children here, but it still seemed crazy. Madeleine was a woman, yet whom could she befriend in this wild place? Was she destined to remain a virtual prisoner in this house, fussing with her china and polishing her silver and reading books about the gentler life she'd been bred to expect?

"Why are you looking at me like that?" Maddie inquired suddenly. Had she discerned a glint of pity in his azure eyes?

Fox gave her a disarming smile. "I can't pretend to be an expert on real ladies, Miss Avery, but I was thinking that it's a rare pleasure for someone like me to be sharing a meal with a genuine lady like yourself." He paused, then dared to continue, "And, although you may not believe I am sincere, I will tell you all the same that you are the most *beautiful* genuine lady I have ever seen in my life."

In return she eyed him suspiciously, even if inwardly she basked in the flattery. What hopes she'd had for this evening! The parlor and the dining table had been as perfect as she could make them before she'd gone to bathe and dress. Finally, minutes before Fox had knocked at the door, she had stood in front of the cracked full-length mirror and known that she was very nearly as lovely as she had ever looked. Her gown had been purchased a year ago to wear to a friend's Society Hill wedding, and it suited her perfectly. The underskirt, of green-and-white-striped taffeta, had two tiers of green ruffles at the hem, and the flounced upper skirt and waist were also of clear leaf green. The cut of the gown accented her tiny waist and high breasts, while at her neck flared a stiff ruffled collar, narrowly edged in green, to pick up the vivid hue of her thick-lashed eyes and set off her upswept apricot curls.

All afternoon Maddie had dreamed of making a good impression. Having prayed for a word, or even a look, of approval, she found it hard not to warm to Fox's compliments.

But she would not like him.

Benjamin pouted with her, but by the time they were eating game hens with cherry sauce, Maddie sensed that her little brother was thawing slightly. After all, Gramma Susan seemed positively smitten with this overbearing stranger, and even their father was chatting with Fox as if they were old friends.

After the two men had exchanged facts pertaining to the

length of time they'd been in the Hills and the general reasons they were there (Fox cited gold and adventure, an all-purpose answer), Stephen said abruptly, "Young man, I don't know how much time you've spent in the West, but you must be aware that these Hills are still Indian land, strictly speaking. Do you have an opinion on the Laramie Treaty of 1868, or what the Sioux Indians are having to suffer to satisfy our lust for gold and more land?"

Fox nearly dropped his forkful of string beans. Straightening on his chair, he reached for his wine and took a sip before replying carefully, "You'll pardon me for appearing taken aback, sir, but that's not a subject most men in Deadwood care to discuss."

"But you are not most men, are you, Fox?" Stephen persisted quietly.

"Why, Stephen, you surprise me!" Gramma Susan exclaimed. "You're more astute than I gave you credit for!"

Fox continued to search the eyes of his host. "I have strong opinions about the Fort Laramie Treaty, Mr. Avery, and I have many opinions about the way our race has dealt with the Indians. Suffice it to say that I think our actions are nothing short of criminal. Just *eight* years ago, we gave our word to the Sioux that the Black Hills would remain theirs forever, and already we're going back on our promises. My feelings about the Laramie Treaty pretty much echo my views on the entire situation with the Indians." Fox relaxed a little, sensing Stephen's approval, and leaned back in his chair as Wang Chee cleared their plates. "You must know, though, Mr. Avery, that opinions like mine aren't exactly popular in Deadwood. I'm not prepared to make speeches on Main Street alongside Preacher Smith."

"You sympathize with the Sioux, and yet you're here yourself—an interloper just like the rest of us?" Stephen wondered aloud.

"Perhaps greed has overridden your new friend's loftier principles," Maddie suggested, rather surprised by the growing sharpness of her tongue.

"Madeleine, that was rude," her father said. "I'm certain you didn't mean to say such a thing."

"Perhaps not." She stared down at her plate, feeling Fox's perceptive eyes on her.

Stephen turned to his guest. "How would you like to take a little stroll outdoors before dessert, Fox? We could continue this discussion in private . . . and I may have a business proposition for you."

When the two men had gone, Maddie bit her lip in frustration. "Hideous, hideous man! Gramma, why must you like him so, and why has fate decreed that *Father* must also take to him like a long-lost son?" She threw down her napkin and made a face.

"I'm startin' to like him, too," Benjamin announced suddenly, grinning at his sister. "Fox calls me *Ben*!"

"Traitors," Maddie muttered, "you're all traitors."

"For heaven's sake, darling, don't scowl so!" Susan rose to assist Wang Chee as he cleared the table. "Come and help us with the strawberry shortcake. Do you know, I think that you're sulking because Fox didn't devote enough attention to *you* throughout supper. You may insist that you despise him, but when he paid you that extravagant compliment, your face betrayed you. No innocent schoolgirl has ever blushed more prettily than you—"

"*Hush up!*" Maddie cried as she followed with a stack of plates. "What a cruel, horrid thing to say! Why, if you weren't so old and your bones weren't so brittle, I'd shake you until you begged my pardon and promised never to tease me so again!"

Susan gave her a knowing smile over one tiny shoulder. "You'd have to catch me first, darling."

Chapter Five

July 12, 1876

AT ONE O'CLOCK IT WAS GROWING HOTTER BY THE moment, yet there was clarity in the air on Deadwood's rock-crowned hillsides and in the deep blue sky overhead that made the temperature more bearable. The mountain landscape *looked* cooler.

The miners went on with their work, though they might pause for whiskey and a nap if the heat became intolerable later in the afternoon. In addition to the cleared land where placer mining was in progress, men used sluice boxes, rockers, riffles, and pans to ply the strips of ground between buildings that backed up to the creek. Some had even begun tunneling *under* buildings to get at the gold dust trapped at bedrock.

Fox stood on the lot he'd purchased from Stephen Avery, wiped sweat from his brow with a handkerchief, and smiled at the clutter of Deadwood that twisted away to the north. It was like a long, narrow hive, buzzing continuously with activity. Now it was to be his home.

The twenty-five-by-one-hundred-foot parcel of land that sat between the Avery house and the rest of Stephen's claims had been offered to Fox the night he'd supped with the Avery family. Stephen had been reasonably certain that all the gold had been already taken from the lot, and he welcomed the opportunity to choose his neighbor. He'd liked the younger man immensely, trusted him; with Fox living next to them, Stephen could leave Deadwood more often and worry less about his family's safety.

Fox himself loved the arrangement. This choice piece of land was like a gift from God, particularly in contrast with the rude bunk for which he was paying Charles H. Wagner a dollar a night. A night's sleep at the Grand Central Hotel, its upper floor still under construction, was worse than sleeping on the ground. The drunken geezer who occupied the bunk above Fox's snored like a steam engine, while the foul-mouthed boy who curled on the floor nearby had a case of lice so severe that it inspired him to scratch and curse most of the night.

Because his own sleep was constantly disrupted by the activities of his roommates, Fox remembered his nightly dreams. The first, in which he was happily among the Lakota people, was pleasant but unnerving. They behaved with great kindness and hospitality toward him, and he would feel as if he had secrets that came between them. Fox's newer dream featured Lt. Col. George Armstrong Custer. The dream was never quite the same twice, but it generally contained scenes in which he argued with Custer. There was always a sense of lost control; Fox would try to reason with the man, feel anger rising, and soon they would be shouting. In response to each thing Fox said, Custer would become more irrational, more furious.

If not for the mud, Fox would have camped on his new land. Fortunately he had the money to pay an enterprising Cornish miner named Titus Pym to speed along the process of erecting a structure he could call home. First, both men devoted two full days to combing every inch of dirt one more time and came up with more than a hundred dollars' worth of gold dust, which Fox used to pay Titus in advance for his help. They also hit upon a deep cache of nuggets for which Fox subsequently received more than a thousand dollars. The money would come in handy. Building a cabin could run three hundred dollars or more, not to mention the price of furniture and other household items.

He and Titus had already had one load of logs hauled up the hillside by mules. Now, Titus was at Judge E. G. Dudley's sawmill, which turned out twelve thousand feet of boards per day. Deadwood's three sawmills were doing a roaring business, and Fox had already decided that if he stayed, that was the work he'd pursue. In the meantime, his cabin would need lumber for its roof, floors, and door. It was good to have the Cornish man to do the waiting at the hot, dust-choked sawmill while he himself saw to some of the other chores.

Fox set about marking off the dimensions of the cabin and smoothing the ground with an iron rake to make an even surface for the floor. As the sun beat down, Fox longed to remove his red calico shirt and the boots that made his trousers seem twice as hot and confining. Unbuttoning his shirt and rolling the sleeves up past his elbows, he mused that a person could probably get rich in Deadwood selling cups of ice-cold water to the sweltering miners.

Leaning on his rake, Fox looked toward the Avery house, which was hidden behind a dense row of pine trees. He knew that the evergreen barrier was meant to separate the rough miners from Stephen Avery's cultured eastern family, but it still seemed odd to Fox that they hadn't noticed *him*. At first, when he and Titus were sifting the claim for overlooked gold, Fox had constantly expected Madeleine Avery to appear like a vision in one of her perfect, proper gowns, every sun-bright lock pinned neatly into place. Best of all, however, would be the wonderful scene she would make, fueled by outrage over his proximity.

But two full days had passed without any sign of the Averys, and now Fox began to wonder. Was it possible that Madeleine really didn't know he was here . . . and soon to be her neighbor? Or, worse, might she know and be indifferent?

It seemed that the logical thing for him to do was go next door, apologize for his appearance, and request a glass of water. Weren't they all friends? Fox ran long fingers through his grimy, wind-ruffled hair, dusted off his pants and hands as best he could, and walked toward the wall of pine trees. At the last moment he remembered that his suspenders

were hanging loose and caught one in each thumb. Drawing
them over his wide shoulders, he smiled to himself and strode
onward. Madeleine Avery would doubtless be disgusted by
the sight of him, but the prospect of seeing *her* was suddenly
more appealing to him than the water he craved.

Maddie was hard-pressed to remember a more distressing
day. First, her father had announced that he would be leaving
Deadwood again in the morning and had gone off to buy
supplies. Then, Benjamin had sliced open his thumb while
playing with a kitchen knife. Gramma Susan and Wang Chee
had taken him, shrieking with fear, to Dr. Sick to see if the
wound needed stitching. Also, for some unknown reason
Gramma had taken it into her head to bake bread today, in
the middle of a heat wave—so Maddie was left behind to
knead the dough, perspiring through the threadbare blue cotton dress she'd worn during the worst of their journey West.
When a visitor came calling she tried to ignore the insistent
knocks, but to no avail.

The garish, painted creature who forced open the front
door and sashayed into the kitchen introduced herself as
"Garnet Loomis." She was carrying several jars of service-
berry jam, which she boasted of having put up herself. Apparently she had met Gramma Susan at Mr. Gushurst's store,
and, she insisted, they were now the closest of friends. The
jam was a present for "Susie," she announced loudly, stack-
ing the jars on the makeshift kitchen table.

Unprepared for company, Maddie was embarrassed to
be seen even by this Garnet Loomis creature. She related
the sad tale of Benjamin's accident, trying to look weak
and preoccupied at the same time, certain that Mrs.
Loomis would apologize for her intrusion and hurry on
her way.

"You poor little thing!" The big-boned old woman jumped
up and shocked Maddie by capturing her in a crushing hug.
"You need help, and Garnet's here to give it to ya! You just
sit down and have a rest. I'll knead that bread dough for ya

and it'll be the best bread you ever tasted, I kin promise you that!"

Overwhelmingly relieved to be freed of Mrs. Loomis's embrace, Maddie staggered backward and dropped onto a ladder-back chair. Her shoulders ached and she was so, so hot, but somehow, watching Garnet Loomis take over *her* kitchen, she felt a surge of renewed energy.

"You are much too kind," she said rather firmly, rising from her chair. "However, I really cannot allow you to do my chores, Mrs. Loomis."

"No, no, I *want* to do this!" The old woman clearly meant to put an end to any protests. She began kneading the dough with such force that Maddie cringed involuntarily; it looked as if Garnet were hurting the stuff. "You're not used to the life out here and we all know it. Takes a while to toughen up. Why, I came to St. Louis forty years ago and I never thought I'd make it through the first winter." Garnet beat on the dough, turning it rhythmically as she continued in a loud voice, "But, I did, and I liked it. Married a French fur trader who brought me to Fort Laramie, went out to set trap lines, an' never came back." She shook her head, laughing at the memory. "Men out there just ain't husband material, if you know what I mean, missy! Anyways, then I had to take up some sort of profession if I wanted to eat, and there wasn't much choice. I didn't mind. Kinda fun, if you can stand the truth. 'Course, now I'm not exactly prime goods, but I look after the younger girls; teach 'em the trade and mother 'em when they need it. Not a bad life for an old broad who loves adventure, huh? Al Swearingen, the Gem's owner, talked me into bringin' some of my girls out from Cheyenne in May, and I thought, Why the hell not?"

Madeleine was quite speechless. Pasting on a polite smile, she helped Garnet Loomis transfer the kneaded dough into an ironstone bowl, which she covered with a towel. "How kind of you to help me. I do believe I am a bit fatigued by the heat, so your assistance was certainly welcome. Now, I hope you won't think me rude, but I must—"

"Oh, I'll go in a minute, honey, but let's set a spell and cool off with a little refreshment. Any whiskey?"

Maddie tried not to betray her shock. "Why—ah—no, I don't believe so . . ."

Looking around the kitchen, Garnet spied a decanter of brandy on a shelf. "That'll do." She plucked an unwashed glass off the table and poured in a generous amount of the amber liquid. Maddie declined to join her, but sat stiffly opposite her guest and conversed as courteously as she was able. As it turned out, there was little for her to do but endure, for Garnet talked almost nonstop, even answering her own questions.

"I hope you won't think I'm bein' rude, dearie, but I'm startin' to worry that you're going to have a worse time fittin' in here than I thought. You're not just weak and timid—you think you're better'n the rest of us, don'tcha?" Garnet tossed back the brandy, then poured another. "Well, that won't do, if you mean to stay. Not if you want friends, leastways. I s'pose you've a notion that all we got in Deadwood is sin and vice and a lot of foul-mouthed miners who spit all day long. Ain't that so?" Maddie opened her mouth to reply, but Garnet spared her the effort. "Yeah, well, this town is growin' to be a place of real class. Maybe you didn't hear that an actual theater troupe is come to Deadwood! It's Jack Langrishe, who's hugely famous—you've probably heard of him even back East—and his wife and two other actresses. They're putting up a theater right this minute down on Main Street, and then there will be plays like *Hamplet* and such, I shouldn't wonder! So you see, honey, there's no cause for you to think you're better'n the rest of us. Take some advice from old Garnet—just join in and throw off those airs. If you don't, they'll just keep gettin' in your way of a good time!"

Madeleine felt dangerously, crazily close to tears when Garnet Loomis reached across the table, pinched her cheek hard, and tugged it to-and-fro. When a tapping came at the kitchen door, she looked up hopefully. Fox ducked his handsome head under the lintel.

"I apologize if I'm intruding . . ." he said hesitantly, glancing from Maddie to Mrs. Loomis with ill-concealed curiosity.

"Absolutely not!" Maddie jumped to her feet and rushed to greet him as if he were a much loved relative returning from the war. "What a perfectly lovely surprise, Fox! How well you look!"

In truth, that was an understatement. For an instant time seemed to stop as Maddie soaked up the picture Fox made framed in the sunlit doorway. He was thoroughly bronzed by the sun, which made his eyes even more crisply blue in contrast, and when he smiled the flash of his teeth was startling. Maddie could see that he was grimy and sweaty, too, but that made him appear stronger, leaner, taller, and more intensely male than ever.

"Could you spare a cup of water for a thirsty man?" he asked.

Maddie hurried to comply, and they all were silent for a minute as he drank. Finally, Garnet Loomis spoke up in loudly flirtatious tones, "Well, well, at last I get to meet the man every girl in Deadwood's pinin' for . . . 'specially little Victoria!" She winked, then stood up and put out her hand as abruptly as a man. "Fox, I'm Garnet Loomis! Come on and sit with us. I've been helpin' Miss Madeleine with her bread dough. You know how these eastern girls are, all weak and pale, fainting at a moment's notice!"

Maddie, who had already been blushing, felt her cheeks flame. With a slow smile that begged her to meet his eyes, Fox said, "Faint? Miss Avery? Impossible! It is tempting, I know, to underestimate beautiful women, but in this case you should know that Miss Avery is a lady of rare character and intrepidity." He clasped Garnet's hand briefly, assessing the situation. "I'm afraid that neither I nor Miss Avery can spare the time to socialize, Mrs. Loomis. I am a very busy man, and I have come to discuss business that relates to Mr. Avery's mining claims. If you'll excuse us . . ."

Garnet all but dug in her heels as Fox steered her toward the front door. "Say, did you hear the news? Jacob Horn rode into town this morning with an Injin head! He's been carrying it around to all the saloons, hopin' to sell it."

"I doubt whether Miss Avery is interested," Fox remarked dryly.

Shaking her head and frowning, Garnet declared, "Injins is somethin' we all have to think about, whether we like it or not. You heard that sayin', 'The only good Injin is a dead one,' well, that's *true*, believe you me. All I can say is that it's a good thing us whites didn't give up until we got these Hills back from those simpleminded savages who never had any notion of how to put this land to use. Some Injin lovers'll tell ya that those bloodthirsty, sneaking Sioux deserved to keep the Hills, but the truth is that they barely tiptoed higher than the foothills 'cause they were scared that those evil spirits they believe in would strike 'em with lightning or some such nonsense. They're no more capable of making proper use of prize land like these Hills than a bunch of animals would be. Not only that—"

"Mrs. Loomis, at the risk of sounding like one of those Indian lovers you despise, I have to confess that I disagree with almost everything you've just said. Unfortunately I don't have time to set you straight about the Sioux, but meeting you has been very interesting." Fox opened the door and waved a dark hand to indicate that she was to exit. "Do have a pleasant afternoon."

A pang of guilt propelled Maddie to the doorway. "I appreciate all your help, Mrs. Loomis. And I know that my grandmother will be so pleased by your gift. It was extremely kind of you to think of us."

Backing away from the little frame house, Garnet Loomis looked uncustomarily befuddled. "You tell Susie that I made that jam from serviceberries I gathered myself!"

"I give you my word," Maddie said sincerely. Then, the moment the door was shut, she looked up into Fox's dancing eyes and the two of them burst out laughing. Maddie clapped a hand over her own mouth and tried to stifle her mirth.

"Don't let her hear you!" she managed to gasp, leaning on Fox's arm. "The poor thing. She means well. . . ."

He stopped laughing then and cocked an eyebrow at her. "The hell she does! If you let an overbearing person like Garnet Loomis call the tune, she'll do her best to tyrannize you." Suddenly he was keenly aware of Madeleine's nearness, the light pressure of her hand on his bare forearm and the fresh green color of her eyes. "Perhaps I am prejudiced against women of her type," he murmured. "She sees the world only through her own eyes and has no patience with those who believe differently."

"And I thought I was being magnificently tolerant because I was trying not to condemn her on the basis of her appearance and manners," Maddie replied, with a laugh. "How could I have known that you of all people would make such a lofty, philosophical appraisal of Mrs. Loomis?" Then, suddenly, a look of horror crossed her face as she remembered her own appearance. Fox, who was just a few inches away, had begun to let his eyes roam over her, smiling to himself as he took in her bedraggled hair, flour-smudged face, and threadbare frock.

Before she could distance herself from him, she found herself backed against the parlor wall. "Don't worry," Fox said, amused, as if he'd read her mind. "I like the way you look. In fact, it's reassuring to discover that you *can* look like this."

"Like a slovenly hag?" Maddie's heart began to pound as she gazed defiantly into his eyes. Fox towered over her, and there was something about him that was perversely exciting.

"A hag?" He laughed. "Hardly. You're a beautiful woman, Miss Avery, more beautiful than you know. But, every time I've seen you, you look like one of those rich society females portrayed in *Godey's Lady's Book*, every hair in place and your body stiff and perfect. *Too* perfect for my taste." A wave of daring caught him by surprise, and he slid an arm around her tiny waist. "You're downright radiant just like this, with your skin fresh and your hair curling the way it wants to. That gown may not be fancy, but it shows your own shape instead of one that changes you with bones and bustles. Most of all, you don't look like you're afraid to move—or be touched!—for fear of disturbing your immaculate countenance. I'm reassured to discover that you are secretly a woman, after all, and not a porcelain doll.''

"Mr. . . . Fox, your overfamiliarity o'ersteps the boundaries that must exist between a well-bred lady and . . . the men of her acquaintance.'' Even as she spoke, Maddie was horrified to realize that her words lacked conviction. In point of fact she was having difficulty breathing. "You . . . must be aware, sir, that propriety further dictates that you and I should not even be alone together in this house, else . . .''

"Else I might attempt to compromise your virtue?'' Fox said in a soft, richly amused voice. He leaned closer, so that she could feel the warmth of his breath on her brow. "Fear not, Miss Avery. If I admire your beauty or touch your waist, what crime is that? Your virtue is safe with me . . . unless, of course, *you* wish otherwise?''

Flushing and dizzy, Maddie felt his body press against her slim form. And she *liked* it. She knew that she ought to utter an outraged protest, but in her secret heart, she was thrilled and tantalized.

Slowly Fox slid his arms around her, loving the way fragility and womanliness blended in her body. She was slightly damp with perspiration, and he thought idly that this must be the way paradise smelled: floral, clean, yeasty, and just a little musky. The feel of her warm curves and her fragrance and the sight of her astonishing marmalade-bright hair made him want to flick open all the buttons on her gown and bring her to life. How much passion must be locked in her prim little soul!

"Would you like me to kiss you?'' Fox inquired, his lips and whiskers grazing her ear.

The sensation of his body pressing against her, and the tickle of his breath on her ear, sent shivers through her body that Maddie had never imagined before. She was deliciously warm, and when the shivers seemed to gather between her legs, she blushed with embarrassment and innocent yearning. "I—I don't know. I mean, I haven't before, and it would be scandalous for me to assent. . . ."

"Are you serious? You have never been kissed?"

"I'm a *lady*, if I may say so without sounding self-important. My mother was careful to protect me from . . ."

"Men like me?" Fox laughed softly. "Well, I mean no offense to you or your mother, but it's high time you were kissed, *Miss Avery*! We'll pretend it's an experiment and no one will ever know. How's that?"

"I'd really rather not have a conversation about . . . this."

"Indeed?" He flashed a grin. "I see. Despite your avowed preference for the rules of etiquette, you secretly wish to cast them off—or have me do it for you. You don't *want* a choice, do you?"

Maddie couldn't look at him. Why must he torment her so? And then, as she lowered her lashes, he took pity on her—and himself. It was alarming to realize how much he wanted her, and of course, a taste was all he could have. It would have to do.

Slowly Fox gathered her into his embrace and tipped back her delicate face. Her eyes were closed, the lids pale and nearly translucent, which made her appear even more innocent. The irony of this scene was not lost on Fox. Here he was in a town filled with wanton women, and he had found the one beauty who clung tenaciously to propriety. Moreover, that same prim but luscious beauty was now nearly swooning in his arms, eyes closed and lips pursed as she waited fearfully for her first kiss.

"Madeleine . . ."

How she wished he would stop talking and simply *take* her! "What is it?" she whispered.

"Look at me."

Swallowing hard, she complied. His eyes, so uncompromisingly blue, were inches away, smiling into her own. And there was another sort of gleam in his gaze that sent a fresh wave of shivers through her body.

"Put your arms around my neck," Fox murmured. "Go on. *Touch me.*"

Her face on fire, she obeyed. Something about the overpowering nearness of him, the strength of his shoulders and neck, the very smell of his male sweat, caused a sudden throb in Maddie's most secret place. As if he felt it, too, or saw it in her eyes, Fox smiled and brought his mouth down over hers. Her lips opened spontaneously, and she felt herself sigh from the sheer unexpected pleasure of the sensations he evoked. No wonder people liked to kiss! All these years Maddie had imagined a strange, dry pressing of one closed mouth against another. Instead it was magical. Fox seemed to caress her mouth with his, kissing parts of it, then tasting all as if she were succulent. To her further surprise, she discovered that she liked the way his mouth felt and tasted . . . and she wanted more. Her breasts had begun to tingle behind the thin cotton of her gown; never in her life had she felt like this, and she was shocked to experience a powerful urge to surrender completely to Fox's masculine spell.

When she began to run her hands through his sun-streaked hair, caressing his neck and shoulders, touching her tongue to his, Fox was thunderstruck and intensely aroused. Madeleine was ambrosia beyond his wildest dreams. The top buttons of her gown were open in deference to the heat, and he glimpsed a dusting of freckles trailing down the ivory skin hidden behind more tiny buttons. Without thinking, he pressed his lips to the base of her throat, burning to open Maddie's bodice, just to *see* her breasts. The remarkable color of her hair had attracted him from the moment they'd met, and slowly he'd allowed himself to wonder about the woman's body that went with hair the shade of rosy-gold dawn. Freckles, he now knew. The thought of her breasts, pale and opulent, with pink nipples, increased his desire to the point of pain.

When Fox kissed her throat, Maddie tasted his neck, reveling in the feeling of the muscular body holding her so effortlessly. Then, quite without warning, a familiar voice brought her hurtling back to reality.

"Ahh-hem!"

They broke apart instantly, and Maddie's knees nearly gave way. Somehow she managed to steady herself and meet the keen, perceptive gaze of Gramma Susan.

"I declare, will wonders never cease?" the old woman remarked, with a chuckle. "Fox, you have exceeded even my expectations of you on this day. I confess that I thought Maddie would be the last person in Deadwood to capitulate to your charm." As she talked, she walked away from them into the kitchen, forcing Maddie to follow. Fox, meanwhile, went over to Benjamin, who stood in the front doorway holding up his bandaged finger.

"Gramma Susan, it's not what you think," Maddie began, blushing profusely, wishing again that she'd never set eyes on Fox in the first place.

"No? What a pity." Susan O'Hara peeked under the checked towel to inspect the rising bread, then looked up with a smile. "It doesn't matter in the least what I think, my dear. I would be the last to condemn you and the first to congratulate you if you've finally tasted the pleasures of—"

"No, no, it was nothing like that!" Maddie cried. "I think I was having a sunstroke, or something like that, and—"

"Don't say you fainted again!" Susan shook her head. "How very tedious."

At that moment Fox himself appeared, filling the doorway, with Benjamin in tow. "Good afternoon, Mrs. O'Hara."

"Fox's going to take me to see where he's building his new house!" Maddie's brother exclaimed.

"I really don't think that's a good idea, Benjamin—"

"Call me Ben. Fox says it's a better name in the West."

Maddie had been too embarrassed to look at Fox before, but this was too much. "I beg your pardon, sir, but I hardly think that it's your place to choose the proper name for *my* brother, who is being raised a gentleman . . . not a crude hooligan!" Stiffly she turned her attention to Benjamin. "You have just returned from the doctor and I won't have you traipsing off to heaven knows where to see a house that isn't even built yet.''

Even Susan was smiling, and Fox bit his lip as Benjamin countered, ''Fox's house isn't going to be in heaven knows where! He's going to live right next to us, on the other side of the pine trees!''

Maddie went pale and had to grip the back of a chair to keep from swaying. Fox's smiling, bearded face seemed to dance before her eyes. ''Wh—what did you say?''

''Maybe,'' Fox himself interjected, ''I forgot to tell you that we'll soon be neighbors. That's why I came here for water; I was working just a few yards away, preparing the land for the lumber that arrives today.''

''Isn't it wonderful news?'' Susan declared. ''I must admit that for once I wholly approve of my son-in-law's judgment. He couldn't have sold that parcel to anyone I'd rather have for a neighbor. Maddie, aren't you pleased?''

''Pleased?'' she echoed, trying to force a smile. ''Pleased? Why, I'm quite . . . overcome!''

PART TWO

I think of thee!—my thoughts do twine and
  bud
About thee, as wild vines about a tree. . . .
            —Elizabeth Barrett Browning

Chapter Six

July 17, 1876

"MADELEINE AVERY, WHAT ARE YOU DOING?" Susan stood at the foot of the stairs, drying her hands on a dishtowel. "You can't hide up there reading all the time!"

Maddie appeared and descended with a book in her hand. "I've finished *The Count of Monte Cristo*, Gramma. Such a witty, sophisticated adventure—and in *France*!" She paused on the last step to sigh, beaming. "It was the perfect escape from this—this horrid wilderness. And now I shall begin *The Scarlet Letter*, as soon as I can locate it among the books still packed in the trunk. How I wish for real bookshelves!"

"*The Scarlet Letter* should certainly cheer you up," Susan remarked, with pronounced irony. "What's that book in your hand?"

Maddie held it up to display the title: *The Lady's Guide to Perfect Gentility*. "It was Mother's. She gave it to me to read at various times over the past few years—probably when there was a noticeable lapse in my manners."

Shaking her head, Susan took the volume and opened it to the table of contents. " 'Conversing with Fluency and Propriety,' " she read aloud. "How terribly boring. Let's go into the kitchen, where I have more interesting activities in progress."

Maddie followed her grandmother, protesting, "It's been very helpful for me to read portions of this book again. For example, I knew that I should not allow myself to fall into the habit of calling Mr. Daniel by his Christian name, that it was wrong, but I acquiesced because that is how everyone seems to address him. This book reminds me that such practices open the way to unpleasant familiarities . . . much more so than one might imagine.''

"Unpleasant?'' Susan echoed, baffled. "If you can bear to hear my opinion, I would say that *book* is unpleasant! Honestly, Maddie darling, why do you allow yourself to be taken in by such life-choking notions? Silly rules like those were only made to prevent human beings from genuinely enjoying themselves!''

The kitchen was hot but colorful and fragrant with the odors of fresh-baked potato bread and apple cobbler. Susan, who had been born into wealth and had become wealthier still during her marriage to Patrick O'Hara, had always believed that money meant freedom—in this case freedom to buy what she wanted in spite of the exorbitant Deadwood prices. Today, that meant paying sixty cents for a pound of butter, seventy-five cents for a dozen eggs, a dollar for a large roasting chicken, and thirty cents for a pound of fresh cheese.

"I thought we might take a picnic basket to Fox and Titus,'' she explained blithely, gesturing toward the still-warm peas and the carved chicken, which had been basted with herbs and butter while it roasted. "The cabin is coming along quite nicely, but it's such hot, exhausting work.''

Maddie looked away. In the past few days she had done everything in her power to push all thoughts of Fox from her mind. But it was no use. During the day, lying on her bed and reading compulsively, she often imagined that she could feel him staring at her open window—that if she were to rise and look through the fluttering curtains, she would see him standing on the other side of the row of pine trees, eyes shaded as he gazed right through the walls of her home. At night he haunted her dreams.

"Who is *Titus*?'' she murmured to her grandmother, wandering over to inspect the cobbler.

"Oh, he's a lovely fellow from Cornwall who is helping Fox. I never dreamed that there were so many different nationalities way out here in Dakota Territory, but it seems that the lure of gold attracts people from all over the world. I've met Cornish miners, and Chinese, of course, and Italians, Swedes, Germans, Jews, Irish, and many Negroes. I find the atmosphere extremely stimulating!'' As she spoke, Susan began putting food on plates and in bowls for the picnic lunch. "Here, darling. Let's just spoon the peas into this jar with a lid and the men can pour out what they want.''

"Gramma Susan,'' Maddie began hesitantly, "what do you think about the Indians? I mean, aren't we all trespassing on their land, strictly speaking? According to your great friend Garnet Loomis, they're savages who didn't know how to use the Black Hills or the rest of the frontier. Yet one can't help feeling a bit uneasy about the way we've simply shoved them aside. . . .''

Susan looked at Madeleine, her brow furrowed. "You needn't refer to Garnet as my 'great friend' in such tones of sarcasm, Maddie. I like her and I respect any person who is unapologetically genuine, but that does not mean that I agree with all her views.'' She brushed back a stray wisp of white hair. "I confess that I'm rather confused about the Indians myself and I mean to learn more. Ignorance and fear form the basis of prejudice, and I think that white people have rushed to judgment. We can't help wanting this wonderful land for ourselves, so we have decided that the Indians are less human than we are. That way we can justify what we do to 'further the development of civilization.' '' Susan pursed her lips thoughtfully. "Well, I mean to meet some Indians one day and form my own opinions.''

Her granddaughter could think of no response to this speech, which was extraordinary for a Philadelphia matron of advanced years. Not for the first time, Madeleine wondered how someone like Gramma Susan had produced so careful and sedate a daughter as Colleen O'Hara Avery.

Everything was ready; two large baskets with handles were

filled with food and bottles of water and ale. Fixing her attention on these items, Maddie took a step backward. "Well, I'd better return to my search for *The Scarlet Letter*. . . ."

Susan laughed. "Don't be silly. Are you so afraid of Fox that you would make a frail old woman carry these baskets all alone? Why, I could fall and strike my head and—"

"I am not *afraid* of Fox—that is, Mr. Daniel," Maddie interjected hotly. "And I think it quite unfair of you to suggest that you might fall because I did not offer to help. The reason I said—"

"Let's simply do what needs to be done." Susan pointed at the bigger basket. "You're young and strong. Lead the way."

Maddie lifted the willow basket and walked toward the door, her heart sinking. Whatever happened, there must never again be a repetition of the shocking scene that had occurred with Fox in the Avery parlor. Quickly she took inventory. Her striped muslin gown was high-necked but cool, and it covered her sufficiently. Her hair was appropriately pinned up in a chignon at the nape of her neck. No jewelry or other unnecessary decorations would lead Fox to believe she was trying to attract him. If Fox would actually be living in a house next to theirs, she must make her position crystal clear.

Affecting a lighthearted, careless attitude, she walked with Gramma Susan between the pine trees that divided their lot from Fox's. For some reason she expected to find him toiling over a pile of rough-hewn logs, attempting to construct a crude little cabin like those she'd seen being thrown up on Main Street. Instead, the sight that met her eyes caused her to stop, staring in surprise.

The parcel of land, which had recently been overrun with Stephen Avery's miners, was now smooth and flat. Beautifully cut long logs and smooth planks were stacked near the house, which appeared to be about half-finished. It *was* a log cabin, but unlike any other Maddie had seen. The frame was at least thirty-five feet across the front and twenty feet wide, and the logs were squared and fit neatly together. Two fire-places and chimneys made of rubble stone laid in lime mortar stood tall at each end of the house. Fox, Wang Chee, and a little man Maddie took to be Titus were setting a log in place on the east side of the cabin that brought the building nearly even with Fox's chest.

As the women drew nearer, Wang Chee looked up. Noticing the smile that spread over his friend's face, Fox wiped his brow and glanced back to meet Maddie's emerald eyes. The sight of her pierced his soul and he was shocked by his reaction.

"Uh-oh," Titus Pym whispered, with a bemused smile. "I've never seen you speechless before, lad."

The Cornishman's words brought Fox rudely back to reality. "Sorry." He gave Titus a sheepish grin. "Just tired, I guess. Hello, Mrs. O'Hara, Miss Avery," he called, smiling politely. "Before I inquire about those baskets you're carrying, I should introduce you to Titus Pym, who is helping me build the cabin."

"We met the day before yesterday," Susan said, leading the way inside the partially built dwelling.

"Of course. How could I have forgotten?" Fox felt a certain loss of control. He made Titus and Maddie known to each other, then turned his attention to Maddie's evident surprise as she gazed around the cabin. "You look shocked. Did you expect a lean-to?"

"Well, no, of course not, but I must admit that I am impressed. You have obviously built this cabin with great care, which I admire . . . and I didn't expect it to be so large, so much like a—a—"

"Home?" he supplied helpfully.

"It does have a look of permanence."

"I like to be comfortable," Fox explained, with a grin and a shrug.

"I say, Bravo!" cried Susan. "How fortunate for us that you encountered Benjamin on that day less than a fortnight ago and brought him home to us! Now we'll have the best possible neighbor, particularly since my son-in-law is rarely in Deadwood. I hate to admit weakness, but there are times when women need the assistance of a man.''

''And I am at your service, Mrs. O'Hara. Whether the problem is a snake in your kitchen or a heavy piece of furniture that needs moving, you need look no farther than your nearest neighbor.'' Fox grinned down at her as he spoke, charming her with the easy familiarity of a loving grandson. He began to peek under the linen towels that covered the baskets of food.

Susan slapped lightly at his hand, laughing, and soon cloths were being laid out on the fresh-cut pine planks that formed the floor. With the vivid blue sky overhead, the smell of sawdust mingling with chicken and fresh bread and cobbler, and the exaggerated cries of astonishment the men uttered as the picnic was spread before them, it began to seem like a party. Feeling awkward and out of place, Maddie stepped backward as the others settled themselves on the floor, beaming. Fox brought in a wooden crate to serve as a chair for Susan, who perched on it and began calling out descriptions of the food.

''Will you be rash and sit on the floor with the heathens, or shall I find a seat for you, too?'' Fox whispered in Maddie's ear.

''I really shouldn't stay.'' She couldn't meet his keen gaze. ''I mean, Benjamin will be coming home and looking for his lunch, and he won't know where we've gone . . .''

''Oh, Ben's been with us all day. He likes to help. He should be back directly.''

Every time he called her brother ''Ben,'' Maddie cringed. ''Well, where on earth is *Benjamin* now?''

''I sent him to town to buy me a new chisel. He thought he saw some sort of commotion down on Sherman Street and obviously wanted to investigate, so I gave him a legitimate errand.'' Fox grinned and turned away to join the others. ''I'm starved,'' he said over his shoulder by way of explanation, and left her there.

Maddie nearly backed right out the door and ran for home, but Gramma Susan stopped her with one meaningful glance.

Sighing, Maddie went to join them. The three men had been gulping water and now filled their glasses with ale. Titus Pym was in raptures over the fresh peas. "Many's the day I make do with little more than a sack of roasted peanuts, some jerky, and mayhap a cup of thin soup and a bite of bread."

For long minutes they all ate happily, sometimes attempting to exclaim something with full mouths. When at last they began to slow down, Susan scooped portions of apple cobbler onto their plates. Titus, proving himself to be both high-spirited and verbose, shared his recipe for a Cornish pastie, which Susan promised to make. Then he went on to tell about his "pard," Henry, who had made the journey with him from Cornwall. It was Henry's habit to fry bacon in a pan in the morning, then use that same pan as a tool to seek gold after breakfast. He called it his lucky pan and always found enough gold dust to buy more bacon for breakfast. Then, one afternoon in May, Henry had discovered a fortune's worth of nuggets in his frying pan. To Pym's dismay, his friend had taken his new wealth and returned to England without delay.

"I was happy for 'im," Titus said, waxing reflective, "but couldn't help feeling a trifle sorry for meself, if you take my meaning. Not only was I all alone in a strange country, but Henry didn't even think to leave me the frying pan." He scratched his pointy sunburned nose and grinned. "Odd, isn't it, how God provides for us if we trust? I was beginning to feel right despondent when along comes me *new* pard, Fox, and now I have a reason to get up in the morning again. I feel useful, and I'm making new friends. Americans! Life's bloody grand, don't you think?"

Maddie felt her heart warming toward the Cornish miner. The mood of conviviality in Fox's half-built cabin was contagious, and when she heard herself laugh aloud, she checked herself instinctively and stood up as if to leave. Fox gave her a quick, perceptive glance.

"Why," he whispered, "are you afraid of pleasure?"

She turned, their faces inches apart, eyes meeting in a way that frayed her nerves. Faintly Maddie could detect the scent of ale and fresh, fragrant food on his warm breath. "You misread me, sir, and make yourself too important. My reasons for departure are unrelated to you or this gathering." She was proud of her cool, precise words. "There are other matters to which I must attend."

"Ah." Fox's eyes crinkled gently at the corners. "Have you secrets, Miss Avery?"

"Hardly. I want to work a bit in my garden before the afternoon grows too hot."

"Your *garden*?" His sun-bleached brows flew up. "Didn't you arrive in Deadwood too late in the season to plant vegetables?"

"I hope to grow vegetables next spring, if we are still here, but for now I have had to content myself with a flower garden. I brought the seeds from my mother's garden in Philadelphia and have done my best to re-create hers, on a more limited scale, of course."

Fox shook his head in admiration and disbelief. Stephen Avery had been away too much to concern himself with planting grass or landscaping, so the lot on the other side of the pine trees had remained a muddy mess. That Madeleine was trying to create a civilized garden in the midst of a bog struck Fox as absurdly touching. "So," he murmured, "we are both reaching beyond our surroundings. Others may think us ridiculous for wasting time in an effort to make our circumstances more bearable, but I won't laugh at you or your garden, Madeleine."

Her face was warm, and she surrendered to a smile. "Perhaps we understand each other . . . in this instance."

"Tell me about your garden. Have you enough sunlight? What have you planted? Are the seeds growing in that soil?''

''Yes, they are growing, but I may not have blooms until August!'' Maddie laughed. ''My mother loved an English garden, so I planted foxglove, pansies, sweet william, columbine, verbena, and . . . oh, much more. If it had been spring, I would have planted a border of primroses, but this year I had to be content with white alyssum.''

Fox had to suppress an exclamation of amazement. ''You are incredible, do you know that?''

''Gramma Susan might use a different word to describe me. She thinks I spend far too much time trying to create a fantasy world that simply does not exist here. I'd rather read about more civilized, romantic worlds than surrender to this one. The prospect of slaving in the kitchen or trying to shop on Main Street, amid the mud and all those unsavory people, makes me feel entirely unsuited for my new role.'' Maddie sighed. ''I only came because my mother died and Father asked that we join him. For Benjamin's sake, I thought that we should be a family, and I dreamed of taking care of Father . . . but he is rarely present.''

''You haven't been here very long—and it *is* a huge change from Society Hill in Philadelphia. Perhaps one day you'll relent and begin to see the good qualities of life here.'' Fox gave her a tolerant smile. ''It's better than most of us deserve.''

''What makes you think I lived in Society Hill?'' she demanded. ''How do *you* know of it?''

''You might be surprised to discover how much I know,'' he replied enigmatically, then rose to his feet. While they had been talking, Susan and the others had finished picking up, and now the baskets were repacked. Fox held out a hand to Maddie and watched as she rose in one graceful movement.

She wanted to press him to say more, but he turned immediately to Gramma Susan, thanking her for the wonderful, nourishing lunch. The old woman basked in the warmth of Fox's tone of voice, then remarked without a trace of meanness, "Maddie told you the truth, you know. It's probably best that she avoids the men here because she'd never make a fit wife for any of them. It's all I can do to get her to take instructions in the kitchen—she's hopeless alone!" Then she turned to Madeleine and added, "It's not your fault, my dear, and heaven knows we love you just as you are. I can't help thinking, though, that we probably shouldn't have come."

"Well, I didn't particularly yearn for marriage in Philadelphia, either, so it really doesn't matter much if I spend a year or two on the frontier. Perhaps by the time we return I'll have been too long on the vine. . . ."

Fox had been taking all this in, but before he could form a comment, Benjamin burst into the roofless cabin.

"Here!" he cried, pushing the shiny new chisel into Fox's hand. Perspiring and wild-eyed, he could scarcely contain his excitement. "There's news, big news! *Guess* who's come to town! All of Deadwood's in an uproar!"

For an instant Fox's heart clenched and he felt the blood drain from his face. Could it possibly be. . . ? "Who?" he asked, his voice deadly quiet.

"Is it . . . President Grant?" Maddie was teasing.

Titus Pym laughed and joined in. "Queen Victoria?"

Obviously Benjamin didn't really want to play this game, for he shook his head as if impatient with them for wasting his time. "No, no! Listen to *me*! I saw Wild Bill Hickok leading a wagon train up Main Street. Saw him with my own eyes! Wait'll I tell Johnny Gordon about *this*!"

Fox's heart gave a jump of relief, then his interest was piqued. "Hickok is in Deadwood? Are you sure it isn't someone who just looks like him?"

"Yeah, I'm *sure*!" With that, Benjamin ran back onto the hillside, his red hair sticking up in spikes. "I'm going to Johnny's!" he yelled before disappearing.

Susan shook her head. "That boy needs a firm hand. Since his father doesn't seem inclined to stay at home, perhaps someone else could step in." She gave Fox a sly sidelong glance, which he acknowledged with a smile, but his thoughts were down on Main Street with James Butler Hickok.

Fox still visited the saloons most nights, not because he liked to carouse better than he liked to lie on his new cabin floor and look up at the stars, but because he still hadn't heard any news of Custer and the Seventh Cavalry. He'd figured out that it took a long time for information to reach Deadwood since it was so far from a river, a telegraph, the train lines, or even an army fort. Still, it did seem odd that no one who had passed through Deadwood knew how the battle had turned out.

And Fox wasn't sure what he hoped for; it seemed that either outcome would make him feel guilty. Lately he'd begun to dream that someone would accuse him of desertion, and this was not improbable. Had anyone else heard Custer order Dan Matthews to leave? To the others, he doubtless appeared to be making a speedy exit to avoid the battle.

Fox stood on Main Street, which was fitfully lit by the coal oil lamps that lent garish illumination to the many saloons, gaming halls, and "theaters." Apparently the wagon train had brought well over one hundred newcomers to Deadwood, for all around Fox crowded men and boys he'd never seen before, as excited as children in a candy store as they contemplated the enchantments before them. Some of the women tried to help the newcomers decide by venturing out onto the street and boldly parading up and down.

"Fox!" a familiar female voice called from above.

He stopped in the middle of the busy, muddy street and looked back, upward toward the Gem's balcony. The plump, petite figure silhouetted against the lamplit window was easy enough to recognize. He raised a hand in greeting and smiled, wondering whether she could see the expression of goodwill in the shadows.

"Where you been?" Victoria wailed. "Come up here!"

Other men paused in the midst of drinking or spitting to look at Fox, who suddenly felt uneasily conspicuous. "I wish I could," he called back. "But I have other business." Shrugging elaborately, he pointed toward Nuttall & Mann's Number 10 Saloon, then waved and continued on his way.

Physically he craved a woman so much that he forced himself not to think about it. Problem was, he'd had a taste of Madeleine Avery, and now these upstairs girls repelled him. He figured he'd reach the point where he wouldn't care and then maybe he'd have a few drinks to kill his finer sensibilities and just do the deed . . . but he hadn't reached that point yet. Maddie was like champagne, and Victoria and the others were like homemade elderberry wine left in a forgotten cupboard for a few dozen hot summers. He'd have to be pretty damned thirsty to resort to the latter.

Tinkling, ill-tuned pianos mixed with the strains of cracked fiddles and the occasional horn, filling the night air with a horrendous excuse for music. However, the shouts and laughter of Deadwood's celebrants would not be drowned out. When Fox crossed the threshold of Nuttall & Mann's, it was as if he'd been assaulted. The more time he spent up on the hillside working on his house, the less tolerance he had for socializing with a lot of loud-mouthed cardsharps and drunks and whores.

Still, he was curious to see Wild Bill again. Their paths had crossed a dozen years ago, when Hickok had been a Union scout and had yet to acquire his dashing nickname. Over the years he'd made a reputation for himself as a professional gambler, army scout, and a sheriff in Kansas, laying down the law and shooting anyone foolish enough to challenge him. However, when he'd accidentally killed a policeman in Abilene while ostensibly trying to keep the peace, he'd lost his job, and word had it that the past five years had not been kind to the celebrated Wild Bill Hickok. Fox was curious to learn for himself whether the rumors of his deterioration were true. Would he even be able to recognize the man? As he made his way through the crowd to the bar, Fox's eyes examined the men at the gaming tables. There were dozens of new faces, but none that struck a chord.

Then he stopped. J. B. Hickok was leaning against the bar, chatting with Pink Buford and Capt. Jack Crawford. He wore his hair and mustache long, but they could not disguise the fact that he had aged dramatically since the Civil War. Fox wondered, not for the first time, whether this was an inevitable consequence of life on the frontier.

Hickok squinted in his direction, tipped his head slightly, then squinted a different way. "We've met, haven't we, pard?"

Fox extended his hand. "Years ago, during the war. It's good to see you again, Mr. Hickok."

Wild Bill nodded slowly. "What name do you go by these days, son?"

"Fox." He grinned suddenly, and when the older man squinted again, Fox realized that he couldn't see well. This was a sad state for a renowned marksman. Looking at Harry Sam Young, the bartender, Fox murmured, "I'd like to buy a drink for Mr. Hickok," and watched as another gin and bitters was placed on the bar.

"No need for formalities, Fox. Bill suits me fine." Hickok lifted the glass and drank deeply, closing his eyes for an instant, then smiling as he opened them.

"What brings you to Deadwood, Bill?" Fox asked.

"I raised some money leading part of the wagon train. We left from Cheyenne and met up with some other wagons at Fort Laramie." Hickok shrugged and remarked softly, "I got married; did you hear it? My wife is Agnes Lake, the circus performer. She's world-famous. I want to make enough money to give her a proper home, and since everyone knows that Deadwood's the richest and the wildest place on earth at the moment, I figured this was the place to do it. . . ."

"Our card game's about to begin," Pink Buford muttered, leaning between the two men.

"Good. I don't feel my best, but I doubt whether that will

impair my talent at cards.'' Wild Bill gave Fox a philosophical smile.

Pressed now for time, Fox tried to act as if he were idly attempting to make conversation. ''Bill, weren't you a scout for Custer a few years back? I hear he's doing some serious Indian fighting up in Montana.''

''Yeah, I've heard that, too. Custer's all right, but too eager for my taste. It wouldn't break my heart to hear that Crazy Horse had killed old George.''

Fox nearly sighed aloud. So, even the wagon train did not have news of the battle. He needed to know now—even if knowing meant that Wanted posters featuring his own face would appear on every building and tent in Deadwood. The uncertainty was eating at him, and his dreams were getting worse.

''Well,'' he remarked as casually as a man who hadn't a care in the world, ''it's good to have you in town, Bill. I'll leave you to your game. Let me know if there's ever anything I can do for you.''

Hickok gave him a crooked smile. ''I'd be obliged if you'd remember to watch my back when we're in the same room, Fox.''

''It would be an honor,'' he replied, and they both laughed.

Chapter Seven

July 20, 1876

IT WAS GETTING HARDER AND HARDER TO STAY IN the house. Maddie nearly gave herself away to Gramma Susan and expressed those sentiments aloud, but she remembered herself just in time. It wouldn't do for her grandmother to know that she was bored with *The Scarlet Letter*, bored with polishing silver, bored even with the shopping trip the two women had made to look over the supplies that had come in on the wagon train. Even a glimpse of Wild Bill Hickok, pointed out to Maddie by E. B. Farnum, thrilled her not at all. Farnum, a merchant who was said to have designs on the office of mayor, spent most of each day sitting outside his store on a flitch of bacon, holding forth on a variety of subjects. None of it interested Madeleine.

She was loath to admit it even to herself, but what did seem to interest her these days were the goings-on next door. Sometimes she would peek between the curtains upstairs, or from the kitchen window if Gramma Susan wasn't watching, and try to see what was happening. This was one of those times.

Her grandmother, having risen at dawn to bake while the house was still cool, was now napping peacefully on her son-in-law's bed, and Maddie was stationed at the window next to the back door. Figures appeared and disappeared in and out of Fox's house, their images flickering as they passed the row of pine trees. Benjamin was over there, giggling madly, and someone was singing what sounded like a sea chanty. Hammers pounded. Fox had brought his horse to live with

101

him on the hill, and Maddie gave her brother treats to take to the roan she now knew was called Watson.

Fox seemed to confound her at every turn. Just when she felt he'd proven himself to be tough and crude, he'd surprise her. A horse named Watson indeed! . . . And then there was the matter of the dinner he'd shared with her family, showing up in his fancy clothes, conversing like a gentleman. Sometimes that day seemed like a dream.

Fox was emerging from his log house, crossing the lot toward the row of pine trees where Watson was tethered. He had something in his hand and Watson was moving his head up and down in anticipation. Maddie dragged over one of their crate chairs and hopped up for a better look.

"Why don't you just walk over there and say hello?"

Maddie nearly toppled to the floor at the sound of her grandmother's voice. Then, to make matters worse, when she glanced back outside she saw that Fox had stepped between the pine trees and was waving to her. The smile he wore was maddeningly wry.

She wanted to die. "Gramma Susan, how *could* you?" she cried, jumping to the floor and yanking the curtains closed.

"Perhaps you were looking for a fly that was annoying you," Susan suggested blandly.

Maddie narrowed her eyes at the old woman and tried not to smile. "How did you know? I'm going out for a breath of air. I may be a few minutes, for I have to check for weeds in my garden."

"Don't rush on my account."

Touching a hand to the cluster of ringlets caught up over her left shoulder, Maddie decided that she couldn't risk giving herself away completely by turning back to look in a mirror. Her mint-sprigged muslin frock was clean and pressed. Her hands were washed, and her hair seemed presentable. She took her gardening apron from its hook by the window, slipped it on, and tied a big bow in back, then drew on her gloves and opened the door.

"I must say, you are more fastidious than I could ever hope to become, even at this advanced age," Gramma Susan remarked. Adjusting her spectacles, she gave her granddaughter an innocent smile. "It must be the difference in the way we were raised. My mother was a little scamp, you know."

"Gramma, how can you say that? Great-grandmother Meagan was the wife of a United States senator!"

Susan shrugged. "Mama could play that part when she had to, but underneath it all she remained a scamp at heart, and we all loved her for it." Handing Maddie her slender, ladylike hoe, Susan said, "Go on and tend your garden now, darling."

Maddie stepped into the sunshine, then remembered the real reason she was there and hesitated. When she turned back toward the safety of the house, she discovered that Gramma Susan had heartlessly shut the door.

Feeling silly, she clutched her hoe and started toward the garden. It hadn't rained for a few days, and the mud had nearly dried up in their "yard." Still, one never knew when a kid slipper might sink into a mushy place that had looked perfectly harmless to the unsuspecting eye. Maddie proceeded with care and tried to forget that Fox was only a few feet away.

Fox absently fed Watson the green stubby end of a carrot as he watched Maddie with a smile. The picture she made in her proper gown, apron, and gloves, brandishing that shiny new hoe, was charmingly incongruous in these rowdy surroundings.

"I think the young lady is expecting me," he whispered to Watson. "Stay right here until I come back." The horse nickered softly, showing his teeth.

Fox approached Maddie with a welcome sense of euphoria. He'd been feeling like a man living, with ragged uncertainty, on the edge, and that unpleasant feeling had been worsening as more days passed without news of the Seventh

Cavalry. It began to seem as if they'd simply vanished off the face of the earth. The house had distracted him for a while, but now it was harder to concentrate. Whiskey at night helped numb the worries, and he'd made more new friends since Bill Hickok's wagon train arrived. But he'd missed Maddie. She was the best distraction of all—and, he sensed, the riskiest.

Maddie had begun to chop the warm earth of her garden with delicate hoe strokes. The seedlings were doing very well, thanks to her trips to-and-fro with a watering can. They'd had only one thunderstorm all month, and Susan had reminded her that new plants needed to be kept wet. Sensing that this was merely a ploy to put her in Fox's way, she'd been careful until today to do her watering in the evening, after he'd gone off to commit whatever indiscretions he was partial to in the badlands.

"Incredible. How have you done it?"

She started and pressed a hand to her heart, even though she'd known he would come. Whirling around, she found that he was standing right behind her.

"Did I startle you?" He put a hand on her arm, pretending to be solicitous, but knowing that it would unnerve her. "My apologies."

"I am quite all right." For a long moment Maddie indulged in the luxury of staring at him, lean and masculine in snug, faded dungarees and a shirt of blue-striped ticking. The blue in the shirt accentuated his eyes, and the snow white background set off his warm, deep tan. Fox hadn't bothered with an undershirt, and Maddie was drawn to the portion of his chest that was visible behind several open buttons. She knew nothing at all about men's bodies, but this seemed to her to be an ideal male chest, with just the right amount of soft yet crisp-looking dark brown hair. It was the kind of chest a woman might dream of resting her cheek against. . . .

"I hope you don't mind that I came without an invitation,

but I've been hoping for a guided tour of your garden ever since you told me about it during our picnic lunch," Fox was saying, quite aware of her dreamy scrutiny. "Look at these seedlings! Why, Miss Avery, you've been taking excellent care of them, yet I never see you outdoors. Have you been weeding and watering by moonlight?"

"Certainly not. What a ridiculous notion." She began hoeing again so that she could turn her face away. "How is your house progressing?"

"Very well, thank you. Titus has been edging nearer a decline with each day that passes without a visit from you. He has decided that you are the most beautiful woman he's seen since leaving Cornwall."

"Gramma Susan and I will have to return for another look. Perhaps tomorrow."

Fox was shaking his head in wonder as he took in the size and complexity of Maddie's flower garden. At least two dozen feet long and five feet wide, it was patterned with many, many different types of seedlings planted in tinier beds in the shapes of squares, rectangles, and crescents. The designs were already interesting because each kind of green plant was unique, but it was easy to imagine how glorious it all would be later in the summer, when the colorful flowers would bloom.

"It will be like a tapestry, I suppose," he mused, still staring. Then he smiled and looked over at Maddie. "Is that the idea? Would you believe me if I said that I am most impressed with your creation, even without flowers?"

The sun emerged from behind a tree, and she shaded her eyes with a gloved hand. Her delicate nose, dotted with one or two telltale freckles, wrinkled slightly as she replied, "Yes, I would believe you. I'm impressed myself! You know, I have always been passionate about gardens, but I never did any of the work. We had gardeners. Mother sometimes went out, wearing an apron and gloves and a proper bonnet to protect her from the sun and soil, and she'd prune a bit and let me carry the basket and help her decide which flowers to cut for the house." Maddie glanced off over Fox's wide shoulder, as if looking back in time. "So you see, I've loved the beauty and order of an elegant garden since I was tiny, but it never occurred to me to grow anything *myself*. When we came out here, I had visions of doing all sorts of work for the first time. I imagined that I'd cook and clean and sew for my father, but I've discovered that it takes time to develop those skills. One isn't born with them simply because one is a female. Nor is one necessarily interested in any of those pastimes because one is female. . . ."

"But the garden is different?"

She looked at Fox's tanned, chiseled face and remembered suddenly how his skin felt to the touch, how he smelled, the frightening rapture of his kiss. "The garden? . . ." she forced herself to repeat. "Yes, I've discovered that I can apparently not only appreciate flowers, but grow them, too. I *love* watching the minuscule changes each new morning brings. When the first bud appears, and then opens, I shall know how God must feel as He surveys the countless miracles of life that are always occurring. To have a hand in creation, even of a few flowers, is simply amazing to me!"

Fox wanted to touch her cheek, but he was afraid that it would break the spell and scare her away again. "I have an idea, I think, of what you are feeling. I've found it surprisingly satisfying to plan and build my house. I've never built a home of my own before, let alone dreamed each detail."

"I thought frontier men were used to building things for themselves," she said. "How long have you been out West . . . and where did you come from?"

Fox hesitated as the glint of curiosity in Maddie's eyes reminded him that he couldn't afford to give away too much about his past. "Now, Miss Avery, you're being polite, but I know better than to imagine that you really want to hear me drone on about my life." He paused to yawn at the very thought. "Instead, I wish you would teach me about the flowers. Do you remember which is which?"

It was an inspired diversion. Maddie fairly glowed with excitement as she handed him her hoe and reached into the deep pocket of her apron. From it she withdrew a folded piece of paper. Fox watched, curious, as it was opened to reveal a neatly plotted map of the garden. Each quadrangle or crescent had the name of a flower printed inside it.

"Across the back are the hollyhocks and foxgloves, then canterbury bells and blue dianthus and larkspur and columbine." Maddie was marching back and forth, pointing with one hand and holding the map in the other. "Here are blue cornflowers, over there is a circular bed of zinnias surrounded by daisies and stock, while this rectangular planting is pansies, flanked by sweet william and forget-me-nots. Behind them—"

"Hey!" The rough, rude shout came from Fox's property.

They both looked up, turning to see a short, homely man waving and advancing toward them. "Who is that?" asked Maddie.

"Damned if I know," Fox muttered. As the fellow drew closer, Fox could see that he had the oddest-looking body, consisting of a soft, squarish torso poised on long, thin legs. He wore gray trousers rolled up partway to display black boots, a dirty blue shirt, a kerchief tied around his neck like a yellow bib, and a crumpled flat-brimmed hat. Reaching his quarry, the man stuck out a hand. "You the fella they call Fox?" he said. "Never mind, I know you are; they told me so over there. Pleased to meetcha. You probably heard of me. I'm Jane Cannary."

"How do you do, Miss Cannary?" Fox replied, without missing a beat. Of course he had heard of Calamity Jane; who hadn't? Bullwhacker, scout, drunk, liar . . . she was the sort of human oddity that could thrive only in the West. Seeing that she was staring openly at Maddie, Fox took a closer look at her face. Calamity Jane couldn't have been thirty years old, yet her skin was as tanned and leathery as a man's, and her small eyes were bloodshot and greenish gray, smudged with fatigue. Her nose was flat, her mouth wide, and she had the bloated appearance of a hard drinker.

Suddenly Jane let out a raucous whoop of laughter, then looked back at Fox while pointing at Maddie. "Is *she* a *joke*? Last time I saw a *lady* all duded up like that it was on the Union Pacific train to Cheyenne. That *lady*—" she paused to spit out a stream of tobacco juice that threatened to dribble down her chin at the end"—was from *London*! Couldn't ya just howl? Daughter of a baron or some such horseshit. Had her nose in the air and a pretty white dress and gloves on just like this one. Bet she didn't last a month in Cheyenne, even for her husband's sake." Calamity Jane gave Maddie a sly glance. "How long you been in Deadwood, dearie?"

Fox intervened, though the spark in Maddie's green eyes told him that she could speak for herself. "Miss Cannary, may I present Miss Madeleine Avery."

"I'd shake yer hand, but I wouldn't wanta get those nice white gloves dirty. Where you from, Mad? You two married or somethin'?"

Maddie tried desperately to disguise her confusion and dismay. Could this—this *person* actually be a woman? "How do you do, Miss Cannary," she murmured. "I've been in Deadwood nearly a month, having traveled here with my family from Philadelphia. And, no, Mr. . . . Fox and I are most definitely not married. We are merely . . . neighbors."

"Well, I'm glad to hear *that!*" Jane leered at Fox, then continued cheerfully, "Philadelphia, huh? Almost as snooty as London, from what I hear. Never been there myself and I don't care—"

"Miss Cannary," Fox broke in, "did you come here with a purpose, or by accident?"

She jammed her hands into her pockets and grinned, showing a set of stained teeth. "Oh, I had a purpose all right. Heard about you, mister, from Garnet Loomis, and decided to come and see for myself. I'm one determined gal, I don't mind tellin' you!"

"I'll take your word for it. At the moment, however, I

have a few things I must discuss with Miss Avery, so I'd appreciate it if you would—"

"Go away?" Jane crowed with laughter. "I kin take a hint, mister. No offense, neither. I'll have my chance. Before I go, I gotta pass along a message from Wild Bill. It's the excuse that got me up here today. Bill says he has some news for you. Says it's about what you talked about before, whatever that means. 'Bye!"

Calamity Jane turned and started walking away, her stride long and loose-limbed. Near the row of pine trees, she pivoted suddenly and shouted, "Hey, pard! If you need another pair of hands to help build that fancy house, I'm damned good with a hammer! I work cheap, too!"

Fox waved to her again, nodding, and didn't look back at Maddie until their outrageous visitor had disappeared from sight.

"I knew there were some very strange characters in the West, especially here, but who was *that*?" Maddie shook her head in disbelief.

" 'That' was Calamity Jane. Have you ever heard of her?" Fox's thoughts were already darting off toward the news Hickok had to impart, but he didn't want to leave Maddie yet—not after they'd gotten along so well today. "Calamity's a legend, but a lot of it's made up of stories she tells about herself, especially after she's had a few drinks. She's strange, but harmless."

"Now that you put it that way, I suppose I ought to feel sorry for her, but it's hard to summon kindness toward someone who has just been laughing at me." She gave him a shy smile. "In a few moments, I'm certain I'll feel more sympathetic."

Fox wanted to hug her, and he did dare to put one hand on her back in a gesture that was halfway between a pat and a caress. "I'm sure that Miss Cannary hasn't had the benefit of your proper breeding. She doesn't know better . . . and if she does, she treats everyone that way, from what I hear. She's cruder than most men."

"How charming." Maddie felt a shiver run down her

back from the touch of his hand. "Aren't you curious to learn what Mr. Hickok is waiting to tell you? Benjamin would be positively agog to hear that you know his hero. He's talked of little else since that wagon train arrived in Deadwood."

"I'll take Ben over to meet Bill as soon as I have a chance, if it would mean that much—"

"Please don't!" she exclaimed, aghast. "I am doing everything in my power to *discourage* his new fascination with desperadoes!"

Fox rubbed his bearded jaw and smiled slowly. "I'm afraid that you're living in the wrong town . . . but then you already know that, don't you." His other hand still rested on her back, and now he drew her closer. A ray of sunlight broke through the trees and illuminated Maddie's exquisite hair. He ached to bury his face in it, then press his mouth to her temple, her creamy throat. Instead, he dared to brush his face against the softness of her hair. "You wish," he whispered, "that someone different lived next door, don't you? A gentleman in every way, who reads the Romantic poets and wears a paper collar as a matter of habit, and always behaves in the best of taste—"

"Don't be silly," Maddie broke in, her voice trembling. "There are no such men in Deadwood."

"And if there were?"

Her heart began to race as Fox drew her closer until her breasts grazed the unyielding surface of his chest. Her cheek touched the starchy fabric of his blue-striped shirt. It smelled fresh and new . . . and yet like Fox. "We—we shouldn't be speaking of such matters, Mr. Daniel." She could barely get the words out.

So close! Each time she came so close to giving way, to yielding to her woman's heart, but always at the brink she recovered. Boldly, as if to taunt her, Fox kept his fingers on her back, raising them slowly to her shoulder in a tantalizing caress. When he felt her quake, he lifted both hands and stepped backward. "It seems I can't be trusted, can I?"

Maddie straightened and gave him a challenging look. "I believe that I can handle you, sir. And now, if you don't mind, I would like to return to my gardening."

She caught one last, maddening glimpse of Fox's flashing white grin before she turned back to her silent, cooperative seedlings.

It seemed that the sound of hammering was incessant these days, whether Fox was on his own hillside above Sherman Street or in the midst of Deadwood's badlands. There were still plenty of stores and saloons located in tents with calico inner walls, but more and more of them were being replaced by hastily constructed buildings. Main Street was still a filthy, stinking swamp, but at least it had a more permanent appearance. Dozens of new arrivals poured in each day, prompting Charles H. Wagner to raise his rates at the Grand Central Hotel.

Fox checked Nuttall and Mann's Number 10 Saloon, the Betwix-Stops Saloon, the Senate, and the Green Front and finally found Wild Bill sitting at a card table in the Gem. He was flanked by Bessie and Victoria but appeared disinterested. There were two other men at the table, one of whom was Capt. Jack Crawford, who styled himself a "poet-scout." Fox found the man annoying and conceited but decided to endure his company in exchange for Bill's.

Fox took a seat and smiled. "I'm not interrupting a game, I hope?"

Hickok shook his head. "No. I feel like hell today, Captain Jack's writing a new poem, and Charley here's about to go to the bathhouse." He shook Fox's hand and then slumped back in his chair. He was paler than the last time they had met. "Have you met my pard, Colorado Charley Utter? Charley, this is Fox. I knew him in the war. A good man."

The third fellow, who wore buckskins and sported a long mustache and shoulder-length hair like Hickok, smiled at Fox. "It's good to know you. Me and Seymour are starting a Pony Express here in town. If you need a job, we need riders."

Fox smiled back, liking Colorado Charley immediately. "I'll keep that in mind, and I appreciate the offer."

"Where you been, darlin'?" Victoria whimpered. When she leaned over his shoulder, the smell of her cheap perfume was overpowering.

"Leave Fox alone, Victoria," Wild Bill said as he poured himself another drink with his left hand. Fox remembered that this was one of his cautious habits, leaving his right hand free. He also endeavored always to sit with his back to the wall and never to the door of a saloon when he played cards. Some laughed at Hickok's vigilance, but he contended that it had kept him alive when many of his contemporaries had been less fortunate. "Why don't you girls leave us for a few minutes. I'd like to speak to Fox without an audience."

Victoria and Bessie flounced away, curves jiggling. Something in Wild Bill's solemn gaze prompted Fox to accept the offer of a drink. "Is this serious?" he said, and as soon as the words were out, he sensed what the subject was. Oddly enough, Fox hadn't thought of Custer once in the past few hours.

"It's about Custer and the Seventh," Hickok said in husky tones. "You asked about them the other night, and I thought you might know someone who was with Custer."

"I did," Fox whispered. Instinct told him to gulp the drink.

"There's been terrible news!" Capt. Jack Crawford exclaimed, unable to restrain himself.

"What do you mean?"

Bill shot Crawford a warning look. "Well, we just got word that last month Custer's men went up against a whole mess of Sioux—up near the Little Bighorn in Montana. June twenty-fifth, I b'lieve it was . . ."

"And?" Fox heard his own voice from a distance.

"Well, it seems Custer bit off more than he could chew.

He was massacred, him and the couple hundred men who rode with him that day.''

''They're dead?'' Fox was certain he must have misunderstood. ''All of them?''

Hickok nodded, stroking his mustache, then reached out with his left hand to refill Fox's glass. ''Story is that they didn't have a chance; there must've been two thousand Indians. Either Custer was one of the greatest heroes who ever lived . . . or the biggest fool.''

As the truth sank in, Fox felt as if his heart would explode.

Chapter Eight

"I HEARD THAT THE ONLY SURVIVOR WAS A HORSE name of Comanche," Charley Utter remarked. "Too bad he can't talk."

Fox's mind was whirling as he thought of Capt. Myles Keogh, Comanche's rider, and then all the other men he had come to know in the days before the battle. Stabbing guilt brought beads of sweat to his forehead. He tried to concentrate. Surely the entire Seventh Cavalry hadn't been killed that day—it had numbered more than six hundred men! Besides, just before Fox had made his exit, Custer had divided the regiment into three battalions, to be commanded by Reno, Benteen, and himself. It sounded as if only Custer's battalion had been wiped out. Perhaps the others, circling the Indians from different directions, had managed to escape.

His thoughts kept returning to one fact: If he and Custer hadn't quarreled so violently, and if Custer had accepted his offer to join the soldiers, Fox would have gone with them to their deaths. Right and wrong no longer mattered; the point was that he had ridden away and they'd all been killed. Good God, why hadn't he tried harder to change Custer's mind? Were his nightmares real? Was it George Armstrong Custer's *ghost* who taunted him at night?

While Fox was lost in thought, it seemed that everyone in the Gem had begun to talk about "General" Custer and the tragedy at Little Bighorn. Colorado Charley Utter, sensing that the drama was about to get out of hand, departed for the bathhouse. A moment later Capt. Jack Crawford stood

up, brandishing the paper covered with his fanciful handwriting.

"Who would care to hear the first verse of my newest
poem, composed during this past hour since word came of
General Custer's demise?" A murmuring hush spread over
the crowd, which prompted Captain Jack to step up onto his
chair and read:

> Did I hear the news from Custer?
> Well, I reckon I did, old pard.
> It came like a streak o'lightning,
> And you bet, it hit me hard.
> I ain't no hand to blubber,
> And the briny ain't run for years,
> But chalk me down for a lubber,
> If I didn't shed regular tears.

People made sounds of solemn approval, while some of the
upstairs girls began to weep. Captain Jack cautioned them
that it was only the first verse, and he couldn't promise that
the rest of the missive would be as profound.

Wild Bill gave Fox a glance and a shrug in critique of
Crawford's talent, but Fox was in no mood for irony. "I—
I'm going to go upstairs for a little peace," he muttered.
"Hope you feel better, Bill."

"Can't say as I blame you, pard. Have one for me."

Fox didn't know if his friend meant a drink or a girl, so
he merely nodded and rose to find Victoria, stopping for a
bottle on the way. Victoria threw a triumphant look back to
her friends as Fox took her elbow and guided her toward the
stairway.

Climbing the slanting staircase, Fox found that he couldn't
shut out the unwelcome thoughts. He'd never experienced
such pain before. What did they call it—survivor's guilt? Images burned in his mind of two hundred soldiers lying dead
under the Montana sun. He had handled Custer badly, letting
his temper override reason. He shouldn't have said the things

he had . . . he shouldn't have left, even if Custer had ordered him to . . . he should have tried something else . . .

But what about the Indians? another voice in his head argued. Would it be better if Custer and the Seventh had butchered the Lakota people instead? Would that have been fair?

Pausing on the top step, Fox stared at the bottle for a moment, then lifted it to his mouth and drank deeply. *Please God,* he prayed silently, *make it stop. . . .*

Titus Pym nailed one of the last shingles in place on the cabin roof, then leaned over to look down at little Ben Avery. "Just about finished. Where d'you suppose that bloke Fox has got to?"

He'd asked the same question of Benjamin and Wang Chee at least a dozen times over the past three days, and of course no answer was forthcoming. Now, Ben lifted his hands and shrugged. "Gee, Mr. Pym, I don't know. He'd of told somebody if he was gonna leave town, wouldn't he?" As Titus crept over to the ladder and descended, Ben's brown eyes lit up. "Maybe he's in the badlands! You want me to go down there and ask around?"

"Certainly not, me young lad!" The older man feigned shock. "But I was thinkin' it might not hurt to inquire at your house. Perhaps he said something to your grandmother or your sister and didn't have a chance to speak to any of us."

"Why would he tell Gramma Susan anything? Or Maddie? Gramma's an old lady and Maddie *hates* Fox!"

"Does she, then? That's a strong word, lad. Let's go along and ask all the same, and if we're lucky, perhaps your lovely grandmother will offer me a piece of cake or pie or whatever dessert is cooling inside the kitchen window today."

Pym put a hand on the boy's shoulder, and they walked across the lot, through the pine trees, and up to the Averys' back door. Titus would have knocked, but Benjamin threw open the door and marched in. Susan O'Hara was drying dishes and putting them away on the shelves. Her face brightened at the sight of the Cornish miner.

"Mr. Pym, how good it is to see you again! I can't tell you how impressed we all are with Fox's beautiful cabin, nor can I thank you enough for keeping an eye on my grandson. I do hope you'll send him home if he's a nuisance!"

"Nay, Mrs. O'Hara, we all enjoy young Ben. Fox especially has taken a shine to the boy."

"Fox is a good man." Susan put down her towel and gestured to Titus to take a chair. "I've just baked a rhubarb pie. You'll test it for me, won't you?"

The wiry, gray-haired man blushed with pleasure. "It would be an honor, Mrs. O'Hara."

As she cut the pie, prepared his plate, and set it before him, Susan inquired, "Where is Fox these days? It seems ages since we've seen him. I hope you won't be horrified if I confess that even at my age, I enjoy the sight of a man as good-looking as he is. Sometimes I steal a glance at him through the window just to reassure myself that I'm still alive!"

Drawn by the sound of voices, Maddie put down her copy of the movingly romantic *Jane Eyre* and wandered over to the doorway that separated the parlor from the kitchen. "Hello, Mr. Pym. It's nice to see you."

Titus grinned in her direction, then sobered. "Likewise, Miss Avery, but I hope you won't think me rude if I say that you're looking pale. I hope you aren't ill?"

"No, I'm fine," she replied, with a wan smile. In truth she was feeling abysmal, but there was nothing physically wrong with her. Secretly Maddie feared she might be heartsick.

"I was just about to ask your grandmother if she had any notion of Fox's whereabouts, but she asked me first," Titus said, attacking his pie with gusto. "We haven't seen him for three full days, Miss Avery, and I've never known him to just run off without a word. Odder still, he didn't take Watson. I've no doubt that he's fine, wherever he is, but I will admit to a measure of concern. . . ."

"Maybe the Injins got him, just like they got General Custer," Benjamin piped up ominously. "Johnny Gordon says that the Black Hills belong to the Injins and they're gonna attack Deadwood and kill us all for trespassing! Johnny says that they cut your scallop off before they kill you, and they shoot arrows all over your body, and—''

"Benjamin Franklin Avery, be silent!" Susan commanded. "You know better than to speak of such things, particularly in the presence of ladies."

"I don't think the Indians've got our Fox," Titus Pym reassured the little boy. "He's been around them before and knows their ways. He told me so himself. They'd invite him for supper, not kill him, lad."

Madeleine joined them at the table. "Did Fox come back to the cabin after that Calamity Jane person left here three days ago?" she asked. "You saw her, didn't you, Mr. Pym? She said she'd been directed to my garden by you."

Titus scratched his sunburned pate and muttered, "Now you mention it, miss, I do remember her. I thought she was a him, but Wang Chee set me straight. And, thinking back, I believe that that was the last time I saw Fox. I saw him walking off shortly after that."

"Well," Maddie said softly, "I may have a clue. Miss Cannary told Fox that Mr. Hickok wanted to speak to him. I believe that he went to find him."

" 'Twould seem, then, that I ought to seek out this Hickok fellow and discover what he knows of Fox's whereabouts," Pym declared, swallowing the last bite of pie and wiping his mouth with a napkin.

"Wild Bill Hickok?" Benjamin cried. "I don't think he'll talk to you, Mr. Pym. No offense, but Wild Bill is *famous*! He's performed feats of daring with his Colt pistol. I read a story about him in Philadelphia that said he'd killed more than one hundred criminals! Strangers must try to talk to him every day, so I don't think you could even get close."

Titus patted the boy on the head and stood up. "This is Deadwood, lad. I don't doubt that Mr. Hickok is treated with respect, but he's hardly the president of the United States. I'm sure he'll have a word with me . . . if I can find him."

"He plays cards in the badlands most of the time, but he's not staying at a hotel. He and Colorado Charley Utter are camping in their wagon alongside Whitewood Creek. Want me to show you where?"

"Benjamin, how do you know these things? Haven't we told you to stay away from that part of town?" Gramma Susan shook her head. "And you most certainly will not go with Mr. Pym. Honestly, you're incorrigible!"

"Lad, I have a task for you," Titus said as he held the door for the sulking boy. "Fox would want us to take the best care possible of Watson. Agreed? I am quite certain he needs to be fed and brushed. Are you up to that?"

Benjamin nodded, brightening slightly. Smiling, Titus turned back to thank Susan again for the pie, assured her and Maddie that he would keep them informed of any news, and bade them good day.

When they were alone, Susan O'Hara turned to study her granddaughter. Maddie tried looking out the window, but she knew that there was no escaping her grandmother's searching regard. "You look terrible, darling girl. Let's have a tiny spot of sherry to put color back in your cheeks, and then we'll talk."

Maddie quaked at the sound of that last word. When Gramma Susan set a small red-and-gold Bohemian glass goblet before her, she sipped from it gratefully.

"Now then," said the diminutive old woman, "you have been wandering around here looking more like a ghost with each passing day. I've been waiting patiently, hoping that you might come to me and discuss your feelings, but I suppose I should have known better. Instead, by the look of you, you've been trying to pretend you *have* no feelings!"

"I—I don't know what they are," Maddie said miserably.

"Aha!" She cried. "So you admit that you're feeling *something*. That's a start. Tell me all about it, and I'll help you make sense of your heart."

"My heart?" The words made almost no sound at all. "I don't know that I'm not simply ill. Who knows what's in the water here? Perhaps I'm being poisoned.'' Seeing that her grandmother was in no mood to waste time, Maddie shook her head in despair. "Oh, Gramma, what *is* wrong with me? I ache, here''—she moved one hand to her breast—''and I can't eat, and I wake up all night long in the midst of unspeakable dreams . . .''

Susan fixed her with an unwavering blue stare. "The answer, I think, is clear if you have the courage to own it.'' When Madeleine looked down, she prompted, "Be honest. Is there not one person who inhabits your thoughts and the dreams you describe as 'unspeakable'?'' Susan reached across the makeshift table and took Maddie's hand. "Those dreams are merely nature's way of prodding you into womanhood.''

"But, Gramma . . . I can't bear it! How could this have happened? Of all the men in the world, why has my heart chosen''—Maddie swallowed audibly, then wailed—*"Fox?''*

Susan clapped. "Oh, happy day! What a relief! You *do* have some Hampshire and O'Hara blood flowing in your veins after all! Maddie, darling, I can only applaud the instincts of your heart. Fox is just the sort of man I would have chosen for you, but feared you would reject. He would have been too much for your dear mother, but not for me or your great-grandmother! This is one of the happiest moments of my life!'' She came around the table, drew a crate up next to Maddie, and embraced her.

Madeleine, meanwhile, was panicking. "Gramma, what you have said is madness! I'm frightened! I feel as if my life has become . . . a runaway horse!''

Susan O'Hara laughed and hugged her again. "Darling girl, celebrate! Life is sweetest when it is carrying us off to unplanned adventures. How could the outcome be less than wondrous with a man like Fox?''

"But we are completely unsuited for each other, and even if that were not a factor, what makes you think that he wants to have more than an amusing flirtation with me? If Fox wanted a—a mate, wouldn't he have chosen one by now?''

"Not necessarily. Few really interesting men settle down

before the age of thirty. And if they are also as attractive as Fox, they may wait even longer.'' Susan patted Maddie's flushed cheek. ''I haven't seen you with such hectic color since you were a little girl. Don't be frightened of the future, darling. Reach out and embrace it, *savor* its uncertainty. I cannot tell you exactly what lies ahead between you and Fox, but I will urge you to go forward and discover the answer for yourself.''

Tears sparkled in Maddie's eyes. ''Oh, Gramma, where is he now? What if something's happened to him?''

The dirty gold light of coal oil lamps suffused the Gem Theatre, heightening its tasteless, raucous ambience. There was plenty of smoke in the air, as well as an assortment of unpleasant body odors, and Colorado Charley Utter had to squint when he entered the saloon. Some of his cronies called out to him, but he merely waved and shouted, ''Not yet, boys!''

The soiled dove who called herself Victoria was having a drink with a cardsharp at the bar. Charley hated to intrude, but he didn't want to wait all night, either. Coming up behind her, he caught a whiff of her perfume and cleared his throat.

Victoria glanced back absently, then recognized him and smiled. She was a pretty girl, Charley decided, with soft white skin and generous curves. Her long black curls were striking. Too bad she had fallen into Al Swearingen's trap.

''You want somethin'?'' Victoria inquired, showing him her dimples.

''Sorry to interrupt, ma'am.'' Charley touched the brim of his hat and gave the man who'd bought her drink an apologetic look. ''I'm looking for a fella, on behalf of Wild Bill Hickok. Bill wants me to have a word with Fox—''

She widened her eyes to cut him off, then turned to the cardsharp and said sweetly, ''Honey, I gotta speak in private with Mr. Utter, then I'll be right back. You won't even miss me. Now, don't move, promise?'' That taken care of, she led Colorado Charley over to the staircase and whispered, "Fox is in my room upstairs. He's been here more'n three days!"

Charley's brow furrowed in thought. "If he's up there, what're you doing downstairs?"

"That's not what he's lookin' for—not that I don't wish different." She shook her head in confusion. "Somethin' is eating him, know what I mean? He's been drunk or passed out most of the time since we went upstairs, way back that day the news came about Custer."

"It's none of my say-so, but don't it hurt your business to have Fox hanging around in your room all the time?" Charley asked politely.

A fleeting look of regret passed over Victoria's pretty face, then she laughed. "Fox gives me money every day he's there. He's generous. Besides, I . . . like him. I'd worry about him if he was lying senseless somewhere else. And even like this he's still twice as much a man as anyone else in this crazy town." She glanced up the shadowy stairway. "You're welcome to have a word with him, if he's up to it. Maybe he'll tell you what's bringing on those nightmares. Never knew anyone to suffer more in their sleep."

Charley thanked her, received directions to her room, and went slowly up the staircase. When he knocked on Victoria's door, there was no response.

"Fox? You in there? It's me, Charley Utter. Bill sent me to look for you 'cause he didn't feel up to it himself tonight. Mind if I come in?"

He thought he heard a sort of grunt and decided it was an invitation. Opening the door, Charley discovered a sad little room with an iron bed, its mattress made up with patched sheets and a quilt, an old bureau with a mirror, and a little table and stick-back chair. An oil lamp on the table was lit, filling the room with flickering shadows. Fox sat on the chair, forearms resting on his thighs, his hands clasped loosely and head bent.

Charley took stock of the situation and decided quickly on a course of action. It was pretty obvious that this fellow wouldn't welcome his intrusion, but his first loyalty was to J. B. Hickok, the truest pard a man could have. He knew that Bill would do what he could to help Fox if he were here himself. So he closed the door and crossed the warped floor, twisting his hat in his hands. At Fox's side, he hunkered down.

"Looks to me like you've got a problem," he said in neutral tones.

Slowly Fox raised his head, and Charley tried not to betray his shock. The man who had been the picture of health just three days before, bronzed and vigorous, now looked as if all the juice of life had been sucked out of him. His eyes were bloodshot, his hair and body smelled stale, and he was pale and hollow-cheeked beneath his tan and beard.

"Wild Bill sent me to find out what's become of you, pard. Seems that a friend of yours, one of them miners from Cornwall they call 'Cousin Jacks,' searched Bill out today. He said there are folks worried about you; people who care about you."

Fox lifted one hand, looking as if he were in pain, and rubbed his eyes. A long moment passed while he sat thus in the quivering lamplight.

"Are you sick?" Charley pressed, hating to do it. "Did someone die? I got to tell Bill something."

When Fox took his hand away, he looked at his visitor with haunted eyes. "Yes, someone died," he said harshly.

"Well, you can't sit up here for the rest of your life! That won't change anything, will it?"

He shook his head. "I . . . can't. Not yet." Reaching into the shadows behind the chair, Fox produced a nearly empty whiskey bottle and drank deeply. When he held it out to Colorado Charley, the man drew back as if repulsed.

"What about your friends? The fellow who came to our wagon today mentioned a little boy who's worried about you and misses you. Won't you at least let me send word to them—"

"No!" Suddenly fierce in his drunkenness, Fox raised his voice. "Get out of here and leave me alone!"

"You don't have to ask me twice." Charley straightened, knees aching, and walked to the door. He paused there and glanced back. The figure who sat in the shadows across the room looked like an old man, bent and broken.

Chapter Nine

July 25, 1876

"I CAN'T BELIEVE MY EYES!" ANNIE SUNDAY
Matthews declared, hands on hips, as she stared at her son.
The tall, handsome woman with the rich chestnut hair wore
a tasteful gown of rich burgundy that set off her eyes. Hazel
and beautifully direct, they never had been able to keep a
secret of her feelings and judgments.

"Ma, what're you doing here?" Fox's mouth was so dry
he could scarcely form the words, and as he lay on Victoria's
bed he found that he couldn't move, couldn't even rise to
greet his mother. Shame broke over him in a mighty wave.

"Look at you, Daniel Matthews! How could you have
allowed yourself to sink so low? I would think you were sick,
but I can smell the whiskey and your unwashed body." There
was no condemnation in her eyes, only sadness. "You're
made of stronger stuff than this. Whatever it is that has laid
you low, you must fight against it. Get up!"

"I can't," he cried.

A hand shook him, gently at first, then more forcefully.
"Fox, wake up. You're havin' another bad dream, honey."

He opened burning eyes and saw Victoria's face above
him. "Where is she?"

"I don't know what you're talking about." She rose from
the bed, clad in lace drawers and a chemise. Her bottom
jiggled as she went over to the mirror and began pinning up
her hair. "You know, honey, I been waiting for you to come
out of this, but I think you're gettin' worse. I like you too
much to let you drink yourself to death in my bed." She

tossed him a coquettish smile over one dimpled shoulder. "Frankly, I had other plans!"

Gingerly Fox attempted to sit up and found that he could swing his legs over the side of the bed. His head didn't pound quite as much as it usually did when he wasn't drunk, and it came to him that Victoria hadn't brought him a new bottle the night before. He'd lain down to wait for her to come with it about nine o'clock and must've fallen asleep . . . or passed out. The twelve hours of sleep had brought him a measure of sobriety; apparently enough to allow Annie Sunday to squeeze into his conscience.

"I appreciate your kindness, Victoria," he said in a husky voice.

She stared in surprise, then rushed to pour a glass of water and bring it to him. "Why, honey, I think you're gonna live after all!"

After drinking the water down, Fox said, "I'm afraid it's true. And I'm going to get a bath and a huge, hot breakfast."

"You're leaving me, aren't you?" Boldly Victoria sat down beside him on the lumpy bed and leaned forward so that her breasts pushed against his arm.

There was a new, heightened cynicism in the half smile that didn't reach his eyes. "You overestimate me. Just because I'm moving doesn't mean I'm hot to get laid." The flare of passion in her eyes gave him pause. "Not yet, anyway."

"I don't know what it is about you, but whatever it is, you sure got it strong." She was practically purring now. "Will you come back? Don'tcha owe me that much, for taking care of you?"

Fox laughed harshly. "Isn't it supposed to be the other way around? You're the one selling it, Victoria."

"Not to you, honey."

She was leaning closer, and her full lips were nearly touching his. What the hell, he thought, and slid an arm around her back. When he kissed her, there was a slight spark in his lower region that gave him hope. Maybe he was meant to live after all, just like Victoria said. He wouldn't be the same man; how could he be? But Fox guessed that it was better to be alive than dead, even if he did feel like he'd lost his honor.

"I gotta go now," he muttered, drawing back.

"I know." She gasped for breath. "Today's Monday, the day all us girls go to the bathhouse. You want to come back tonight and have me when I'm all clean and powdered?"

Fox stood up and stretched. "I appreciate the offer, but don't wait for me. I need a lot of fresh air. I don't know when I'll be ready to come back inside the Gem."

He dressed, ran a hand through his grimy hair, and caught a glimpse of himself in the hazy bureau mirror. It was a sobering sight. His eyes were bloodshot, his color was terrible; he looked like a man near death. For an instant the memory of Annie Sunday in his dream returned. Fox was disgusted with himself.

Victoria held the door for him and he escaped. Suspenders dangling, he descended the stairway. His head had begun to ache as if his brain were swollen, and his eyes felt as if they were on fire. Rounding the corner, he nodded to the few men playing cards. The saloon was nearly deserted this early in the morning except for Bessie and a few other girls. He barely glanced at them, but that was enough.

There was only one female he'd ever seen in the world with hair that color. Fox saw only the girl's back as she talked, gesturing, to Bessie. Her marmalade hair was arranged in a cluster of ringlets, and she wore an immodest gown of puce silk.

Fox didn't think; he acted. Stars seemed to flash before his eyes as he strode to the bar, grabbed the girl by the arm, and pulled her toward him. "What the hell do you think you're doing?" His voice was raw with anger.

The girl cried out, frightened, and when she tried to break free he saw that she wasn't Maddie at all. Fox felt as if he were in the midst of another crazy dream. Bessie stepped between them and scolded, "Fox, what's got into you?" She put an arm around the new girl, murmuring, "Don't you pay him no mind, Lorna. He's just come from a . . . sickbed, I guess it was, hmm, Fox?''

He rubbed his face, then peered at the frightened Lorna over the top of his hand. "Ma'am, I apologize. I was struck by the color of your hair, and I thought you were someone else. It didn't occur to me that two women could have such beautiful hair, especially in the same town."

Lorna, who was now calming down, managed a philosophical smile. "I reckon you're right about that, 'cause I sure wasn't born with this color."

Al Swearingen came up behind Fox and clapped him on the back. Known around the badlands as the "whore man," Swearingen was a person Fox went to great lengths to avoid. "Good to see you up and around, pard. I'm sure you'll understand if I charge you for the accommodations. Say . . . three dollars a night?"

The ingratiating tone of Swearingen's voice made Fox want to shoot the man and put them all out of their misery. It was a pleasant thought, anyway. Instead he paid up, even though he'd already given Victoria more than this much. But he had no intention of telling her employer that, for fear the snake would demand his share from her. Intellectually Fox realized that the girls at the Gem and the other sporting houses were not prostitutes because Swearingen or anyone else was holding a gun to their heads, yet he had always felt an urge to liberate them.

This morning Fox told himself to mind his own business like everyone else in the West. Now honor and ethics were muddy territory for him. If he tried to maintain his old conscience, he would never sleep through the night again.

When Swearingen had stuffed Fox's payment into the bag of gold dust he kept in his trousers, he turned to Fox and clasped his shoulder. "What's yer hurry, son? A minute ago you looked hungry for an introduction to our newest girl." Al gave her a meaningful look. "Lorna, say hello to Fox, one of Deadwood's finest."

She smiled dutifully. "Hello."

With a nod, Fox said, "Sorry again if I was rude." As

they exchanged pleasantries, he looked her over, astonished at how closely she resembled Madeleine. It really was ironic . . . and oddly reassuring. The way he'd begun to feel when he was near Maddie was disturbing, to say the least—especially now that he saw himself as permanently tainted by his guilt over Little Bighorn. If he began to sense that he was losing control with Maddie, he could come to Lorna. A vaguely cynical smile played over his mouth as he took her hand, remarking, "I hope to see you again, ma'am."

"Do come soon to hear me sing!" she exclaimed. "Mr. Swearingen's brought me all the way from Cheyenne, he admires my voice so much! All I need's a few lessons."

Bessie glanced at Fox from behind Lorna's back, lifting an eyebrow, and Al cleared his throat. "In that case," Fox replied, straight-faced, "I'll be looking forward to your performance."

With that he made his farewells and headed out into morning sunlight. The sights and smells of the badlands had never appealed to him until now. Life, even tarnished, was welcome, and it was bliss to be outdoors.

His first destination was Wang Chee's laundry, located up Main Street in Chinatown. Fox's senses were nearly overwhelmed by the exotic panorama. Tiny tumbledown shops were heaped with Chinese embroideries, silks, teak, precious china, sandalwood, and carved ivory. Merchants squabbled, then with wheedling tones endeavored to entice Fox to buy. And here and there were opium dens and gambling games. Plenty of whites wandered through Chinatown when they were looking for a good time; the aura of foreign-steeped danger added to the excitement of misbehaving.

Fox wasn't interested personally, but today he enjoyed the drama. In Chee's laundry, where the clothes were as thoroughly washed as the gravel in the creek, Wang Chee's wife was elated to see him, though Fox could see the concern in her eyes as she took in his appearance. The fact that he had come at last for his clean clothes seemed to reassure her.

Carrying the neat package, he made straight for the bathhouse, striding down the bustling wooden sidewalks that stopped and started along the muddy street. There, after making Old Frenchy haul in a double load of fresh water from the creek, he scrubbed himself twice, then shaved his neck and trimmed his own beard so that it followed the chiseled contours of his jaw. Finally, clad in boots with light gray trousers tucked in the tops, a loose red calico shirt, and suspenders, Fox gave old Frenchy the rest of the money he had on him and emerged onto Main Street feeling almost lighthearted.

Preacher Smith was standing on his crate on the corner. Spying Calamity Jane among the small audience, Fox kept his head down and hurried to the Grand Central Hotel. Other restaurants were now doing business in town, particularly in the Chinese quarter, but Fox had a craving for Aunt Lou Marshbanks's flapjacks.

Just outside the hotel door, a grizzled old man was selling copies of the *Black Hills Pioneer*. "You heard that Custer an' all his men gone up the flume?" he asked when Fox paused to buy a copy. "It was a bloody bizness, but then you know how those red devils are. Now they're raidin' the Hills, probably comin' for Deadwood next. You kin read all about it in here." The shriveled old-timer fixed Fox with a watery eye. "Wish I could read."

Fox took the paper and arched an eyebrow. "Sometimes I wish I couldn't."

He waited until his second cup of coffee and the flapjacks, fried eggs, and sausage patties were placed before him before he looked at the newspaper. Slowly he ate the breakfast and absorbed the printed words.

Among the exaggerated advertisements for local businesses were columns of news. It seemed that more facts and rumors had been gathered concerning the "slaughter" of Custer and 225 of the Seventh Cavalry. Just as Fox had known instinctively, Company C had been among those who'd fought and died with Custer. Major Reno and Captain Benteen, commanding the other two battalions, had taken different routes and met the Indians first, according to the newspaper account. Custer had proceeded onward and apparently decided to attack without reinforcements. Rumor had it that the "massacre" had been attended by gruesome mutilations and, the *Pioneer* concluded:

> There is but one settlement on the Indian question here. The hostile Sioux should be exterminated and white men engaged in trading ammunition to them should be hung wherever found. Let the government call out the Black Hills Brigade and put it in the field.

Fox put down his fork and pushed the plate away. He went on to read the accounts of recent raids made by bands of "hostiles" so near to Deadwood that the townsmen were cautioned to stop shooting their rifles and revolvers indiscriminately. "Save your ammunition, boys," the newspaper advised, "until things become a little more pacific in regard to the Indian question."

Sighing, Fox leaned back in his chair and nibbled at more of his breakfast. Images flashed in his mind of the morning of June twenty-fifth, when he'd ridden away, of the animated men who now lay baking on the Montana hillside, of Custer whooping, "I could whip all the Indians on the continent with the Seventh Cavalry!" What was it Bloody Knife, the scout, had warned earlier? *"There are more Sioux ahead than we have bullets . . ."*

A chill ran down Fox's spine at the memories. Bloody Knife was dead, too, the *Pioneer* said. He'd been with Reno, in relative safety, yet was hit in the forehead by a stray Sioux bullet. He began to wish he were back in Victoria's room, where he could escape in solitude. He wished he could put out his thoughts like candle flames. Questions of ethics and the fact that Custer had ordered him to depart seemed irrelevant. He just couldn't shake the sense of guilt.

Rising, Fox paid, then turned to exit. In the doorway he nearly collided with a young fellow who looked like an eastern banker in his brown frock coat, double-breasted vest, spotless white shirt, and slim fawn trousers. When Fox murmured a word of apology, the man's face lit up.

"No, no, pardon *me*! I haven't the least notion where I'm going. I've just arrived and, to be honest, you are the first person who's said a civil word to me." He removed his bowler to reveal a fine head of curly blond hair and put out a smooth hand. "Permit me to introduce myself, sir. I am Graham Horatio Scofield the Third, of the Boston Scofields."

"Ah." Nodding, Fox bit his lip in an effort not to grin. "Good to meet you, pard. I'm Fox." When he saw that the newcomer was waiting for more information, he added, "Welcome to Deadwood. Here, take my newspaper. It should answer a few of your questions."

"That's very kind of you. Are the rooms decent in this hotel?"

Fox cocked his head. "If you've come looking for decency, I'm afraid you may have stumbled into the wrong town, friend. The Grand Central's food is first-rate, though, and if you ask around you may get some better advice about hotel rooms. There are a few new ones I haven't tried."

"Thank you!" Scofield shook his hand with enthusiasm. "It's very kind of you to help me. I appreciate it more than you know."

Fox felt a little tug of sympathy for the young man as he watched him wander into the chaos of the hotel's dining room. He'd rarely seen anyone who looked more like a fish out of water. However, he was hardly the man's keeper; he had problems enough of his own. And with that in mind Fox turned away and started walking home.

"When's Fox coming back?" Benjamin asked Titus Pym for the hundredth time in five days. The two of them were sitting in the cabin doorway, staring at the cloud formations above the opposite side of the gulch. Sometimes Titus would whittle for a few moments, then stop.

"I've told you, lad, I can't say for certain, but I believe it will be soon. Quite soon."

"Are you sure he's all right? What if the Injins got him

like they did General Custer and all those soldiers? What if—"

"Ben, you remember, don't you? Wild Bill's friend Charley Utter saw Fox and spoke to him. He's just been . . . ill these past few days, and staying with friends until he feels better."

Benjamin sighed heavily. "I sure miss him."

"As do I." Titus looked around, taking in the nearly completed cabin. He'd done all he dared without Fox's instructions. The roof was finished, and the windows and stairs, but he had a feeling that Fox wanted something special for the front door, so he'd left that. For the past five days he'd slept on the rough pine floor, missing the view of the stars, cared for Watson, and waited. Now, his stomach grumbled loudly. "Ben, me lad, why don't we pop into your house and see if your dear grandmum has any crumbs of food she'd like to give us. . . ."

"Okay!" The boy jumped up, glad for a diversion. "I think I saw her baking something with brandied pears in it this morning. I bet you'd like it a lot, Mr. Pym!"

"I don't doubt that for a moment." Titus clambered to his feet with a groan, and they started toward the Avery house. Watson was, as usual, tethered to one of the pine trees, and as Titus and Benjamin approached they saw that Madeleine was there, stroking the roan and feeding him a handful of oats.

The face she turned up to the sunlight was pale, and Titus noticed that her green eyes looked tired and dull with pain. Still, she was dressed neatly, in a buttercup-yellow gown with her white gardening apron and gloves, and her hair was the hue of a blushing peach. On the ground was a trowel and a pan lined with seedlings, their roots protected by clumps of dark earth.

"We got tired of waiting for Fox and so we thought we would go eat something," Benjamin explained, strutting beside Titus like a little man.

Quickly Maddie's eyes met Titus's. "There's still no sign of him? No further word?"

"Sorry, Miss Avery, but no." The Cornish miner put on a cheery smile. "He'll be along, though. Meanwhile, what're you doing on this fine day? Don't say you mean to feed all those pretty plants to Watson!"

Warm color suffused her cheeks. "Actually . . . I thought I might plant a few flowers around . . . the cabin. It looks so nice now that it's all done, and it occurred to me that a bit of color might be nice."

"Won't Fox be pleased!"

Her blush deepened, and she bent to pick up the pan and trowel. "Well, I was just searching for something to occupy myself . . ."

"C'mon, Mr. Pym!" Benjamin called, fidgeting. "I'm *starved*!"

Maddie watched them go, then gave Watson a last caress and continued on toward the cabin. Her heart ached. The log house looked handsome and new, a rare example of care and craftsmanship in a town where dwellings went up in hours and came down just as suddenly if the wind blew hard or objects like fists, wagons, or bullets struck them. Fox's cabin symbolized the man who had created it, Maddie now realized.

Bending down next to the opening where the front door would fit, she began to dig with her trowel. The sound of Fox's voice, the sudden magic of his grin, the uncompromising blue of his eyes, everything about him haunted her dreams and tormented her days. Gramma Susan was right. As much as it hurt to feel as she did about Fox, she would not wish to go back now. She felt gloriously, excruciatingly alive for the first time.

Where was he? The question echoed in her mind and soul for the thousandth time. Restlessly she began to nestle the seedlings into the ground. Mr. Hickok had assured Titus Pym that Fox was safe. Had he used the word *indisposed* or *ill*? It didn't really matter, for Pym's manner gave him away. He was a poor liar, staring at his feet and clearing his throat and flushing redder with each question put to him. A little voice in the back of Maddie's mind began to suggest that Fox had gone off for a few days of wanton revelry with one of the soiled doves in the badlands. Rather than have such fears confirmed, Maddie had stopped quizzing Titus. Deadwood's half world, north of Wall Street, catered to every vice known to man, it seemed, and no one batted an eye. A different set of values prevailed in the West, and Fox was certainly human. Beyond that point Madeleine dared not think.

She patted dirt around the last plant, which would yield daisies, and wiped a bead of perspiration from her brow with a gloved hand. In the distance Watson made a low nickering sound, and Maddie's heart leaped. When she rose to her feet and turned, there was Fox.

"Miss Avery, what are you up to now?" he inquired, with a touch of irony.

Tears tightened her throat. She walked toward him haltingly, tingling with joy and yet aghast to see how he had changed. He was thinner and paler than he had been just five days ago, and there were dark smudges under his eyes. Then, drawing closer, she saw that he had been through some sort of ordeal. He was changed in other ways; he looked haunted.

"I—I was planting a few flowers by your front door. Do you mind?"

"They'll probably die," he replied.

Her chest hurt. Where was the handsome, irresistible man who had teased and taunted her with his words, and his touch? "Fox," she whispered, "I'm glad you're home. I mean— everyone has been worried about you."

Maddie stood so close to him that her breasts nearly grazed his calico shirt. Old feelings stirred, like the embers of a stubborn fire. When she turned her face up to him, Fox saw the truth in her eyes. He didn't move as she leaned gently against him for a moment, her scent wafting upward tanta- lizingly.

Too bad, Fox thought. *I'll have to break her heart.*

Chapter Ten

July 27–July 30, 1876

LIKE EVERYTHING ELSE IN DEADWOOD, THE phases and colors of the days were dramatic. Because the town was set low in a gulch, soft, creeping dawns and sunsets were out of the question. Instead the sun would appear abruptly, round and golden, like a jewel atop the twisting canyon's crown of white rocks. Then, at around ten o'clock, the sky would deepen to a clear blue.

On this particular morning Fox had been up for hours by the time the full sun popped into sight. He'd just hung his beautifully crafted front door and sent Titus down to Main Street to purchase another latch since the first choice was too short.

The sun signaled the beginning of warmer temperatures, causing Fox to push up the sleeves of his white undershirt and unbutton it to the middle of his chest. He had just turned in the doorway to search inside for some bread and fruit when he spied Madeleine Avery approaching with a basket.

Fox wished he could disappear. He wasn't much for conversation these days, and he didn't have the patience to be polite—especially to Maddie, who had taken to gazing at him with her heart in her eyes. As if that weren't bad enough, his lust for her burned hotter each time she came near. It had all been a lot easier when he'd been a decent, lighthearted man and she the cool, prim ice maiden. Those days seemed long ago.

"I see you have a door!" she said brightly, stopping a short distance away as if to gauge his mood.

Fox leaned against the rugged frame, nearly filling the space, and nodded. "What can I do for you?"

"Gramma . . . asked me to bring you these muffins." She took a step forward and gestured toward the basket.

"You both shouldn't have bothered."

Twin spots of color stained Maddie's cheeks. She couldn't fathom what had come over Fox since his disappearance. "There's no reason for you to be *rude*! Gramma Susan happens to be a very nice woman, and she's grateful to you for allowing Benjamin to spend so much time here. Is it a crime for her to do you a kindness?"

"No, it's not a crime," he replied harshly, "but I'd rather be left alone."

She stared in outrage as he turned and went inside the cabin. Tears threatened, but she forbade them. Instead she followed Fox, holding fast to the basket. When she entered the cabin, she had to wait a few moments for her eyes to adjust to the shadows. Then, slowly, she took in the table constructed of wooden crates and planks, the assorted barrels and stools, and Fox's bedroll, spread out in a corner. Fox himself was sorting through some tools piled on the open stairway, so Maddie went over to the table and set the basket on it.

"You may as well have these," she said.

He glanced over his shoulder as if he'd forgotten who was speaking, then nodded again. "If you say so, Miss Avery."

Biting her lip, Maddie picked up a book from the table. She had planned this visit for too long to be chased away by his discourteous treatment, especially when she suspected that that was his intent. For some mysterious reason Fox could no longer bear to be close to her—just at the time when she wanted it more than anything else.

" '*Leaves of Grass*, by Walt Whitman,' " she read aloud from the title page. Poetry! Now here was yet another incongruity: a rough-edged western man who read poetry? "I've heard so much about Whitman's work, but my mother wouldn't permit me to buy *Leaves of Grass*. She said it was shocking." Maddie smiled slightly at the memory.

Fox took the book out of her slim hands. "Your mother was right. Some of it probably would seem shocking to you, and that's exactly why I like it." His eyes met hers in a momentary flash of blue ice. "Beware, Miss Avery."

"Don't you take that attitude with me!" she heard herself shout. To her further indignation, Fox simply walked away. "Wait just one minute!"

She was right behind him, reaching for his arm, which felt as though it were made of iron. It came to Maddie that he could flick her away effortlessly, yet he did not. "What's wrong with you? Why won't you tell me? Why have you changed so? If there is anything to be done, you need only ask for help. You have friends who—"

His face stormy and forbidding, he turned back and grasped her delicate arms, lifting her up and away. *"There's nothing to be done!* There; are you satisfied? There's nothing to be done and nothing to say, to you or anyone else. Just go away and leave me alone!"

Her eyes swam with tears. "Oh, Fox . . ."

The sight of her evoked feelings that were so painful they made him angry. "What the devil do you want from me?" he demanded, his voice raw. "This?" He pulled her against him and covered her lips with his own, kissing her until she was compelled to respond. "Is this what you want?"

How many hours had she lain awake dreaming of his kisses and the touch of his hands? Maddie was unschooled in the details of lovemaking, but she didn't need to know what came next. Tentatively she lifted her hands to his shoulders and parted her lips, just as he'd taught her that day in the parlor.

Yet everything was different this time. Fox lifted her off the floor, and moments later they were facing each other, kneeling on the padded surface of his bedroll. It seemed that every inch of Maddie's body ached with needs she couldn't fathom, and the sound of her beating heart filled her head. Fox's hands nearly spanned her waist when he drew her hard against his body. She had never felt more fragile, more thrilled by the contrast between men and women.

She longed to hear him speak tenderly; but he did not. She yearned to have him caress her slowly, so that she might savor each new sensation; but he would not. Instead, he was rough. His mouth was so hot; the pressure of his lips and hands would not be denied. When he bent her back, kissing her neck, Maddie panted involuntarily as waves of innocent arousal washed over her. He smelled of sweat, but on Fox even that scent was intoxicating. She wished he would slow down so that she could touch his chest, kiss his face and learn its contours, taste him. Maddie tried to move in Fox's embrace, but it was unyielding. The first sparks of confusion and panic flared at the edges of her ardor.

"Fox—" she managed to gasp.

Deftly he worked at the fastenings that marched down the back of her peach crepe bodice. The high neckline opened without resistance. Moving like a lean, hungry panther, he pulled Maddie's gown away from her body, then drew back to stare at her breasts, thinly covered by a fragile chemise. God, but they were beautiful: full and taut, with pink nipples visible through the lawn. Quickly he lowered the straps of her chemise and freed her breasts. Maddie made a sound when he cupped them in his hands, then reached around to clasp her buttocks and bring her against him, hip to hip. His kisses were ravenous. It seemed that he could devour her as he tasted the pale, soft sweetness of her throat, shoulder, the curve of her breast, a tender, puckered bud.

Maddie's face flamed. Tears spilled onto her cheeks, and when at last he lifted his head to kiss her and she could feel the hardness between his legs pressing against her, she began to struggle in earnest.

Fox tasted salt on his tongue. Dimly it came to him through a haze of raging passion that she was resisting him, crying out. Her tiny fists struck at him blindly, and he drew back.

"What the hell—?" Shame spread through him like a dark stain, but he could not let her know.

Hair spilling down and cheeks tear-streaked, she clambered to her feet, tripping once over the hem of her skirt.

"You *forced* yourself on me!" she sobbed. "How dare you? I thought you were a man of honor!"

"Don't go blaming me for what just happened. You all but asked for it with a signed document." Fox rose, too, and had to restrain himself from reaching out to help when he saw her fumbling with her chemise in an effort to cover herself. This accomplished, Maddie straightened her shoulders, lifted her delicate chin, and presented her back to him.

"You'll have to repair your damage," she said stiffly. "I cannot reach the fastenings."

They were silent as he worked, his fingertips grazing her skin occasionally. Fox wished it didn't have to be like this, but there didn't seem to be any other way to scare her off. This unequivocal rupture would be best in the long run, for both of them.

Her clothing restored, Maddie smoothed back her hair and pinned it into a loose chignon. Then, without looking back, she walked to the door and opened it.

"The basket—" Fox said hoarsely.

She turned at length, haloed in the radiant sunlight that filled the doorway. "The muffins are for you and Titus," she said quietly. "I should tell you that in spite of what has transpired between us, I know what sort of man you truly are. I cannot guess what has happened to wound you so deeply, but I do know that I am too strong to be scared off so easily."

His eyebrows flew up in astonishment at this speech, and an instant later Madeleine disappeared from the doorway. Fox stood as if paralyzed, then strode across the cabin. Reaching the door, he shouted after her slim, exquisite departing figure, "Miss Avery, I don't give a damn about you!"

Maddie continued walking as if she hadn't heard.

The next day Stephen Avery returned home. He didn't say much about where he'd been and in fact seemed much more interested in sleeping than talking, but his homecoming kept Maddie busy and distracted—or so Fox hoped. For his own part, he avoided the house next door. When the last muffin had been devoured by Titus, he ordered the older man to return the basket. Happy to comply, Pym feasted on chicken stew at the Avery house and returned with a whole, aromatic plum cobbler.

"Stop bringing food from the Averys into this house!" Fox burst out, pacing as if Titus had committed a capital offense.

The Cornish miner was taken aback. "Eh? What's amiss, sir?"

"I'm tired of having their dishes and baskets and plates cluttering up *my* house, that's all." He directed a menacing glare at the cobbler pan.

"Never mind, then, I'll see to it." Titus reached protectively for the pan, which sat on the makeshift table. "You don't have to go within touching distance of Miss Avery, if that's what's got your back up."

"Why the devil should you say a thing like that?" A muscle twitched in Fox's jaw.

"Were you supposing I'm an idiot? I have eyes, son."

It was unsettling for Fox to face the fact that he didn't seem to be fooling anyone—including, it seemed, Maddie herself. No one believed him when he said he didn't want her. Since the truth was impossible, he resolved to try different tactics. Tomorrow he would go down to Main Street in search of Graham Horatio Scofield III.

Stephen Avery, lounging in his bed, looked up from his breakfast tray when Madeleine peeked into the bedroom. "Hello, darling." He smiled weakly and patted the quilt, which had been painstakingly stitched by his late wife. "Sit with me for a bit."

It was late, nearly eleven o'clock, and Maddie searched his face with worried eyes as she drew near. Her father had been sleeping more and more of the time since his return to Deadwood. Something wasn't right. To make matters worse, he wouldn't tell them where he had been or why. At first Maddie had accepted his stories about business dealings in Custer or Hill City, but now she was beset with doubts and worries. Gramma Susan didn't say much, but her eyes were keen and watchful behind her gold spectacles.

This morning, observing her father's curiously flushed face, Maddie decided it didn't matter where he had been or what his secrets were. He had a right to privacy, and she was beginning to think that secrets were normal. She had a few of her own. . . .

"You look prettier each time I see you," Stephen said, gazing at her proudly. Madeleine's violet-and-cream-striped taffeta gown, with its heart-shaped neckline and fitted bodice, was proper yet provocative at the same time, and her bright curls were cunningly caught up in a series of loops that curved partway down her back. She was a breath of fresh air to him, and his eyes shone with the depth of his love.

"Thank you, Father." Smiling, she perched on the bed and clasped his hand. "You haven't eaten very much of your breakfast. How are you feeling?"

"Oh, I suppose I may have picked up a touch of the ague while I was away. It's no use pretending I'm not ill; you can see for yourself."

She sighed with relief. "Well, then, let's send for Dr. Sick—"

"The most ironic name," Stephen interrupted, laughing and then coughing. At length he added, "Who knows what sort of outdated potions they try to pass off as medicine around these parts. The redoubtable Dr. Sick might kill me with his cure."

"But, Father—"

"Just wait a bit, my dear. You may send for him if I take a turn for the worse." Attempting to allay her concern, Avery took a bite of coddled egg. "There, you see? I'm just a bit weak; nothing serious. Now then, tell me what's been happening in my darling daughter's life? How have you and Fox been getting on? His cabin looks amazingly impressive from the window."

"Why do you link my fortunes with Fox's?" she asked, coloring immediately.

"No reason, really. Perhaps it was wishful thinking on my

part. I know that there aren't many men to choose from in Deadwood, but Fox seemed different. Sometimes while I was away, I would think about you before falling asleep, and I confess to imagining tender scenes between you two.''

Maddie stiffened. "Wishful thinking, indeed, Father. That man hasn't a drop of tenderness in his body as far as I know. However, his house is very fine, just as you observed, and he has been indulgent regarding Benjamin. He gives him simple chores to do which allow him to feel important.'' She hesitated, then continued, "As I have told you several times since your return, I'm adjusting well, I think. My garden is healthy and some of my flowers have buds on them. I have no personal life to speak of, but that's not a source of concern to me."

It was clear to Stephen that his daughter was holding back all that truly mattered, but he saw that her pride would resist any attempt he might make to pry. A silence fell between them, then suddenly Maddie straightened.

"I almost forgot!" She withdrew a creamy envelope from the pocket of her skirt. "Look at this—a little Chinese boy brought it to the door about an hour ago. Go ahead and read the note inside. Perhaps it will make some sense to *you*."

Stephen looked at the envelope. On the outside, in a flowing hand, was written "Miss Madeleine Avery.'' The paper was expensive, all but unheard of in brawling Deadwood. Frowning, he took out the neatly folded note and read aloud, " 'Greetings to Miss Avery. My name is Graham Horatio Scofield the Third, of the Boston Scofields, and I am newly arrived in Deadwood. I have been given to understand that you share this rather awkward condition, and also that we may come from similar backgrounds and have similar characters. I beg that you will forgive my abrupt address, but I perceive no other way. I ask that you receive me today at noon so that I may introduce myself. I expect nothing; I hope for friendship. Yours respectfully, Graham Horatio Scofield the Third.' ''

"Do you know this man?" Maddie inquired, clearly flustered after hearing the missive read aloud.

He shook his head slowly. "No . . . and I am inclined to think that I would remember someone so singular to these environs."

"Well, I suppose I shall have to meet Mr. Scofield," she replied, with a sigh. "I can hardly turn him away. Noon is fast approaching, so I'll find Gramma Susan, warn her, and see what refreshments we have to offer this unsolicited visitor."

She took Stephen's nearly untouched tray with her. When she paused in the doorway to glance back, she saw that her father was already asleep again.

When Maddie joined her grandmother in the kitchen, Susan was experimenting with a new recipe for small Cornish pasties shaped like turnovers. The fragrance of the diced steak, potatoes, onions, and pastry all baking together was heavenly.

Susan O'Hara took Maddie's news with typical good humor. Of course any newcomer was always welcome, as far as Susan was concerned, but she agreed with her granddaughter that in this case, something besides pastie ought to be served. Bustling about happily, she prepared tiny triangular sandwiches filled with thin-sliced chicken and cucumber and arranged them on a tray with plates of orange segments and oatmeal cookies. To make the cookies look more refined, she cut them carefully into quarters. Tea was brewed and lemons sliced. Maddie was just assembling little cups and saucers that matched the exquisite Canton teapot when a polite knock sounded at the front door.

"Just pretend I'm the maid when I bring all this into the parlor," Gramma Susan hissed as Maddie prepared to greet her guest. "There will be time enough later to identify me if you and Mr. Scofield form an attachment." The whimsical smile she gave her granddaughter told her how much stock she put in that likelihood.

Looking every inch the decorous, gently bred, and tasteful young lady, Madeleine opened the door. Facing her was a man who could have been plucked from one of Philadelphia's excruciatingly refined dancing assemblies. He wore an immaculate gray cutaway coat, light trousers, a brocade vest with a rolled collar, and a stiff white shirt, celluloid collar, and a perfectly executed four-in-hand tie set off by a scarf pin. He carried a violet nosegay and doffed a bowler hat to reveal curly blond hair parted in the center.

"You must be Miss Avery," he said, awestruck. "Word of your beautiful hair has preceded you! Uh . . . allow me to introduce myself. I am Graham Horatio Scofield the Third, of the—"

"Boston Scofields?" Maddie couldn't resist exclaiming.

"Ah, I see that you are familiar with my line," Graham said. "I am not surprised. Philadelphia and Boston are not so far apart, after all, and it is my experience that the better families are acquainted all along the eastern seaboard."

Maddie was momentarily at a loss, then she put out her hand. "It's a pleasure to meet you, Mr. Scofield. Won't you come in? I was just about to have tea and hoped you would join me. How kind of you to send a note in advance."

"I brought these for you." He presented the violets and sketched a bow. "Somehow I felt that you would be the sort of lady who would love flowers."

Maddie paused in the act of pressing her nose into the blooms to inhale their perfume. "It's most unexpected to meet a man like you in Deadwood, Mr. Scofield."

"And even more unexpected to encounter a true lady like yourself, Miss Avery," he replied earnestly. "It's as if I have discovered a treasure much more valuable than gold."

"You are . . . too kind, sir." Despite an occasional prick of amusement, Maddie could not help responding to his compliments and admiration. After the treatment she had received from Fox of late, Graham Horatio Scofield III's effusive kindness was almost soothing . . . for an hour or two, at least. Goodwill bubbled up in Maddie as she watched Gramma Susan darting in and out of the parlor to serve the tea, apparently delighting in her little masquerade. Mr. Scofield, though unfailingly polite, treated Gramma Susan with a condescending air that made Maddie want to giggle. Still, she was entertained. They discussed all the latest news from

the East, sipped tea, exchanged opinions about Elizabeth and
Robert Browning, Harriet Beecher Stowe, the movement for
women's suffrage, Napoléon III's Second Empire in France,
and Dickens's *A Tale of Two Cities*, which Graham had read
on the train from Boston to Chicago. Maddie was beginning
to quite enjoy herself, feeling that she had found a friend
who could help her to escape mentally from Deadwood when
the need arose.

"Have another sandwich, Mr. Scofield," she invited
warmly. "Let us speak of anything other than our arduous
journeys West, Custer's massacre, and the current price of
gold and land in this hideous town. I don't even want to know
why you came here."

He laughed, perhaps a bit too loudly. "I know what you
mean, Miss Avery, and I am happy to comply. I fear that I
have made a mistake coming to the Black Hills, but it isn't
one that can be rectified by wishing. It's such a long way
back to Boston. . . ."

Desperate to steer the conversation away from reality, she
said, "What poets do you enjoy? Longfellow?"

"Yes, I like Longfellow and Tennyson and Shelley most
particularly. I find that I'm rather put off by some of the newer
poets, like Whitman, who I know you'll agree is occasionally shocking in his approach."

Maddie stared at him as his last words sank in. A torrent
of unwelcome questions surged up within her. How had Graham Scofield heard of her and how did he know so much
about her? How did he know she was from Philadelphia?
Only one person could have informed Scofield that she had
used the word *shocking* to describe Walt Whitman's poems.
It was too neat to be a coincidence.

"Pardon me, Mr. Scofield," she said, with her sunniest
smile, "but have you met a gentleman called Fox? He's quite
amiable—a tall, strong fellow with dark hair and a short
beard. He lives next to us, and if you haven't met him, I think
you should. I am certain that the two of you would become
friends."

Graham had gone pale as she spoke, then gradually looked

relieved. "As a matter of fact, I have met your friend, Fox. He is splendid! He's given me invaluable advise about purchasing land here in town, and I owe him an immense debt."

"So immense that you might attempt to court me if he asked you to?" Maddie inquired sweetly.

Scofield broke out in a sweat. "Hot today, isn't it? Horrible weather."

"Would you mind terribly if I asked you to see yourself out, Mr. Scofield? I've just remembered a very pressing appointment."

With that, Maddie stood up and marched into the kitchen. She didn't even pause to speak to Gramma Susan before throwing open the back door and emerging into the sunlight. Through the pine trees, she could see Fox and Benjamin in front of the log cabin, sawing a piece of wood supported between two sawhorses.

Her tiny hands were balled into fists, and she felt as if fire were flashing from her eyes as she strode up to them. Fox looked up, wiped his wet forehead with his rolled-up shirtsleeve, and then went back to sawing as if Maddie didn't exist. Benjamin glanced between them, confused.

"Benjamin, you must hurry home right now. Gramma Susan needs you." She was too angry to think of anything except a lie. While the little boy was running toward the other house, Maddie turned to inspect the flowers she had planted. "Don't you water them? You have to water them or they'll die."

Fox merely shrugged and continued sawing patiently.

Maddie threw herself at him, striking his face with her fists, hearing her underarm seam rip, grappling for his shoulders as if she could bring him down and overpower him. "I hate you!" she sobbed. "How dare you let my flowers die? Are you killing them to hurt me? What kind of man are you? And that person you bribed to come into my home and lie to me! Did you think I wouldn't know he was a fraud? Do you take me for a *fool*?"

Fox caught her wrists and held her away from him. "Good God, have you lost your mind?"

Tears were streaming down her face. "Why—why—?"

Fox's jaw tensed and his blue eyes hardened as he stared at her. "Because I can never give you what you want, Maddie. Understand? I want you to *forget all about me*."

His voice was like a steel blade that penetrated her heart. Maddie thought she might die from the pain, but then she heard another voice, high-pitched and frightened, crying out from the row of pine trees.

"Fox, Fox! Come quick!" It was Benjamin. "Something's really wrong with Papa! He says he has to talk to *you* right away!"

Chapter Eleven

July 30–August 2, 1876

MADDIE LIFTED HER SKIRTS AND RAN, OBLIVIOUS of the mud that spattered her ivory kid shoes. Fox sprinted past her across his lot, between the pine trees, and then he disappeared inside her house.

By the time Maddie burst into the kitchen, her face was scarlet from the exertion, her hair a fiery tumble of curls down her back. Susan O'Hara was waiting for her. "Gramma, what's happened?"

"There's no cause for alarm, darling," the old woman replied in soothing tones. She took Maddie's trembling hands and looked into her eyes calmly. "Your father has had a . . . spell of some sort. He had a pain in his chest that went down his left arm, and he began to sweat, but it has passed now. Apparently, however, it frightened him enough to disclose some of the matters he has so clearly been keeping to himself."

"But . . . what about a doctor . . . ?"

"Benjamin has run for Dr. Sick, who may or may not be in Deadwood. Failing to find a physician, he will seek advice from one of our friends on Main Street."

"Well, I'm going to Father right now!" As Maddie started toward the doorway to the parlor, Susan caught her torn sleeve.

"My dear, he's asked to speak to Fox. We must allow them some privacy."

Her granddaughter whirled around, emerald eyes ablaze. "That's *ridiculous*! Why, Father could die without seeing

149

anyone except that vile *Fox*. I do not believe that there is anything he wishes to say to him that he would not wish me to hear also!''

Susan stepped back. ''Have it your way.''

Maddie knew a momentary pang of shame for shouting at her grandmother so angrily. ''I'm terribly frightened . . . about Father.''

''Of course you are.'' Susan's voice was neutral.

Precious seconds were ticking away. Maddie gave the old woman a faltering smile, then hurried toward the doorway to her father's bedroom.

The door was locked.

''Father?'' she called, knocking. ''It's Maddie. May I come in?''

A mumbling sound was followed by the click of the latch, and then the door swung open. Fox stood before her. ''You must be very calm, and if he asks you to go, you mustn't argue, Maddie.''

She pushed past him, pausing only long enough to cry, ''I'll thank you not to instruct me regarding my own father, sir!'' An instant later she was sitting on the edge of the bed, holding Stephen's hand. He was shockingly pale and drawn, and for the first time she noticed that his wavy black hair was flecked with gray. ''Papa,'' Maddie whispered. ''How are you?''

He managed a brave smile, but there was fear in his eyes and he made no effort to move. ''No doubt I'll recover, my dearest. What of you?''

''I?'' she echoed.

''You . . . look as if you've been in an accident,'' he remarked, still smiling faintly.

Maddie felt Fox's eyes on her like a brand as she fingered her flurry of unbound curls and with her other hand felt for the ripped seam in her sleeve. She laughed. ''I did have an accident of sorts, but it was nothing serious. I'll be *much* more careful in the future.''

''Well, then, if you have set your mind at ease, my dear, I would ask you to grant me time alone with our friend Fox.''

Bristling, Maddie tightened her grip on his hand. "Father, how can it be that you would share confidences with him and yet deny your own daughter the same honor? Am I not worthy of your trust? Please, can't you see that I'm a woman now and not a child?"

"Miss Avery, your father hasn't much strength." Fox put a hand on her shoulder. She jerked away as if scorched.

"Never mind, Fox," Stephen whispered hoarsely. "Madeleine is right. She is an adult and I should not try to shield her from the secrets of my past if she prefers the painful truth. Besides, it may be necessary that someone here understand what is transpiring over the next weeks . . . in case I do not recover." He gestured for Fox to sit down on a nearby stool, which his friend did, hitching it closer to the bed.

"You are going to be fine, Father," Maddie murmured, tears pricking her eyes at the very thought of losing him so soon after they had been reunited.

The room was oppressively hot, and Fox rose to throw open a window and roll up the sleeves of his shirt. Then, settling himself on the stool, he looked over at Stephen expectantly.

"I don't have the strength to explain everything I've done the way I'd like to, Maddie," Stephen said, begging her with his eyes to understand. "I do want you to know that I loved your mother . . . though I realize I wasn't always the husband she deserved."

"She loved you, too, Papa," she replied.

"I was away too much, but the urge to seek adventure and explore new land was too powerful for me to resist. Your mother seemed to understand that I would not be happy if I remained in Philadelphia and followed the rules. It has occurred to me that she, who never bent if she could remain erect in life, allowed me to bend for both of us." Stephen pointed to the bottle of brandy on the table beside his bed, and Fox poured him a small glass and helped him to drink it.

"Father, you can explain all of this to me another time. Whatever it was that you did when you were away from us,

I shall understand,'' Maddie reassured him, fearing that he might have another spell that would render him incapable of speech.

He sighed deeply; a resolute expression appeared on his haggard face. "I . . . had other lives when I was away. I was sometimes lonely, but . . ." He looked away from Maddie and sighed again. "When I was returning East from the Nevada silver strike in '59, I encountered surprise snowstorms that forced me to seek shelter not far from east of here with a band of Teton Sioux Indians. I traded with them, began to feel at home with them, and stayed so long that I had to wait out the winter."

Fox sat forward at this news but said nothing. Maddie looked slightly bewildered.

"Life among the Indian people is impossible to describe. We whites have woefully misjudged the depth and richness of their culture. I was happy there." Stephen's eyes misted for a moment, then he recovered. "There is a purity and harmony in their way of life that we have lost in our constant striving for progress. But you must not misunderstand me, Maddie. I did not forget about my family, and when the thaws came in spring, I was anxious to return to you and your mother."

"Is that your secret?" she whispered, hoping against hope.

"What I have just said is . . . the box that holds the secret."

Her heart began to beat very fast then, and she held tighter to her father's hand. "Dr. Sick may arrive at any moment, Papa. You must take the secret out of the box."

Looking at them, the oft-absent father and the daughter who strove for security and order, Fox felt an unexpected wave of sympathy. A box, indeed, he thought.

Stephen was nodding. "I'm not ashamed, you know, but I don't expect you to understand, my girl. The truth is . . . that I had tender feelings for a young maiden in the Sioux village—or Lakota, as they call themselves. Her name was Yellow Bird, and she was very kind to me that winter. I think she loved me, but she understood that I could not remain

among them.'' He began to take shallow breaths. ''The day
I left, Yellow Bird told me, quite sweetly, that she carried
my child.''

''Father!'' Maddie gasped, unable to disguise her shock.

''You certainly were not the first white man to have a child
with an Indian woman,'' Fox said in a firm voice. ''The
Indians say that Custer himself had a Cheyenne wife, perhaps
even a child, yet he deeply loved his wife, Elizabeth. You
were human, sir, as are all of us.'' He gave Maddie a warning
stare. ''I might venture to suggest that even your daughter,
whose fine qualities we all admire, is human.''

''Well, of course I am!'' Her eyes were brilliant as she
looked from Fox to her father. ''What happened then? Did
Yellow Bird have the baby? What has become of them?'' The
notion that she might have a half-Sioux sibling was more
than she could comprehend at that moment.

''Yes, Yellow Bird had a baby daughter, whom she named
Sun Smile . . . but I didn't know this until I came out here
last autumn. As you doubtless remember, Maddie, I never
went West again after the war and Benjamin's birth. Your
mother's health was failing, and she needed me . . . and I
suppose I felt guilty. It wasn't until Colleen died nearly a
year ago that I felt I could return to the Dakota Territory and
search for news of Yellow Bird and the child.'' The difficulty
Stephen was having in telling his daughter the truth was now
evident. A droplet of sweat—or a tear—trickled down the
side of his cheek. ''Not that I raced off and failed to grieve
for your mother. You know better than that, Madeleine. But
I heard about that first gold strike on Whitewood Creek in
August of '75 and felt that old thrill . . . and to be honest, I
welcomed the chance to escape my pain, and my regrets. . . .''

''How did you find Yellow Bird?'' asked Fox, steering him
back to the subject.

''She was visiting her father at the Red Cloud Agency
south of here. I went there to look, to ask about her, and by
chance she was there. She was married, of course, and had
other children. We spoke as old friends, which was oddly

comforting to me. Yellow Bird was a kind and gentle woman.''

Maddie had to swallow hard before she could find her voice. "And . . . Sun Smile? Did you see her as well?''

"No. Yellow Bird told me that Sun Smile was never fully accepted by her husband, so when she was old enough to marry, she did so. Sun Smile married a Miniconjou Sioux who shunned the efforts of whites to herd Indians onto the Great Sioux Reservation. They were among the disconnected bands who had chosen to throw in their lot with Crazy Horse and continue to live freely, roaming and hunting where they chose.'' Stephen was growing tired, but he caught the glint in Fox's eyes. "I know, I know . . . Crazy Horse's warriors were the ones who demolished the Seventh Cavalry.'' He paused, accepting another sip of brandy when Fox offered the glass. "It was enough for me, at first, to know that Sun Smile was alive and happy, according to her mother. But, as matters with the Indians worsened, I began thinking more and more about her, wondering if I didn't owe her something as her father. Before the news came about Custer, I went back to the Red Cloud Agency, hoping against hope that she and her husband might have returned there to be safe. When I heard the news about Crazy Horse and Custer, my heart sank. And . . .'' Stephen closed his eyes for a moment, then murmured, "I learned, from Yellow Bird's father, that she and her own husband and one of their sons all died this past winter of cholera—another of the white man's gifts to the innocent Indians.''

Maddie felt her heart opening as she began to understand the sadness and conflict her father had suffered. She warmed his cold hands in hers and gave him a tremulous smile.

"What is it you want me to do, sir?'' Fox asked.

"Well, this may sound quite mad to you. . . . It probably is, but never mind. When I was returning north from the agency, I encountered a village of Oglala Sioux camped a few miles east of the Black Hills. They gave me a meal, though there isn't much food now that the buffalo is nearly gone and the rations distributed at the agencies are so pathetically inedible." He was breathing harder, and Maddie squeezed his hands. "At any rate, what they told me hit me like a bolt of lightning. They were going to strike the village that next day and head south . . . because word had reached them that Crazy Horse and his people were in Dakota Territory!"

Fox rose at this news and began to pace at the foot of Stephen's bed. "It could be a rumor," he said, trying not to betray his own excitement.

"I don't think so. These people were deadly serious; one of their young warriors had seen Crazy Horse himself, and after riding back to inform his own people, he announced that he was going to join the hostiles. This band is convinced that Crazy Horse will bring the 'bluecoats' to this area like a swarm of bees and that all Indians who happen to be nearby will be slaughtered. That's why they are hurrying to the safety of the agency."

Fox's brown hands coiled into fists as he stood at the bottom of the bed and stared at the older man. "Did they say exactly where Crazy Horse and his people are?" he asked carefully.

Avery nodded, unable to suppress a smile. "Yes. Bear Butte—or very near. Do you know the place?"

"Quite well." He rubbed his bearded jaw thoughtfully.

Maddie looked quickly from Fox to her father and back again. "What are you two up to?"

"I planned to go myself," Stephen said. "I ought to do this myself, but it seems that by the time I am well enough, Crazy Horse may have moved on and I may have lost my only chance to find Sun Smile."

"You aren't suggesting that Fox should appear in the midst of a camp of hostile Indians who have just massacred General Custer and more than two hundred of his men? That would be suicide!"

"Why, Miss Avery, it almost sounds as if you care!" Fox arched a brow at her and grinned. "Actually, on a more serious note, it would not be suicide. I spent time among various Lakota tribes myself, including the Oglala, Miniconjou, and Hunkpapa. I do not think that even the Crazy Horse people will kill me.''

''Excellent!'' Stephen smiled with undisguised joy. ''You'll go, then?''

''It would be an honor, sir, to do this favor for you.''

Avery saw that an offer to pay Fox would not be welcome. Instead he murmured, ''I cannot express what a sense of relief I feel. If you can only find Sun Smile and convey to her my concern and good wishes, that would be enough. But if she is in need of a safe haven, I hope that she will consider returning to Deadwood with you. I have no doubts that my family—*her* family—would open their arms to her. Would it be so wrong for Sun Smile to learn more about the other half of her heritage?''

Maddie's mind was spinning with a million confusing thoughts while the two men continued to make plans for Fox's journey to Bear Butte. As she thought about the half-sister she had never met, a feeling began to come over her that she had never known before. Suddenly she realized that she wanted to go with Fox. Yet, watching the two men, she knew without doubt that neither would consent if she asked straight out to go to Bear Butte. Even if she and Fox were more congenial, he would laugh at the notion of taking her on such an adventure.

Nevertheless, she was determined to go. Somehow this seemed to be a part of her destiny, and not even Fox could be permitted to stand in her way.

Dr. O. E. Sick arrived that night with Benjamin and Titus. He administered an ''elixir'' that smelled strongly of gin, and Stephen lapsed into a deep sleep that lasted until the next noon. Maddie, wandering in from time to time to see if he had awakened, thought that her father wore an expression more peaceful than any she had seen since their arrival in Deadwood. Unburdening himself had probably been a more effective treatment for his ills than any medicine Dr. Sick could prescribe.

And Stephen had no more cause for worry about Sun

Smile. If she was anywhere near Bear Butte, Fox would find her. Of this her father was certain, and in truth, so was she.

Over the next three days Fox made careful preparations for his journey. He was in and out of the Avery house because Stephen had frequent suggestions to make. They argued about whether Fox should take a wagon along in case Sun Smile decided to return to Deadwood. Fox believed that like all the Indian women he'd ever known, Sun Smile was not used to being spoiled and would be perfectly willing to ride a pony. What if she didn't have one? Stephen fretted. What if Crazy Horse's people couldn't spare one? Sun Smile, who was bound to have doubts anyway, might lose her nerve. Stephen was determined to make it as easy as possible for her to come.

Fox simply didn't want to be bothered with a wagon, especially on the mountain roads. And it would slow him down. Only when Stephen began to embellish his plans did Fox listen seriously.

"You can take supplies to the Indians," Avery declared, sitting up in bed and eating one of Susan's delectable Cornish pasties. "Imagine how quickly they must have been forced to strike the village at Little Bighorn! And they haven't been able to go near the agency for rations in months. If you take a wagon, we can pack it with dried beef and eggs and fruit and . . . everything they might need. Why, a few pounds of sugar and coffee and they'll treat you like a king!"

"Sir, you know that I'm not interested in being lionized by the Sioux," Fox replied evenly. However, the plan appealed to his humanitarian instincts, and his eyes flickered thoughtfully.

"Of course you're not." Stephen was earnest. "I only meant that if you brought some of the things the Sioux need most and they are grateful for your help, they may be more inclined to encourage Sun Smile to go with you when you explain about . . . me."

Fox raked a hand through his chestnut hair and sighed. "I'll think about what you've said, Mr. Avery."

"You know, we haven't much time. Today's the first of

August. I think you should go during the night tomorrow, so it would be helpful if you could make up your mind. Let me make one more proposition that may tip the scales. Why not take along a crate or two of rifles and an ample supply of ammunition? If Crazy Horse and his followers are going to be hunted down and punished for prevailing over Custer and his men with such apparent ease, they will surely need every assistance to make this a fair fight. . . .''

"All right, all right!" Fox raised his hands, laughing. "I give up! I'll take a wagon, I'll take food, and I'll take guns and ammunition. And if I'm going to leave tomorrow night as my commanding officer has planned—"

"I only thought that it would be wiser if all of Deadwood didn't see you go," Stephen hastened to explain. "I mean, it seems that a few precautions would not be out of order. Do you agree?"

"Obviously, sir, you have given this entire situation a great deal more thought than I, so I shall defer to you from this moment onward. However, as I was about to say, if time is short, there's a lot for me to do. I'll send Titus to hire a wagon and have him look into purchasing some rifles."

"Good thinking, my boy," Stephen said approvingly, and beamed. "It would be better if you aren't seen making any of the arrangements for this journey—just in case. Isn't there an itinerant miner we could pay to procure the guns? And perhaps you know a woman who could buy foodstuffs . . . ?"

"I may." A wry smile played over Fox's mouth. "I'd better be on my way then, sir."

"Let me know what the costs are and I shall reimburse you."

As Fox stepped on a squeaky floorboard near the open door leading to the parlor, Maddie scampered quickly into the kitchen. Rounding the doorway, she bumped straight into Gramma Susan, who had been leaning to one side with a hand cupped to her ear. At eighty-three she had better hearing than Benjamin.

"Oh!" cried Maddie in surprise, then clapped a hand over her own mouth. When she heard the front door close and peeked to see that Fox had departed, she turned on her grandmother. "What on earth were you doing, Gramma?"

Susan O'Hara smiled impishly. "I was listening, just as you were, darling."

"Oh . . ." Maddie didn't know how to respond.

"I know you want to go with him, and I know the reasons why." Pursing her lips, she nodded in a way that brooked no argument. "*All* the reasons. Don't worry, and don't waste energy on a debate. I think you *ought* to go, Maddie dear, and I shall help you devise a plan."

Chapter Twelve

FOX FOLDED HIS LAST CLEAN SHIRT AND STUFFED it into the bag along with the rest of the clothes he was taking to Bear Butte. The cabin was still bare, almost sad-looking, and he told himself that he would make an effort to turn it into more of a home after this journey was over. Glancing at the crates of rifles, ammunition, and foodstuffs that were piled in one corner and covered with a woolen blanket, he realized that part of the reason he had volunteered so readily to leave Deadwood was because it gave him an excuse not to confront his own life and future. Some nights, lying on the floor on top of his bedroll and brooding about the debacle at Little Bighorn, Fox felt so guilty that he thought he'd never be able to enjoy life again. At such moments the chance that he might not return from Bear Butte rather appealed to him. Certainly it would solve a number of issues that might never be settled otherwise.

Fox didn't think the Sioux would kill him. He didn't even fear Crazy Horse, who was only fighting for his freedom. However, the West was fraught with dangers; men died accidentally all the time. . . .

"What the hell's wrong with you?" he muttered. Sighing, he pulled on his boots, buttoned his faded blue shirt, and started for the door. Titus was off making arrangements for the wagon, which he would bring that night. Then, once it was loaded, Fox would leave Deadwood and go in search of Stephen Avery's daughter Sun Smile. It was an awfully peculiar world, no doubt about that.

Opening his new front door, Fox inhaled the warm morning air an instant before his gaze fell upon Madeleine. She was standing in front of the border of flowers she'd planted without his permission. This time, holding a watering can, she was frozen in midair like a statue. Only the slow flush that crept into her cheeks betrayed her nervous anticipation.

Inexplicably Fox felt a surge of rage every time he saw her. She was another of those questions in his life that couldn't be answered. "What are you doing?"

Stung by his stone-cold voice, Maddie bit her lip and continued to water the blossoming zinnias and daisies. "I don't want them to die."

"You are trespassing," he heard himself say. It sounded like a stranger's voice, and a part of Fox thought, *Was there ever a worse bastard?*

"And you're ridiculous, to put it politely," Maddie replied. "I have done nothing to deserve such unkind treatment from you."

Fox felt a pang of admiration for her spirit. Her little chin was lifted proudly. Why was she so stubborn? He hurt every time he saw her, and now that pain made him long to rip her precious flowers from the ground.

Instead he wrested the watering can from her. "Go home, Miss Avery. *I don't want to be near you!*"

Fox's voice was ragged with suppressed emotion, and Maddie's eyes flew up to search his face, sensing a little of the truth, the only part that mattered to her right then. "You give yourself away, Fox," she whispered.

When she touched his hand, reaching for the watering can, a strange shiver traveled up his arm and followed his spine downward. It was hard to breathe, and his eyes burned. Dear God, how glorious her hair looked in the morning sunlight! He remembered how it smelled. . . . And then dozens of memories assailed him—of the freckles that dusted her milky skin, the inexpressible sweetness of her mouth, the astonishing beauty of her breasts . . .

"I—" His voice was barely audible. He released the watering can and stepped backward. "I have to go."

Maddie's legs trembled as she watched him disappear through the pine trees. A moment later Fox had mounted Watson and the sound of hoofbeats could be heard on the sloping lane leading to Sherman Street. A secret smile curved Maddie's pretty mouth before she walked back to her own house to enlist the aid of her little brother.

Fox went straight to the Gem Theatre without even making a conscious decision. A mule train blocked most of Main Street, and bullwhackers were either unloading goods or drinking in the saloons.

Garnet Loomis stood a few feet inside the Gem's front door, apparently striking a deal of some sort with a disgustingly filthy bullwhacker. When she glimpsed Fox, she smiled broadly. "Hey, honey!"

He paused beside her. "Thanks again for ordering that food for me, Garnet. I appreciate it."

"You already paid me. I didn't deserve no five dollars for that little bit of work. Are you gonna tell me what all that food's for?"

"The poor," Fox answered, with a cryptic smile. "Where's Lorna?"

Garnet's penciled brows rose. "What? Poor Victoria!" Then her eyes narrowed, and she slapped his arm, grinning. "I get it! Lorna reminds you of that starched prissy little lady who lives next to you, don't she?" The sudden flash of danger in his eyes stopped her. "Lorna's been real busy lately, if you know what I mean. Last time I saw her, she'd just come back downstairs. As you can see, there's some new fellas in town."

Enjoying the sense of degradation, Fox went over to the bar, ordered coffee, and slowly examined the crowd for Lorna's coppery curls. He remembered how much she'd resembled Maddie the morning they met. They were nearly identical, Fox told himself, and felt an involuntary stiffening in his crotch. He wondered if he were cursed.

There she was, standing in a crowd near the stairs, talking to a lean, unshaven miner. Seen at exactly the right angle,

Lorna *did* appear to be Maddie, but when she turned the illusion would fade. Still, he thought, she'd do.

Lorna's face lit up when she saw Fox approaching. She didn't look as innocent as she had that first morning, but she was still a damned attractive woman.

"What can I do for you, pilgrim?" she inquired playfully.

"I'd like to talk to you. That's all . . . for the moment, anyway." Fox smiled and saw her green eyes melt.

"Now just a durned minute!" cried the young miner.

"You can wait for me," she told the boy firmly. "Have another drink. I'll be right back."

Spurning common sense, Fox took Lorna's hand and pulled her out the front door and onto the dirty wooden sidewalk. Then, pressing her against the Gem's front window, he enfolded her in his powerful embrace and kissed her so forcefully that she made a gasping sound deep in her throat.

"Mercy!" she panted when Fox let her draw a breath. Then he kissed her again, ravenously, and Lorna could feel him, almost frighteningly erect, pressing through her frilly gown of cheap silk. "You need it bad!"

She didn't taste like Maddie, and in the daylight it was even more obvious that her hair color was artificial, but Fox told himself that a pale imitation was, in this instance, preferable to the genuine article. "Lorna, do you like me? I realize that you haven't had much opportunity to get to know me, but I don't think it would be presumptuous of me to say that I'm an improvement over the majority of other men you . . . meet here." He smiled. "I take a bath every day that I can; I've been told that I am not a strain to look at; and I have money."

"Why, Mr. Fox . . . are you *proposing*?" Lorna squeaked.

"Not marriage, if that's what you mean," he said dryly. "How would you like to take a little trip with me? I have to leave Deadwood for a few days, maybe even a couple of weeks, and I've just decided that a little female companionship would be in order. I'll pay you more than you'd make here, and you'll have a hell of a lot more fun."

"Well . . . *sure!*" Lorna agreed, feeling giddy. "Can I bring wine?"

"Whatever your heart desires." He bit back a laugh and added, "You must give me your word that you will tell no one about the particulars of this journey, however. Don't even mention my name. Can you do that?" When she nodded, Fox continued, "Bring what you need in one bag and wait for me in the alley"—he pointed to the opening between the buildings—"at midnight. If there is a change in plans, I'll send word to you. Do you understand?"

Clapping her hands, Lorna nodded and stood on tiptoe to give him a shy kiss. "I can hardly wait! Sounds like a regular adventure!"

"In more ways than one," Fox replied in a low, amused voice, and chuckled when she blushed. "I'm off to the bathhouse, but I'll see you later."

Lorna skipped back inside to tend to the sulking young miner while Fox strolled toward the bathhouse on the corner of Wall Street. Not until he had disappeared inside did Benjamin Avery peek out of the alley next to the Gem Theatre. After looking right and left, he dashed out and ran all the way home, his wheat blond hair sticking up in sweaty spikes.

James Butler Hickok was walking from the Pony Express office to Nuttall & Mann's Number 10 Saloon when he saw Fox emerging from the livery stable, leading Watson. He called out a greeting.

"Bill!" Fox walked up the street to meet him halfway and they shook hands. "How have you been?"

Hickok shrugged philosophically. "Well, I'm alive, and that's a start. What about you? Has Jane Cannary been chasing you? I thought maybe she'd cornered you in your room at the Gem Theatre and forced you out at last."

"I appreciated your concern, pard," Fox said warmly. "Charley's visit helped me to see that I had to straighten up, and so I have. I've meant to visit your camp and thank both of you."

"Charley's been away most of the time, riding for the Pony Express," Bill said.

"And what about Calamity Jane? She offered to help me build my cabin, but I eluded her then and have continued to avoid her since. I assumed she was busying herself with *you*, or that she'd found religion through Preacher Smith. I saw her among his audience one day, positively starry-eyed."

Hickok laughed and shook his long, wavy hair. "That's rich, son! Jane and Henry! But, I shouldn't amuse myself at Preacher Smith's expense. He's a fine man, and I hear he left a family behind to come West and labor in his Master's vineyard." He stared soberly at the ground for a moment, then one side of his mouth twitched. "Anyways, we're all safe from Jane for the moment. She's gone to Rapid City, determined to find a bull to ride on Main Street. That's the rumor."

"It's a good one." Fox fell into step with him and, still leading Watson, walked along to Nuttall and Mann's Number 10. Wild Bill was congenial and unusually talkative. He told Fox that he'd just sent off a letter to his wife, Agnes Lake, "the famous circus performer." Bill always added this last identifying phrase and Fox couldn't decide if it was inspired by pride or a feeling of unworthiness.

A new, crudely lettered sign hung outside a makeshift building as Fox and Hickok passed. When Bill saw Fox glance at it curiously, he read it aloud: " 'Office of Star & Bullock, Auctioneers and Commission Merchants.' I met Sol Star and Seth Bullock earlier this morning. Just came in from Helena, Montana, with a huge wagon full of goods— chamber pots, Dutch ovens, dynamite, mining equipment. Haven't even been here one day, and already they're an asset to Deadwood! They have plans to start building a handsome store right away."

"Hard to believe how fast this town is changing," Fox remarked. "I was here when there were no towns at all, just the most beautiful mountains and valleys, streams and flowers you ever saw."

"How'd you manage that? Were you with the Custer expedition in '74?"

"Not exactly." Fox felt a dull ache starting in his temples. They had reached the door of Nuttall & Mann's and Fox put out his hand. "I'll say good-bye here, Bill. I hope you won't think I'm being too sentimental, but I am grateful for your friendship, especially in a town like this."

"Likewise, pard." Hickok grinned, which changed the shape of his drooping mustache. He turned then and went into the Number 10. Fox watched for a moment, noting that the only empty chair at the card table faced away from the door.

"I got your lucky chair," cried one of the cardsharps, whooping with laughter. "Too bad you was late, Wild Bill!"

Hickok glanced back over the top of the swinging door and gave Fox a bemused smile.

"You want me to watch your back?" Fox rejoined, half in jest.

"Never mind. If it's my time, I'm ready."

Fox was glad to get away. He wanted to go home and take a nap; give his brain a rest.

"I feel like a traitor," Benjamin whispered loudly. He sat between his sister and grandmother at the new pine trestle table in the kitchen. "If Fox knew I'd been spying on him, he'd boil me in oil!"

"Hardly," Maddie replied absently as she experimented with different styles of handwriting on a sheet of paper. "Your loyalty to your family must override your loyalty to a mere *neighbor*. Besides, all this is for Fox's own good. Just wait, Benjamin. He'll thank you later for your help."

The little boy brightened at this, for he loved sneaking around the badlands, hiding in dark corners, eavesdropping on adult conversations. "I don't understand what's going on, but I hope you're right." The boy cocked his head at Maddie, studying her as she boldly printed words. When he'd returned earlier with his report—that he'd seen Fox kissing a lady from the Gem Theatre who looked like Maddie—he'd expected his sister to faint or something. Instead, Maddie and Gramma Susan had looked at each other in a funny way, like they were sharing a secret or something. Then, when he'd told them how Fox had asked the lady to go away with him and to meet him at midnight in the alley, his sister had thrown her arms around Gramma Susan, giggling, then clapped her hands and exclaimed, "Thank you, God!"

Benjamin's grandmother was acting awful peculiar, too. Now she was saying to Maddie, "Oh, if only I could take your place! How I would love to visit an Indian village and find out the truth about them!"

"An Indian village?" Benjamin echoed. "Who's going there? I want to go!"

"I must have been having a spell," Gramma Susan said, winking over his cowlicks at her granddaughter. "That happens when you get very old. Sometimes I might say things that don't make any sense at all!"

Shaking his head, the little boy got up and went to the door. "I'm going outside. This is boring."

"Stay near the house, Benjamin," Maddie cautioned. "I'll have another errand for you soon. And don't forget—if you see Fox, don't mention one word about anything you've seen, heard, or done today. Understand?"

The boy nodded. "I just wish someone'd tell me what's been going on around here."

"I promise to tell you tomorrow morning," Susan said. "How's that?"

"Everything?" His freckled face was stern.

"If your father agrees, yes. I'll speak to him."

Visibly cheered, Benjamin went outside to climb trees. Once he was out of sight, Madeleine handed her grandmother a freshly lettered piece of paper. "How does that seem?"

Susan O'Hara read aloud in a hushed voice:

My dear,
I have thought better of my invitation to you to accompany
me. I fear it is an impossible plan. Do not come to the alley
at midnight.

Regretfully, FOX.

Before Susan could comment, Maddie hastened to explain, "It's a bother not being certain of her name. Benjamin thinks Fox called her Laura, but who knows for certain if he got it right. I only pray that the rest of his details were correct." She bit her lip, cheeks flushed with anticipation of the night to come. Would Gramma Susan be so supportive of this scheme if she knew just how confusingly intimate Maddie's relationship with Fox had become?

"I think it sounds fine," Susan O'Hara said, peeking over the top of her spectacles. "And the printing is quite masculine-looking, yet legible. Now, do we dare send Benjamin into the Gem?"

"What choice do we have?"

"Why don't I go?—Now, now, don't fly into a dither. Do you imagine that I should be shocked by the Gem Theatre? In truth, I am much better suited to this errand than Benjamin. I'll just put on a bonnet that conceals my face and hair, and take this letter to Garnet. She'll be able to direct me to Laura, or whatever her name is." Susan O'Hara rose and straightened her tiny shoulders, filled with pride at her own ingenuity. "Garnet knows that Fox is our neighbor. I'll say that I was on my way to the store and volunteered to deliver his note. Who would doubt the word of an eight-three-year-old woman of breeding?"

"*Gramma . . .*" Maddie began in a strangled voice.

"*Phhshh!*" Susan waved her hand dismissingly. "It will be effortless. Believe me, I'm much more dependable than Benjamin." With that, she took the missive Maddie had composed and went in search of a proper bonnet for her escapade into Deadwood's half world.

The evening passed swiftly. Susan O'Hara, escorted in the wagon by Wang Chee, stopped off at the Bighorn Store for supplies and then wandered farther north on Main Street for a few crucial minutes. When she returned home, she smiled at Maddie from under her bonnet. "Everything is taken care of," she said conspiratorially. "I saw her read the note myself. By the by, her name is Lorna. She appeared disappointed, but then that nice young man with blond hair who was here for tea offered to buy her a gin and bitters, and she cheered up immediately. When I left, they were already laughing together."

Maddie blinked. "Do you mean Mr. Scofield?"

"Of the Boston Scofields," Gramma Susan confirmed, with a sober nod. "None other. . . . So, now that Lorna has been disposed of, are you certain you still wish to undertake this adventure? Any fears or doubts?"

"No, Gramma." In truth, Maddie was filled with terror. But overriding her trepidation was the sense that she was destined to make this journey, to spend this time with Fox, and to find her half-sister. "I think perhaps I'll go upstairs and lie down for a bit," she said, rising, "since I doubt I'll get much sleep during the night." She embraced her grandmother with uncustomary feeling and kissed her soft, wrinkled cheek. "You're a remarkable woman, Gramma. I'm grateful to finally be able to see that clearly."

Upstairs, Madeleine visited first with her father in case he was asleep when she arose. Then she retired to her room and lay down on the narrow bed under the eaves, the little china doll with real golden curls on the pillow next to her. Unless Fox sent her back, she reflected, or coldly endured her presence as he'd been wont to do of late, her innocence would soon be lost along with the careful childhood symbolized by the china doll she'd never named.

Maddie's heart raced at the thought, and she was filled with a panicky sort of anticipation, as if she were on a river headed for the most thrilling and terrifying of waterfalls. Eventually she slept, a smile on her elegantly beautiful face.

Fox, meanwhile, had risen from his own nap. Night came suddenly, stealing the rosy light that softened the gulch, and soon Titus appeared with the wagon and two disgruntled mules. Fox eyed it all with consternation. The wagon was a battered prairie schooner, no more than an ordinary farm wagon with sturdy wheels and a canvas cover lashed over its frame.

"Couldn't you do any better?" he asked.

Titus gave him a dark look. " 'Twas a stroke of great good fortune that I was able to lay claim to *this* on such short notice."

With exaggerated patience Fox listened to his friend's instructions regarding the mules, which apparently responded with minimal cooperation to all but the words "Gee" and "Haw." "I certainly hope I'll be able to manage without you," Fox said when Pym paused for breath.

"I don't appreciate your tone," Titus shot back, his voice rising in the purplish shadows. "Perhaps I'm worried about you, and perhaps I've simply done the best I could!"

Fox smiled wearily and placed a tense hand on the smaller man's shoulder. "And perhaps I'm behaving like a bastard again. I apologize."

Titus wished his friend would reveal what had been tormenting him these past days, but he knew that whatever it was was a secret. And secrets were like poison. He was about to say something obliquely along that line when the sound of gunshots reached their ears. At first both men only listened, since the rowdies who crowded the badlands often fired a few shots when drunk.

Fox was the first to walk around the cabin and out to the edge of his land, which overlooked Sherman Street. Titus followed. Main Street was too far enough north to make anything out, but the sound of shouts and screams had joined the ongoing gunfire.

"Would you mind taking a look?" Fox asked Pym, his voice absent. Odd worries pricked at him, and he tried to push them away. "I'll go next door and bid Mr. Avery farewell, then start packing the wagon."

"I'll discover what's afoot and return to help you," Titus agreed, nodding.

The evening passed swiftly into night. Fox conferred one last time with Stephen Avery, ate the chicken with biscuits and gravy pressed on him by Susan O'Hara, joked with Benjamin, and finally asked after Madeleine as he rose to leave. It was almost a relief to hear that she was sleeping. Lorna would be easier to enjoy if Maddie's memory weren't so fresh in his mind.

Packing the wagon properly took some time, but Fox welcomed the activity. When he put in the last wooden box of supplies and stowed blankets and his own belongings in the back, he took out his pocket watch and was shocked to see that it was eleven o'clock. Where was Titus?

A disquieting sense of apprehension crept over him. He brought Watson to the wagon, tied him gently to the back, and was feeding him a carrot when Titus appeared, riding his own bay mare. Fox called out to him, but the Cornish miner made no reply. Instead he dismounted and walked over to Fox, who then could see that his friend's face was dead white and his eyes wild.

"What happened?" he demanded. "Tell me."

Titus pulled a tin flask from his shirt pocket and took a swig. "It's—it's Wild Bill Hickok. A dirty coward walked up behind him while he was playin' poker at the Number Ten and shot him clean through the head. Poor fellow. He never knew." Pym drew a ragged breath, then continued, "The town's in an uproar, of course. I arrived right after the shootin' and left once I'd heard that the villain had been apprehended."

Fox felt as if he'd been blindsided. "Who shot Bill?"

"E. B. Farnum said he gave his name as Jack McCall. No one seemed to know him. Another of those stray tomcats who drift in and out of towns like this, intent on nothing more than breaking the law." Titus patted the younger man's arm. "I know that Hickok was your friend. I'm sorry."

Awash in moonlight, Fox looked stunned. "I suppose it must have been his time," he whispered at last.

"Who's to say? If any of us wanted to be safe and die of old age, we'd've stayed where life's more civilized."

Fox knew this was true. The West was dangerous—there was no guarantee when you woke up in the morning that you'd see the stars again. James Butler Hickok knew that better than anyone.

Dazed and melancholy, Fox bade Titus Pym good-bye,

adding that if he didn't return, his friend was to own the cabin. Then he swung up to the driver's position, took the reins, called out "Gee!" to the mules, and the wagon lurched forward into the night.

It seemed that the entire town was awake and in the streets. Everyone was talking about Wild Bill's horrific death, how he'd been sitting with his back to the door, how he'd been holding "aces over eights," how the miners' court was about to convene, and so on. Fox's heart ached as he guided the mules and the heaving wagon through the mass of worked-up people.

Suddenly a girl called out to him, and he glanced over to find that he was passing the Gem Theatre. Reining in the mules, he turned his head and saw a flame-haired female running out of the alley. She wore a shawl around her shoulders, which came loose from her head as she waved at him, nearly dropping her carpetbag and satchel in the process.

Good God, Lorna! He'd completely forgotten her—and now, frankly, he wished she'd forgotten him, too. Sighing, Fox decided that he'd send her back with the first party he encountered that was Deadwood-bound. In the meantime the diversions she would offer might be more welcome than ever. "Can you climb up on your own?" he called.

The girl nodded. Fox looked back, under the canvas that arched over the wagon, and saw her throw her belongings up into the wagon and clamber on board herself.

"I'm . . . all set!" she exclaimed breathlessly.

"Why don't you try to get some sleep," Fox replied. "I'll wake you later, when we're well on our way."

Maddie nodded, then collapsed gratefully on her back. The boxes of supplies and rifles provided an effective shield between her and Fox, and obviously he hadn't recognized her. She pressed her hand over her mouth to smother a giggle. The wagon rolled onward, lumbering through the crowds and then up the twisted roads that led northeast out of Deadwood Gulch.

PART THREE

Press close bare-bosomed night—
    press close magnetic nourishing night!
Night of the south winds—night of the large
    few stars!
Still nodding night—mad naked summer
    night.

                —Walt Whitman

Chapter Thirteen

August 3, 1876

RAINDROPS HAD BEGUN TO PELT THE CANVAS THAT shielded the wagon. Opening her eyes, Maddie felt confused and disoriented until, slowly, her memory righted itself.

Where were they? The wagon was stopped; Watson had been untied from the back. Throwing off quilts, Maddie crawled tentatively to the back of the wagon and peeked outside, terrified that Fox might come around the corner and surprise her.

They were in a clearing of pine trees. The moon shone overhead, dimmed intermittently by the silvery rain clouds scudding across the summer sky. The air was warm, sultry, and pine-scented. The world seemed to have shrunk, consisting only of the clearing and the wagon filled with wooden boxes, frayed quilts, and Maddie. She felt thrillingly alive as she lay back and listened to the spattering raindrops, waiting to discover what would happen next.

After a few minutes the occasional rustling sounds outside became more focused. Maddie heard Watson stepping through the clearing, followed by Fox's whispered reassurances. The very sound of his voice acted on her like some wild aphrodisiac. She didn't care what the consequences might be. She didn't care if he cast her aside afterward, sent her home on foot, vowed never to speak to her again. As long as she could have him this one time, she cared for nothing else. There was no other man in all the world save Fox, and tonight he would lie with her.

Even the quest for Sun Smile was forgotten as Maddie

feigned sleep, listening as Fox tied Watson to the back of the wagon. He must have taken the horse to a nearby creek and brought water back, for she could hear liquid pouring into a tin pan, then splashes and muffled sighs. Fox was washing. She opened her eyes, peeking just enough to see him haloed in moonlight, shirtless, running his hands through his damp hair. Crystal droplets fell from his beard onto the tapering splendor of his chest. Fox drank deeply then from a canteen and climbed up into the back of the wagon.

Maddie's heart thundered as she felt his gaze linger on her. Could he see the color flooding her cheeks? A moment passed and she peeked again, just as he was pulling off his pants. She caught a glimpse of bare, muscular flank, the hard arc of his buttocks . . . and felt herself responding with a shock of hunger mixed with panic. Dear God, what now?

Fox, of course, shared none of her apprehension about the situation. It had been so long since he'd been with a woman, and he was done with holding back. Little Bighorn, Maddie, Wild Bill . . . a storm of conflicting emotions swirled within him, clamoring for relief. Well, Lorna would be happy to accommodate him—and with no strings attached. She would numb his feelings and demand nothing for herself, which was lucky because he had little to give.

Stretching out beside her on the rumpled quilts, Fox marveled again at the uncanny resemblance Lorna bore to Madeleine. It would be so easy to pretend . . . and the mere thought sent desire's hot blood coursing through his veins. He touched her cheek with the back of his forefinger. When her eyelids fluttered, he whispered, "Hello," and felt for the tiny buttons down the back of her gown. He smiled to himself when he found that she'd done up only every other one. "Don't worry, honey, this won't take long. I'd just like to see a little more of you."

He'll know as soon as he looks into my eyes, Maddie thought, *and then everything will be different. He'll be with me then. . . .*

But Fox had no time to waste on romantic gazes. He buried his face in her tumbled marmalade curls and allowed himself to believe that it was Maddie's scent he inhaled. How warm the night air was! His mouth was hot on her brow, temple, and the tenderer spots that trailed down her neck. Almost roughly he pulled the faded calico gown from her body. When he saw that she wore no undergarments, he made a low sound of approval that only fanned the fire of Maddie's misgivings.

He bared her breasts and touched them softly, marveling at their beauty. When his mouth teased a puckered nipple, the feel of it against his tongue made him suddenly mad with need. With an urgency that left no room for any gentler sensibilities, he finished undressing her and pressed her back into the quilts. Her warm, lithe, enticingly curved body was all that he had fantasized, and more. She even smelled like Madeleine. Outside the Gem Theatre she'd reeked of the same strong, cheap scent that all the whores seemed to share. Tonight, though, in the misty, rain-washed, moon-silvered woods, her skin was pure and unmarked and smelled faintly of fresh flowers.

Her waist was narrower than the span of his two hands. Her hair was like liquid silk. Her mouth was delicious. Even her ears, delicate as buds, were clean and sweet. Fox began to feel as if some fairy had cast a spell on this clearing in the trees, granting him the fulfillment of his most extravagant longings.

Desire raging more fiercely by the second, he at last surrendered to the fantasy. Deft fingers found her secret places, and each touch revealed delicate beauty. "My God," he whispered, "you're beautiful. . . ."

There was no reply, merely a soft sound that struck him as vaguely tragic. But when he kissed her, he tasted the salty warmth of tears. He would have pulled back then, but she stopped him. With a tiny hand she reached down and touched him, guiding him toward her essence. And when she arched her hips against him and opened her thighs, Fox released the animal he'd kept leashed inside for so long.

The sensation of entering her body, which was soft, snug, warm, moist, and welcoming, was bliss beyond his experience. She clutched his back, gasping, as he thrust deeper. Cupping her bottom with work-roughened hands, he fused their bodies completely and then drew back, repeating the movements until they were caught together in a pounding rhythm so primitive that all thought was obliterated.

"Ah, Maddie . . ." Fox breathed against her ear.

Madeleine felt a burst of joy when she heard her own name. *He* does *care*! she thought triumphantly. Giving herself over at last to the act of love, she met his thrusts eagerly, running her fingertips over Fox's shoulders and the chiseled lines of his face. When he looked down at her, she gave him an incandescent smile and whispered, "Yes, yes, it is I . . . Maddie!"

Fox felt his heart stop for an instant. The shock nearly drained the blood from his body, but his manhood had a life of its own. So close . . . he was so close . . . and now, as his climax built to uncharted heights, he shut his eyes and willed his thoughts to cease. Release came in an explosion of pure ecstasy, pleasure so intense and new that he realized he would never be able to erase its memory.

In the wake of his fulfillment came despair, shame, disbelief . . . followed almost immediately by a flood of questions. Drawing away from Madeleine, he reached for one of the quilts and threw it over her hastily.

"What the *hell* are you doing here?" he demanded. "Have you lost your mind?"

"No." She met his angry stare, her green eyes luminous in the moonlight. "I made careful plans, aided by Gramma Susan. I knew what I was doing." She prayed he couldn't see the blush that suffused her cheeks or the tears that stung her eyes. "I wanted—I wanted this."

The knot of tenderness in Fox's chest only made him angrier. "Damn you! Did it ever occur to you that I might *not* want *you*—especially under these circumstances? Didn't I make myself plain enough in Deadwood when I told you to stay away from me?"

"I didn't believe you," she murmured.

"Oh, you didn't?" His eyes burned into hers. "You tricked

me! I didn't want to go near you, my dear Miss Avery, yet you took it upon yourself to override my wishes and—"

"But, Fox," she interrupted, "this *was* your wish. You said my name in the middle of the love act."

Furious, he jumped out the back of the wagon and pulled on his pants. "*Damn* you! I thought you were a lady! How could you give yourself to a man who didn't want you—who thought you were someone else . . . For God's sake, put something on! I'm going for a walk."

"But . . . what shall I do?"

"Walk back to Deadwood for all I care," Fox replied in a voice jagged with iciness.

Dawn crept over the pine-studded hilltops in lambent shades of gold and coral. As Fox approached the wagon, he inhaled the air, freshened by the brief rain shower, and wished that his own mind and heart could be cleansed as easily. The more he thought, the more confused he became as feelings of anger and longing rose up to complicate matters. Of course, he knew that there were no solutions to this problem with Madeleine. An attachment between them was impossible; he had too many secrets, too much guilt, and a nagging feeling that he wasn't entitled to love and the deep happiness it would bring him. Besides, a woman like Maddie deserved better. Fox felt tainted now, broken.

His eyes burned as he leaned against the back of the wagon and gazed at Maddie's sleeping form. How in the name of reason had this masquerade of hers failed to arouse his suspicions? He wasn't a fool! Now, despite his efforts to do the right thing where she was concerned, he'd taken her virginity and possibly gotten her with child without even realizing it was she with whom he was coupling.

The possibility that he *had* suspected, deep down, was one he refused to consider.

And what was he to do with her now? His heart ached to look at her, her delicious body swimming in *his* shirt, legs twisted in a threadbare quilt, long curls swirling outward like a halo of flames. Maddie's face, strong, delicate, and vulnerable all at once, was dearer to him than he cared to contemplate. And that terrified him. If only she could turn into Lorna. Lorna would open her arms to him and then shake his hand when she returned to Deadwood. She'd know better than to expect anything from a man like him.

A man like him . . . *You know better than that,* Annie Sunday's voice scolded softly from a corner of his mind. *You're not like the others . . . and Madeleine knows it. Isn't that why you're afraid of her?*

He rubbed his eyes with strong, tanned fingers and shook his head. God only knew what he could do with Maddie, but for now he had to get some sleep or he'd be a madman for the remainder of the day. Smiling ruefully, he climbed into the back of the wagon, settling down beside Maddie on the quilts.

This time, however, he kept his pants on.

The scolding cry of a blue jay awakened Maddie to the full light of morning. The bird had glided over and perched on the back of the wagon, eyeing a piece of apple Watson had apparently dropped on the ground. The horse nickered at the jay, which promptly flew away.

Even under the canvas that canopied the wagon, it was growing warm. Maddie felt drowsy but oddly content. Stretching, she turned on her side and her face touched Fox's. Her breasts brushed against him and her hand fluttered uncertainly above his chest. He was breathing deeply.

Tears filled her eyes. She yearned to rest her hand on the crisp hair covering Fox's chest, to snuggle against him and listen to his heart beat. What had passed between them in the night did not seem real, despite the soreness between her legs. Of course she had wanted passion, and she had been determined to uncover the mysteries of mating, but now she realized that most of all she wanted to *touch* this man who made her feel so acutely, excitingly alive. She wanted to learn his body, all its secrets, and to share hers with him.

Reluctantly Maddie sat up, sighing as Fox's shirtsleeves slipped below her hands. Dreams were all well and good, but for now they would have to remain dreams. Fox still kept the door to his heart bolted, guarding it jealously, as if he knew it would open spontaneously to Maddie if he relaxed his defenses for even a moment.

It was almost pleasure enough just to look at him now, she thought with a smile. He was so handsome! . . . Every detail of his face more than measured up to the fantasies she'd nurtured since childhood. Those challenging eyes, safely closed now, usually warned hers away, so this opportunity to stare was a luxury.

Satisfied at last, Madeleine crawled carefully, silently, to the back of the wagon, plucked her satchel from a corner, and emerged into the morning sunlight. Watson watched as she stepped behind a tree, rifled through her bag, then dressed quickly in a plain lawn chemise and tan cotton gown sprigged with green flowers. None of the clothes she'd brought were particularly attractive because she'd opted instead for her coolest work dresses.

Maddie fastened up the back of her gown, then groomed her hair with a silver-backed brush and tied it with a ribbon. Finally, after buttoning her feet into embroidered kid slippers, she took a long look around.

The wagon had been stopped in the middle of a verdant clearing above the rutted road that led eastward out of the Hills. On one side the mountain slanted upward, covered with a rich mixture of ponderosa pine, spruce, and quaking aspen. To the left, the hillside swept down to an open meadow bathed in sunlight. Through the nearest part of the meadow rambled a stream where two mule deer were drinking, their black-tipped tails flicking in the warm breeze. Jackrabbits raced across the far side of the dew-spangled meadow, while meadowlarks sang in a nearby stand of paper birch trees. Wildflowers bloomed in profusion among the meadow grasses: delicate blue harebells, purple shooting stars, orange wood lilies, yarrow, yellow-blossomed prickly pears, and even wild roses. Maddie stared in open wonderment for long minutes, watching the mule deer until they lifted their heads and disappeared into the forest.

The stream, rushing over worn stones, beckoned to her. From her satchel she withdrew a tin cup, flannel cloth, linen towel, and a bar of rose-scented soap, then found a shallow spot where she could kneel beside the water and fill her cup.

The water tasted incredibly delicious. After emptying two cups, Maddie felt a wave of euphoria sweep over her. In spite of Fox's attitude, she sensed that this journey was necessary for both of them, whatever the outcome.

She set about washing then, soaping the cloth and scrubbing her face, neck, hands, arms, and, after a quick peek around, between her breasts. It wasn't a proper bath, but it was quite lovely and refreshing. She bent over the stream, skirts hitched up above her knees, and began to rinse the soap away.

"I should have known," a male voice remarked from some distance behind her. "Only Miss Madeleine Avery would attempt to bathe in nature as if Philadelphia society were watching and waiting for a lapse in propriety!"

She pressed the linen towel to her face, straightened her shoulders, and turned unhurriedly. "Well, if it isn't the unfailingly charming Mr. . . . What was your surname again? Or don't you have one?"

Bare-chested and sleepy-eyed, Fox walked down to her side. "It's not that I don't *have* one, my dear, but simply that I don't *need* one. That's the beauty of life in the West. One isn't confined by a lot of stiff-necked rules." He gestured toward her bar of scented soap and the linen towel discreetly monogrammed with Maddie's mother's initials. "You call that a bath?"

"It will have to suffice for the moment," she replied warily.

Fox nodded. "You mean until we reach that elegant hotel where there's a hand-painted bathtub and two maids waiting to wash your hair and dry you off? There's bound to be one between here and Bear Butte."

"You needn't be sarcastic," she replied. "I shall simply make due as the need arises. It's really none of your concern."

"Well, if you don't mind," he said, strolling downstream where the stream deepened, "I believe I'll have a bath myself. There's nothing like the water in the Hills to make you feel alive, especially when a trout swims against you."

Maddie stood watching mutely as Fox began stripping off his pants. At first she felt certain he was only teasing her, but then it became embarrassingly clear that he was serious. At the crucial moment she turned away and heard him laugh. Splashing sounds followed. Peeking between her fingers, she saw that he was waist deep in water. She took her hands away. "Why are you laughing?"

"Because, Madness, you seem to be of two minds. Last night you were a brazen temptress, insisting that passion burned in your soul, unashamed. This morning you are covered from neck to toe, bathing like a spinster and blushing in horror when I choose to take off my clothes and wash effectively!" His blue eyes danced and he reached up with both hands to push back his wet hair, thereby giving her an unobstructed view of his magnificent chest. Sunlight percolated through the birch leaves to dapple him with gold.

Light-headed, Maddie protested, "You are far more skilled at this verbal sparring than I, and it is evident that you are used to extricating yourself from amorous entanglements. If you mean to confuse me, you are succeeding. I am no match for you in this game, sir."

Fox smiled with slow appreciation. "Modesty becomes you, but I know better than to take you at your word. You won the first encounter of this *game*, as you call it, quite decisively last night—before I even knew that a contest was in progress."

"I will not be drawn into this—"

"At least *you* have a choice!" he shot back, the bantering tone now gone from his voice.

Maddie's eyes flashed, but she remained silent. The fact that there was more than a little truth in what Fox said about her hypocrisy did not make her feel any kinder toward him. She wanted to run back to the wagon, but instead she gathered her shaky dignity and walked along the edge of the stream until she was only a few feet from Fox.

"Yes?" he inquired coolly, soaping his shoulders and chest with a white chunk of soap.

"I thought I should inform you that I did not climb into the wagon last night simply to force myself upon you . . . and since the experience was apparently so repugnant to you, I assure you that henceforth I shall refrain from trying to convince you otherwise." She hesitated, uncertain of herself and hating Fox for making her so. "I . . . admit that I do have feelings for you, but I can accept your refusal to reciprocate them."

"Why, that's very civilized of you," Fox drawled. "Too bad you didn't take me at my word before last night. I *told* you to stay away from me. Virtue's a valuable commodity for a woman in your class—even in Deadwood. You think a *gentleman* will want you if he knows you're . . . damaged goods?"

Her chin trembled. "That's my concern, not yours. What I really want to say is that you mustn't send me back. I know you mean to, that you can't bear my presence, but I am begging you to allow me to go with you to Bear Butte."

"Why the hell should I?" he demanded, lathering his wet hair.

"Because I want to meet my half-sister!" Maddie cried. "I have wanted to go ever since Father told you about Yellow Bird and Sun Smile. I knew you wouldn't take me if I asked you, and I knew Father would forbid it, so Gramma Susan and I took matters into our own hands."

"So I noticed."

"I object to your arrogance, sir! Just because you are male

and stronger and more self-sufficient in this environment than I, that does not make you a superior human being! On the contrary—"

To her horror, Fox bent over and began rinsing his hair, exposing his buttocks as he did so. As he straightened and shook his wet locks he took advantage of Maddie's momentary speechlessness to say, "I admire your conviction, Maddie, but I cannot stand here in the water all morning while you hold forth. Why don't you return to the wagon and sort your ribbons, or whatever it is that you do before breakfast, and I'll join you shortly. After I am dry and fed, I'll decide what to do with you." The sight of her flushed countenance made him want to smile, but he refrained.

Maddie whirled around, started off blindly, and nearly tripped over her skirts in the tall grass. "I—I will wait for you, then, expecting to conclude our discussion," she said, striving to appear composed.

"I don't know that you're in a position to make the rules," Fox answered in an offhand tone. When she started away from him up the hill, he allowed himself a grin, then dived under the water like a fish. *Paradise*, he thought, and popped back out of the water.

Maddie stood at the edge of the trees, waiting. "I have a question."

"Hmm?" He was looking for the soap.

Willing herself not to blush, Maddie said evenly, "I would appreciate it if you could tell me where the chamber pot is packed."

Fox stared, certain at first that she was joking. Then his brows flew up and he gave a shout of laughter. "Miss Avery, brace yourself for a shock." He paused, savoring the moment. "There *isn't* a chamber pot. When one is in the woods, one does one's . . . business behind the nearest tree."

Maddie nearly wept with embarrassment and shock. "I see," she replied in a strangled voice, and turned to continue on her way back to the wagon.

"Are you *sure* you don't want to go home now?" Fox called after her, grinning.

Maddie glanced over one shoulder with an imperious expression. "Quite," she replied, then lifted her faded skirt and marched up the wooded hill.

Chapter Fourteen

August 3–4, 1876

FOX DIDN'T SEND MADDIE BACK TO DEADWOOD. As they ate bread, jerky, and apricots for breakfast, he remarked matter-of-factly that he couldn't spare the time to return her there himself, though he dearly wished to be rid of her. As he stared into her eyes, Maddie found herself unsettled by the sheer intensity of his gaze. Clearly he was angry with her, and more. She'd been quite certain that the "more" was a tender emotion he couldn't bear, but she was beginning to realize that Fox was much more complicated than that. Over the next days his complexity would fire her own love for him and make her despise him, often at the same time. Yet she was learning how truly willful she was—and she set about exercising her willfulness as if it were a muscle in need of strengthening.

Their first full day was quite taxing, traveling through the Black Hills toward the eastern edge, where they would then turn north and journey over the plains to Bear Butte. Fox could not allow himself to soften toward Maddie. Hours passed without a word spoken between them. Still wary of his temper and fearful that they'd encounter someone passing them en route to Deadwood, Maddie stayed out of sight in the back of the wagon. Perhaps Fox would forget about her, she mused hopefully. If other pilgrims journeying to the goldfields came along, he might not do any more than wave.

Maddie found herself dozing despite the stifling heat and the jouncing of the wagon. Sometimes she murmured to Watson, who walked behind patiently. At one point in the afternoon she awoke to find that she was damp with perspiration, and for a moment she was disoriented. Then, remembering where she was, and why, Maddie reflected on the changes she had undergone since leaving Philadelphia—and especially since meeting Fox. The Madeleine Avery of yore would have been appalled by the mess Maddie had made of her life. Here she was, in a rickety wagon, dusty and sweaty, without even a chamber pot, making a journey to an Indian village with a man she had made love with and who claimed to want absolutely nothing to do with her . . . and yet she felt as if she were awash with happiness. She felt free, liberated from all the stringent standards of behavior her mother had instilled in her since childhood.

In fact, as she knelt on the quilts and peeked at Fox over the stacks of crates, it almost seemed to her that she was enjoying the sort of enormous adventure she'd missed during childhood. Her mother had overprotected her and had never allowed her to go off with the children of the Avery servants to play in the woods, building castles out of rocks and branches or sailing little boats down creeks that might carry them all the way to China. Maddie had never played house or donned old clothes and disguises, nor had she put notes in bottles and thrown them into the Schuylkill River in hopes that someone in France could try to decipher her secret language.

Other children had spent long, happy hours indulging in such energetic and imaginative pastimes. When Madeleine heard their stories, she pretended to disapprove, but in truth, she'd been intrigued. Even as a girl, however, she knew that her mother would never permit adventures of that sort. Colleen had believed that a young girl should pass her days with needlework, music, etiquette, and school studies, while keeping herself immaculately clean at all times.

Now Maddie knew what she had missed. Every time she tried something that would have horrified her only a few weeks before, a little voice cheered in the back of her mind. She felt brave, a trifle crazy, and utterly ecstatic to be sharing this adventure with Fox. Just the sight of him made her feel intoxicatingly giddy. She loved every moment.

When they made camp that night, Fox looked drawn, and he treated her as if she were a stranger who had begged a ride. Maddie was feeling oddly serene, however, and smiled from time to time as she helped him prepare a cold meal and then tidy up before bedtime. Before darkness enveloped them completely, Fox took Watson out for a ride. Maddie sensed that it was as much to get away from her as to exercise the roan, so she cleaned her teeth, took a deep breath and went behind a tree to attend to certain needs, and then climbed into the back of the wagon.

When Fox returned and tethered Watson behind the wagon, he looked in and saw Maddie curled as far to one side of the quilts as she could get. The moon was bright, bathing her in its luminous glow. God, how she worked on him, he thought—like a drug he could not avoid or resist! Shaking his head, he went to join her. He couldn't recall ever being more exhausted, but still he rolled up an extra quilt and put it between them, like the old-fashioned custom of bundling.

Exhausted or not, there was no guarantee of safety if Fox had to sleep next to Maddie. . . .

By the next afternoon Maddie found that the rosy glow was fading from her adventure. Fox's taciturn behavior was making her sulky, and she had never known such heat or dust, not even during the rigorous journey westward from Philadelphia. Of course, most of that trip had been spent on trains and a riverboat, and the overland leg across Dakota had taken place in June. August in the Dakota Territory was quite a different story.

The prospect of enduring the rest of this day and night covered with grimy perspiration made Maddie scowl. When the wagon rolled over a large rock, jarring her, she glared at Watson and muttered an oath.

"What?" Fox yelled from the driver's perch.

She couldn't believe he'd heard her. "I didn't speak," she replied loudly. "Your ears fool you."

"I don't think so," he said, with a dry smile, but he didn't press the matter.

They were coming down, out of the Hills, when Fox guided the mules off the rutted road and onto a grassy plateau. Eagerly Maddie scrambled out of the back of the wagon to take a look.

The shallow canyon that lay before them emerged from the pine-studded hillside with the flourish of a rushing waterfall, narrowed, and then opened gradually until the distant prairie spread it flat and marked the stream with cottonwood trees.

"How lovely!" she exclaimed, shading her eyes in the late afternoon sunlight. The cheerful splash of the waterfall made her lick her lips.

Fox pulled up the blue kerchief knotted around his neck and wiped the sweat from his brow. "I thought we'd make camp here for tonight. The heat will be even more relentless once we're on the plains."

"I'm slowing you down, aren't I?"

"You mean am I altering the pace out of concern for your feminine sensibilities?" He nearly smiled. "Hell, no. Are you saying that I've somehow made this journey pleasurable for you? If so, that was hardly my intent. I care only for my own comfort. Since you came uninvited, I'd prefer to ignore your needs altogether." Fox freed the mules from their harnesses, then unbuttoned his shirt, lost in thought. "I'll see to the animals before I wash up. In an hour or so you can cook us some supper. I intend to turn in early so that we can start for Bear Butte before dawn, while it's cool."

A thin rivulet of perspiration drizzled down Maddie's back. She wanted to scream. Instead she repeated through gritted teeth, "Cook?"

"I wouldn't want to put you to any trouble, ma'am," Fox shot back sarcastically.

Their eyes met for a long, angry minute, and spots of color stained Maddie's cheeks. He knew perfectly well that she could scarcely cook in a kitchen, let alone out here in the wilderness, but of course this was his way of needling her, of forcing her to acknowledge that she was a useless burden and had been wrong to come.

"I might be able to make you a fire," he said slowly.

"How kind you are! That would be simply lovely. All we lack is matching china." Maddie yanked open the tiny buttons at the top of her bodice. "Do you know, I believe I'll have a bath myself. That is, if you'll *allow* it, sir."

Fox's brows flicked upward at her announcement. He went to fetch Watson, who was demanding attention, and as he led the roan past Maddie he said, "Do you mean a *bath*—or more prim dabbing at your neck with that pretty pink cloth?"

"To be quite honest with you, I'm finding that the tenuous hold I had on civilized conduct has deserted me entirely." She reached into the wagon for a towel and soap, pretending not to notice Fox's bemused expression.

"In that case, don't delay on my account, Miss Avery. I'll be happy to wait my turn . . . unless, of course, your sense of propriety has disappeared to the extent that—"

"No," Maddie interjected sweetly, "I draw the line at communal bathing."

Off she went then, leaving Fox to stare after her with the sort of appreciative smile that he tried to keep hidden from her. The feeling in his chest, however—like a clenching fist that alternated with a sense of frightening, blessed surrender—was growing more difficult to ignore. Fox was an honest man caught up in a maze of secrets that seemed to beget one another, yet the prospect of revealing the truth to Maddie was intolerable to him.

Running his lean hand over Watson's side, he murmured wryly, "I'm not even sure myself what's true, let alone what's right. . . ."

Nearly tearing off the buttons, Madeleine stripped off her faded gown, then her petticoat, stockings, and shoes, until she stood on the bank of the stream in her oldest muslin chemise.

The sensation of blazing sunlight on her naked arms and legs was stunningly novel and liberating. *Mother would be scandalized,* she thought involuntarily, and discovered that it was a relief to have that out of the way. Colleen's code of etiquette was like a piece of baggage, a hatbox, perhaps, that had fallen off the wagon long ago. It wasn't important or relevant to her new life; it only restricted her.

Maddie laughed aloud as she looked down in happy amazement at her bare limbs, remembering Fox's taunts during her performance with the soap and cloth the morning before. It was simply ludicrous for her to cling to Philadelphia standards out here in the wilderness! Besides, she was hot and dirty; it was time to get clean.

Stepping tentatively over the gravel shore, Maddie looked down and glimpsed her full breasts through the sheer fabric of her chemise. A sense of horror jarred her momentarily, for the pink crests of her nipples were clearly visible, out here in broad daylight! Then she stopped and hugged herself, smiling again. It was as if she were on a seesaw between the past and the future, between the proper lady her mother had raised her to become and the spirited, passionate woman who was emerging a little further with each moment that passed. Maddie couldn't help the pangs of anxiety that threatened to hold her back, but she fought them and let herself flow with the inexorable currents of destiny. Part of the exhilaration she felt was due to Fox and the magic of her love for him; yet there was a grander design at work—a design that was altering the fabric of Madeleine's inner being.

With the innocence of a child, she stepped into the water and waded in to her waist. It was cool, rushing around her, startlingly pleasurable against her bare legs. There was a warm glow in her heart, a feeling of wonder and joy, as she raised her face to the sun and, eyes closed, basked in its glory.

The waterfall beckoned. Maddie opened her eyes and splashed toward the shower that streamed over a canyon shelf. She paused to pull down the wet chemise and toss it onto the bank, and then she drew the pins from her dusty hair and let the sunset-bright mass spill down her back.

Fresh and invigorating, the waterfall cascaded over her arm, then her shoulder, and finally, as she stepped forward, Maddie's entire body. It was glorious. She rubbed the bar of soap over her skin and watched the froth rinse away in the next instant. When she stretched up her arms to wash her hair, the sensation of water streaming down her exposed breasts, belly, and thighs was sheer ecstasy. Through the blurry curtain of water, Maddie saw the china blue sky, the shallow curve of the stream bank, a hawk gliding in the distance . . . and Fox standing high above her on the rim of the gulch, shirtless, staring.

By the time Fox finished his own bath and returned to their campsite for supper, Maddie had spread a picnic over a quilt on the ground and the sun was setting behind the hills.

Hearing him approach, she felt suddenly shy and busied herself with plates and forks. She had no regrets about the shower, which she felt had cleansed her in every sense of the word, but instincts had a way of rising up unbidden. Her cheeks flamed at the memory of that moment, when she had seen him watching her under the waterfall, and later, the fire in his eyes when she had climbed the hill from the stream to the plateau where they camped, wearing only the damp chemise.

What point was there in struggling back into her gown when she was wet and the sun was beating down on her—and Fox had already seen her completely naked? Still, to walk right up to him in broad daylight clad only in an undergarment that left nothing to the imagination . . . !

"I see that you decided to put on some clothes," he remarked now, hunkering down next to her on the quilt.

"A few." She was furious at herself for blushing like a schoolgirl, for feeling shy with him when she was supposed to be reveling in her newfound abandon.

Fox didn't know what to think. He shrugged into the clean shirt he'd unpacked earlier, ran his hands through his wet chestnut hair, and marveled at Maddie, who was wearing loose pants, probably borrowed from her father, and a smaller shirt that most likely belonged to Benjamin. The latter was unbuttoned in front so that her sweet chemise peeked through. Never had Fox seen a more innocent undergarment—or one that aroused him as acutely. It was an insane situation.

The more he told himself that he could not, must not, have her, and could not, must not, *care*, the more insane he felt.

One moment she was cavorting naked in a waterfall; the next moment she was dressed like a boy, her luxuriant hair caught back in a ribbon, her face turned away to hide a demure blush. Her mouth looked more delicious than the array of food she had spread before him.

"I hope this will suffice," Maddie said. "I decided to forgo your offer of a fire. It's still so warm, and I've no desire to reek of woodsmoke."

"Fine with me." His eyes wandered over the meal—a loaf of Susan O'Hara's rye bread with a chunk of sweet butter set next to it, a bowl of dried apricots and raisins, some thin slices of smoked ham mated with cubes of cheddar cheese, and a plateful of oatmeal cookies. Not only did it all look tasty and tempting, but the colors and arrangement of the food and dishes pleased Fox in an aesthetic sense. He considered sharing his pleasure with Maddie but decided it would be wiser instead simply to eat. Inside, he might feel warm, peaceful, and intensely alive, but perhaps it would be better to keep his feelings to himself.

Maddie tried to eat, but found herself watching Fox most of the time. The embers of twilight burnished his chiseled features and sun-bleached beard; coral-tinted shadows moved slowly over the lines of his strong body. For a time, Fox ate half sitting in a crouch. His companion didn't speak and her movements were almost soothing as she sliced bread and replenished dishes. Night sounds mingled in the stillness; frogs and birds and crickets and the distant howl of coyotes drifting in on the warm breeze.

At last he unfolded his lean-muscled legs and stretched out across the quilt. Lying on his side, propped up on an elbow, he slowly met Maddie's intent gaze. Her heart skittered.

"God, what beautiful country this is," he whispered. "I've never seen such sunsets in my life as we have in Dakota. Just . . . breathtaking."

She swallowed hard. Fox was talking about her and the way she looked bathed in the fiery hues of the setting sun. She knew it. After a moment he leaned forward, past her, and pulled something from his haversack.

She saw that it was *Leaves of Grass*, by Walt Whitman, whose controversial works had so shocked Colleen Avery and her friends among Philadelphia society. Maddie eyed the slender volume with curiosity. "Will you read a poem aloud?" she dared to ask.

Amused, he lifted a brow and opened the book. "Are you hoping for descriptions of the honest pleasures of the flesh; of men and women writhing together in feverish abandon? If so—"

"You are simply horrid!" she burst out, cheeks aflame. "Why are you treating me this way?"

"I don't know what you mean," Fox replied coolly as he thumbed through the pages. "Never mind; there's no need to take everything I say personally. I was only referring to the fact that everyone seems to think Whitman is the most scandalous of characters—some sort of hedonist left over from ancient Rome. The truth is that he writes about *life*. All of it."

Maddie began gathering up the dishes. "That sounds reasonable."

"Listen: this is called 'A Prairie Sunset.' " Fox breathed deeply of the fresh evening air before he began to read:

Shot gold, maroon and violet, dazzling silver, emerald, fawn,
The earth's whole amplitude and Nature's multiform power consign'd for once to colors;
The light, the general air possess'd by them—colors till now unknown,
No limit, confine—not the Western sky alone—the high meridian—North South, all,
Pure luminous color fighting the silent shadows to the last . . .

His voice drifted off so that each word had time to sink in. "Incredible, isn't it?"

Maddie was awestruck. "I've never heard more perfect words. 'Pure luminous color fighting the silent shadows to the last.' That's exactly what's happening now."

"When we're above the Hills and the western view is only prairie, the sunsets will be even more spectacular."

Fox felt as if he were floating in a world of fantasy. Maddie herself was like a fantasy: hazy gold, fresh and sweet, her green eyes gleaming with both innocence and intellect as she contemplated her first encounter with Walt Whitman. He longed to take her in his arms, to smell, taste, and touch her. He yearned to feel pleasure again.

Flipping onto his back, he stared at the gathering stars and pondered the knot of guilt his life had become. Until that day in June near Little Bighorn, Dan Matthews had been both introspective and adventurous, devil-may-care yet committed and courageous when the situation demanded. Now, lying on the threadbare quilt, brown arms crossed above his head, it came to him that these days he was ruled by his tormented conscience. It stifled all other facets of his personality. He was possessed by guilt for failing to pacify Custer . . . and guilt for surviving when his comrades were dead . . . and guilt for the moments when he caught himself enjoying life. Anger and resentment were children of Fox's guilt, and all the more frustrating because he didn't know where to direct them.

"Fox," Maddie said softly, "can I ask you a question?"

He felt a little thrill of anticipation when he turned his head and saw her leaning forward. Her face was shadowed and golden above him; he caught the floral scent of her soap when he inhaled. "What?"

"Why do you hate me so?"

Fox's voice, when he found it, burned. "I don't hate you, Madness . . . but I cannot give you what you want from me, and sometimes, when you are near me, wanting, it makes me angry." She was staring at him so intently, trying to make sense of what he was saying, that the clenching pain started again in his chest. "I'm not really angry with you—more like at life."

"I don't understand."

"Neither do I, particularly."

"Do you have a wife somewhere else? Back East?"

He very nearly lied to her. "No. I just—just can't love anyone right now, and I can't explain, either." His voice was harsh. "If you were a different sort of woman, we'd have a love affair, I suspect."

Tears of frustration pricked her eyes. "You called me 'Madness.' Why?"

Fox's face softened at last and he put a hand up, caressing her cheek. "I didn't mean to say it aloud; it's what I call you in my mind because that's what you do to me. You're my Madness."

"*This* is *madness*!" she exclaimed, moving closer until her breasts touched his chest and she could feel the telltale thud of his heart. "Here we are, a million miles from places where they worry about silly details like what 'sort' of woman one is, and yet you are denying both of us fulfillment for that most inane of reasons! You've told me over and over again to stop clinging to my rules of ladylike behavior, to let go and enjoy life, and yet—"

"It's not that simple," he protested, catching her hands in his. "You know better, Maddie."

"I can't make you explain to me what's standing between you and a whole life, but whatever it is, it isn't here tonight. Fox, I have never felt like this before. Ever! I don't care if there's no future for us. All I care about is this moment." Madeleine's face was inches above his, her eyes starry-lashed and aglow with desire. "Stop punishing yourself for whatever it is that's weighing on your mind. Stop punishing me. Give us both a reprieve . . . just for tonight."

Still holding her delicate hands, Fox drew her nearer and lifted his own head just enough to surrender a slow, melting kiss. "Yes," he replied at last.

"Just for tonight," she repeated, as if fearing he would

change his mind or she had misheard. Joy coursed through her veins like liquid fire.

Of course, Fox knew better, but he nodded. Reaching around, he pulled the ribbon from her hair and watched it cascade toward him like the sunset itself. Every single inch of him ached for her. Fiercely. As she came to him, lying against him on the quilt fashioned of scraps of calico and chintz and gingham, Fox gazed into her eyes and managed a ragged whisper:

"My own Madness . . ."

Chapter Fifteen

August 4–6, 1876

SOFT GUSTS OF EVENING AIR WHISPERED AGAINST Maddie's flesh, thrilling her as the sunlight and water had earlier. Fox removed her clothing almost reverently, and she gazed at him through her lashes.

In the burnished twilight, she was extravagantly luscious. Fox bit his lip against the desire that surged outward from his loins. "Sweet Jesus," he muttered disbelievingly. Her breasts, the graceful arc of her arms raised above her head, fingers tangled in that glorious hair . . . she was exquisite.

"What?" Maddie murmured. Sensing his approval, she allowed herself a Mona Lisa smile as she watched the play of emotions cross his face.

"You're beautiful." Fox barely recognized his hoarse whisper. "Too beautiful. Dangerous. . . ."

Madeleine couldn't even blush in this dreamworld. "You know me, Fox. Sometimes I think you understand me better than I do myself. I'm not dangerous." She studied his dark, arresting face. "If anyone's dangerous, it's you."

Her slim hand reached toward him, touching the portion of his tanned chest that showed between the unbuttoned halves of his shirt. Fox drew in his breath, shocked by the fierceness of his response, but he didn't allow himself to wonder what it meant. Instead he moved slowly, deliberately, with tenderness. First he tugged at the waistband of her trousers and drew them off along with the rest of her chemise, then he pulled off his own clothing and stretched out beside

199

her on the quilt. The sun had nearly set now, leaving behind lavender shadows.

"I don't mean to be dangerous." His fingertips traced the curve of her hip.

"I know." And she did, somehow. Their eyes were inches apart, and for that moment Maddie saw inside him. There were no answers to the riddles that twined about Fox, but she knew that underneath the pain he felt and could not help inflicting on her as well, there was honest goodness and laughter and courage. He'd hurt her again if she stayed around . . . but not tonight.

"One of the reasons I was so mad at you about what happened between us in the wagon . . . is that it was all wrong," Fox said softly. He laced his fingers through hers, kissed her hand, then continued, "I still can't give you what you really need, which is my heart and a future to go with the lovemaking, and that's why it never should've happened—No, don't try to convince me otherwise because I know a hell of a lot more about the world than you do, Miss Avery. You're a baby when it comes to the workings of the human heart."

Maddie swelled inside with pure joy just to have him talking to her this way. "Mmm-hmm."

"I mean it! You should've kept your distance; it makes me furious that you went against every warning I gave you. But, since we can't undo what happened, I can at least try to amend the experience for you. If I'd had any idea that it was you . . ."

Now she did allow herself a smile. "You wouldn't have laid a finger on me!"

"Better than taking you for the first time as if you were a whore."

She stared, her smile fading. What did he mean? "But, you weren't unkind or rough," she protested.

"My dear," he said grimly, "you have no concept of what you missed. However, tonight I can give you the experience you deserve"—Fox slipped a hand down her back and drew her hips against his—"for the first and last time—with me, at least."

Maddie was confused, yet so excited that her heart pounded in her ears and a long, slow chill swept down her body, prickling her flesh. "I don't—"

"But you will," Fox cut in, "if we stop talking." His breath tickled her ear, then he was kissing her eyes, temples, brow, cheeks, and finally, her waiting mouth.

Maddie melted utterly, a slave to Fox's skillful hands and lips as she lay shivering and gasping. How could the simple sensation of touch evoke such delicious arousal? With excruciating deliberation he kissed her throat, feathered her inner arms with his fingertips, all the while making low murmuring sounds that dissolved the last of her inhibitions. Maddie opened her mouth, feeling the balmy night air sigh between her parted thighs. Could this possibly be real?

Fox saw her breasts swelling, straining toward him, and he turned Maddie's supple form away. This was his gift to her, these moments of pleasure as nearly perfect as he could manage; selfishly he realized that it was also a gift he was giving himself. He knew that he would carry the memory of this fantasy-made-real for the rest of his life.

Lifting her hair, he touched his lips to her nape, then nipped at her graceful shoulders, the sensitive sides of her back, down her spine . . . At last his hands cupped her buttocks. For one thrilling instant, Maddie felt the hot tumescence of him press her there, but then it was gone. His strong fingers kneaded her bottom, gently and then more deeply, sending needle pricks of electricity over her nerves. Then, painstakingly, Fox explored each curve and hollow of her shapely legs. He knelt and lifted her foot, kissing the instep while his eyes devoured every detail of her naked form.

When he lowered his head and pressed a kiss to her inner thigh, Maddie moaned and her hips bucked involuntarily in response. Fox nipped her there and then pushed her thighs farther apart. She was blushing, lifting her head to look down in panic, and Fox glanced up to meet her sparkling gaze.

"Shh," he reassured her. "You're afraid of yourself, not me. I won't hurt you. Quite the contrary, in fact."

The sight of his roguish grin brought tears to her eyes, and love for him swept through her body in powerful waves. She reached down to touch his chestnut hair, grateful for the burnished light that allowed her to see the response in his eyes. In the next instant he came toward her, covering her with his powerful body and meeting her lips with a heartfelt kiss. This was truly dangerous; Fox knew it, but he no longer cared. Not tonight.

While her arms twined about his shoulders and their mouths fused in a wildly erotic dance of passion, Maddie felt as if she were soaring above the clouds. Every inch of her flesh was unbearably sensitive as a result of Fox's ministrations; but even more sublime was the simple pleasure of his body against her own and the chance to embrace and kiss the man she loved. Maddie's hands were hungry. In the midst of endless kissing, she buried her fingers in his hair, felt the curls that had enticed her for weeks as they fell over Fox's collar, and then touched his muscled shoulders and back. He was warm and hard all over; surprisingly familiar in a curious way, as if they had done all of this before. The smell and the taste of him made her giddy.

Fox wasn't certain how much longer he could last. He freed his mouth from Maddie's kiss despite her whimpered protests and ventured lower. Her breasts were exquisite: full, creamy, and ripe, their pink nipples darkened slightly with arousal. Fox shook his head; this was torture of the finest sort.

When, after long moments of slow caresses, Fox's warm tongue circled her nipple, Maddie made a low noise that didn't sound quite human to her own ears. He had to cup her breast in his hands while he suckled because she'd thrown her head back, writhing with pleasure. Dimly it occurred to her that her legs were parted and she was thoroughly wet there. The yearning between her legs intensified; her hips seemed to have a life of their own, surging against Fox.

"Let it come," he encouraged, his voice ragged.

Although Maddie didn't know what he was talking about, her body seemed to understand. She was clenching her teeth, feeling the heat of his blue eyes on her even though her own were closed tight.

"I need . . ." a voice sobbed, and she recognized it as her own.

A few heartbeats passed while his fingers continued to massage her aching breasts, then something wet and warm touched the very core of Maddie's desire. A cry passed her lips. Fox's tongue quivered expertly, she gasped and gasped, and finally a tide of euphoric sensations emanated from that spot. Horrified, Madeleine realized that she was not only weeping but also pressing closer to his mouth as the contractions intensified.

When the tremors began to subside, Maddie shocked herself by experiencing, not shame, but a sense of bliss and fulfillment. And she felt closer to Fox than she had ever dreamed possible. Not only had he shared the experience with her, it was he who had been her guide.

Ablaze with his own passion, Fox was astonished to hear Maddie's uninhibited giggle. She pulled at his hair and he went to her, kissing her ravenously. Her legs embraced his hips, her mouth beamed under his, and then she touched him, undaunted by his state of arousal. Fox was ready for her—achingly ready.

"If I hurt you," he whispered, "stop me."

"You can't," Maddie replied giddily. "We were created to be together."

Just for tonight, he'd believe it, too. The sensation of thrusting into her, snug and moist, was so agonizingly pleasurable that Fox thought for a moment he had died—and he didn't care. She was right; they fit together as if they'd made love a thousand times. The scent of her hair and the curve of her neck against his face were perfect to him. Their rhythms matched magically. Maddie met each deep thrust while Fox quickly realized that he was no longer able to choreograph their lovemaking. His body threatened to leave him behind; the blood pounded in his head, and thoughts were obliterated by the driving force of a passion more intense than any he'd experienced before.

Although Fox had planned this last scene of Maddie's perfect love-play, the initial scalding pulse of his climax came with unexpected suddenness. Maddie's fingers gripped the muscles of his back as he cried out. Her tightening embrace encouraged him to groan again, and his eyes stung as the last of his burning spasms subsided.

A wave of serene confidence surged over Maddie. She gazed at Fox's slightly averted face and saw that he was both stunned and completely vulnerable. Pushing back his damp hair, she touched his jaw with her lips and smiled.

"Christ," he breathed at last, overwhelmed and more than a little embarrassed.

Maddie's skin prickled when Fox disengaged and rolled away. The air was turning cooler and an owl hooted in the distance. "Fox?" Her voice was barely audible. "Is something wrong? I mean—wasn't I—?"

Staring at her, he said flatly, "Good God, it isn't you—it's *me*." He sat up, his wide back and strong head silhouetted against the violet sky. "That's what comes of having the devil's own conceit. What made me imagine that I could give you something perfect? That is—" He broke off, staring into the distance. "Hell, I'm making an even bigger ass of myself trying to explain."

She was incredulous. Scrambling onto her knees, she wrapped her arms around him and cried, "You are right about one thing: this *is* nonsense! Every moment was perfect, beyond dreaming. I don't have any idea how you think you failed, but I do know that I wish you hadn't mentioned it. I was *happy*!"

It came to Fox then that she was right. Why couldn't he dwell on the pleasure rather than his own self-perceived shortcomings? Perhaps it had been a mistake for him to believe that he could throw off the shadow of Little Bighorn. As long as he carried that burden, Fox reflected, he probably wouldn't be able to freely enjoy pleasure . . . let alone accept real love.

"Fox?" Maddie murmured, both stung and perplexed by

the sense that his thoughts had taken him away again. "Have you heard anything I've said?"

He turned to face her and she saw the raw emotion in his eyes. "Of course I heard you . . . and I agree with you. It was thoughtless of me. Unforgivable. But then, I warned you, didn't I? I told you that I cannot give you what you need."

"Stop saying that!" Madeleine cried. Anger flashed in her emerald eyes and she tossed her hair, which rippled over her bare shoulder like honeyed fire.

Fox bit his lip, then gathered her into his embrace. They knelt in the evening breeze, holding each other fast, while Maddie blinked back tears.

"I'm sorry. . . ." His words were scarcely audible. Slowly he tipped her face up, kissed her salty eyes and cheeks, and then her mouth. It was rosy, almost bruised, from their lovemaking, and the kiss they shared now grew sweeter by the moment.

"I'm not," Maddie answered at last. A mischievous smile played over her face.

Laughter welled in him and his heart ached to release it along with the pain that stubbornly refused to leave. Finally he did laugh. He saw the surprise and answering joy in Maddie's eyes before she drew him back down onto the quilt, where they laughed and loved together. In time, the starry sky covered them like a blanket of black velvet and diamonds.

Miracles seemed to crowd Maddie's life after that night. The land itself was a miracle once they reached the plains. Why hadn't she noticed when she'd first crossed the Dakota Territory with Gramma Susan and Benjamin? The endless sea of prairie grass sent roots two feet down, Fox told her, to provide nourishment for the buffalo whether it rained or not. Above them sprawled the sky, a canopy of Wedgwood blue decorated with a fanciful variety of clouds. Some were piled in mounds, like a profusion of whipped cream, while others were striated as if pieces of white cotton had been stretched and pulled apart.

Even more beautiful was each night's sunset. Together, Maddie and Fox would take in the spectacle as it unfolded across the boundless sky. Each sunset and sunrise seemed more breathtaking than the last. Each was a miracle.

And no less miraculous to Maddie was Fox. She was constantly intrigued and surprised by his mind, likening it to a puzzle with key pieces that he kept carefully locked away. So much remained uncertain between them, there was so much he insisted he couldn't give her, that she indulged in what was tangible.

The night after Maddie's awakening, Fox had been congenial but physically wary. It wasn't until the moon had risen high in the ebony sky and their fire was reduced to embers that Maddie rose out of a deep sleep, tempted by delicious pleasures. She was nestled against Fox's warm, bare chest. He had thrown one leg over her and, with a sleepy sigh, run his hand over her as if by instinct. The rough, long-fingered hand she adored fitted itself to the curve of her bottom, then slid up under the man's shirt she wore in place of a nightgown. Eventually, when Maddie was tingling all over, aroused even more by this wordless passion that built between them at this unreal hour when one always slept, Fox's mouth found her own. As if this episode didn't count, or might be passed off in the morning as a dream, he gave vent to his need, ravishing her with kisses, caressing her with burning hands, suckling her nipples until they ached, and finally pushing into her eager body.

With the dawn, Maddie awoke to find Fox breaking their camp. Her cheeks colored at the sight of him, but he met her gaze unflinchingly. Still, nothing was said. Both knew what had occurred, yet it was easier to pretend that each had dreamed something slightly shameful.

It was afternoon now. Madeleine rode next to Fox, sharing the silence as she contemplated the simple beauty of the prairie and the miracle of her lover's body. How exotically he was made compared to her, all lean, sinewy strength, with wrists and hands and thighs that made her own seem child-like. He was the first man she had ever seen naked, and that made him all the more alluring and mysterious. She yearned to touch him. Finally, to fill the thundering silence of her thoughts, Maddie spoke.

"Fox, I hope I'm not mentioning a subject that is too painful for you, but I did want to say that I was sorry to hear about Mr. Hickok's death. Wasn't he a friend of yours?"

Fox's chin rose slightly, his hands clenched once on the reins, and then he turned to let his blue eyes rest on Maddie. "Actually it's kind of you to mention Bill. He was a rare man. We did become friends during these past weeks and, to tell you the truth, I don't think I've accepted the fact that he's dead. It all seems like a dream, doesn't it? The night we left Deadwood amid the chaos following Bill's murder—and all that's happened since, for that matter." One brow arched wryly. "I think I'd be more upset about Bill if I didn't have a feeling that he was ready to go. He as much as said so." Fox fell silent, returning his attention to the mules. There hadn't been anything much for him to do during the past few miles of open, gently sloping prairie, but now they were coming around an out-cropping of hills that blocked their view of the vast sea of pale green grass that lay beyond. After he navigated the mules and wagon around these last obstacles, they ought to have their first glimpse of Bear Butte.

Maddie's thoughts were in another realm entirely, having fastened onto one ill-chosen phrase Fox had spoken. *So,* she brooded, *it's all like a dream to him.* Was that his way of dealing with the situation developing between them? She gave him a winsome smile. "As long as you mean a pleasurable dream—not a *nightmare*—I'll agree with you. Of course, I'm not referring to Mr. Hickok's shooting. I can certainly understand that you might want to pretend that that night was not real."

Fox was staring ahead, concentrating on the rocky, precipitous path that the mules were navigating. Behind them the covered wagon clanked and groaned, until the ground eventually evened out and they emerged from the last stand of pine trees. Fox drew back on the reins, and Maddie followed his gaze. In the distance, a tall, pointed island seemed to rise out of the pale green ocean of prairie grass.

"What is *that*?" she breathed.

"Bear Butte." Memories pushed up forcefully from his past, grasping him like an unseen hand. Fox felt his palms go clammy, and perspiration beaded on his forehead. Christ, how much of his time with the Sioux had he buried at Little Bighorn? His conflict, it seemed, had been greater than he'd imagined. Staring now at the granite sentinel rising more than a thousand feet above the prairie, it came to him that he, like Maddie, had personal reasons for this journey. Glancing at her, he said, "It's inspiring, don't you think? The Sioux, or Lakota, have long regarded Bear Butte as a sacred place, and a convenient spot to gather as well. They usually come here at the end of the summer to fatten their ponies, do a bit of trading, and send smoke signals to other bands if the need arises. . . ." He spoke almost unconsciously, and when he ran out of words, his voice trailed off.

"That's where we're going, isn't it?" Maddie queried in an effort to absorb reality. Their adventure was no longer a lark; soon she would be in the midst of the same Indians who had recently massacred more than two hundred American soldiers.

"Yes." Fox lifted his brows. "You aren't afraid, are you?"

She swallowed hard but managed a smile. "Perhaps. A little." No sooner were the words out than her heart began to beat like one of the Indian tom-toms she'd read about as a child. "Fox, you told my father that you spent time among the Sioux. Maybe you've even been to Bear Butte yourself before. Won't you tell me what to expect? I think it would help if I had knowledge beyond the myths I've heard about Indians."

He squinted into the sunlight, thinking.

"They are *myths*, aren't they?" Maddie pressed, her voice rising.

"Mostly." He looked down at her pale face and laughed. "Where is the spirited, headstrong woman who came, uninvited, to find her sister and discover for herself what the Sioux were really like?"

"I—I still feel that way!" she protested, licking her lips. "It's just that . . . I mean, I can't help feeling a qualm or two . . . about the unknown, I mean."

Fox took pity on her. "Yes, I know what you mean. In fact, I'll tell you a secret. I wasn't prepared for the onslaught I felt myself when we first glimpsed Bear Butte—and I've been here before." He paused for a moment, then continued, "I wish I could tell you exactly what to expect, Maddie, but I'm not sure myself. A lot's changed since I spent time, a long time, in fact, among the Sioux. They still believed most of the white man's promises then. They still had enough freedom to carry on their way of life. That's over now, in spite of the Indian victory at Little Bighorn. I don't doubt that the people who are following Crazy Horse are even angrier and more frustrated than the rest of the Lakota, which is why I'd've preferred that you stay in Deadwood. It was a shame that you listened to your grandmother rather than your father and me. She's a fine woman, but in this case I fear it was the blind leading the blind."

"You don't really think they'll *harm* us. . . ? You told Father that you believed you would be safe, that you had friends among the Sioux, even among Crazy Horse's renegade bands!"

Fox shrugged. "Do you really imagine that I would have voiced any fears to your father even if I had them? I cannot give you guarantees, but a few short years ago I would have. The majority of the Lakota people I have known have been the finest human beings I have ever encountered. Your father and I have both told you what we feel about the Indians."

"But you aren't sure whether they are still like that?" Maddie knew she ought to leave it alone, but she could not help worrying the matter like a dog with a bone. Was she going to be cooked alive over burning embers or torn apart by four horses running in different directions?

"I don't know what else to say to you. These people feel hopeless and betrayed, and they may feel that way toward all white people. Others whom they have befriended have turned against them, so they may not trust me, either." He took a dried apricot from his pocket and chewed it thoughtfully before adding, "The Lakota are wise, though. They will remember that I did not ask for anything from them, nor have I broken any promises. I shared only friendship and laughter and work with them during my years on the plains. There is no reason for them to punish me for the transgressions of other white Americans. I believe that we will be safe."

Maddie sighed audibly and a smile spread slowly over her lovely face. "Well, then, that's good enough for me. Now I can indulge in pure excitement over the next chapter in our adventure. We'll be *safe*!" She repeated his words with added emphasis, as if that would lend them more credibility.

Fox sighed, too, but there was a weight on his heart. He and Maddie would probably remain safe . . . as long as Crazy Horse and his Lakota followers didn't discover that he had been among the bluecoats who'd been hunting Indians that infamous day at Little Bighorn.

Chapter Sixteen

DUSK WAS GATHERING, WASHING THE LANDSCAPE with hues of amber and rose, when the pair of mules pulled their wagon and two passengers to the crest of a gentle ridge. Bear Butte loomed before them now, filling Maddie's vision. The flatland that lay below the ridge and stretched up to the laccolith's base was threaded with cottonwood trees.

Fox drew back on the reins and narrowed his eyes at the distant trees that shimmered in the gentle breeze. "Those cottonwoods mean water. They grow along streambeds, and that's where the Indians make camp." He shaded his eyes and wished he'd thought to bring a spyglass. Suddenly it occurred to Fox how careless he'd been—probably because his mind had been clouded by a lot of nonsensical visions of Maddie. Why hadn't he realized that the Indians might attack them before he could establish contact, before he and Maddie even knew they were there! How the hell was he going to communicate if he didn't see someone he recognized early on? And the words—! Panic swept over him as he struggled to remember the rudiments of the Lakota language he'd nearly mastered a few years ago.

Sensing the tension that emanated from his body, Maddie said, "What's wrong?"

"Nothing," he murmured, and gave her a smile of calm assurance. "I was just thinking . . . wondering how best to approach this situation."

"Shouldn't we search for the village?"

"Oh, I don't doubt that it's down there, shielded by the

211

cottonwoods. In fact, my guess is that they already know we're here.''

Maddie tried to swallow, but it seemed that something was lodged in her throat. Reality penetrated at last: Fox really had no guarantees about what would happen when they came face-to-face with these renegade Indians.

"Maybe it would be best just to sit here for a little while and wait—give them a chance to come to us,'' he decided at length. "I believe I'll eat while I can.''

She stared in disbelief as he rooted around behind them in the wagon and brought out a hunk of rye bread, some jerky, and a couple of plums, all of which he offered to Maddie. "No, thank you,'' she cried in a strangled voice. "I've no stomach for food at the moment.''

"Sorry to hear it,'' Fox replied laconically. He ate with relish, washed it all down with cold coffee, wiped his mouth, then got out to give Watson and the mules water from a bucket. When he returned to his seat, Maddie was fairly wringing her hands.

"How can you be so composed at a time like this? Why, I—''

"Don't raise your voice,'' Fox interrupted. "It carries on the breeze. Would you be happier if I gnashed my teeth and begged God to spare us from torture and death? Do you want me to sweat and roll my eyes and tremble and hide?''

Before Maddie could speak again, Fox lifted his head, put a finger to her mouth, and listened. "They're coming,'' he whispered.

Sheer terror flooded her. For an instant she thought she might faint, then her innate strength of character bobbed to the surface. "Shall I get a rifle?''

Fox gave her an endearing smile and caressed her cheek with a brown hand. "My darling Madness, it would do you no good in the face of a band of Indian warriors, but I do admire your pluck. I believe that you'd defend us both if you had to.''

Tears blurred her vision and she wiped them away furiously. "There must be something we can do!'' A symphony of hoofbeats reached her ears, rising out of the flatland below them.

"Just this." He slipped his strong arms around her and drew her into his embrace, still smiling at her with fond blue eyes that crinkled at the corners. "There's no point in worrying. Better to believe the best." He kissed her then, bending her backward, his mouth working on her tense lips until he felt them soften and respond. Finally he kissed his way down her cheek and throat, murmuring, "Shhh . . ." so soothingly that she went limp in his arms.

Fox was relieved that Maddie was able to respond to him in the midst of her fear. He knew that the sight of the braves, with their war paint that was meant to frighten and intimidate strangers, would terrify poor Maddie, and he'd hoped to distract her. At length, lifting his head, he saw that five of the lean young men, clad in buckskin leggings and fierce-looking in their bright paint and feathers, had formed a line astride their agile ponies. Two of the other riders were galloping the rest of the way up the gentle slope. One of them wore paint on his face that made him resemble a ferocious bear; he wore his hair unbraided, and his naked upper body was streaked with more paint. His companion, whose face was painted mostly white with green circles around his eyes, wore a blue short coat that had once belonged to a white army officer. Fox wondered if the blue coat was a treasure from Little Bighorn.

"Oh, my lord . . ." Maddie breathed, the words scarcely audible.

The two braves made a menacing show of their approach to the wagon, reining their horses up short, brandishing decorated spears, and shouting a challenge in the Lakota language.

Fox was surprised to discover that he was calm. A sense of déjà vu enveloped him like magic. Meeting the fierce stare of the first man, he declared, *"Kola!"*—uttering the Lakota word for "friend." He pointed to himself and then to Maddie. Emboldened, he added the exclamation of pleasure: *"Hun-hun-he, kola!"*

The five-man escort party began to murmur among themselves while the young man wearing the army officer's coat glared at his companion and grunted something unintelligible to Fox. It was the first man with whom he felt the unconscious rapport, so he continued to meet his thoughtful stare. At length the fellow spoke slowly in Lakota and Fox translated his words mentally: "I think we have met before, bold friend, as you call yourself. My name is Kills Hungry Bear. Are you. . . ?"

Flooded by elation and recognition, Fox half rose and exclaimed, "My old friend! I am the one your people called Fox-With-Blue-Eyes."

Maddie stared at the two of them, stunned, as they greeted each other as brothers. Kills Hungry Bear was introduced to her, and she managed to smile. Then the other Indian nudged his companion. His fearsome expression was now rather sulky, like a boy being excluded from an important event.

Laughing, Kills Hungry Bear gestured sideways and presented Striped Owl, who was, he explained, one of the Cheyenne who had joined with the Lakota bands who resisted reservation life. When greetings were exchanged among Striped Owl and the white visitors, Kills Hungry Bear asked Fox why they were there.

"I have come to meet with your people. I did not know that you would be among them," Fox replied, surprised to discover how readily the Lakota words returned to him. "Miss Avery and I are searching for someone whom we believe to be with those who follow Crazy Horse."

"I must trust you," Kills Hungry Bear replied solemnly. "You have never lied to me, so I believe you. There are many among your race who would lie to gain access to Crazy Horse so that they might strike him down, but I shall explain to my people that you and your woman are different."

"The Lakota people have been very good to me. I owe all of you a great deal," Fox said. "You may trust me; I hope that you will."

"Then let us go to the village. You both look hungry and tired, so we will offer you food and rest, and then we will talk."

As Kills Hungry Bear wheeled his buckskin pony around, Fox noticed the symbol of a hand wiped across the animal's flank. He remembered then that it meant the rider was in mourning. Memories of his friend's family, who had treated him like a relative, returned with stinging clarity, and Fox spoke. "Kills Hungry Bear . . . I see that you are in mourning." He chose his words carefully, avoiding a direct question that might offend.

The young man glanced back, his shining black hair flying behind him in the evening breeze. Twilight accentuated his clay-colored skin and the shadow of sadness that passed over his proud features. "Do you remember my brother, Aiming Fast? In the Moon of Making Fat, he was killed at the Greasy Grass River by Long Hair's bluecoat soldiers."

Fox managed to nod, then slapped the reins against the mules' backs so that they would carry the wagon rumbling down the hill after the seven proud young Indians astride their ponies.

Maddie clutched Fox's arm and whispered excitedly, "We're safe, aren't we? I don't know what you were saying, but I could tell. Everything's going to be all right, isn't it?" She paused to wait for his nod, then rushed on, "What was he talking about at the end?"

"Why do you ask?" Fox's voice was low and harsh.

"Did I say something wrong? I just meant that . . . well, it's very *odd* to be frightened out of one's wits by people who have dressed up to accomplish that very purpose, and then, when they speak, not to be able to understand a word that's being said! I'm just curious, that's all. I wish you'd translate all of it for me so that I don't feel quite so lost!" She pushed back the wayward tendrils that blew around her cheeks and brow. "He's your friend; I can see that much—and there was something very touching about the expression on his face at the end. Won't you tell me what he said?"

"*His* name is Kills Hungry Bear," Fox reminded her.

"He's as worthy a human being as anyone you know, so you may as well call him by name." A sigh rose aching from his heart before he finished, "The last thing I spoke to Kills Hungry Bear about was the symbol of mourning painted on his pony's flank."

"And?" Maddie prodded gently, thinking at the same time that she would never be able to learn what everything meant in this extraordinarily foreign culture.

"His brother, whom I once knew, was killed at Little Bighorn by one of Custer's soldiers." Fox's eyes burned as he spoke the words. Why did life have to be such a damned bloody mess? Would he ever find his way out of this labyrinth of guilt and confusion? Annie Sunday had taught him that good and bad were easy to separate if one searched for the truth, but in the world that was being reshaped on America's frontier, everything seemed to be painted in shades of gray. Right and wrong just depended on a person's point of view.

Or did it?

"How terrible," Maddie was saying sympathetically. "Still, it hardly seems fair to blame the white people for that, since the Indians killed every one of Custer's men in return!"

"I'm afraid it's not that simple."

The Indians who led the way on horseback had followed the upper curve of the ridge and now began to descend, heading down into the valley that emerged in front of the shielding cottonwood trees. As the mules clambered in the ponies' wake, Maddie gasped and pointed at the spectacle that lay below.

There, nestled against the glimmering trees and a curled ribbon of azure water, was the Indian village. Splendidly picturesque, like the paintings by Philadelphia artist George Caitlin that had fascinated Maddie as a child, the tableau before them held her spellbound. Dozens of tipis fashioned of buffalo hide and topped with graceful fans of willow poles, huddled in the carnation pink depths of twilight. Figures with black hair and tan garments moved about, and a herd of hundreds of ponies raised soft clouds of dust as they grazed in the shadow of Bear Butte.

"It's amazing," Maddie murmured, and felt Fox's answering smile. "I feel as if I've dropped into one of the stories I used to read in *Harper's Weekly*. I never dreamed . . ."

Fox thought of many responses to make, but none seemed sufficient. At length, as they drew nearer, he queried, "You're not frightened anymore?"

A few older children were frolicking in the stream, and their giggles joined with the clear, musical sound of adult laughter. Maddie saw some men playing a game with stones while a group of women gathered wildflowers and wove them into one another's braids. "Frightened?" she echoed. "Of what?"

Kills Hungry Bear, Striped Owl, and their escort of five rode ahead into the village. Moments later, the laughter stopped. People began to point up the hillside at their clumsy mules and wagon with Watson bringing up the rear. Kills Hungry Bear spoke animatedly to a group that formed rapidly. The men surrounding him appeared to be important, and Maddie wondered if Crazy Horse was among them. What if he proclaimed that she and Fox must die to pay for the sins of their race?

Fragrant wisps of woodsmoke rose out of the tops of the tipis, which Maddie noticed were of varying sizes and generally larger than she had imagined. A great deal about the village was different from what she had imagined. Although the people had fallen silent as they watched the white intruders, moments before they had acted like human beings with minds, wits, and skills as well developed as anyone else's. These Indians appeared charmingly civilized. Who could say that this simpler style of living was less enlightened than the rowdy mayhem of white settlements like Deadwood? Maddie sighed, contemplating the seemingly endless series of paradoxes.

"Don't worry," Fox said. "They're more frightened of you than you are of them."

They had come to a stop a few dozen yards away from the

group of conferring men. Fox reached over and absently squeezed Maddie's hand, and for an instant her world was condensed to his power to move her and the force of her feelings for him.

The sound of whispering roused her. The young women who had been picking wildflowers stood quite near to the wagon, frozen with fright and curiosity. When Maddie looked at them, they gazed back with dark eyes alight with intelligence and pride. Strong emotions stirred deep in Maddie's soul. These young women, whatever the tint of their skin or the manner of their dress and culture, were kindred spirits.

Kills Hungry Bear returned to the wagon in the company of another, older man with penetrating eyes and an aquiline nose. Fox translated for Maddie as he was introduced as He Dog, a comrade of Crazy Horse's since childhood. It seemed that Crazy Horse himself was not in the village, but He Dog and the other men who formed the core of the last resistance against white efforts to manipulate the Indians in the Dakota Territory had agreed to allow Fox and Maddie to come into their village.

"I thank you for your efforts on our behalf," Fox said, with a relieved smile.

Kills Hungry Bear replied, "We need the rifles and ammunition you have brought to us, and some of the other men remember you when you lived among us on the plains. We do not trust as readily as we did then, but all agree that you earned and held the regard of the Lakota people for many seasons. This means more than promises on a piece of paper."

He Dog nodded once, then spoke. "I, too, remember you, Fox-With-Blue-Eyes. I knew your father. He was there during my first real buffalo hunt when I was a boy. The land was black with buffalo and the ground shook under my horse. Your father urged me on when he sensed that I was frightened. His kindness stayed in my mind." A bittersweet note crept into He Dog's voice as he stared into the distance, back into the past. "Those times have gone with the buffalo. The whites have done us much harm, but I have not forgotten that there are real human beings among you.''

Fox couldn't speak for a moment as he imagined his father, whom he missed and loved so fiercely, hunting buffalo among the Lakota people. Even when Fox had first visited here, before Custer's expedition discovered gold in the Black Hills, the halcyon days of buffalo herds a million-strong and limitless freedom for the Indians were over. Zachary Matthews had been fortunate to dwell among the Lakota people when he had.

With quiet dignity, the village welcomed Fox and Maddie into its midst. Kills Hungry Bear did not ask why Maddie was with Fox, or if they were married, and she didn't argue when he gave them his tipi to share. Secretly she was immensely happy for the opportunity to spend more time alone with Fox.

She ducked down to enter, Fox followed her, and the flap dropped behind them. Surprised, Maddie stared at Fox with wide green eyes. ''Is he leaving us now for the whole night? What about Sun Smile? When will we be able to ask about my sister?'' She had already begun to wonder if Sun Smile had been one of the women who had gazed at her with such eloquence upon their arrival.

''There's a certain amount of . . . etiquette, for lack of a better word, that must be observed,'' Fox replied. ''After we rest a bit and settle in, I'll visit with Kills Hungry Bear for a while. With luck, the opportunity will arise for me to mention Sun Smile.''

A little furrow appeared in Maddie's brow. ''Why can't you simply *create* an opportunity?''

''The Lakota people don't admire our tendency to just blurt out whatever question is on our mind. They prefer to be patient and allow life to reveal itself to them when the time is right.'' Seeing her frustration, he murmured, ''I'll learn what I can, Rashness.''

Maddie nodded, accepting that as the best he could offer, and turned her attention to their quarters. The tipi was thoroughly alien, yet surprisingly comfortable. Its compact frame consisted of a dozen willow poles over which were stretched soft buffalo hides neatly stitched together. In the middle at the top was a smoke flap; directly under, on the ground, were the remains of a fire. The rest of the floor was covered with grass and wildflowers, over which were spread rawhide rugs with the hair side turned up. Maddie reached for a velvety buckskin pillow, squeezed it, and asked, "What do they stuff them with?"

Fox grinned. "Cottonwood floss."

"How lovely!" Her face glowed with wonder.

He pointed out other features of the home. Although at least two beds were customary in a tipi, to accommodate a family, Kills Hungry Bear had only one. Roomy and inviting, it consisted of a mass of buffalo skins and pillows. Against the back wall was a painstakingly decorated hide that depicted the history of Kills Hungry Bear's family.

"That can be removed from the wall and worn as a robe for important ceremonies," Fox explained. "Those bags hold all of his, and his family's, worldly goods. Do you see how they're decorated? Kills Hungry Bear's wife spent many hours mixing berries and earth to make paints, then she made each one into a work of art." He leaned over to pick up one of the handy rawhide bags and showed Maddie the added decorations of colored porcupine quills.

She fingered them in amazement, then peeked inside the bag's opening. "What sorts of things does an Indian own?"

Her curiosity was so artless that he succumbed. "I'll take Kills Hungry Bear's belongings to him when I go, but perhaps first we might look at one or two. Don't tell him, though!"

"How would I do that?" she countered, with a wide smile.

Fox's brow curved upward. "I am grateful for the language barrier. It's the only hope I have of censoring you in front of our hosts." He looked into the bag then and drew out a soft leather case. "This was made to hold a comb." Out of it he pulled a long, painted object that bore only a passing resemblance to the imported silver-plated comb Maddie owned.

"Oh!" she exclaimed, reaching out to touch it while making a face.

"It's a porcupine tail," Fox explained, straight-faced. "Clearly these people are clinging to their old ways, because a comb would be easy enough to trade for." Then he produced a smaller painted bag and opened it. "This is the art kit, you might say. Here are the brushes, and the turtlebacks they use for paint pots." When he held one out, Maddie touched it and smiled slowly. "In the other bags are clothing and moccasins. Over there is Kills Hungry Bear's own supply of food, and his utensils. It doesn't look like he has much, and I would expect him to have more beds, a bigger tipi, and more painted decorations. It's almost as if he doesn't have a family."

"Does he have a wife?"

"I'm certain he had just married when I left his tribe three years ago. Little Dove was her name, I think." Pensive, Fox gazed at the tipi walls, where the usual array of long, carved pipes hung in fringed cases, along with a bow and arrows in a quiver, and a bag that held Kills Hungry Bear's war bonnet looped over the tripod above the bed. It was all normal enough, but there were no feminine touches. "Well, I suppose I should take these things to him and see what he's prepared to tell me."

Maddie watched as he gathered up Kills Hungry Bear's painted bags and felt a tremor of anxiety. She was quite hungry, too, and warm.

Throwing back the door flap, Fox scrambled into the violet-hued evening air and reached back inside to collect Kills Hungry Bear's belongings. Then, as if seeing into Maddie's mind, he said, "I can open other flaps around the tipi if you're hot. It's common practice during the summer. You'll be much more comfortable if you don't mind a few curious looks from your new neighbors."

"Not just yet, I don't think," she said doubtfully. "But perhaps I'll keep this flap open."

"It's a sign of welcome for guests," he warned.

"Oh, Fox, I can't keep track of all these new rules!" Maddie gave an exasperated sigh. "I'll just take my chances with the guests, as long as they are friendly . . . and you bring me something to eat right now!"

After he'd fetched their own sack of food, kept until now behind the wagon seat for them to nibble on between stops, Maddie chewed vigorously on a strip of jerky and watched him go off into the village in search of his old friend. Consumed by curiosity and a nagging flutter of trepidation, she continued to gaze outside, but stayed well back in the shadows. Children and dogs continued to scamper through the village. One man passed, laughing, with his son riding on his back. Families were beginning to gather inside their tipis, lowering the side flaps since the night promised to be cooler.

Maddie's heartbeat quieted as she absorbed the sense of peace and harmony that prevailed. No one was going to leap on her and scalp her if she let down her guard. Edging nearer the opening of her tipi, she leaned forward to get a better look. The stream purled in the distance and the shiny leaves of the cottonwoods gleamed silver in the light of the rising moon. A young woman led her pony back from the stream. As she neared Kills Hungry Bear's tipi, Maddie swallowed a gasp. What could be the matter with this girl? She was filthy, streaked with some sort of brownish grayish mess; her dress was ragged and dirty, her hair uncombed and apparently unwashed, and she chanted to herself as if she were mad.

Maddie drew back as the woman passed, uncertain whether or not she might be dangerous. Actually the girl was quite lovely, Maddie noticed, under the dirt that caked her skin and hair and the ragged buckskin garments. Her form was lithe and gracefully curved. Her features were almost classically delicate, unlike the broader faces of most of the other Lakota women. How tragic it would be if someone so young and lovely had descended into madness!

Then, as if feeling Madeleine's stare, the girl turned slowly and gazed into the tipi's opening. To Maddie's further consternation, the haunted eyes that met hers were dove gray, thickly lashed, and eerily familiar.

Chapter Seventeen

August 6–7, 1876

AFTER FOX TOOK KILLS HUNGRY BEAR HIS belongings and the young man had handed them into the tipi where he would sleep during the white visitors' sojourn in the village, the two friends went off to unload the rifles and supplies from the wagon. Exclamations of surprise and pleasure were heard as He Dog and some of the other Lakota men joined in. They built a bonfire nearby so that they could see the crates as they were opened. Everyone was shocked by the quantity and quality of the gifts Fox had brought from Deadwood.

"You have been very generous," He Dog said as he inspected bags of sugar and coffee. "Our supply of food is small. Buffalo are scarce and, of course, we do not take rations from the agency. However, we have a priceless commodity that is not available at the agency: freedom." His nostrils flared as he spoke the word. "Your people think that the land belongs to them or to us, when in truth it is no man's to buy or sell. The land and the sky and all that lies between belong to *Wakan Tanka*, the Great Mystery—the Grandfather of us all! Your people do not listen to simple truths. They take what they want if it is not given freely! Your people—"

"Please." Fox held up his hand. "I know you are angry at the white people, but as you said before, we are not all the same."

"No." He Dog sighed, calming. "That's true. I have been unfair. As you said, we are angry."

"Why did you bring so many guns and so much food?" Kills Hungry Bear asked. "It is very good of you!"

"I brought them, but they are a gift from a man named Stephen Avery. Do you know of him? He spent a winter with a band of Lakota people many seasons ago. In fact, the woman who came with me is Stephen Avery's daughter." He waited to see if anyone would encourage him to continue.

"Huh." Kills Hungry Bear looked bored and the other men had begun carrying the crates of rifles away. "Those are repeaters? Most of us are spoiled now for the bow and arrow since we found repeating rifles."

The abrupt change in topic let Fox know that Stephen Avery's name was known to Kills Hungry Bear and the others. Perhaps his old friend even guessed why Maddie had come, but clearly no one wished to talk about Sun Smile— at least not yet. The Lakota took life one event, one subject, at a time and did not believe in rushing things. Fox was familiar enough with their ways to realize that Kills Hungry Bear would give him a cue when the time was right. His only problem was explaining the concept of patience to Madeleine.

When the work was done and Watson and the mules had been watered and fed, Kills Hungry Bear suggested that Fox and he climb up Bear Butte and smoke.

They didn't go far. The bonfire was still in sight when they hunkered down on a rocky ledge and exchanged Kills Hungry Bear's pipe. Its bowl, of soft red stone, was carved in the shape of a bear, and its long stem was fashioned of gray ash wood. Plainly made, Fox recognized that this was his friend's everyday pipe, yet the ritual they shared would always be meaningful. When both men had smoked and shared a few minutes of silence, Fox spoke in a quiet voice.

"Your tobacco is good. Not too strong."

Kills Hungry Bear nodded, his eyes closed. "I mixed it with some willow bark and bearberries. Maybe a little bit of sumac leaves, too." He drew slowly on the pipe, then said, "The bluecoats are coming for us, I suppose. That is why you brought so many rifles. I guessed that it would happen, after we killed Long Hair and his soldiers at the Greasy Grass River. Some think that they will leave us alone now, but it will not happen. For every white man we kill, countless more come to take his place. They will not let us have a victory. We will be punished for fighting for our lives and our freedom.''

Fox said nothing at first. He looked at Kills Hungry Bear with his melancholy black eyes, proud features, and bronzed skin. Strips of fur were twisted around his freshly braided hair. As the pipe was handed back to him, it came to Fox how remarkable this simple ceremony was that they shared. When men passed the pipe and opened themselves, they could, together, cross a bridge from the earthly world to the spiritual. How little the white race knew of the mysteries of the universe.

"You do not answer," Kills Hungry Bear remarked.

"I was thinking how much I have missed the ways of your people," Fox said honestly. "But I will answer you. I think that you speak the truth, although I have no real knowledge. I do know that people in the Black Hills are very angry about all the bluecoats who were killed with Long Hair."

Kills Hungry Bear's eyes hardened. "Did you know that *he* was the one who made the Thieves' Road into our sacred land, *Paha Sapa*, which you call the Black Hills? I will never understand why your people must have everything you see, no matter who is hurt. The whites believe that we are foolish. It must be because we have followed their advice so readily. For many years, we believed the promises that were made to us, but the only promise that was kept was the promise to take our land." He shut his eyes again. "I do not like this feeling in my heart, but it has been put there by the treachery of your people. Some of the Lakota are tired of resisting. Only a few of us remain to fight for what has belonged to us since the Great Spirit created our world."

Listening to Kills Hungry Bear's plainly spoken truths, Fox felt some of the clouds of guilt and confusion break up inside him. "I agree with you, my friend. I am sorry for the wrongs my race has done. I wish I could change what has happened.''

The Indian laid the pipe down between them and surveyed the boundless star-strewn sky. ''Do you know Crazy Horse?''

''I saw him only one time, but I have heard many stories about him.''

''He is a great leader. I would rather die fighting beside him than live by the white man's rules.''

''Where is he now?''

Kills Hungry Bear grinned, his teeth strong and white in the darkness. ''He is making life hard for the whites who are trying to steal *Paha Sapa* from us. How much I have come to understand by his side! He has spent his whole life seeking the true path through visions from *Wakan Tanka*, the Great Spirit. Many men do not understand such things fully until they are old, but Crazy Horse knows that *this* world is only a shadow of the *real* world. Since he was a boy, he has been able to get into the real world when *Wakan Tanka* gives him dreams.''

Fox knew that it was through dreams that Lakota youths found their names as men. ''I have heard that Crazy Horse was called Curly when he was a boy, and that in his visions he saw his horse dancing so he took the name Crazy Horse.''

''Yes!'' Kills Hungry Bear was pleased by his friend's knowledge. ''Crazy Horse knows much. He has watched the ways the bluecoats fight and thought about how to use that knowledge in battle against them. He also has learned that if he goes to the *real* world, through his dreams, before a fight, he can bear any test. *Wakan Tanka* also gave him special powers that helped him lead us that day we killed Long Hair and all his men.''

''Crazy Horse is a great warrior,'' Fox observed. It was hard for him to think too much about the underlying story, the tale of that day at Little Bighorn. Each time it came into his mind, he felt a dark weariness. The answer eluded him and he had no heart to search for it yet.

''Crazy Horse is a great human being,'' Kills Hungry Bear said. Then, without further ceremony, he picked up his pipe and got to his feet. "I am glad you came to us, Fox-With-Blue-Eyes. The guns and food you have brought us are sorely needed. We are grateful."

As they returned to the village, Fox asked casually, "Do you have a wife, my friend?"

"Yes. She was afraid and so I sent her to the agency. I don't know what to do yet." He sighed softly and shrugged. "Sometimes I think I should take another wife, but I miss Little Dove. We have children. It is hard to think of courting another wife. Some men can manage more than one, but I am not sure, if Little Dove and I are reunited, that I could do this."

Kills Hungry Bear had stopped outside his tipi. It had grown late and the village was quiet except for the muffled stirrings of the pony herd and the occasional owl hoot or coyote howl in the distance. Knowing that Maddie would be anxious for news, Fox decided to trade on the renewed intimacy he felt with his friend after their long conversation. "Kills Hungry Bear . . . I wonder if there is a woman here in this village who is called Sun Smile."

The warrior gave him a sidelong glance and lifted the opening flap of the tipi. A sleeping figure could be glimpsed inside and a small dog rose to greet the latecomer. "I am weary. We will talk some more later. I hope that you and the woman with fire hair sleep well and wake refreshed."

A moment later, Fox stood alone in the dark village.

Maddie was conscious first of an odd smell. Slowly she opened her eyes and it seemed that she must be dreaming. A soft coral light illumined strange objects and a painting on rawhide. A fire, surrounded by a ring of stones, burned low so that only molten embers remained. Her face was pressed against thick brown fur and it came to her that this was the source of the smell. Not unpleasant, but . . . foreign. *I am lying on a bed of buffalo fur,* she thought, *in an Indian tipi!* Then she remembered that she had finally grown bored and tired waiting for Fox and had lain down on the bed, hoping that no rodents or insects would crawl over her if she closed her eyes. Now it must be the middle of the night; it seemed that an eternity had passed. Where was Fox? Had something happened to him? The thought made her heart beat faster.

"Uhm-gh," groaned a low, masculine voice. An instant later, a lean-muscled arm rounded Maddie's waist and drew her close.

Joy welled up in her. In his sleep, Fox cupped Maddie's breast and nuzzled the side of her neck, then made another sound of contentment that slid into the deep breathing of slumber. Tears sprang to her eyes as she looked down at the strong, brown hand that held her fast. It was all she could do to resist turning in his embrace and kissing him awake. Instead, she touched his warm fingers, snuggled her bottom backward against him, beaming, and gazed into the orange fireglow. This wasn't a dream. Much was uncertain, but for tonight, this was enough.

This was everything.

"I am called Strong," the Lakota woman said to Maddie in halting English. "Because I can talk with you, you come with me." A proud smile shone on her angular face and she added, "Today."

Madeleine had been warned by Fox when he went off to hunt antelope with the men that someone might come for her. If the women wanted to make her feel welcome, rather than leaving her alone in the tipi, it was a good sign and she must not turn them away. However, he added, with a backward glance, Maddie must not ask about Sun Smile. She must leave that matter to him.

"How do you know English?" she asked Strong, emerging with her from the tipi into the sunlight.

"I stay at the . . . agency a long time. I want to learn what white people are saying about me. I ask the agent's woman to teach me to speak the words." Strong smiled again at Maddie, started to reach for her hand, then drew back shyly. "Come. I will show you our ways."

Maddie soon found herself working alongside the women of the village. First, Strong gave her a drink to freshen her mouth. Pure cold spring water filtered through fresh mint leaves tasted so good that Maddie drank deeply, then smiled at her new friend. She watched as some women scraped the hair from skins that were staked to the ground while others did washing with a soap Strong called *haipajaja*.

Strong took Maddie with her and a few other women and children to dig *tinpsila*, a root plant that grew plentifully in the shadow of Bear Butte. The women tied them in bunches, then hung them on racks to dry after returning to the village. Strong explained that the white roots could be eaten raw, cooked in soup, or dried and stored for winter.

Many of the other fruits had passed their season. Gone were the strawberries, chokecherries, and wild currants, but the prickly pears were just beginning to ripen, and Strong picked one for Maddie to sample. The bright red fruit grew like jewels on the cactus and proved to be deliciously sweet and juicy.

When the sun rose high in the cerulean sky, Strong, Maddie, and the group of women and children filled their arms with the bunches of *tinpsila* and walked back to join the others in the village. Though dusty and perspiring, Maddie found that she enjoyed the sense of camaraderie that the women shared. It would be very pleasant to talk their language, she thought, to have a name that spoke for her, and to wear a soft, loose buckskin dress decorated to her own taste. White women rarely worked together this way, so they couldn't enjoy the conversation, laughter, and sympathy that accompanied shared tasks.

"I am learning much about your people that I like," she said to Strong, with a slight flush.

"It is good that you can learn," her new friend replied as they approached the village's edge. "Many of your race look down on us. They think that we are the ones who must learn."

"I regret that my people couldn't let yours live in peace," Maddie said honestly.

"Everything has changed. They have killed all the buffalo, which were our . . . livelihood." Strong gave a sad smile as she found the word. As the day went on, her English returned with more facility.

Maddie listened closely as Strong explained how the women had tried to adapt to life without the buffalo—or, at least, with far, far fewer of them. Now that white hunters had laid waste to the millions of buffalo that had once thundered over the plains, the Lakota tried to make do with deer, bear, antelope, even prairie dogs. Once, she said, a woman's work centered around making careful use of every part of the buffalo except the offal. Nothing else was wasted. Not only were the meat and hide essential, but even the ribs became sleds and toys, the horns were made into spoons, the outer lining of the stomach was used as a container for water, and the hooves were boiled for glue.

"We treated the buffalo with respect," Strong maintained. "We killed only as many as we truly needed, just as the Great Spirit intended."

Maddie averted her eyes, ashamed for the wasteful plunder of the white men. No one else spoke of it, but the sadness of change was in the air. Life was not the same as it had been since the world was created, and everyone seemed to understand that there was no going back.

"They make this food that they're so proud of!" Maddie whispered excitedly to Fox as they tended to the mules and Watson. The wagon was a few hundred yards from the village, but still she spoke as softly as she could, fearing someone would overhear and take offense. Everything that she had seen and learned that day was stored inside her, waiting to be shared with Fox. Now, as he brushed Watson and listened with fond attention, the words spilled out. "Strong called it *hash*, but it wasn't like any hash I ever heard of before. They had bones chopped up that they boiled until they were soft and grease came to the top. Then they skimmed the grease off and put it aside. Next, they roasted dry meat and pounded it with a special stone hammer and added some chokecherries. What a recipe! Finally they melted the grease and mixed it with the pounded chokecherries and meat. Strong said that if this hash were properly kept, it would harden and remain edible for a long time.'' She stuck out her tongue and made a comical face to let Fox know what she thought of that.

He laughed, stroking Watson's silken flanks. ''You're talking about *wasna*, and it's considered a real delicacy.'' He shook a finger at her in mock reproval. ''Your new friends surely thought they were doing you a huge favor by teaching you that recipe, so keep your opinion between us!''

''Oh, I wouldn't hurt Strong's feelings for anything. What a wonderful day I had! When the real work was done, all the women bathed together in the stream, and it was such fun! They laughed and splashed one another and played like fish, and soon I was playing, too, as if it were the most natural thing in the world.''

''It is,'' he said dryly.

Maddie blushed. ''I know, but it's hard to undo the habits of a lifetime.'' She fell silent for a time, thinking of the quiet activities that had filled the women's afternoon. During this hot part of the day, the entire village relaxed, either napping or resting together, or occupying the time with tasks like moccasin making or beadwork. Most of the men came back and either lay down with their families or fashioned arrows or other articles of war. The promise of battle hung always in the air. ''What did you do this afternoon?'' Maddie asked Fox. ''I thought you might come back to our tipi.''

''Kills Hungry Bear and I, along with some other men, unpacked the rifles from the crates and I showed them all how to load them. There are nearly six hundred warriors here, so there are still not enough guns for all, but they'll be a help.'' Straightening, Fox stared out over the prairie with crisp blue eyes, then sighed harshly. ''Of course, the eventual outcome is inevitable. Perhaps it's not a favor to delay it.''

Maddie's heart hurt at the thought that these people were doomed. Disturbed, she sought to change the subject. ''Fox? . . .''

''Hmm?'' Suddenly he looked tired and came over to lean against the side of the wagon, his arm brushing hers.

"I saw a woman today who was most unusual. At least, I think it was a woman. It must have been, because she was called Woman's Dress and wore a dress and was helping the other women to make hash . . . but she had a deep voice and broad shoulders—"

Fox's laughter cut her off. "You are charming. Did Woman's Dress bathe with the rest of you? . . . I thought not. She, or more accurately *he*, is what the Lakota people call a *wintke*. There are just as many men like Woman's Dress among the whites, but they are usually forced to pretend to be other than the way they were born. The Indians have a wonderful philosophy about *wintkes*. They believe that each man's destiny is revealed to him in a dream provided by the Great Spirit—at about the time boys begin to become men. If some men behave more like women, it is accepted and they have an important place among the people." As the clouds darkened and swelled in the west, Fox shaded his eyes, watching as he continued, "*Wintkes* help to take care of the women in the village when all the men are away. Often they tend to the wounded after a battle. Thinking back, I remember meeting Woman's Dress a few years ago. Someone mentioned him and I expected a woman when I heard the name. As I recall, Woman's Dress was a childhood friend of Crazy Horse's, called Pretty One then. It would seem that they've remained friends." He smiled. "The Lakota people have a basic respect for God. They aren't quick to ridicule His creations."

Maddie listened with wide eyes. "Indians have an astonishing gift for living!" she exclaimed at last. "How wise they are!"

"We can learn a great deal from them," he agreed, "but don't elevate all of them to sainthood. These people are as human as you are." He paused as he realized that she was not receptive to his words. Everything and everyone here was so new to Maddie—no wonder she was a bit spellbound. "You're happy, aren't you?"

"Very." Maddie gave him a radiant smile.

"It's hard to believe that you are the same stiff-backed

proper *lady* I met just a few weeks ago." Slowly Fox trailed a fingertip down her slim arm, then raised her hand and kissed the palm.

"I was never stiff-backed," Maddie protested weakly.

"My *dear* Miss Avery, you most certainly *were*!" He narrowed his eyes at the clouds again, then appeared to smell the breeze. "I think a storm may be brewing. Shall we go back to the village?"

"First, can I ask you about one other person?"

As he led the mules and Watson to the shelter of the cottonwood trees, Fox looked back over his shoulder. "I'm listening, sweet."

The casual endearment made her heart skitter. Trailing in his wake, she described the woman she'd seen last night, so soon after their arrival in the village. "Is she mad, do you think? I saw her again today and she looked just as hideous as before. Why doesn't someone help her? Under the filth, she's pretty, but I could swear that her legs and arms are scarred, and that she's rubbed mud or something into the wounds! There may be bugs living in her hair, but when we all bathed today, she just sat on the shore and watched." Maddie paused for breath, then hurried on. "She needed a bath more than all the other women combined, but she didn't even wash her face, and no one seemed to think that this was the slightest bit unusual. Now, don't tell me *she's* a winky, or whatever you called them, because it's very obvious that she's a female!"

"Now, Miss Avery, what could you mean by that?" Fox teased. Slipping an arm around Maddie's waist, he grinned and gave her a squeeze, then let his fingers drift caressingly over her hip and, more daringly, her bottom. "Is that what you mean?"

"Stop that and answer me," she scolded, with mock severity.

The smell of meat cooking wafted out to them on the evening air, and Fox suddenly realized that he was ravenous. "The woman you describe is almost certainly in mourning," he explained while guiding Maddie back toward the village.

"That's the way Lakota wives behave when they've lost their husbands. It's normal, which is why none of the other women appear disturbed by her appearance. New widows wail and cut themselves and generally wallow in their own dirt for about a year—"

"What?" Maddie interjected, horrified. "But, that's so—so uncivilized!"

Before Fox could elaborate further, his attention was diverted by the sight of a cloud of dust moving rapidly across the prairie. Now he could make out a horse and rider, galloping like the wind toward the village from the south. The approaching Indian rode bareback and brandished a lance in one raised hand, and his dark hair flew behind him like a banner. Others in the village had also sighted the rider. Cries of welcome multiplied as people emerged from their tipis and rushed to meet the man.

"What's happening?" Maddie asked, filled with fresh curiosity. "Who is that? Do you know? Is he dangerous—or important?"

"You might say that," Fox replied cryptically. "That's Crazy Horse."

Chapter Eighteen

August 7, 1876

EVERYONE WAS CURIOUS TO SEE WHAT PLUNDER Crazy Horse had brought back from *Paha Sapa*, the sacred hills now overrun by whites. However, after sliding from the back of his yellow pinto, Crazy Horse spoke not to the adults but sent the village's crier to bring the children to him.

Fox and Maddie were caught up in the crowd of people who rushed toward the stream to meet the great Oglala warrior. He removed the things he had slung over his pony's back and now led the animal to drink, standing quietly to one side. Maddie saw that Crazy Horse did not have the commanding physical size she had expected of so renowned a warrior and hero. Of barely medium height, he was lithe, with dark hair that might have been more brown than black, a high, sharp nose, and ebony eyes that remained alert despite the long day's travel.

He wore paint: a lightning streak on the side of his face and hail marks on his body. A single spotted eagle feather at the back of his head substituted for the innumerable feathers he could have claimed if he were counting coup for each enemy he had struck down in battle. Around his neck, Crazy Horse wore a war whistle fashioned from the wing bone of an eagle.

Hanging back with the other women, Maddie was struck by his manner of dignified intelligence. A kind of weary valor seemed to radiate from his bronzed body. His burdens were many, but Crazy Horse's courage and strength appeared to be unflagging.

Fox, who stood a short distance from Maddie, spoke as if to himself, "An extraordinary man."

The children were crowding near now, and Crazy Horse smiled, lifting two large skin bags from the assorted items that included his Winchester rifle, a war club, and an artfully crafted bow and quiver of arrows. Now, opening the bags wide, everyone could see that they bulged with raisins, which he invited the children to eat. Their little hands plunged in to gather samples of the treat, but they were careful not to be greedy in the presence of this man whose stubborn bravery sustained the entire village.

Strong, Maddie's new friend, had come up beside her. "He loves the children more because his own daughter died," she said.

Maddie looked over in surprise. "How sad! What happened to her?"

"One of your race's sicknesses . . ." Her brow furrowed as she tried to remember the word. "Cholera? Yes. So sad, but grief made Crazy Horse stronger in his will to fight back against the whites. And grief brought him closer to his wife, Black Shawl." Strong nodded toward the woman who stood waiting outside Crazy Horse's tipi. Maddie recognized her as one of those who'd been making hash that afternoon. It surprised her somehow to think of Crazy Horse as a family man. As if reading her mind, Strong added, with a small smile, "Black Shawl's mother lives in their tipi, too. They take very good care of their man."

Maddie found that she wanted to know more about this side of Crazy Horse. "Was his daughter very young when she died? What was her name?"

"She was called They-Are-Afraid-Of-Her. I believe that Crazy Horse made her name," Strong replied. "She was at the age when a child is easiest to love when death took her. Crazy Horse was a devoted father. He heard her first words and delighted in watching her learn to walk, then teaching her to dance."

Strong sat down beside a cottonwood tree, as if waiting for the excitement to subside, and Maddie joined her. Strong related the story of another occasion when Crazy Horse returned to his village from a raid against the whites. In his absence, the village had moved from a spot near the Little Bighorn River to a site by the Tongue River. He and the other members of his war party tracked them there only to learn that They-Are-Afraid-Of-Her had fallen sick and died before the village moved.

"How long ago was this?" Maddie asked.

Strong shrugged. "I only learned about your time when I stayed at the agency. It was in the time you call summer, when Long Hair and his bluecoats were making the Thieves' Road to *Paha Sapa*. I think it was Crazy Horse's grief that kept him from fighting more to keep Long Hair from invading our sacred ground."

"Custer's expedition into the Black Hills was in 1874," Maddie said. "Two years ago."

"A dark time for us," Strong replied. "And Crazy Horse . . . when he learned about They-Are-Afraid-Of-Her, he made his father tell him where the little girl's scaffold was. It was far away, a dangerous place in Crow country, but he went there all the same. When he found it after two days, Crazy Horse climbed up beside They-Are-Afraid-Of-Her and lay beside her for three nights and days. She was very tiny, wrapped in a buffalo robe . . ."

Maddie's eyes brimmed with tears. "That is a very sad story."

Shrugging again, Strong said, "Yes, but it made Crazy Horse a bigger man. He has never wanted power, only to fight for his people. Every blow that he has suffered as a man has made him stronger, quieter, more modest yet wilder, rasher in his acts of defiance against the whites." Standing again, Strong brushed off her butter-soft buckskin skirt and added, "So you see, Crazy Horse is not an easy man to know. Yet without him, I do not know what would become of all of us who are not only from his band, the Oglala, but all the other bands of Lakota as well as Cheyenne and more. Anyone who wishes to fight rather than surrender meekly

to the whites can join forces with Crazy Horse. He makes
miracles. . . ."

Maddie loved the cozy interior of the tipi she shared with
Fox, especially now that night had fallen. She enjoyed the
small tasks that let her feel she was taking care of him: folding his clothes, arranging their food and supplies, and keeping things tidy. They had just finished a satisfying meal of
dried meat and one of the prickly pears the women had
brought back from the prairie, and now, as she watched Fox
laze on their bed, bathed in the golden light of the fire, she
told of her earlier conversation with Strong. Fox listened
quietly, his smile tinged with irony as she repeated Strong's
final words: "He makes miracles. . . ."

"Miracles, yes," Fox agreed ruefully, "but I fear that
even miracles and Crazy Horse can't hold off the army forever. There simply are too many soldiers."

"But what about his raids into the Black Hills? And what
if the army can't find Crazy Horse and his people?"

Fox ran his hand over the buffalo fur that cushioned his
body. "These raids are annoyances to the whites more than
anything. Do you think Crazy Horse can really change anything by stealing an occasional pack mule or bolts of cloth
for summer leggings or beads for moccasins? It's all for show.
Even the other warriors have tired of going with him. They
want a rest from fighting, but Crazy Horse cannot rest."

"Fox-With-Blue-Eyes," a voice said quietly outside their
tipi flap, which was partially lifted.

Maddie leaned over to admit Kills Hungry Bear, who apol-
ogized for the interruption before announcing that the important warriors were gathering in the council tipi to meet
with Crazy Horse. Fox was invited to join them.

"But, if he hates the whites so much, is it safe for you to
appear?" Maddie asked worriedly after the Lakota words
were translated.

Fox was already getting up, running a hand through his
hair and straightening his clothes. "Crazy Horse is too intelligent to punish me for the sins of my race. One of his best

friends over the years is a white scout called Frank Grouard—
I don't think I have anything to fear.''

"I have already asked Crazy Horse. He suggested that you
come after we told him that you have been living in the town
you call Deadwood," Kills Hungry Bear told Fox as they
walked toward the huge council tipi. "He hopes that you can
give us help to decide how to get your people to leave *Paha
Sapa*."

Fox said nothing, although privately he wished the solution were that easy. Crazy Horse knew better, too. Overhead,
the moon was full and bright, casting its glow over the countless tipis in the shadow of Bear Butte. Suddenly Fox was
reminded of another night not so very long ago when he had
been called out of a tent to attend a council meeting. A chill
prickled the back of his neck as memories returned to him
of the officers gathered in George Armstrong Custer's bivouac, and of Custer himself, his hair tamed by cinnamon oil
and his sunburned face and short beard set off by a scarlet
cravat.

I didn't belong with them; I shouldn't have been there, Fox
thought now as he looked down at his soft buckskin trousers
and the moccasins Kills Hungry Bear had given him this
morning. They were nearing the council tipi; raised voices
clashed in the night air. *But if I don't belong with the whites
can I claim to be one of these people? Would I adopt the
identity of the Lakota and risk my life for their sakes?*

He was spared having to answer the question as He Dog
appeared beside the two men and led the way into the large
council tipi.

It was warm inside the council tipi and the air was heavy
with the scents of woodsmoke, tobacco, and the sweet grass
and herbs that were placed in the fire as a sort of incense.
As the Pipe Ceremony came to an end and all the men were
silent, searching their hearts for words of truth, Fox felt almost disembodied. Dreamily he took in the wonderful, vivid
scene; a scene that was nearly extinct now, or at least con-

ducted more for ritual among the agency Indians than for any functional purpose. The agency Indians had little say in their destiny, but these men here tonight clung proudly to their ability to make decisions about the future; it was a key aspect of Lakota life. The tribal consciousness that guided the course of their society and behavior was the reason they could live together so harmoniously: the council made decisions for the entire village, and those superceded the wishes of the individual.

Fox thought disparagingly of the chaos that reigned among the greedy, lawless whites in places like Deadwood. How foolish they were to imagine that they were more civilized than these men who filled Crazy Horse's council tipi.

"I saw them," Crazy Horse said at last, his tone even. His face, weary yet alert, was set in an expression of forced concentration. "I try not to let fury overcome me when I think of them, digging in the hillsides of *Paha Sapa* like greedy, tireless prairie dogs. I stood high above them on the top of the canyon and saw how they have cut down the trees and turned the forest to a swamp with their waste. It is desecration. I wanted to snuff them all out. I wished I were a prairie fire and they were field mice. . . ." His black eyes met Fox's for an instant before he added, "But the truth is this: they are the fire and we are the mice. Is this not so, Fox-With-Blue-Eyes?"

Fox felt light-headed as countless heads turned in his direction. Smoke stung his eyes while conflicting emotions stung his heart. "I—I am only one man. I don't have enough knowledge to offer an opinion that important."

"Are you not among us as a friend?" Crazy Horse pressed.

"Yes."

"He has brought us many rifles," He Dog told his childhood friend, "in case the bluecoats attack our village."

"I do not want to sit here, like rabbits who have grown tired and frightened after being hunted for a long time by dogs, and wait for the bluecoats to strike our village." His voice grew stronger. "Have we not just won a magnificent victory? They thought that we were beaten and that they need only ride into our land and round us up and kill us like so many of their docile long-horned spotted buffalo, but they misjudged us. They misjudged us!''

The ''spotted buffalo'' so.scornfully referred to by Crazy Horse—and looked upon as objects of ridicule among the Indians in general—were, Fox knew, the cows whites had introduced to the Lakota people as an alternate source of meat. Cattle were the source of an unpleasant odor, they maintained, and it was thought that their meat must be impure, a pale imitation offering from the white man.

Once again Fox felt a twinge of uneasiness, recognizing his tendency to straddle the two worlds, white and Lakota. And as he absorbed the atmosphere in the council tipi, his uncertainty grew. No matter how welcome they made him feel, he couldn't forget that just a few short weeks ago he had hunted these very warriors with the Seventh Cavalry led by George Armstrong Custer. He was also a citizen of Deadwood, one of the white people Crazy Horse wished he could snuff out like so many bothersome, invasive prairie dogs. Now he glanced down at his bare arm, comparing it with that of his friend Kills Hungry Bear. One was tan, the other deep mahogany: the two men were as different as the buffalo and the cow. Why pretend otherwise?

He Dog was speaking. In the respectful atmosphere of the council tipi, the warriors took turns, listening attentively to one another's opinions before settling on the direction tribal consciousness would take.

''My friend,'' He Dog said, looking at Crazy Horse, ''you must see that it is pointless for you to make more raids into *Paha Sapa*. The bluecoats have been shamed by our victory over Long Hair and his men. They are searching for reasons to retaliate against us. If you strike at them without cause, it will be one more excuse for them to break the Laramie Treaty completely and openly take *Paha Sapa* from us. They will say we did not deserve to have such valuable land. They will say that we are savages—''

Crazy Horse's body tensed and his black eyes blazed. In

a breach of etiquette, he spoke when He Dog paused to take breath. "I cannot live according to what the white man will think or the tricks he will play! When I give my word, it is done, but the whites know nothing of this! Their words are all lies and tricks. Would you have me try to think like they do even if it means betraying everything I believe is right?" Rage and frustration nearly overcame Crazy Horse's usually dignified manner. "I *know* more about the ways of the whites than I like. I have already studied them in order to triumph over them in battle." His tone dropped to one of calm finality. "I will not muddy our ways with thoughts of theirs. I can only do what is right, what I have seen in the real world."

"But, what of the safety of the people in this village?" He Dog persisted. When Crazy Horse received this in silence, his friend's broad face grew stormier. "You are past the foolish years of the wild young warrior! You belong to the people now and must think of them, not giving them such uneasiness!"

Others spoke, their voices blurring in Fox's mind. He could see, and he knew that the others could see, that Crazy Horse would not change the course he had charted. He would fight to the death for what he believed to be right for the Lakota people.

Maddie was awakened by a deafening crack of thunder. Raindrops were pelting the covering of the tipi and the steady, musical sound was immediately reassuring.

The storm, which had been threatening all evening, had arrived at last. It felt like the middle of the night, but Maddie remembered that she had curled up to sleep early, waiting for Fox, thinking just to rest for a bit. Where could he be?

Thunder boomed again, sounding as if it were rolling across the prairie, perhaps destined to collide with Bear Butte in an explosion of silvery light. The rain beat harder on the tipi; droplets found their way past the smoke flap at the dwelling's apex, sizzling as they plopped into the molten embers of that night's fire.

Maddie shivered, drawing her buffalo robe up to her chin.

She felt more lost and alone than at any other moment since she had stolen away aboard Fox's wagon the night he'd left Deadwood. As a little girl she'd been scared of storms, and childhood didn't seem so far away at the moment.

My mother wouldn't know me, she thought tearfully. Then she laughed. *Never mind Mama . . . I don't know me!* At length, as she listened to the rushing of the rain and the mournful wail of the wind and the aching thud of her own heartbeat, Maddie found her way back to sleep.

When Fox ducked into the tipi, his hair and beard dripping, he was mesmerized by the sight of Maddie asleep beneath the buffalo robe. Even Crazy Horse had noticed the bright-haired white woman traveling with Fox-With-Blue-Eyes, and had mentioned her to him when they had a moment alone at the end of the council. The name Crazy Horse used was new to Fox, however, who was uncertain whether it had been coined by the great warrior or repeated to him by someone else in the village. Whatever the source, it was perfect for Maddie, especially as she lay with her hair splayed over the buffalo robes, framing her delicate face and echoing the color of the embers.

"Fireblossom," he whispered, tasting the name tenderly.

Tonight, "Madeleine Avery" seemed as distant as "Daniel Matthews." Even the mere intrusion of his Christian name made Fox burn inside. He began to tear off his wet clothing, fighting the frustration in his gut that festered and poisoned him, demanding resolution.

Fox went to Maddie like a drowning man to shore. His body was damp, shivering, tense. Naked, he drew her against him and inhaled the wildflower scent of her luxuriant hair. She wore one of his shirts; Fox ripped it from her, embracing her totally.

Maddie's first sense of panic was swept aside by the tidal wave of Fox's need and her own yearning response. Her arms clasped his shoulders and back, but she was so slight against him that she seemed insubstantial. One of his hands cupped her bottom, drawing her fully against the hot steel of his manhood. Maddie ached as she strained to meld with Fox; her breasts swelled and her rib cage arched to make a hollow where her tummy usually curved softly. Every ounce of her was taut and eager.

Fox ran his other hand down the length of Maddie's slim, tantalizing form. Her flesh was like priceless ivory, pale and glowing against his dark, rugged body. She was smooth, her symmetry broken only by the rosy-gold curls between her legs and the pink crests of her nipples. True, there were freckles sprinkled here and there, but in the burnished light it appeared that Maddie's throat and cheeks and thighs, and the curve of each shoulder and breast, were all dusted with fire sparks. Fox thought that she was the most extravagantly lovely woman he'd ever seen.

"Fireblossom . . ." Whimsy and rich passion infected his voice, and before Maddie could question the endearment, he was kissing her and she sank giddily into a sea of sensual pleasure. He grew more ravenous by the second, and she met him kiss for kiss, ravishing his delicious mouth with equal hunger.

Maddie did not notice when Fox's lovemaking crossed the invisible danger line. At first, the edge of roughness in his touch thrilled her and allowed her to vent her own pent-up ardor. Their ragged breathing mingled with the slashing gusts of wind and rain outside the tipi. Maddie was flushed, digging her nails into Fox's back as they kissed and touched and their need for consummation grew. Then, Fox's hand twined in her mane of marmalade hair until he held it, wound around his fist like a rope. Maddie couldn't move her head and that made her try harder. That's when the first splinter of alarm pricked her. Fox's kiss felt . . . out of control somehow, his driving need no longer in synch with hers. Her first protest was muffled by his hard male mouth. She was confused; still aroused, still wanting and loving him, yet aware that something was wrong.

He was lying on top of her now; Maddie was pinned like a butterfly. Anger rose in her, anger and outrage, but in her heart she also understood that something was breaking inside

Fox and the outcome might depend on how she handled this situation. She had been trying to wedge her hands under his chest to push him away, but now she stopped. Fox lifted his head, and for a moment their eyes met.

In the depths of Maddie's emerald eyes, gleaming with bittersweet love, resolve, and tenderness, Fox clearly saw his own reflection. For weeks he'd felt blurred, his identity riddled with uncertainty and guilt. He'd been a stranger to himself, but now, in the eyes of this woman, he saw a familiar person. There was no going back; Fox had been changed forever by that day at Little Bighorn and its aftermath, but he was still whole, still valuable. Maddie loved him, and that meant a great deal.

The weight of Fox's body lifted slightly and Maddie could breathe again. The hand that had gripped her hair now caressed it. Tender kisses aroused the hidden places at the back of her neck, in the hollow of her throat, her inner arms, her breasts, her temples. When at last he met her gaze once again, she saw that his eyes were agleam with tears.

"Oh, Fox . . ." she breathed, and put her hand up to his bearded jaw.

Later, in the afterglow of slow, sweet lovemaking, Maddie moved her cheek against the crisp hair on his chest and blinked back the tears that stung her own eyes. How could she convince him to share his problem with her? That whatever tormented him could be defused and banished if he would only speak the words? She felt closer to him now, closer than ever, yet there were huge barriers in their way— barriers that only Fox could breach. Maddie could help him, but only if he let her inside.

"Maddie?" Fox's voice was hoarse under the drumbeat of the rain. At least the thunder and lightning had stopped and the wind had died down.

She rose on an elbow and studied him, lying on his back on the bed of furs. Flickering shadows from the last of the fire played over his chiseled face, and although he appeared relaxed, Maddie could feel the tension in his body. Was he going to confide in her at last?

Smiling, she traced the edge of his sun-bleached beard with her fingertips. "You called?"

He gave her a perfunctory smile that failed to erase the pain in his eyes. "I have to tell you . . ."

"Yes?" Maddie leaned nearer, all her love focused on him.

"I'm not sure what possessed me earlier, when I was so . . . forceful. If I ever treat you like that again, or even yell at you, my advice is to walk away from me and never come back." Fox cupped her chin, thinking that he didn't deserve her devotion and patience. "I've never mistreated a woman before, though, so I think I can safely promise that it'll never happen again."

Maddie was disappointed. Instead of sharing his feelings, his problems, *himself*, Fox was discussing his behavior, keeping her at arm's length . . . still. "Oh, don't worry about me, Fox," she said at last, with a jaunty smile. "I'm not helpless! I may be a lot littler than you, but I'm resourceful. I would find some way to incapacitate you!"

He chuckled, rubbing his eyes. "I'll bet you would. Well, now that I've got that off my chest, I feel like I could shut my eyes and be dead asleep. I'd forgotten that those councils go on for hours and hours, smoking, talking, and smoking and talking some more." He yawned. "Let's go to sleep, shall we, Fireblossom?"

"And what's this 'Fireblossom' all about?" Maddie demanded, with a playful shake of his shoulder.

He opened one eye. "It seems to be your Lakota name. Not every day they have a red-haired woman in their midst! Now come on and lie down here. It's almost dawn."

Snuggling into the crook of his arm, Maddie fidgeted, her eyes open wide. "Fox?"

"What?"

"Aren't we ever going to talk about the real truth?"

He tensed slightly. "You mean Sun Smile?"

"No, that's not what I mean," she said, with a pang of guilt as she realized how little she had thought of Sun Smile that evening. "I know that you'll let me know as soon as there is word of her, and I understand that these things take time." She took a deep breath. "I'm talking about your secret. The shadow that haunts you. It's what causes your moods, you know, including the one that made you act that way earlier. You can't keep running away from whatever it is, Fox. You have to face this, and—"

His eyes opened and he fixed Maddie with a clear, ocean blue stare that caused her to stop speaking in midbreath. "I know," Fox said plainly.

She gulped, shocked. "You *do*?"

"I'm not as obtuse as I pretend to be, sweet. I know everything you've just said and more. And, if you can be patient for a little while longer, I think I'm just a few steps away from doing battle with my demons." Smiling at the look of joy on her face, Fox closed his eyes again and added, "But first I need my rest. Lie down, woman!"

Grinning broadly, she complied.

Chapter Nineteen

August 8–9, 1876

THE MORNING WAS MAGICAL. FOX ROSE EARLY, IN spite of his protestations about his need for sleep. He whispered to Maddie that he was going with Kills Hungry Bear to swim and maybe hunt a bit on the other side of Bear Butte. Eyes closed, she gave him a sleepy kiss and went back to her dreams.

Among the Lakota, it was customary for a tribal elder to go to each tipi at dawn and call *"Co-o-o!"* to let the people know that it was time to start the day. When the village was on the move, everyone was especially prompt, but at times like these it was less imperative to obey the caller. Maddie heard the call twice outside her tipi door and still she dozed, smiling to herself, thinking about the name Fox had called her. Fireblossom. It was so beautiful that she was afraid to hope the Lakota could have really given her such a lovely gift.

Eventually Strong came to the tipi and called to her new friend. "Fireblossom? Are you sick?"

Maddie scrambled up and threw back the tipi flap. "It's true, then! I have a new name!"

Strong smiled. "Do you like it?"

"It's the most wonderful name I have ever heard in my life!"

"Your hair is much admired. The people could not resist giving you a name that honors your hair and your fair face and form. It is said that you are very pretty, like a flower, and your hair is like a new blossom. That is the best way I can explain it.'' Suddenly she looked worried. "I was afraid that you might wish for a name that celebrated your spirit. You are not offended?''

"Of course not! I never dreamed that I could be accepted enough by your people to even earn a name. I treasure it. I am honored.''

Strong nodded politely, then fell silent. It was clear that she did not understand why Maddie was still inside past dawn, but good manners kept her from inquiring directly. "There are new strawberries growing along the banks of the stream,'' she volunteered. "It is unusual to have more of them in these hot days. The women have just noticed them now that they are red, after the rain. We are going to pick them.''

"If I hurry and dress, may I come?''

"Why do you think I am here?'' Strong teased. "Do not hurry, there is no need. The berries are for all of us to share.''

As she struggled into a chemise and drew a frayed gown of red calico over her head, Maddie inquired, "What is your word for strawberries?''

"Wazusteca," Strong replied. She was fascinated by the sight of her friend trying to dress unassisted.

"Waz-us-te-ca,'' Maddie repeated carefully. "That's pretty.''

"Uh . . .'' Strong hesitated. "Do you ever think that your clothes are . . .''

"Foolish?'' Maddie supplied cheerfully. "When I lived in a city and everyone dressed like this, I didn't think about it, but it became harder and harder to get into my gowns after we came West. I don't know why they are made so that a woman cannot dress herself. Will you help me?'' She turned her back and gazed beseechingly over one shoulder. Strong obliged, staring at the fastenings with an expression of bewilderment—truly only a white person could have made something so impractical and silly! Maddie added fuel to the fire by spinning a hilarious description of a corset, the white woman's self-induced torture to lace that undergarment ever tighter, and ended with a brief account of that ultimate frivolity: silk stockings. By the time she'd finished, Strong had the back of Maddie's gown closed and both women were breathless with laughter.

"At least I have these now," Maddie said as she reached for the moccasins Kills Hungry Bear had brought as a gift. "I'll never be able to squeeze my feet into high-heeled, pointy-toed leather slippers again!"

"You are very happy today," Strong observed as she ducked to emerge from the tipi.

"It is a wonderful day!" She lifted her face to the morning sunshine and immediately beheld a truly spectacular rainbow. Its pure colors appeared to be overlaid by a golden haze and it arched from the western horizon backward to disappear behind Bear Butte. "Look! It's a rainbow!" With childish enthusiasm, Maddie lifted her hand to point.

"No!" cried Strong. She pulled her friend's arm down before Maddie had time to extend her finger. "You must not!"

"What do you mean? I wasn't doing anything wrong!" Stung and surprised, she felt an urge to pull her hand free and point again.

"That is a *wikmunke*," Strong scolded. "It means 'trap.' The *wikmunke* circles the earth and holds it. The Great Spirit has painted it in the sky to trap the rain and bring it back to us."

"That's very charming," Maddie replied a trifle sulkily. For the first time, she wondered how intelligent people could actually believe such nonsense. Many of their stories explaining the existence of various animals or facets of the world were like fables—entertaining yet far too simplistic for anyone with real knowledge to believe. She gave Strong a patronizing glance. "And why, pray tell, can't I point at your precious rain trap?"

"Because my people believe that it is dangerous. The *wikmunke* is so powerful that, if you point at it, your fingertip might be made sore and swollen."

When she saw that Strong was completely in earnest, Maddie was ashamed of her condescending attitude. Even if the Lakota explanations were childlike, they were more entertaining than the lessons she had been taught as a child. They knew as much as they needed to in order to carry on their idyllic way of life . . . but how would they fare if they were forced into the white world?

The very thought sent a shiver of foreboding down Maddie's back.

Gazing up at one side of Bear Butte and a portion of a rainbow's arc, Fox gave thanks for his life. Cool, sweet water held his body suspended, caressing his naked flesh. He lifted one arm, brought a plum to his mouth, and took half of it in one bite. Juice drizzled into his beard, then into the water. Fox thought he felt a fish brush his buttocks, but he was too relaxed to flinch. Instead he smiled, squinted, and wondered how far Kills Hungry Bear had drifted.

"I would like it," a voice murmured to him from a short distance downstream, "if time could stop and my life could stay just as it is now."

"You don't mean that, Kills Hungry Bear," Fox replied, amused and content. "There are too many pleasures you would miss if you spent your lifetime drifting on your back in the water."

There was a long silence. A breeze blew over their wet bodies and the mood shifted. "Perhaps. I know, too, that I must face the challenges that lie ahead, but it is hard to feel brave, as I do before even a terrible battle, when I can see so clearly into . . . what is your word?"

"The future?"

"Yes." Kills Hungry Bear had paddled gently toward Fox and now he reached out to touch his friend's cheek. "I know you can see the future, too, and that is why you refuse to answer Crazy Horse's questions."

"If I thought that anything I know would help the Lakota people, I would fill his mind with my knowledge," Fox said, "but I do not know the bluecoats' plans, and what I can guess would only sadden Crazy Horse and your people more. It's hard enough to see all that has changed since I last lived among you. So much has been lost—''

Kills Hungry Bear stood up abruptly. The water reached his chest and he pushed his way through it back to shore, saying, "You may find these changes sad, but agency life would be much sadder! It is''—he looked back at Fox, eyes flashing as he groped for a word—*"pathetic."*

The two men sat together on the bank, dappled with sunlight that filtered through the leaves of the great cottonwood trees. They remained unclothed, their hair wet. Fox's hair curled a little at the base of his neck as it dried; Kills Hungry Bear's hair streamed down his dark back like ink.

"I remember your body turned red from too much sun when you first came to us," Kills Hungry Bear said, with a grin. "It seems a long time ago. We were very young."

"You more so than I." He noticed that his friend was observing not only his lighter skin, but also the hair on his chest, arms, and legs. Kills Hungry Bear would never say so, but Fox knew there was a measure of repugnance mixed with his curiosity. Like the "spotted buffalo," a man who had body hair was considered undesirable and unclean compared with the Lakota men, whose skin was smooth. They sniffed and made jokes about the hairy whites with their unkempt beards and matted chest hair who went for days without washing. The Lakota people bathed daily, even when they had to break ice to have a plunge at the start of their day. Zachary Matthews had told Fox about the habits of the Indians, so when he'd traveled West the first time, he had been clean-shaven. Now, if he were not determined to separate his new self from Matthews, clean-shaven special adviser to Custer's doomed Seventh Cavalry, he would dispense with the beard again, if only to mesh more easily with his Lakota hosts.

"Crazy Horse has returned to *Paha Sapa*," Kills Hungry Bear said at last. On the opposite bank of the stream, a jackrabbit paused to nibble a tasty clump of leaves. "Touch-The-Clouds came to the village while we slept and he went with Crazy Horse to see the town where the white men burrow into the hillsides. Short Bull and Black Fox also went, but He Dog refused.''

"I would like to see Touch-The-Clouds again," Fox said, with a nostalgic smile, as he conjured up memories of the seven-foot-tall war chief of the Miniconjou band of the Lakotas. His impressive size and dignity inspired fear, but Fox had discovered that he was a fine human being. "It's good to know that such old friends are still with Crazy Horse."

Kills Hungry Bear shrugged. "Many chiefs are not. Some have been blinded by the white people's promises. Some are jealous of Crazy Horse. I am afraid that he might be killed by his own people as easily as yours." Pausing just long enough to turn his upper body toward Fox and fix him with a level stare, he said, "I am weary of this talk about other people and of problems that cause us pain because we have no power to solve them. Instead, let us talk about *you*, Fox-With-Blue-Eyes."

Fox felt as if the wind had been knocked out of him. He tried to smile casually but succeeded only in avoiding his friend's penetrating eyes. "What do you want to know?"

"Ah, I see that my sense was true! Ever since you and Fireblossom came to our village, I have felt a shadow hovering over you, even when you are laughing and acting like the friend I used to know. There is something wrong."

Even as panic swept over him, Fox felt an answering swell of relief in his heart. Still, the words wouldn't come. His secret was the kind that made him a traitor to everyone; neither white nor Lakota could forgive him.

When Fox didn't reply, Kills Hungry Bear said gently, "Perhaps I will understand better if you tell me how you came to the town you call Deadwood?''

Fox sighed harshly, then shook his head. "I won't lie to you, my friend, and I cannot tell you the truth."

"I am happy to hear that you respect me enough not to deceive me. And, it's respect for yourself." He sat in silence and pondered the situation for a few moments before adding, "My father told me the same thing before I went to sleep, every night that he was in our tipi. He said, 'A Lakota may lie once, but after that no one will believe him.' I used to think that my father thought of this wisdom alone, but I later discovered that all good Lakota fathers repeated that to their sons!'' Kills Hungry Bear chuckled softly at the memory.

Lulled by the atmosphere of affectionate conviviality, Fox declared, ''Amazing! *My* father said that to *me* about a thousand times during my boyhood, but instead of 'Lakota' he just said 'man.' '' He laughed, remembering.

Kills Hungry Bear patted Fox's sun-warmed back. ''I suppose that they were wise men, our fathers, to recognize the importance of that lesson.'' Now he fixed his eyes again on Fox's face and continued, ''Do you know that other Lakota saying, *Wowicake he iyotan wowa sake*?''

Slowly, with the sound of his heart pounding in his ears, Fox translated, ''Truth is power.'' He lay back in the lush grass bordering the stream. ''I know the truth *is* power, but somehow it seems that my case must be different. You said a moment ago that respect for myself is one reason I won't lie to you, but I have the kind of secret that has tormented me so much that I'm not sure I do respect myself anymore.''

''The secret is keeping you like a prisoner,'' Kills Hungry Bear decided. ''The truth will destroy it and then you'll be free.''

Fox opened one blue eye and arched the brow above it. ''I wish it were that simple.''

''It can be, my friend.'' He gave him a maddeningly serene smile. ''Wait. I'll get my pipe and we'll smoke. Then you should have some answers.''

Fox closed his eyes again. ''My mind is filled with questions but never any answers.'' He lay in silence, listening to the sounds of Kills Hungry Bear preparing the pipe and making sparks to ignite the dry tobacco. As the fragrant smoke wafted down to him, Fox propped himself up reluctantly and reiterated, ''It's not going to be this simple.'' His tone was stubborn. ''You people think that the pipe can solve any problem, but if all I needed was tobacco I'd've fixed this mess I'm in long ago!''

Kills Hungry Bear held out the pipe. "You know that you are speaking nonsense. Tobacco won't provide the solutions, Fox-With-Blue-Eyes. Everything that you need to know is already inside your heart. You need only believe in yourself, trust yourself, and let the Great Spirit guide you."

Fox's chest hurt; he felt raw inside, but as he took the pipe tears of hope sprang to his eyes.

Watching with satisfaction as his friend began to smoke, Kills Hungry Bear couldn't resist murmuring, "Listen to the voice within you. If a man is to do something more than human, he must have more than human power. . . ."

It wasn't simple, but Fox struggled onward. Kills Hungry Bear counseled his friend to pray for a dream that would lead him to freedom. Perhaps it would be necessary to pray and fast for several days. Although Fox responded to that suggestion with a skeptical glance, it appealed to a part of him—the part, nurtured over the years by Annie Sunday, that viewed suffering as a way to atone for his sins. The adult man preferred to regard the coming hours as an opportunity to wrestle with the events that had caused him so much guilt, a chance to discover a way to make peace with himself. Couldn't there be a logical solution? For all his admiration for the Lakota culture, there were some beliefs that he just couldn't swallow. The notion that dreams took one into the "real world," for instance, seemed as farfetched as the idea that the three-quarter moon that hung in the sky that night had assumed that shape "because someone took a bite out of it!" as one of the Lakota men had cheerfully remarked.

Tonight, sitting alone under this three-quarter moon on the other side of Bear Butte, Fox found his thoughts careening down a familiar blind alley. *I don't belong in either world. I've been too well educated in the white world to adapt to the Lakotas, and I've been too enlightened by the Indians to respect my own race.* He rubbed his temples. This was ground he'd covered countless times, and each attempt to conquer the maze only increased his frustration. Perhaps it was time to try Kills Hungry Bear's method.

What do I have to lose?

At the edge of the stream, Fox stripped off his clothes, folded them, and waded out into the nearly still water, glimmering silver and black in the starlight.

I'm scared, he thought, and the realization gave him some relief. *Scared of what? Myself? Maybe. The truth? Time to get some real courage. Spirit courage, not that posturing and recklessness stupid men call courage.*

Fox took a deep breath and sank into the water, acutely conscious of each sensation as the liquid, cool and pure as night, rippled outward from his body. He stretched out on his back, fighting the urge to tense up, gradually relaxing. At length the upper part of his body floated above the surface of the water. Toes, knees, hipbones, penis, sculpted belly and chest, chin, nose, and forehead all floated. Fox saw himself becoming lighter and lighter until even unlikely places, like his ankles, shins, elbows, throat, and temples, floated. His thick hair swirled gently behind his head, caressing his nape and shoulders when he tilted his neck back a bit.

The more he relaxed, the more magical he felt. He lay thus, floating on the stream, floating into himself, for an unmeasurable portion of time. He told himself to stop fighting. Eventually the urge and even the thought of struggling left him. When at last he opened his eyes, he looked up through a frame of lacy black cottonwood leaves to view the sky. The profusion of white stars, sizzling across the heavens, was wondrous. It was as if he beheld a miracle, performed tonight for the first time. A tear trickled down Fox's cheek and melted into the cool water.

It came to him then. He could almost see the hand reaching down toward him. All he had to do was accept it. He thought of Annie Sunday, who was always so certain about life and God. Sometimes, as a young adult, her unwavering certainty about what was right annoyed him, but he had to admit that her ideas made sense and her own life seemed to bear out her wisdom.

God will never desert you, she would say. *He waits patiently, even when you believe you don't need help from anyone. But come the day your back's against the wall, God's grace will intervene. You just have to humble yourself,* Annie Sunday would explain. *When you get there, you'll know it, and then you'll* really *be a man.*

Funny . . . Kills Hungry Bear had said almost the same thing. Perhaps Annie Sunday and Crazy Horse reached the same destination when they prayed. . . .

A wave of sheer, joyous peace rolled soothingly through Fox's body. Closing his eyes, he slowly lifted one hand to the starry sky. He continued to float. In a clear internal voice he prayed, *God, please help me. Direct me toward the answers that will bring me peace. Help me, with Your grace, to discover the wisdom in my own heart. Please lift me with Your strength.*

As if pulled by an unseen hand, Fox came out of the water. With a calm sense of purpose, he dressed and began the long walk back to the village.

"You are changed," Kills Hungry Bear said approvingly. "It is good." Then, holding back the flap opening the tipi where he was staying, he pronounced the traditional Lakota welcome: *"Hohane,* Fox-With-Blue-Eyes."

Entering, Fox saw that Kills Hungry Bear's woman and dog slept together on one side of the tipi. The fire looked fresh; it appeared that Kills Hungry Bear had not slept, preferring instead to wait in case his friend returned to the village in search of him.

"I am glad to find you awake," Fox said.

"I could not close my eyes at such a time. Come. Let us sit and smoke. Then I have something to give you that I made tonight." He led the way to the back of the tipi, took the host's seat, and gestured to Fox to sit on his right, facing east. "I hope that you will tell me then what has happened. I can see in your eyes that the story of your adventure will be important."

Fox's grin flashed white in the amber light of the tipi. He

was eager to share everything with Kills Hungry Bear, but his sense of peace gave him patience. They smoked together for a long time; neither felt sleepy. Then Kills Hungry Bear laid the pipe aside and reached behind his bed for one of the soft buckskin bags that held his possessions. From it he plucked a narrow necklace.

Holding it out to Fox, he said proudly, "I wanted to give you a present that I made for you, in honor of our brotherhood and the journey you have taken this night under the moon." The necklace was just long enough to encircle Fox's neck, and it consisted of tiny blue beads with a thin, sharp tooth marking the halfway point. "I searched and traded here in the village until I gathered enough beads of this color. This seems close to the color of your eyes. And *this*"—Kills Hungry Bear pointed to the tooth in the center—"is the tooth of a fox! I have been saving it for a long time, thinking of you whenever I took it out of the little pouch where I keep special things."

Fox was very moved. He looked into the dark eyes of his friend and said in a tone weighted with meaning, "I will wear this gift always. I am very grateful." He held the beads in his hand for a minute, admiring the care and thought that had gone into Kills Hungry Bear's present. He saw that the beads and the polished tooth had been strung on a narrow strand of buffalo sinew. There were inches of plain sinew at each end and he lifted those and tied them together at the back of his neck. "A perfect fit."

"Yes!" Kills Hungry Bear searched in his bag and produced a mirror, acquired long ago in trading with white men.

Fox stared at his reflection. The tooth nestled in the hair that curled past the hollow of his throat and the blue beads did indeed echo and accentuate the color of his eyes. It was more than an attractive gift; it was symbolic and would enable him to carry a mark of his Lakota experience with him into the white world. "I am very fortunate to count you as a friend, Kills Hungry Bear."

"I hope that you will share your story with me, but only a part of it. Some things cannot be explained. Those feelings belong to you alone.'' He lit the pipe again and drew on it as they both reclined against the pillows behind them.

"The Great Spirit, that I call God, has taken the shadow from my heart,'' Fox said. As he spoke the words, he felt lighter still. "I knew the things that you said to me at dawn. I remember hearing the same wisdom from my own mother. What came to me tonight to lift the weight from me was the understanding that I cannot let others tell me what is right and what is wrong. I must listen to the voice in my own soul, follow it, and not waver.'' He accepted the pipe, smoked for a moment, then added, "This has become difficult for me because of my ties to my own race's culture and the bonds I also have to the Lakota people.''

"Ah.'' Kills Hungry Bear nodded as comprehension dawned. "You have felt caught between these separate loyalties?''

"More than you know.'' Fox's eyes began to burn. "Caught to the point of feeling unbearable pain and guilt no matter which way I turned. Tonight, though, when I opened myself and asked God for guidance, I saw that I do not have to choose. I can do what I feel is right in my own heart as I confront situations that arise.''

"I believe this, too,'' Kills Hungry Bear replied seriously. "It is not you who is wrong because your loyalties are confused, it is fate! You love your race, but some of the things other whites do make you angry. How hard this must be for you, my friend!''

"I've tortured myself long enough trying to make sense out of a world I didn't make. I cannot subscribe completely to either side, so I must carve out my own road.'' He paused. "I realize, too, that it is fruitless to brood over the past. I followed my conscience, unable to see what lay ahead, and because of the actions of others I have spent untold hours regretting my own part in the matter. If I could have looked into the future, I might have acted differently, but only God has that power.''

"I do not know what experience you regret, but I do know

that you have found wisdom tonight. Did you see something when this dream came to you?''

Fox knew that Indian men treasured the visions that accompanied their dream-journeys. "I—well, yes . . . I saw stars. Powerful stars.''

Delighted, Kills Hungry Bear exclaimed, "This is an important day, my friend! I think that you should have a new Lakota name to mark the dream that has changed you. When you came among us before, we named you like we are named as children—for the way you looked. But when Lakota boys make the dreams that carry them into manhood, they take new names.''

"Crazy Horse was Curly as a boy, wasn't he?''

He nodded emphatically. "I think you shall have a new name, too. You shall be Star Dreamer.''

Fox felt a jolt of pleasure. "I like that very much. I would be proud to have such a name.'' Then he felt the old, familiar pang of his torment deep within him as he remembered a certain day in late June. He knew now that it was time to reveal his guilty secret, to unburden himself.

"Star Dreamer,'' Kills Hungry Bear murmured in a satisfied tone. He smoked a bit, smiling, then repeated, "Star Dreamer! It is a fine name. Tomorrow we will feast and dance to celebrate the new beginning for Star Dreamer and the end of the worries you have been carrying.''

"Wait.'' Fox held up his hand as Kills Hungry Bear tried to pass him the pipe. "There is more. I must tell you a secret. I only hope that when you hear it, you will not kill me.''

"Never!'' his friend scoffed.

"I . . .'' Fox took a deep, burning breath and started again. "On the day when the Lakota and Cheyenne fought Long Hair and his bluecoats on the banks of the Greasy Grass River . . .''

Kills Hungry Bear scowled. "Yes? What about it?''

"I was there, too. I rode with Custer!''

Chapter Twenty

"YOU ARE MAKING A JEST!" KILLS HUNGRY BEAR shouted, then lowered his voice when his woman stirred and opened her eyes. "I must tell you, Star Dreamer, that I do not laugh about this."

"It's not a joke; it's the truth." Fox suddenly felt incredibly tired.

"Do you forget that I was there as well?" the other man hissed angrily. "If you were with Long Hair, you would not need to worry that I would kill you tonight because you would have died with Long Hair. The bluecoats shamed themselves, begging for mercy, but we killed every man! We made *certain* they were dead."

The flat tone of Kills Hungry Bear's voice sent a shiver down Fox's spine. The hideous tales of mutilations performed by the Indians on the dead soldiers rose up unbidden in his memory. His mouth was dry when he spoke again. "That day has been the main reason for the shadow in my heart. I should explain . . . that I was only riding with the Seventh Cavalry because President Grant—the Great White Father—asked me to go, to watch Long Hair, because he didn't trust him. I went because I thought I might be able to talk sense to Custer if he appeared to be on the verge of doing something crazy to the Lakota people." Fox flicked up a brow as he spoke. "Well, I was idealistic and stupid. Custer has never been known to listen to reason or err on the side of caution, and my discussions with him led to arguments. You can't imagine how I felt when it became clear that Custer was going to go ahead and lead the cavalry into battle against your people.''

Kills Hungry Bear continued to scowl. ''I am listening. Be quick.''

''When Custer and I quarreled for the last time, not long before the attack began, he became so angry at me that he ordered me to leave—not return to the camp, but *leave*. I was a constant source of aggravation to him. And I admit that, in spite of my opinion of the situation, riding away made me feel awful.'' Fox had been speaking in a harsh, almost angry tone, but now his voice was choked with emotion. ''I had been a hero in America's war to free the Negro slaves—a warrior for *my* people—so to ride away that day before a battle was hard. I felt uneasy. I traveled to Deadwood, weeks passed, and then I heard that every single one of those men who followed Custer had been *killed*. The guilt began to eat me alive. I blamed myself for not finding the right words to convince Custer not to attack.'' Fox paused. ''I have never agreed with any of my country's policies regarding the Indians, and I felt even more so about that particular battle. I'd met Crazy Horse. I knew there might be friends of mine fighting beside him . . . and I thought that your cause was just . . .'' He rubbed his eyes again. ''I'm exhausted. Talking in circles.''

Slowly the furrow relaxed in Kills Hungry Bear's brow. He sighed. ''It took great courage for you to tell me this story, Star Dreamer.''

''I had to,'' Fox said plainly.

''Yes. I understand much better now. You have truly been torn apart in spirit, but now the mending is begun. I thank you for leaving the bluecoats that day.'' A grim smile flickered over his lips. ''I would have been very sorry to kill you.''

''I would have been sorry to die . . . but the guilt has almost been worse. If only I could go back and change the words I spoke to Custer. I should not have allowed myself to become so angry—''

"But you cannot go back; none of us can! Everyone has regrets sometimes—but how could you know what would happen to those soldiers? My friend, you did what you could to change the outcome," Kills Hungry Bear argued. "Isn't that what your dream taught you—that a true human being charts his own course rather than follow a misguided flock? You whites have no war council, where all the warriors can speak about the coming battle. Long Hair listened to no one, and his men had no choice but to obey. There is no *wouncage*, no tribal consciousness, for the bluecoats. I pity them!" He waved a hand as if to indicate that there was no reason for them to waste any more time on this conversation. "I do not think that anything you could have said would have changed Long Hair's mind, do you? And if you had not ridden away from the Greasy Grass River, joining the bluecoats in battle instead, the story would not be different—except that one more white would be dead. You!"

"That's a good point," Fox said dryly. "And, of course, I wouldn't really change my decision that day. That's what I healed tonight when I understood that I could not change what the army did. I followed my own conscience, which seems to follow a road that winds somewhere between the Lakota world and that of my own race." He leaned forward. "What I am doing now is releasing the secret. Has it changed your respect for me?"

Kills Hungry Bear shrugged and rolled his eyes. "After hearing the entire story, I understand . . . but I do not think you should 'release the secret' too freely in this village. There are angry warriors here who would not care for the idea of sheltering a survivor from the battle with Long Hair here in Crazy Horse's own camp!"

They shared a smile over the irony of the situation. "You speak wisdom as usual, Kills Hungry Bear," Fox said. "I thank you for your care, your words, the beads, and my splendid new name. But now . . . I find that I am so, so tired . . ."

Kills Hungry Bear watched with affection as Star Dreamer yawned and put his head back to rest. He mumbled some words about leaving, then slumber overtook him and he began to snore.

Fox was still slightly blinded by the midday sunshine as he headed toward the place where the stream wound nearest the village. There, in the shade of the cottonwoods and enjoying a fine cushion of grass, the women did the work that occupied them most of their waking hours. Later, when the sun blazed hotter and the women and children had taken baths in the stream, the village would rest. Not yet, though.

Fox stood a short distance from the busy scene and looked for Maddie's distinctive gown. Most of the Lakota women were refining hides that had already been scraped clean by rubbing them with sandstones to make them softer, and softer still. Another group filled pale skins with fresh water from the stream, wading in partway. Finally Fox's eyes fell on a circle that included a few women and many children. In the middle was a big carved bowl full of strawberries. A young boy was pouring what appeared to be sugar from a coarse bag over the berries. Squeals of pleasure nearly drowned out the voices of all the women, who conversed contentedly as they worked.

"Star Dreamer."

Fox pivoted in surprise and saw the girl who was Kills Hungry Bear's companion in the absence of his wife. What was she called? He realized he didn't know. How had she learned of this new name of his, a name that was only a few hours old? Fox felt uncertain, so he merely smiled and greeted her deferentially.

"You do not know me," she said, her nostrils flaring a bit. "I am called Runs Away. Are you looking for your woman, the one with the fire hair?"

"I am glad to know you, Runs Away," Fox replied as he tried to decide if she liked him, and if not, why.

"I will take you to Fireblossom, but first I hope that you

will tell me . . . why you say to Kills Hungry Bear that he should not marry me.''

Taken aback, he blinked. ''I have not said this to him, Runs Away.'' Fox saw by the way she set her mouth that she didn't believe him so he added softly, ''I give you my word. But you know that Kills Hungry Bear already has a wife, don't you? You know that his family waits for him at the agency?''

Her eyes flashed like a midnight storm. ''There is room in his tipi for more than one wife. I am not afraid of fighting!''

Fox glanced over her and reflected, in the detached yet carnal way of males, that Runs Away was undoubtedly a wildcat in bed. She wasn't kind or gentle, but no doubt she offered Kills Hungry Bear something that his beloved Little Dove did not. The only problem was that Runs Away wouldn't be happy about being scorned. Fox said, ''I can assure you that Kills Hungry Bear has not sought my advice about this.''

''He would listen to you,'' she said pointedly.

Squinting as a ray of sun emerged between the leaves overhead, Fox replied, with a touch of impatience, ''I would not interfere. I am sorry. Now, if you will take me to Fireblossom . . .''

''She's over there,'' Runs Away snapped, then stalked off in the opposite direction, toward the village.

Although he had an uneasy feeling about what had just happened, Fox's mind was overflowing with thoughts about his own life, and about Maddie. Runs Away had directed him toward the crowd that ringed the bowl of strawberries, but he still couldn't see anything except women garbed in buckskin dresses and moccasins. Then, as he drew nearer, one of the children moved just enough for him to glimpse a mane of marmalade hair. Yet this woman appeared to be Lakota. She wore a pretty dress of doeskin, fringed and beaded, and seemed to be in charge of the gathering. Even as Fox reached forward, past the excited little boys, to touch the kneeling woman's shoulder, she was speaking a lilting phrase of the Lakota language. A baby girl came toddling toward her, plump cheeks smeared with berries and sugar, one hand outstretched to receive another treat.

"Hun-hun-he!" the woman said, laughing, as the baby toppled into her lap.

Fox realized that she hadn't noticed his touch in the midst of all the activity. He saw Maddie's friend, Strong, watching him from across the circle. She looked amused. Feeling slightly annoyed, Fox bent down and once more tapped the woman's shoulder.

Time seemed to slow her movements as she turned and looked up simultaneously. The silky, curling, dawn-colored hair swirled out to make a graceful frame for Maddie's glowing face.

Fox knew that his mouth was open, but he felt frozen. Before he could react, Maddie had jumped up, hugged him, and pirouetted with her pale arms outstretched. "What do you think?" she exclaimed. "Isn't it gorgeous? I feel so much *better* now that I'm dressed properly. I mean, I know that I'm still out of place with this hair of mine, but ever since Strong gave me this beautiful dress, I've sensed a change in the way the other women treat me." She ran her hands over it admiringly, then looked straight into Fox's eyes with an irresistible grin. "Don't you think it's flattering, too? I feel so *free*—so unrestricted! Well? What do you think? Honestly, Fox, if you don't approve . . ."

Managing finally to close his mouth, Fox shook his head and laughed. "Madeleine Avery, you are the prettiest little Fireblossom this side of Sioux City! Is that better?"

Maddie pulled him by the hand until they were nearly hidden by a giant cottonwood tree, then threw her arms around his neck. "Are you certain?" she coaxed.

"Completely." Captivated, Fox lifted her off the ground in his arms, wound his fingers through her long curls, and then kissed her. Maddie's mouth was ambrosia, opening to welcome him while she squirmed happily in his embrace. At length he lifted his head and observed, "You feel damned good in that dress. I don't miss all that underwear of yours a bit.''

She giggled. "Neither do I!" Then her features softened and she caressed his neatly trimmed beard. "I've *missed* you."

His brows flew up in disbelief. "Looks to me like you've been busier than a prairie dog these past couple days. You've worked a lot harder to fit in here than you ever did in Deadwood, and a lot of people never would've believed you could manage this. At least in Deadwood you could get by speaking English, living in a house, wearing the gowns you brought from Philadelphia, eating the same kind of—"

"Boring," Maddie interrupted gaily. She had opened her mouth to continue when something caught her eye around the back of their cottonwood tree. Standing on tiptoe in her soft moccasins, she drew Fox's head down and whispered, "Do you remember the young woman I told you about who never bathes and rarely speaks? There she is, sitting in the grass under that far tree, watching everyone else eat strawberries. Her eyes are so sad. I want to speak to her, but I confess that I'm a little frightened."

Fox leaned around the tree and looked at the woman who sat alone a few yards away. She wasn't very old, but her appearance confirmed his guess that she was in mourning. Maddie was right: under ragged garments, matted hair, and dirt-and-ash-smeared skin, the girl was pretty. Now, as if feeling his thoughts, she lifted her chin and stared directly into his eyes. Even from a distance, her gaze was haunting.

Fox stepped back behind the tree, oddly shaken. "I—I'm sure she's in mourning. There are other widows in the village, but my guess is that this one is more visible and disturbing because she's so young." He paused, thinking. "She reminds me of a beautiful bird that was struck down unexpectedly. She's lost someone she loved deeply, and her dreams died, too."

Maddie seized this theme. "Yes! She reminds me of a bird whose wings have been broken!"

He wrapped an arm around her and kissed the top of her head. "You're developing a very tender heart, sweet."

"Won't you ask Kills Hungry Bear about her?" she begged. "Perhaps there's something we can do to help her."

"Yes, I'll ask him. In the meantime, let's take a walk, just the two of us. I need to talk to you about something important."

Maddie fell into step beside him as he strolled away from the group of women and the village. A deep, abiding happiness surged up inside her. For nearly two days she had kept as busy as possible, trying to keep her mind off Fox, wondering what he was doing and how he'd be changed when he returned. When he'd told her before he left that he was on the verge of banishing his demons, Maddie had sensed that the gulf between them was narrowing at last. He was coming closer and closer to the place where she waited for him . . . and now she felt a little shy and nervous.

"Do you have news of my sister?"

Fox looked over to see that her cheeks were pink, her eyes shining through the veil of her lashes. Beguiled, he managed to reply, "I mean to look into the matter this very day. I've been a little . . . distracted. I apologize." He squeezed her hand. "Do you mind if we talk about me first?"

Maddie discovered that they were all alone. The village was tiny in the distance; she hadn't realized how far they had walked. The grass that grew along the stream bank was lush and the two of them sat down in it and faced each other. It was as if there were an aura surrounding Fox that hurt her eyes. "Is this going to change us?" she murmured.

His handsome face was grave. "Maddie, I'm ready to tell you that secret. Do you still want to hear it?"

Burnished pastel light heralded an especially glorious sunset. Maddie lay beside Fox in the deep grass. She felt sore inside, her heart aching, her eyes swollen from crying.

"How in heaven's name could you have kept so much hidden for so long?" she queried.

"I didn't see that I had a choice."

"Now, you must tell me *everything*."

He was exhausted. "I have!" The story had taken an eternity—the gaps in his past he'd never filled for her, the details of his dilemma at Little Bighorn, the guilt-soaked weeks he'd spent in Deadwood, and, finally, a careful account of the last few hours he'd spent with Kills Hungry Bear, then making a new beginning in the cool, starlit stream.

"You men! You think you've given a complete explanation when you serve up a lot of bones with no meat on them!" Maddie sat up, animated again. "I can't tell you how angry it makes me to think about Custer, forcing all those men to follow him on his quest for glory. You were the only one with any sense, Fox! You did the right thing rather than blindly obeying like some kind of—sheep!"

"Well, there's truth in that—female truth." He smiled wryly. "The fact is that soldiers have to obey. That's how they're trained. Wars couldn't be won if each man decided to question his superior officer. No doubt there were others among the Seventh Cavalry who had reservations about our policy, but arguing with Custer wouldn't have changed anything."

"But you spoke up! You voiced your doubts that night in Custer's bivouac!"

"Yes, but he didn't have the power of God over my future. I explained, didn't I, that I went only as an adviser, and the commissioned title I took was a formality? I was there in Grant's service, not Custer's. Also, I didn't share the other men's loyalty to the Seventh Cavalry. I'd been with them only a few weeks before the battle." Fox leaned up on an elbow and looked into Maddie's eyes. "The other soldiers had spent a long, long time enduring hardships on the western frontier. They'd grown accustomed to looking at the world through Custer's eyes. The abnormal had become normal to them . . . but I was too fresh from Washington, too long out of the army, and too exposed to the *true* story of the Indians, to fall so readily into formation." He ran a hand through his sun-streaked hair and added, "Custer knew it, too. He saw that I had another agenda—when we were on the train together from Washington. That's why he was so defensive whenever I challenged him. You know, I sensed that I was wading into a mire when I acceded to the president's wishes. I knew I'd encounter a lot of moral conflicts, but my mother argued that they'd be there whether I went or not. She felt I was hiding my head in the sand by staying out of the mess we were making with the Indians. She said I might be able to do something to help, to shed light on the truth, if I took a chance and joined the Seventh Cavalry.'' Fox's gaze softened as he recalled his mother's words. ''Annie Sunday is a rabid idealist, very brave and confident. Like most of her theories, this one sounded unimpeachable when it came out of her mouth—but became less workable the farther West I got. It's really a shame that the Indians couldn't have enlisted my mother to speak for them in Washington. No one would dare break a promise to Annie Sunday.''

''Isn't her last name Matthews?''

''Strictly speaking, yes . . . but she's never been good at living in the shadow of a man.'' His tone was warm, affectionate.

Maddie was beginning to adjust to the revelations of the afternoon and now she realized how little she had really known about Fox. ''I always knew that you were hiding something . . . I mean, I could never get a straight answer out of you about your full name, for heaven's sake! But now, listening to you talk about your mother, and piecing together what little you've told me so far about yourself . . . well, it's as if I'm meeting you all over again. You even *talk* differently now! Before, you spoke like an educated man from time to time, but—''

''I'm good at talkin' like a frontiersman, ma'am,'' he agreed. ''Can't go around saying words like 'unimpeachable' and 'agenda' or folks'll look atcha funny. Wouldn't want anyone to get the wrong idea an' think I'm a dude like that fancy friend of yours from the Boston Scofields!''

She cuffed him in mock outrage, and Fox caught her hand and held it, kissing the sensitive surface of her palm. ''Gra-

ham was *not* my friend! If he thought that he was, it was
only because you encouraged him, Mr. Daniel Matthews!''

"Star Dreamer to you, Fireblossom.'' Chuckling, Fox
drew her down until she lay on top of him, happily ensnared
in his embrace. "Oh, Maddie, I've been afraid for so long.''
He kissed her, then kissed her again. "The secrets begat
more secrets, until I felt like a stranger even to myself. A
fraud.''

"And now?''

He grinned. "It's as if I've been let out of jail. I didn't
understand it before, but I needed to come here and be with
the Lakota people, the same ones who killed Custer and all
those soldiers, in order for me to finally sort through it all.''
Maddie's silken tresses rippled downward, making a curtain
about their heads. Tenderly Fox caressed her cheek, fingers
feathering over the alabaster softness of her throat . . . "I
feel a thousand pounds lighter. There's light ahead of me
instead of darkness. I can live with myself.''

Tears sprang to her eyes. "Oh, Fox . . . now, if we can
find Sun Smile, everything will be *perfect*!''

"You sound like my mother, tying all the loose ends into
a pretty bow. I agree on one score: you and I have both
learned a lot about ourselves in the few days since we've
come to Bear Butte.'' He sighed. "I know now that the line
dividing human beings isn't that clear-cut. I can't be all white,
blazing my way through the West with the rest of my race,
but neither can I turn my back on my heritage and live as an
Indian.''

"We'll sort it all out after we go back to Deadwood,'' she
replied firmly. "The first thing you can do is assume your
true identity.''

Maddie had been pressing herself against him, kissing his
ear, so it took Fox a moment to realize what she'd said. When
he did, he rolled her over into the grass so that he was looking
down at her. Seeing her face, winsome with its dusting of
freckles and big, beautiful green eyes, he was struck again
by the power of his attraction to her, his need *for* her—all of

her. He didn't understand it, but it was there, spellbinding and insistent. With an effort, he forced himself to speak.

"I just want to say one more thing, Madness, now—before I lose myself in your eyes. . . . I can't be Daniel Matthews after we go back to Deadwood. I may feel brave again, but I'm not stupid. Confiding in Kills Hungry Bear and in you doesn't qualify this secret for public consumption, sweet. We can't tell anyone else."

She was shocked, confused. "What? Why not?"

Fox gave a short bark of ironic laughter. "Have you forgotten the public's view of the massacre, as they call it, at Little Bighorn? If *I* berated myself for riding away from the Seventh before they met their doom, what do you think everyone else would think of me? I'd be a pariah in Deadwood or anywhere else I went for the rest of my life!" Fox scowled, his mood darkening to one that was more familiar to them both. "I'd be notorious. The only survivor of the infamous bloody massacre!"

"But, Fox . . ." Horrified, Maddie tried to think. "If everyone who was with Custer died, how would anyone know that you were at Little Bighorn? Lots of people in Deadwood are lying low. No one would be suspicious if you took back your full name and became more open and respectable, if"— she blushed charmingly—"if it was obvious that you were in love."

"Ah." He gave a sage nod. "I see. Deliver me from any more of these neat little female maps for my future! How anxious you are to civilize me, to believe that true love and marriage will suddenly erase the events of that day from my past."

"I didn't mention marriage," she protested hotly. "Let me up!"

Fox complied and sent her an uncompromising stare. "You didn't have to. But that's not the issue. Far from it, in fact. You have conveniently forgotten, Madeleine, that the Seventh Cavalry was divided into three separate battalions that day, just minutes before I rode away over the hill. All of *Custer*'s men were killed, but most of the others survived.

Because Reno and Benteen's battalions fought on the other side of the hill from Custer, people tend to forget about them." He ran a hand over his eyes, wearily. "I cannot."

Maddie's heart seemed to be caught in a vise. "You mean . . . that some of those other soldiers might have seen you ride away before the battle? And some of them could point a finger at you if they heard Dan Matthews was living in Deadwood?"

"Only Custer and I know what really happened—that I left because he ordered me to—and Custer's not here to back me up. The rest of the men don't know what was said, and it's not hard to guess what they thought when they saw me ride away from them, in the opposite direction of the camp. If one of them met me in Deadwood, I wouldn't stand a chance. I'd make a convenient scapegoat."

Her frustration with him melted away, replaced by surging love and a tug of despair. Maddie hitched up her doeskin skirt and crawled onto his lap. "Oh, Fox, why does life have to be so difficult?"

"Damned if I know." He bent his head to kiss the pulse points on her throat. "Lucky for us, there are distractions. . . ."

Chapter Twenty-one

August 10, 1876

"YOU MUST SAMPLE THE *WASNA* RUNS AWAY HAS made," said Kills Hungry Bear. He unwrapped a skin made from tripe to display the chokecherry-meat-grease hash that the Lakota considered a delicacy. "She worked very hard to have a good supply for our celebration last night in honor of your dream and name, but then she became shy and kept it hidden. She feared that her *wasna* was not as tempting or delicious as that made by some of the other women." Kills Hungry Bear shrugged slightly and whispered, "Do not repeat this, Star Dreamer, but I think Runs Away might be right. She is not as good a cook as my wife, Little Dove. I do not like the idea of living at the agency, but I miss my family. I hope that the dangers will pass and she will not be afraid to come to me." He watched as Fox, yawning, tasted the hash. "I talk too much. Too much excitement and not enough sleep these past days."

Fox nodded agreement. He could barely swallow Runs Away's *wasna* and hoped that his friend wouldn't expect him to eat any more. "I, too, am tired, but the dancing and feasting last night made many warm memories. I am grateful to the people for giving me such a fine celebration."

"Fireblossom was very fetching in her new clothes," Kills Hungry Bear observed. "She enjoyed herself?"

"Very much. . . ." Fox fell silent as his friend sampled the *wasna*; he waited to see what the reaction would be.

"Hmm . . ." Kills Hungry Bear chewed slowly, nodded, chewed, nodded, wrinkled his brow, puckered his lips, then finally cried out, "Bleh! Ugh!" He spit the bite into his hand, stared at it accusingly, then turned his shocked stare on Fox. "How could *you* swallow that—that *offal*? I always thought that you were a person of refined tastes, but—"

"Now, stop right there!" Outraged and amused, Fox protested, "I felt as you did, old friend, but I didn't want to offend you by suggesting that Runs Away cannot cook!"

"Why not?" Kills Hungry Bear queried mildly. "She is not my wife."

Laughing, Fox fell back on the buffalo robes and looked up through the smoke hole at the patch of blue sky high above. "Ah . . . I sometimes think I could stay here forever. It's a nice dream."

"You whites always want to be Indians after you see how well we live. You are one the people could accept, and I would like it if you stayed, but I know it is not what you really want. You are ready to put all the pieces of your life together. Is this not so?" Kills Hungry Bear used a quilled tamping stick to prepare his pipe for smoking. "If I were to say all that I think, I would tell you that I sense you are more than ready to do these things. You are making plans to leave our village and return to the town you call Deadwood."

"Yes." Fox watched the fragrant smoke swirl upward and wreath Kills Hungry Bear's face.

They were silent for a moment, then the Lakota warrior passed the pipe to his friend. "You have noticed a young girl in mourning? A sad sight. Her clothes are torn, she has slashed her arms and legs and rubbed ashes in the cuts, and her hair is ungroomed." He shook his head. "She was once the most beautiful maiden among all the Teton Lakota band. She had sparkling eyes the color of a goshawk and long, shining, sweet-smelling hair and a smile that made strong men weak."

"Do you know, I have promised Maddie—Fireblossom— to ask you about that very woman. Fireblossom feels tender toward her. She wonders if there is something she could do to cheer the girl."

Kills Hungry Bear shrugged. "She is not meant to be

cheerful. She is in mourning. She loved her husband very much and it is right that she show her grief.''

Exhaling smoke, Fox wondered why his friend had suddenly started talking about the young widow. There had to be a reason. ''Her husband must have been a good man,'' Fox ventured, testing the waters.

He rearranged the eagle feathers on the back of his head, eyes averted. ''Yes. Yes, he was. He was my brother, Aiming Fast.''

Odd, Fox mused, that he should feel guilty for Aiming Fast's death when he hadn't even fought on the side of the bluecoats. ''Aiming Fast was lucky to have such a wife, and such a brother.''

''I have to take care of her now; she has no parents here.''

Fox narrowed his blue eyes and tried to read his friend's expression through the haze of smoke. ''Is there a problem?'' Why was Kills Hungry Bear telling him all this? Where were they going with this talk?

''A problem,'' the other man repeated. ''Maybe. I am not sure I know what is best for this girl. She has many gifts and much to offer in life, but she has sunk into a pit of gloom since Aiming Fast died. She rarely speaks . . . and I am not the best person to help her carry on with life. This will sound mean-spirited, but part of me likes to see her moaning and weeping, hurting for her lost husband. It honors him.''

''Are you looking for advice from me?'' Fox finally asked straight out, tired of playing the waiting game so integral to the Lakota way of life.

Kills Hungry Bear met his eyes in surprise. ''No. I have been thinking about this matter ever since you and Fireblossom came to our village.'' He paused. ''Ever since you told me that Fireblossom is the daughter of Stephen Avery.''

Fox held his breath.

''I have not spoken to you about Stephen Avery since that night,'' Kills Hungry Bear went on in a rush, ''because I guessed why you had come to us. I needed time to think. I have reached a decision.''

''Yes?''

"I hope that you will take my brother's widow with you when you leave for Deadwood. She will wither away if she remains here among our people. I dreamed last night that Aiming Fast was sitting here with me in this tipi and asked me to help his wife to find a new life. He says that he still loves her even though they are in different worlds. He says that she is too young, too special, to die of grief."

"Aiming Fast is more talkative in death than I remember him in life," Fox muttered under his breath.

"What did you say?"

"Nothing of importance. I'm just trying to make sense of all this." He stared hard at his friend. "There is more, isn't there?"

Kills Hungry Bear stared down at his pipe and nodded slowly. "Yes, Star Dreamer, there is more. My brother's widow is called Sun Smile. The man you call Stephen Avery is her father." He sighed. "I believe that *Wakan Tanka*, the Great Spirit, sent you to bring Sun Smile to her other family."

Fox managed a feeble smile. "Well . . . this is . . . So, that's Sun Smile. Maddie will be so . . . *surprised*!" He stood up, suddenly stifled by the warm, smoky air in the tipi. "I'd better tell her right away. She'll be anxious to meet her sister." Fox ducked under the door flap, nearly colliding with Runs Away as he hurried out.

"You have been eating the *wasna* I made," she called after him.

He paused in midstride, turned to offer her an appreciative smile. "Yes! Thank you, it was . . . unforgettable. Now, if you'll excuse me . . ."

"Wait, Star Dreamer! Please, tell me, did you speak to Kills Hungry Bear?"

"Yes, I spoke to him."

"You told him that he should make me his wife?" Her voice rose with excitement.

Fox shook his head. "No, Runs Away, I did not. And I will not. Now, the matter is closed—I do not wish to speak

of it again!'' And with that, he started for the tipi he shared
with Maddie on the other side of the circle.

Watching Fox stride off, Runs Away had bad feelings in
her heart. ''You should not have treated me that way, Star
Dreamer,'' she muttered. ''You and Fireblossom both think
that you are favored because you are white. But you bleed
when you are cut just as my people do. . . .''

Before Fox broke the news to Maddie, he took her back
to the spot in the deep grass, well out of sight and earshot of
the village. It was important that she be able to vent her
feelings, as she had the day before when they had discussed
his secrets.

''How can this be true?'' she cried after Fox had repeated
everything Kills Hungry Bear had said. ''I didn't expect—''

''I know, sweet.'' He watched her pacing furiously in the
tall grass, his heart aching for her.

''I don't mean to sound selfish or hard-hearted, but I hoped
that I might find a sister I could learn to love!'' Tears crept
into her voice. ''There would be all sorts of problems to
bridge even if Sun Smile had been—you know, *normal*! Even
if she were someone like Strong, it would have been hard to
take her back to Deadwood and expect her to fit into that
world, but this . . . just . . . seems . . .'' Maddie had begun
to sob. ''It seems crazy! That woman is like an animal. She
doesn't talk, she wails to herself, she's dirty and refuses to
bathe. . . . I mean, how can we do it, Fox?'' Tears of frustration spilled down her cheeks.

''How can we not? Sun Smile *is* your sister, Maddie.''

She pressed both hands to her face, angry with herself. ''I
know! I know she is! Oh, Fox, I think that maybe I knew
deep inside when I saw her the first night we were here.''
Biting her lip hard, she said, ''Even though she looked like
a mad savage, when our eyes met I had this eerie sense of
recognition.'' Her chin trembled. ''She has Father's eyes! I
don't have his eyes, but *she* does!''

''Maddie, you have to calm down. This isn't the end of
the world.'' He reached for her, and she let him hold her for

a minute before jerking away. "Just because Sun Smile appears to be unreachable now, that doesn't mean she'll stay that way. She's mourning. But Kills Hungry Bear says that she was a lovely girl, bright and beautiful and cheerful."

"Do you really imagine that she'll come back to herself if we take her to Deadwood—to a completely alien world?" Maddie's doubts grew as she spoke. "I don't think so! She'll probably crouch in a corner and—and throw things at my family and—"

"Maddie, stop this." Fox was firm. "Remember your father. This was his wish. Kills Hungry Bear says that it will probably be best for Sun Smile, given the situation the Lakotas face out here now. They're considered hostiles. The army could attack and kill your sister if we leave her here!" He caught Maddie's hands and squeezed them. "If it doesn't work out, we'll take her to the agency. Is that fair enough?"

"I don't seem to have much choice, do I?" she replied. Her cheeks were flushed with the force of her disappointment. "I'll feel more like I'm returning with a wolf than a sister."

With that, Fox tumbled her into the grass and lay down on top of her, grinning. "Why is it that I feel like laughing when I'm near you, even when you're in a foul temper?" His beard tickled her as he kissed her ear and the tender spots along her hairline. "You'll feel better soon. You just need a little time to adjust to this situation."

"I—Oh! Suppose so . . ." When Fox held her thus, loving her and making her feel cherished, Maddie's fears and doubts seemed to vaporize. There was no room in her heart for anything except pure, bursting love. At moments like these, as she caressed his curling hair and thrilled to the sensations of his mouth, Maddie felt so happy, so lucky, that she was sure she could surmount any obstacle.

It was agreed that it would be best for Maddie to meet her sister through Strong. There were long-standing Lakota traditions governing the interchanges between male and female relatives, and these customs kept Kills Hungry Bear from speaking directly to his sister-in-law unless he had no alternative. Fox explained all of this to Maddie while Strong waited outside their tipi. Maddie threw up her hands at the senselessness of such conventions, but secretly, beneath her froth of complaints, she was relieved that Strong would be the one to bring her together with Sun Smile. There was enough to be nervous about without the intimidating presence of Kills Hungry Bear.

Fumbling in her carpetbag, she drew out a piece of velvet with something wrapped inside. She clutched it in her hand as a child might.

Fox was curious, but he didn't ask her what it was. The excitement and fear that she felt were plain to see in the flush of her cheeks and the little furrow in her brow. Clearly, despite Maddie's reservations about Sun Smile's appearance and demeanor, she cared more than she could admit.

"Well . . ." She paused before him, kneeling gracefully on the buffalo robes. "Wish me luck."

"It's just another door, sweet. Go on in."

Touched by the tenderness in Fox's eyes, she kissed him and put her fingertips on the azure beads and fox's tooth that encircled his strong neck. "Sometimes I feel as if all of this is a dream. How can I be here with you like this? How can all these things be happening to us?"

"Never mind how, Fireblossom. Just accept that they are. Now off with you!" Chuckling, Fox patted her doeskin-clad bottom, then turned his attention to raising the nearby edge of the tipi cover nearby to let air in. It was a warm day, and the approaching afternoon promised to be hot. The breeze felt good and Fox lay back and closed his eyes. Soon enough they'd begin the journey home and these halcyon interludes would be ended forever.

The women had mixed green wood into the fires to make more smoke and keep the mosquitoes at bay. The scent of that smoke mingled with the other life smells that Maddie had gradually become accustomed to since arriving among the Lakota people. Today, as the women continued to cook food that would keep for the days when the village was on the move, there were the smells of boiling meat and fat dripping onto the coals. The warm breeze also carried the scent of human waste from the tall grass behind a row of willow trees, and of the huge pony herd that remained near the village while grazing on the luxuriant prairie grass. Someone had been brewing coffee, sent as a gift by Stephen Avery, and Maddie's now skillful nose picked up a clear minty scent as she and Strong neared the stream. Looking around, she saw the light blooms of marsh hedge nettle that had opened since yesterday. It was lovely how all these life smells harmonized: the smells of the land, the animals, and these people who were careful to honor the gifts of nature.

On the edge of the trees, where the light was best, Strong and Maddie encountered Woman's Dress. The *wintke* was seated on a log, painting the outline of a sandhill crane on a rawhide canvas secured to a willow frame. Woman's Dress smiled a greeting to the two women before returning to his painting. Nearby, Crazy Horse's wife, Black Shawl, stood in the shade of a cottonwood tree and fed pieces of a juicy prickly pear to old One Moccasin. Strong explained that One Moccasin had been in ill health since being hurt by a grizzly bear and was known to faint sometimes in the heat.

Children were splashing in the stream or simply floating, too hot to play. Even the village dogs lay quietly in patches of shade. It was in that setting that Strong and Maddie eventually found Sun Smile, propped listlessly against a tree and surrounded by several dozing dogs.

Maddie hung back, beset by fresh doubts, but Strong took her wrist and drew her forward. The dogs reluctantly were roused, moving just enough to clear space around Sun Smile.

"She's filthy," Maddie whispered to Strong when she was close enough to realize that it was her half-sister whom she smelled rather than the animals.

The older woman gave her a sharp look. "Sun Smile knows many words in your language," she warned.

Studying Sun Smile, Maddie found that hard to believe. In fact, the animals were more responsive than this matted, glassy-eyed, squalid creature. Dismayed, Maddie realized that the pity she had felt previously toward Sun Smile had been transformed into horror once she'd discovered that they were sisters. When Strong knelt beside the young widow, smiling, and spoke soothingly in Lakota, Maddie could only think, *This wasn't the way this adventure was supposed to turn out! How can I take this mad savage home to Father?*

Sun Smile finally looked at Strong, focusing with an expression of acute pain, then she turned her face away and began to moan softly to herself.

"What did you say to her?" Maddie asked. "Is she acting that way because she doesn't want anything to do with me?"

"I have told her that she suffers too much, that Aiming Fast would not want her to torment herself this way. I said that it is time for her to reenter life." Seeing the anxiety in Maddie's expression, Strong added, "I will tell her now about you, just a little, then you can speak to her and I will try to say your words in Lakota so that we are certain she understands."

Maddie's heart raced as she watched her friend take Sun Smile's dirty hand and murmur a few gentle sentences. Then there was silence. Sun Smile stared into space, unmoving, for a full minute. Strong waited; Maddie held her breath. Slowly the widow shifted and then looked at Strong, who nodded to confirm the words she had spoken.

Madeleine was unprepared for the wave of emotion that swept over her when Sun Smile turned her face up and looked at her. Again she was unnerved, seeing her father's eyes staring out at her in the very foreign face of a Lakota woman.

For an instant Sun Smile's beautiful gray eyes betrayed intelligence and sensitivity and wonder; then they went blank again. Maddie didn't know what to do. Nothing in her past had prepared her for such a situation. She was wishing she could mumble something polite and run away when Strong suddenly reached out, took her hand, and placed it in Sun Smile's grimy fingers.

"Sisters," Strong said, with a nod of finality, and then she spoke to Sun Smile in their language.

"What are you telling her now?" Maddie inquired, alarmed. "I really wish that you would let me know what you are going to say so that I can decide if you really ought to say it. I mean, you know . . ." Hot color crept up her face.

"You may wish that you could change what is real, but you cannot, Fireblossom. I have only spoken the truth to your sister. I think that she knows of your father. Yellow Bird was the kind of woman who told the truth, and we always knew that Sun Smile was a little different. Whiter." Strong paused, letting her words sink in, then added, "So, I am telling her the name of the father you both share."

Maddie heard her father's name leap out of the singsong Lakota words Strong spoke, and she heard her own voice echoing, "Stephen Avery. Our father." Again there was that brief, keen look from Sun Smile, like a shaft of sunlight breaking through storm clouds, and it heightened Maddie's skittish excitement. Part of her didn't want to feel this way, or to care at all. This smelly, ragged girl was nothing like her fantasy sister. But the past few weeks had changed her. No longer could she deny her true nature, suppress her impulses and emotions for the sake of propriety.

She took out the piece of velvet, unfolded it, and withdrew a golden locket. "This was my mother's," she explained in a trembling voice. Sun Smile had looked away again, trying no doubt to return to her own world, but Maddie was resolute. Fingers shaking, she opened the locket. "Sun Smile, please look. This is Stephen Avery. This is our father."

Sun Smile inched away, staring at the bark of the cottonwood tree instead of the daguerreotype. It had been made years ago, probably about the time Sun Smile had been born, and it showed a pale, solemn, handsome young man with curling dark hair, a stiff white collar, and luminous gray eyes.

"Tell her to look!" Maddie cried to Strong. "Tell her that this is our father!"

Strong obeyed, murmuring to the young widow, but Sun Smile hunched over farther, as if to protect herself. Maddie was outraged. "You ought to be proud to have Papa as your father!" she declared, leaning closer, pushing the open locket in front of Sun Smile's face.

For just an instant the woman's haunted eyes touched their near reflection in the miniature, then she struck at it with the back of her dirty hand. "No!" It was impossible to tell whether she meant to speak the English word or was merely emitting a grunt of protest.

Maddie jumped to her feet, her eyes stinging with tears. "I wish I hadn't promised Father," she said to Strong, "but I did, and now I have to honor that promise. Tell Sun Smile that she will be coming with me when I leave for Deadwood. I will be taking her to meet her father whether she likes it or not, and she doesn't have any choice about it! Kills Hungry Bear *wants* her to go!" Clutching the locket to her heart, Madeleine started to march away, then tossed back a parting shot: "I think Kills Hungry Bear is glad for an excuse to be rid of his brother's wife, and I don't blame him!"

Strong sighed, watching as Maddie strode away. Meanwhile, Sun Smile stared into the distance, glassy-eyed and moaning softly to herself, as if unaware of anyone or anything. At last Strong left her, heading back to the village.

When Sun Smile saw that she was alone, she reached down and plucked something from the powdery dirt under one of the dog's tails. It was the scrap of velvet that had protected the locket.

Sun Smile gazed at the precious cloth for a long while. Finally she leaned back against the tree trunk, rubbing the velvet against her cheek while tears slowly gathered in her beautiful gray eyes.

* * *

"Good-byes are easier among the Lakota people," Fox explained to Maddie as he finished packing the wagon, "because you don't have to say them. Everyone understands that it's time for us to go and it would be considered rude to beg us to stay longer."

Maddie was nervous as she peeked out the back of the wagon. Without the crates of guns and supplies, there was much more room. She had created a cozy place for Sun Smile and decided that she would sit in front with Fox all the way back to Deadwood. "I feel all mixed up now. I've been happy, but I, too, know that it's time to return to our real home. I wish it weren't so impossible to blend the two worlds. I wish I didn't have to go back to wearing corsets and petticoats—back to saying and doing things I don't mean because they're expected of me."

Fox lifted her down and ran a hand up and down her slim back comfortingly. "I know; it's hard, once you've tasted this simpler way of life, to go back. But, we have to, Miz Fireblossom. We're *white*!"

She laughed in spite of herself, then pressed her face against his shirtfront. "Oh, Fox, what about Sun Smile?"

"What about her?" He was careful to keep his tone even and reasonable. "We're taking her back to meet your father, just as he asked. We succeeded in our quest; not only did we find Sun Smile, it's working out that she can return to Deadwood with us. In fact, I'd venture to say that we're helping her in the bargain. Sun Smile doesn't really belong with Crazy Horse's band at the moment. She needs to be sheltered until she recovers from her grief."

"Do you believe that's possible?" Maddie was ashamed of the hateful note that crept into her voice. "I have my doubts."

"Give her time," Fox advised. "Just be patient, Madness."

There wasn't time for further discussion. Watson was prancing around, delighted to be embarking on another journey, and Maddie suggested that Fox exercise the roan while she guided the mule-drawn wagon.

At last, when everything was on board except Sun Smile, she appeared from the tipi she shared with other members of her dead husband's family, holding a buckskin bag and looking lost and frightened. Strong took her arm and led her over to the wagon. Maddie hung back as her friend explained to Sun Smile that she would be safe and well cared for. Then, Fox and Kills Hungry Bear showed her the little nest that would be hers during the journey to Deadwood. Sun Smile sat down on the quilts, dirty and smelly and yet graceful in her movements. She fixed her eyes on her lap and remained thus, frozen, as various friends and relatives reached into the back of the wagon to wish her well.

Runs Away declined to speak to the departing trio, but she watched with narrowed eyes. Strong let Maddie embrace her and thank her for her friendship, but they did not say good-bye.

"Do not fight the will of the Great Spirit," Strong told her, looking into Maddie's green eyes. "You have many blessings. Be grateful for them, and be careful. Others will be envious of your good fortune."

Maddie wasn't certain what those cryptic words meant, but she stored them away in her memory. So many feelings churned inside her as she looked back at the picturesque village and thought of all she had learned and what this place and these people had come to mean to her. One thought, sharp as a dagger, kept recurring: *This life is nearly past for all Indians. Even now, these people are clinging to the end of the dream. . . .*

It hurt too much to realize that there could be no victory for Crazy Horse's followers. Soon, they would have to surrender to life on the agency.

Nearby, Kills Hungry Bear was admitting this same fact to Fox. "I don't know if I can do it, when the time comes," he said in a low voice. "Can I live behind a fence and pretend that cattle are buffalo? It sounds very tedious."

Fox looked over to see that the wagon was ready and Maddie was perched on the high seat, holding the reins. He could offer no words of consolation to Kills Hungry Bear or any of the other people here; they all knew it. Instead he swung onto Watson's back, touched the fox's tooth at the base of his neck, and smiled.

"*H'g un, kola.* Keep up courage, my friend. I will never forget, and if you have need of me, call and I will come."

They started on their way then, slowly moving south from Bear Butte, Crazy Horse's birthplace, toward the Thieves' Road that George Armstrong Custer had made into the Black Hills.

Watson was overjoyed to be loose again and he galloped merrily ahead of the wagon with Fox giving him free rein. The sky was robin's-egg blue and dotted with whipped-cream clouds while the prairie spread out around the tiny travelers, a sea of golden green grass. Maddie watched Fox and Watson run in the sunshine, but she felt none of their pleasure. Her mules seemed to crawl toward the distant Hills and the silence was oppressive.

From time to time she glanced back into the wagon, where her half-sister sat facing the other way. She was glad that Sun Smile couldn't see her because she wouldn't have known what to say or do.

It was bittersweet to wish that life could imitate dreams. Maddie longed for more from Fox, and she had imagined that Sun Smile would be very different from the way she was.

But, Maddie decided, perhaps she didn't have to relinquish her dreams. Who could say what the future held?

PART FOUR

He fumbles at your spirit,
    As players at the keys
Before they drop full music on;
    He stuns you by degrees . . .
            —Emily Dickinson (1830–1886)

Chapter Twenty-two

THE FRONT DOOR BANGED, THEN BANGED AGAIN as the wind caught it and slapped it backward against the house. Stephen Avery, still as pale as his pillows, winced slightly.

"I have asked your son repeatedly to take one additional moment to *close* the door securely on his way in and out of the house," said Annie Sunday Matthews from her chair beside Stephen's bed. Removing her spectacles with one hand, she put aside Nathaniel Hawthorne's *The House of the Seven Gables*, which she had been reading aloud.

"My dear Mrs. Matth—"

"Annie."

Stephen sighed. "Annie, you know how pleased we all are that you've come to Deadwood, and I can never thank you enough for all you've done to entertain me during my convalescence, but I do hope that you'll remember that this is the West." He had the sense, watching her back stiffen, that his chances of swaying her were equal to stopping a railroad locomotive with his bare hands. "What I am trying to say is that Benjamin is just a boy. He doesn't mean any harm. His mind is off on a hundred pursuits of childhood."

"Believe me, Stephen, I *fully* understand the ways of male children. However, understanding Benjamin's behavior does not mean that we must also condone it. A few simple rules are good for him."

Watching as Annie rose to her full, statuesque height, Stephen was struck again by her unadorned good looks and the

291

forceful purity of her character. The woman was at once mesmerizing and frustrating. Physically she was quite a handsome representative of her sex, with glossy chestnut-and-silver hair drawn back in a plain chignon, clear hazel eyes, and a taut body complemented by the simple, high-necked dresses she wore. However, she was definitely a force to be reckoned with. She had appeared a fortnight ago looking for her son, accepted their welcome, and then set about improving the Avery household. Now, Stephen feared, she was about to stride into the parlor and collar his son, who would probably leave the door ajar twice as often in retaliation.

"Benjamin?" Annie called in a calm schoolteacher's voice.

The bedroom door burst open and Benjamin entered with a shout, nearly crashing into Annie Sunday. "Hey! There you are! Where's Gramma Susan, for Pete's sake? An' Titus?" His sandy hair stood up in sweaty cowlicks and his freckles were bright with excitement. When Fox's mother held his shoulders in an effort to quiet him, Benjamin wriggled free, yelling, "Leggo of me, lady!"

"Benjamin, mind your manners!" his father ordered.

"Listen to me! This is *important*!" He stopped, panting, until he was certain that both adults were giving him their attention. "Maddie an' Fox are coming! I saw 'em and Watson and the wagon, with Maddie driving, coming down Sherman Street! They're prob'ly on the way up the hill by now!"

Stephen was agog. "Dear Lord. I wonder . . . Oh, my." He began to struggle with the bedcovers. "Where is my dressing gown?"

"Daniel? . . . Daniel's coming? Right now?" Annie Sunday tried to make sense of Benjamin's announcement. She'd been waiting to see her son since the day she'd left Washington, D.C., after receiving word that he was living in Deadwood. She'd grown so used to waiting that the notion that he was finally going to be in front of her was almost more than she could take in. "This is so sudden," she murmured to no one in particular.

"Papa, I don't know if you're supposed to get outta bed," Benjamin was saying doubtfully as he brought Stephen's dressing gown.

"I'll be fine. I won't go beyond the front door, but I have to see . . . just in case . . ." Stephen felt invigorated, as if a magical cure had suddenly taken effect. Knotting the sash of his brocade robe, he slipped his feet into half-shoes, glanced down at the bare calves that showed pale beneath the hem of his nightshirt, then stepped out with dignity. "Benjamin, I believe your grandmother said that she was going to lie down upstairs and take a short nap. Go and see, will you? And then look around Fox's house for Titus. We should all be present at this moment." Extending his arm to Annie Sunday, he added, "I shall escort Mrs. Matthews to the front porch."

Benjamin nodded, then started out the door, only to be halted once more by his father's voice.

"Son . . . did you see them? I mean"—he cleared his throat—"I realize that you were above, on our hill, looking down, but I thought that perhaps you might have seen if there was anyone with them. Another young woman, perhaps . . . ?" His voice throbbed with hope.

"Huh?" Benjamin tossed back an impatient look. "I saw Fox riding Watson and I saw Maddie driving the wagon. I could tell it was her by her hair. That was all. Nobody else."

"I see, I see." Stephen nodded nervously. "Well, that's fine. Let's go forth to greet the travelers, shall we, Mrs. Matthews?"

Annie Sunday, now slightly recovered, beamed at her host. "By all means, sir, but you must take *my* arm!"

They made an odd little group, clustered on the porch, but Fox found that his heart swelled with affection at the sight of these people he'd known only a scant few weeks. He had brought Watson alongside the mules to help Maddie navigate the wagon up the deeply rutted hillside drive that led to their homes.

"Oh, look, Fox! It's Father! He must be feeling better."

With the reins still in her hands, Maddie shaded her eyes against the sunlight and tried to get a better look. "How wonderful to see him out of bed! And there's Gramma Susan, and Titus, and Benjamin . . . and a woman. Oh dear, I hope it isn't Garnet Loomis—she'd alert the entire town to Sun Smile's existence."

Fox shrugged. "Word will spread quickly enough, I fear. You may as well brace yourself."

"Poor Father." She stole another look into the depths of the wagon, where her half-sister had hunched in silence for more than three days. If not for her smell they might have forgotten she was even present. "I don't know if he'll be glad we brought her or not."

"Of course he'll be *glad*," Fox countered, a trifle exasperated. "For God's sake, Maddie! Don't you think it's crossed his mind that she might not be the pristine Indian maiden you'd obviously hoped for? He wants to see his *daughter*, just as she is—even if she *doesn't* smell like a bed of roses!"

Chastened, Maddie nodded. Fox was right, and the knowledge made her ashamed of herself. Sun Smile had left behind everything familiar to her—she would need loving-kindness and sympathy, support and encouragement. And it was up to Maddie as her sister to take care of her, not find fault with her!

They were rounding the crest of the drive and Maddie could see Benjamin jumping up and down. Titus was holding the back of his shirt to keep him from rushing out to meet them. Her father was smiling, but . . . "Fox, who *is* that tall woman? Do you recognize her?"

Now that they were in the clear and he didn't have to worry that the mules would misstep off the side of the hill, Fox placated her with a hurried glance toward the porch. Susan O'Hara waved at him, and he waved back. And then he saw her.

"Fox?" Maddie felt a pang of worry at the sight of his open mouth and wide eyes. Watson nearly wandered into the mules. "Fox! Who *is* that woman?" Please God, no more surprises, she thought. *"Fox?"*

Suddenly his mouth was dry as dust. "I—" He swallowed and dragged his eyes from the figure on the porch to look at Maddie. "I can't believe it. Maybe you should pinch me. I think that's my *mother* up there!"

Pandemonium reigned over the next several minutes as Maddie and Fox were drawn into the different family dramas that awaited them. After hugs, greetings, and introductions were exchanged on the porch, Fox gave all his attention to his mother. Annie Sunday had traveled two thousand miles to visit her son, and they had a great deal of catching up to do. Maddie, meanwhile, was left to deal with her father, who fixed her with the questioning look she'd been expecting.

"I could take a switch to your legs for running off like that, Madeleine," he said sternly, then gave her a smile. "However, now that you're home safely, I am anxious to hear your report. I'm grateful to Fox for going on my behalf and for looking after you, but this *is* a family matter, and I'm rather glad that you were there as well." Stephen leaned on Benjamin and smiled sadly. "I gather that you were unable to find Sun Smile."

"Actually . . ." Maddie plucked at her threadbare calico skirt and searched for Fox beyond Annie Sunday's head, trying to catch his eye. "We did find her, Father."

Fox moved through the group to her side. "We did as you asked, sir. Sun Smile is with us, in the wagon, but I ought to explain a few things before you meet her."

"Fox, why don't you three sort this out," Susan suggested, "while Benjamin, Titus, Mrs. Matthews, and I go inside and prepare a light meal."

Annie Sunday obviously didn't want to leave her son, but in the interest of Stephen's health, she complied without protest. Fox brought a chair out to the porch for Stephen to sit on. Then, as concisely as possible, he and Maddie told their story.

"She's really here?" Stephen murmured, staring at the

wagon in disbelief. "What must she think of us, leaving her out there in the heat?"

"I believe she's having a nap," Fox assured him.

"Father, you may not be prepared for Sun Smile," Maddie began uncertainly. "She's—"

"I understand what it means for a Lakota woman to be in mourning," Stephen interrupted. "And I'm aware that she must be frightened now. Fox, please, bring her to me."

Maddie stood beside her father's chair and watched with him as Fox went to the wagon, roused Sun Smile, and helped her down. In this more civilized environment, the girl looked more than ever like a wild animal. The sunlight showed every detail of her filthy appearance and she blinked and cringed, looking around her warily, as Fox led the way to the house.

Kneeling beside her father, Maddie prepared to comfort him, prepared to see him recoil from Sun Smile. Instead she saw that he was weeping softly.

"How much like Yellow Bird she is," Stephen murmured. When Sun Smile approached him on the porch, their eyes met in recognition. "She's been told who I am?" Stephen asked.

"Yes," Maddie said doubtfully. "But she doesn't speak, and it's rare for her to communicate with anyone."

"That's part of the reason Kills Hungry Bear, her brother-in-law, thought it would be best for her to come here," Fox explained. "Given the uncertain future of the Lakota, it seemed best that Sun Smile have someone to look after her."

Stephen seemed not to notice any of the aspects of appearance or behavior that so distressed Maddie. He reached out to touch Sun Smile's arm and she curled up into a protective ball on the porch step. "She's going to get better," he said quietly, firmly. "We'll see to it."

"Kills Hungry Bear says that she was fine until her husband was killed at Little Bighorn," Fox told him.

"Well, no wonder! Little Bighorn was just a few weeks ago, and Crazy Horse's people have been on the move ever since! Our poor Sun Smile hasn't had a chance to recover, and the Lakota mourn for a year, as I recall. So this is nothing out of the ordinary. . . ." His voice trailed off uncertainly, and for a moment there was silence as each contemplated the obvious contrast between mourning and Sun Smile's total withdrawal from life. At last Maddie sighed.

"Well, what shall we do with her now?" she asked.

"Your sister will sleep upstairs with you and Gramma Susan," Stephen said.

Maddie's eyes widened. "But, Father—"

"I know that you must be as pleased as I to have brought Sun Smile into our family," he cut in. "We shall all have to make certain sacrifices to ensure that she feels welcome and is able to conquer her grief with all possible speed. We must give her a great deal of love, unfailingly, and show her what it means to be a member of the Avery family."

After a brief hesitation, Maddie nodded. Again she had the uncomfortable sensation that those around her were more generous of spirit, and purer of heart, than she. She resolved to try harder. And whatever her feelings now, she would acquiesce gracefully—not just to please her father, but for her own sake as well.

"Well, well, I'd say that you have undergone a few *changes*," Gramma Susan murmured as she and her granddaughter washed dishes. "I always heard that living with Indians would change a woman, and I guess that's so."

"Oh, honestly, Gramma!" Maddie cried, then glimpsed the twinkle in the old woman's eyes. "You're teasing, aren't you? I'm sorry, I suppose I'm tired." She paused. "Gramma, would you think me very horrid if I confessed that I'm not altogether enchanted with my new sister?"

"So I perceived," Susan said. She dried an ironstone plate and set it on the shelf.

"How can I come to love—truly love someone who—who behaves like a rabid dog?" she exclaimed defiantly.

"Shh. You're acting rather like one yourself, my dear," her grandmother warned.

"But to sleep in the same room with that *smell*—! If she would at least bathe . . ."

"In case you have not noticed," Susan interjected, "Sun Smile has yet to set foot inside this house, and I highly doubt whether she will in the foreseeable future. Unless I miss my guess, that poor child will stay in the wagon where she can be alone and feel a bit more at home. She'll be more comfortable under that canvas top with a view of the outdoors, fresh air, and privacy. You're not the only one who is making adjustments, you know."

Maddie stood with her hands in a dishpan of soapy water, thinking. "Do you think that Father would let her stay outside in the wagon?"

"If it is her *choice*, of course he'll let her. He'll allow whatever is necessary for Sun Smile to feel comfortable. You might try to see someone else's side now and then, Maddie." Gently Susan reached up to smooth back an errant curl from her granddaughter's brow. "I've never been a great admirer of your father's, but I'm proud of him now. He must have been very guilty all these years whenever he thought about Yellow Bird and Sun Smile. He's taking a big chance, trying to bring her into this family, and I'm quite certain he's more scared than he'll let on. You might show him a little compassion, sweetheart."

Gramma Susan's voice made her wish she were little again and could crawl onto her lap. "Oh, Gramma, how good it is to be home with you! You are so wise!"

"Am I?" Susan rubbed the tired place low on her back and tottered over to one of the kitchen chairs for a rest. "I have a confession to make, dear. I've been having some horrid, selfish feelings of my own lately."

"Oh, Gramma, how delightful!" Maddie clapped her wet hands, dried them on her apron, and rushed over to pull a chair next to Susan's. "Tell me everything! No, wait, let me guess first. It's . . . Fox's mother, isn't it?" She giggled when Susan gave a reluctant nod. "I'll own that I was shocked to find her here, but I've been so preoccupied with everything else that I haven't had much of a chance to ponder Mrs. Matthew's character. Is she terribly overbearing?"

"*Please.*" Susan rolled her eyes. "Maddie, she came in

here, a complete stranger, and started running the house! Now, I may be old, but I'm not feeble! And I may not have been the most eager nurse your father could have, but I am not a servant who can simply be bumped aside without discussion."

"Of *course* you aren't!"

"Don't patronize me, Maddie. I don't mean to make myself more important than I am, and I must admit that Annie is a very nice woman. Her goodness makes me feel even worse for feeling as I do." She reached for the sherry and poured herself a thimble-size glassful. "Let's just say that I'm glad you are back . . . and glad that Fox is here, too, so that Annie can redirect her attention toward him."

Maddie chewed on her lower lip for a long minute, digesting this. Susan finished her sherry and poured another for her granddaughter. "Hmmm . . ." She sighed at last and drank down the liquor. "Aren't you going to tell me how matters stand between you and Fox?" she asked at last, out of patience. "After all, I did have a hand in this match."

Maddie grinned. "Yes, and it's lucky you weren't anywhere near when he discovered that I'd stowed away. I thought he might soften if I mentioned that you had given the scheme your blessing, but—"

"Oh, honestly, Maddie, sometimes I think you haven't the sense God gave a grasshopper! Fox is not a person I would choose to have mad at me. I'm surprised he didn't give me a lecture tonight over the pound cake and coffee!"

"Oh, don't worry, he got over it." Maddie gave her grandmother a coy smile. "We made peace, so to speak. We are very close now . . . but a long way from marriage, if that's what you're wondering. Fox warned me all along that he wasn't ready for that kind of entanglement, so I knew what chance I was taking—and I wouldn't change a thing."

"You two are in love?"

She blushed prettily. "Yes, I believe so. Sometimes I believe it more than others, but at least now I understand that Fox's life is complicated by matters other than me. If he's not ready to take a wife and settle down, it's not because he doesn't love me enough.'' She stared into space and sighed again. ''*But*, I will admit that I had hopes of realizing those dreams in time, after we came back to Deadwood and Fox had time to sort out his life. Living near me yet apart, I thought he might miss the closeness we shared while we were with the Lakota. Oh, Gramma''—she looked up, her emerald eyes bright—''it was the most wonderful time of my life. I learned so much in a short period of time—about myself, and about Fox, and about life.''

Gramma Susan gazed out the window reflectively. ''You've heard stories since you were born about my father's career in the United States Senate.'' She waited for Maddie's nod, then continued, ''You remember, don't you, that Benjamin Franklin was his mentor? My brother, and your brother, were both named after Dr. Franklin. I remember discussing the Indian problem with Papa during my youth, and he repeated something that Dr. Franklin had told him—that most of the time when white prisoners have been raised among Indians from a young age, they refuse to be reclaimed by their own race. He spoke of cases where the white person, often female, had been ransomed and treated with all possible tenderness by their English brethren, yet he or she would escape back into the woods at the first opportunity . . . never to be seen by white faces again.'' Dusk was gathering in the kitchen, heightening the poignant effect of her story. ''Fascinating, isn't it? When I was young I often dreamed of somehow tasting that experience for myself. I'm glad that you were able to, my dear, before that culture disappears completely.''

''Yes, Gramma, I am glad, too.'' Maddie's throat was tight with emotion.

''But, you were speaking of your dreams for you and Fox,'' Susan said briskly. ''What shall we hope for from that young man?''

''I wish I knew.'' Maddie rose to light the lamps. ''I was thinking earlier that everything has changed now, hasn't it? Fox's mother is here, and who can say what that will mean?

In any case, I hardly think that he'll be anxious to bring a wife into his home as long as she is staying there.''

"I can't imagine what you've been doing with yourself these past weeks, Daniel!''

Annie Sunday Matthews stood in the middle of her son's spacious house, arms akimbo, and gazed around with undisguised chagrin. Her eyes touched the rumpled bedrolls in the corner, traveled past the open staircase that ascended to the loft above, then lingered on the second stone fireplace, a table and chairs that consisted of planks and barrels, and some crates of supplies and kitchen utensils. "I must say it: I am shocked. How can you live like this?''

Titus Pym had been sitting in the open doorway drinking a mug of ale and watching the sun sink behind the top of the gulch. Now he rose, embarrassed. "I'd best be off, me lad. 'Tis glad I am that you and the lady are back.''

"Titus, where are you going?'' Fox asked in consternation.

"Why, I'll go down to the Custer Hotel. Now that Mrs . . .'' His voice trailed off in confusion.

"Matthews,'' Fox supplied.

"Aye. Now that Mrs. Matthews is here to take care of you and will be staying in this house, she'll be wanting some peace and privacy. It's best this way, at least till we build some proper rooms.'' Pym ended with a broad grin and bowed to Annie Sunday.

She went to the door to wave good-bye to the Cornish miner, then surveyed the daisies and zinnias blooming cheerfully in front of the log house. "I see you have *flowers*. How surprisingly civilized of you, my dear boy.''

Fox bit back a sarcastic reply and tried instead for his best boyish smile. Wrapping an arm around Annie Sunday, he implored, "Don't be so hard on me, Ma. Look at this house! It's a palace compared to the others in Deadwood. I just haven't had time to furnish it properly.''

"Nonsense. You've chosen to live like a heathen, sleeping

on the floor, eating beans out of a can, and washing in a tin basin.''

"Now, that's not true!" he protested. "I go down to Main Street to the bathhouse practically every day, especially when it's hot. I even pay extra for fresh water!"

"My, my, you must be the talk of the town with such shockingly cultivated habits." Annie looked away from his appealing face.

"Ma, you know that I admire you more than anyone, but I've got to be honest. This attitude doesn't suit you. Aren't you happy to see me?"

Her chin trembled slightly. "Of course I am. Perhaps I've just missed you too much, and I've tried to maintain a semblance of composure in the midst of this very foreign place and a lot of strangers. I'll own that I was beginning to worry that something might have happened to you. Can you imagine my fears when I arrived here only to learn that you had gone off to deal with *Crazy Horse*?" Her words were spilling out quickly now. "Oh, Daniel, when I heard about that terrible massacre at Little Bighorn I sobbed for days, certain that you had been killed."

"You, sobbing? Impossible!" Fox chided gently, kissing his mother's shining hair.

"No, no, it's quite true," she insisted. "Thank God you had the presence of mind to send word to me of your safety and your whereabouts. I was so overcome with relief that I determined to come here without delay. I think, were I completely honest, that I felt as if I were falling back in time, back to the days when your father left me in Washington to journey to the frontier. I used to live in fear that he wouldn't come home, that he'd be killed and mutilated by the Indians he sympathized with so, but I never said a word to him, and eventually he stopped leaving." Annie Sunday pulled herself together, calming her voice and smoothing her skirts. "You must be right. I'm tired—and so very happy to see you, darling. You don't mind that I've come?"

"Mind?" Fox echoed. "I love you, Ma. It's wonderful to see you, too."

"Well, that's settled, then. And it's quite clear that you need my help with this house, too! It needs a great deal more than a few flowers, Daniel.''

"Actually you can thank Maddie for the flowers. They are her doing." His eyes drifted toward the pine trees separating their houses.

"Who? Oh, yes, Miss Avery. She seems to be a very nice young lady. I've grown quite fond of her father." Annie Sunday searched her son's face for a moment, then brushed away the fears that threatened her cheering mood. "Let's see what we can devise for my bed tonight, shall we? Then tomorrow we'll go down to Star and Bullock's store and buy you some proper household goods. Goodness, we'd better get a sound night's sleep, Daniel! Tomorrow will be a busy day!''

His mother went bustling off around the house and he walked outside, looking his property over for the best spot to build a new cabin. It wouldn't have to be very big; just large enough for Annie Sunday.

Chapter Twenty-three

August 16, 1876

Fox found J. B. Hickok's grave in Deadwood's cemetery, inventively named Boot Hill. The graveyard was located in a natural clearing partway up the side of the gulch east of town. Fox went there while the sun was still rising on the other side of the white rocks that rimmed the canyon and he found Bill's grave easily among the others. It was still covered with flowers. On the face of a treestump the facts were inexpertly carved: Hickok's name, age, and the circumstances and date of his death.

Fox had bathed at dawn, then awakened Wang Chee's wife to pick up his clean, starched clothes at their laundry. It felt good to be scrubbed, shaved, and clad in a ticking-stripe shirt and faded blue pants that smelled of sunshine, soap, and the hot breath of Mrs. Chee's iron. Although he always felt a pang of longing when he thought of the Lakota, this was where he belonged. Even with its glaring flaws and inconsistencies, Deadwood was home, and he had returned with a new sense of his own worth. Maybe he was flawed, too, but he still had a purpose—and it felt good to know that again. It was as if the flame in his soul had been rekindled.

From Old Frenchy at the bathhouse, Fox heard the details of Bill's death, already embellished, certainly, for the sake of legend. He'd been holding aces over eights, now called the "deadman's hand." His back had been to the door of the saloon when Jack McCall came up and shot him through the back of the head. Some said the assassin was just a drunk, others thought he'd followed Wild Bill to Deadwood to avenge his brother's shooting, at Hickok's hands, in Abilene. Anyway, the miners' court, convened at the Gem Theatre, had seen fit to let him go. So much of the story was muddy that Fox made up his mind not to brood about the circumstances of his friend's death. It was just his time, Fox mused, staring down at the drifts of wildflowers that marked the grave.

"Hey, pard," a voice spoke from a few yards down the hill. "I heard you was back."

Fox saw Colorado Charley Utter approaching and put out his hand. "Good to see you."

"I was gone that night," Charley said. "Didn't get back from Cheyenne until after they buried him. I've been trying to piece it all together, but seems like everybody has a different story. Anyway, nothing I can do now to bring him back." He shrugged, breaking off as his eyes began to water.

"I was just thinking that same thing." Fox's heart went out to the other man; he'd lost his best friend. "I'm going to miss him a lot. It was an honor to know him. I just hate to see this town turn him into some kind of myth—another means to make money, you know."

"That's the kind of town Deadwood is, though . . . Do you feel like breakfast? I was thinking about payin' a visit to Aunt Lou Marchbanks at the Grand Central. Want to come? Her biscuits are beyond compare. Bill loved 'em; we can eat in his honor."

A slow grin spread over Fox's face. "I'd really enjoy that, Charley. It's damned good to be home."

As they clambered down the hillside and crossed the rickety wooden bridge spanning Whitewood creek, Charley said, "I'm gonna make a headboard for Bill's grave. I been thinking about what to carve on it and I thought I'd say, 'Pard, we will meet again in the happy hunting ground to part no more.' " He gave the younger man a sideways glance, waiting for a reaction.

"Those are fine words, Charley. Just what Bill would like," Fox replied. "Let me know when you're going to do it and I'll give you a hand if you need one."

"Much obliged."

* * *

Fox wished that he could confide fully in Colorado Charley Utter, but it seemed like too big a chance to take. He was sure he could trust him to keep a secret but, what if he talked in his sleep or something? So, instead, they ate biscuits and gravy and eggs and sausage, washed it all down with lots of coffee, and talked in generalities about Fox's journey to Bear Butte.

"The folks around here really hate the Sioux," Charley observed when his stomach was full. " 'Course, that's mostly fear, and guilt, too, even though they don't know it. Everybody yells about the advance of civilization and how it's our duty to do it since the Indians are too simple-minded and savage." He dropped a chunk of brown sugar in his coffee and stirred. "I don't know the answer. I don't think that the Lord sent us whites to advance civilization; seems to me that we'll prob'ly end up wrecking a lot of this beautiful country. But on the other hand, I don't want to give it back . . . and I don't want to *go* back. Do you?"

Fox rubbed the bridge of his nose for a few seconds. "No. No, I don't. But I don't see why it has to be either us or them."

" 'Cause we're too arrogant to share."

"Damn. I know it."

"You might be different, but that's just you."

"It's sad to see it from the other side, Charley." Fox leaned back in his chair, which groaned in protest. "Those people just want to be left alone to live the way they've always lived, in harmony with the land. They want the open prairie and the buffalo, and if we could give them that freedom, we wouldn't have to worry about teaching them to farm or giving them rations."

"Yeah, but that would mean admitting that there are other ways to live besides our way, and we're too damned arrogant for that, too! We gotta turn 'em into white folks or kill 'em trying."

Fox thought about the way Custer had behaved before Little Bighorn and how the hundreds of men had gone along with his orders. "You have to admire a man like Crazy Horse, you know. The day after we started back here from the village, we met up with him and a couple of his men who were leaving the Hills after their latest raid. I don't think they accomplished much—certainly not enough—but Crazy Horse was holding a red sunshade that he'd gotten hold of. He was taking it back to an old Indian called One Moccasin who's been fainting lately in the heat. He was proud to be returning with that red sunshade. Even a little victory like that, which was more symbolic than anything, keeps his spirits up. There's something truly noble and admirable about a man like Crazy Horse, who refuses to give up in the face of impossible odds."

"Yeah, I guess," Colorado Charley muttered doubtfully. "Kinda stupid, too, though, don'tcha think?"

"To the outside world, maybe, but not when you're next to him. There's an aura around him that's so strong, you almost believe he might pull it off."

"I know what you mean; Bill had that. Look what happened to him, though . . . and Crazy Horse'll go down, too. Crook's out there, I hear," Charley said.

Fox nodded. "Crazy Horse told me the general's been trying to chase them down ever since Little Bighorn. His scouts just sighted ol' Three Stars and his troops camped on the prairie a fair distance north. Crazy Horse had enough sense to burn the grass behind his people as they moved south from Montana, but Crook underestimated the Sioux again and now the word is that his horses are starving and the men are about out of rations, too."

"There's nothing stupider than a white man in Indian country," Charley observed. "Y'know, I wouldn't publish an account of my adventures with Crazy Horse in the *Pioneer* if I was you, Fox. There's lotsa folks in Deadwood who might wonder just how friendly you got with the Sioux. Maybe you didn't hear that the *Pioneer* was calling to hang any whites found to be trading ammunition to the Indians—?" After wiping his mouth with a napkin, he pushed back his chair. " 'Course I know you wouldn't do nothing like that.

Bringing an Indian squaw into town is one thing, but there's a big difference between the two.''

"You heard about Sun Smile?" Fox said, with mild surprise, as they walked toward the sunlit doorway of the hotel.

"Your ma likes to talk. She was over at Star and Bullock's store last time I looked. Prob'ly still there since she seemed to have a long list of things to buy."

Fox bade Colorado Charley a hasty good-bye, thanking him for the breakfast and conversation and agreeing that they would meet again soon. Charley wandered off into the badlands, while Fox went over to Deadwood's new store on the corner of Main and Wall streets.

Annie Sunday Matthews made a striking picture. She stood in the middle of the plain, rustic store, which still smelled of freshly sawn pine, wearing a tasteful polonaise walking suit made of cream broadcloth with sapphire-blue buttons and trim. Although the suit was simply tailored and she wore no jewelry except her diamond wedding band, Annie Sunday exuded taste and breeding. Her hair was drawn back softly into the usual chignon that set off her handsome face and fine hazel eyes.

A dark-haired man who was most notable for his bushy eyebrows and mustache was holding an animated conversation with Fox's mother. Another man with an angular face and thinning brown hair was seated behind the store's desk. A surprising amount of merchandise filled the room.

"Why, Daniel, how delightful to see you," Annie Sunday greeted him, extending a gloved hand. "I wondered where you had gone when I awoke this morning. Have you forgotten simple courtesies like writing a note to inform others of your whereabouts?"

Fox was spared a reply to this incredible question by Seth Bullock, who stepped forward to introduce himself and his partner, Sol Star, who then bowed from behind the desk. Both men wore suits and paper collars. "How proud you must be to have such a remarkable mother," Bullock proclaimed. "It took great courage and resourcefulness for her to come all this way alone. She's just the sort of woman Deadwood *truly* needs.''

"You won't get an argument from me," Fox agreed obliquely.

"Mrs. Matthews has been telling us that she taught school for a good many years," Sol Star put in. "That's what Deadwood needs—a first-rate teacher to educate our children."

"I can't think about such a project yet," Annie demurred. "My son needs me first."

"Ma! What are you saying? How could I be so selfish to keep you to myself when the children of Deadwood are in dire need of a *teacher*? It sounds like you were destined for such a position; makes me think that the hand of God led you out here"—Fox swept his arm overhead—"to the wilderness!"

"Certainly I'll consider it," she murmured, directing a sharp glance at him. "I must say that I find the civic spirit in this town to be very . . . fervent. Why, Daniel, did you know that Mr. Bullock has taken on the job of sheriff? He's just been telling me that the reward has been raised to fifty dollars in clean, merchantable gold dust to anyone bringing in an Indian's *head*!" Annie Sunday paled slightly. "Truly there are aspects of life here that shall be difficult for me to adjust to. I certainly pray that no one will think of harming our dear Sun Smile.''

"I don't think that's the kind of Indian the reward is about, Ma," Fox assured her, while trying to figure out how to get her out of the store before she said his real name again or anything else he'd regret. He should have known better than to let her out of his sight without explaining that the people here didn't know him as Daniel Matthews. Of course, she'd been in Deadwood for days. Had she already spread his real name all over town? "Would you mind waiting for me outside?''

"But, my purchases—"

"I'll take care of everything, Ma," Fox told her through a clenched smile.

"Well, since you put it that way . . . Gentlemen, I must

bid you good day.'' Regal as a queen, she nodded to them both and swept out the door.

Fox asked to see a list of the items his mother had bought. Most of the furniture was on order and he asked Star and Bullock to hold off on their search for the pieces she'd requested. Everything else that wasn't a matter of personal taste, he told them, might be delivered at their convenience. "I'll return in a few days to pick out my other household goods personally,'' he said before paying them and taking his leave.

Annie Sunday was perched on the seat of the Averys' open wagon. Little Ben sat next to her, holding the reins. There was a moat of waste and mud separating the store's wooden porch from the wagon, so Fox was forced to stand a few feet away and converse with his mother. "I appreciate what you're trying to do, Ma, but I'm a grown man. I'd like to do my own shopping.'' His tone was gentle. "We can discuss this better at home, I think. Why don't—''

"You never cared one bit about picking anything out for yourself before,'' she interjected. "If I didn't know better, I'd think that you were about to take a wife!''

"We'll talk about this later. I'll meet you at home at midday.''

With those parting words, Fox set out in search of Preacher Smith.

Maddie was nearing her wits' end. At her father's behest she had spent the better part of the morning trying to coax Sun Smile to come out of the prairie schooner and into the house. However, each time she tried to interact with her half-sister, the effort seemed to widen the chasm between them. Sun Smile was adamant in her rejection; it was impossible to pretend otherwise or to stem the tide of hurt and resentment that swept over Maddie after she'd been pushed away.

With a great deal of trepidation, she approached the wagon again at noon, carrying a plate of sliced chicken, fried potatoes, buttered rye bread, and a plum. When she poked her head under the canvas cover that arched over the wagon, the smell was overpowering. Sun Smile was cloaked in shadows, huddled against a trunk that had been filled with her few cherished possessions. As soon as she heard Maddie's step, she averted her face so that all that was visible was a snarled mass of black hair.

"Sun Smile, aren't you hungry? . . . I know that you can understand me," Maddie said, speaking slowly and clearly. "I have brought you food. Father hopes that you will come into the house. We want to take care of you."

Sun Smile made pushing motions in the air with one grimy hand and began to moan, softly, her mourning song. At last Maddie shook her head, set the food inside the wagon, and turned back toward the house. However, her attention was soon captured by a horse and rider nearing the top of the drive leading to the Avery home. The man was waving—and moments later she could see him clearly.

It was Graham Horatio Scofield III.

Maddie sighed. The last thing she wanted was to play hostess to a social call. But at least she looked presentable, even pretty, in a graceful amber faille walking suit that set off her brilliant hair and showed her figure to advantage. She moved forward to greet her guest as he hailed her.

"Ah, my dear Miss Avery!" Scofield dismounted a trifle awkwardly and clasped his derby in his hands. "My eyes gasp at your beauty!"

"Do they?" Maddie asked whimsically. Then she smiled. "It's nice to see you, too, Mr. Scofield."

"Ah, you have not forgotten! How can I describe my relief? And I cannot refrain from remarking on the amazingly similar clothes you and I have chosen to wear today. Is it not singular?" He bent his curly blond head to sweep a hand downward, encouraging her eye to follow. Indeed, Scofield did wear a light brown suit, a cinnamon-colored vest of watered silk, and a brown silk tie over his stiff-bosomed shirt and celluloid collar.

"Quite singular, sir." And, as it was inevitable, Maddie succumbed to propriety and invited him in for a glass of lemonade.

When they were seated on the settee, Scofield whispered, "I must make a confession."

Maddie could see her father through the doorway to his room and knew he was listening. "A confession?" she repeated weakly.

"Yes. Yes, it's true. I heard this morning that you have been among the Indians. I want you to know that this knowledge does not in any way alter my opinion of your character, Miss Avery. In truth, I must tell you that you appear to be unblemished by the experience."

"Umblemished? I'm not sure I understand you, sir."

He set down his lemonade and tried to take her hand, but she eluded him. "I mean, my dear, that I know you are too fine to allow anything you may have been forced to experience to tarnish your character. Perhaps you have, instead, become more . . . how shall I say it? More womanly, as a result." He blushed and began to perspire. "Miss Avery, I know that you and I did not strike up the sort of friendship I had hoped for after my first call here some weeks ago. However, a great deal has changed since then. I have become more and more discouraged in my quest for a suitable wife in this godforsaken town. My mind doth ever return to *you.*" Graham caught her hand this time and clutched it fast in his damp grip.

Startled, Maddie tried to pull away. "Really, Mr. Scofield, I don't—"

"Wait! Hear me out! Has it not occurred to you, my dear, that there were already few enough suitable men out here for you to choose from? Now, after your little journey . . . Well, need I say more? However, *I* am willing to overlook it!" he announced triumphantly. "In fact, I might even regard it as a sort of . . . aphrodisiac . . ."

"Mr. Scofield!" Maddie gasped. "I'm certain I did not hear you correctly!"

"Dare to believe it, Madeleine!" he exclaimed passionately. "It's quite true: I am asking you to become Mrs. Graham Horatio Scofield the Third!"

"Of the Boston Scofields?" It was Stephen, calling from his bed in tones of mock wonder.

Graham jumped to his feet, still clutching her hand, and cried, "Yes! Yes, sir, the very same!"

Maddie was dizzy with the urge to giggle when another voice spoke from the kitchen. "Now, hold on." The door swung open and Fox seemed to fill the room as he strode in and loomed over the younger man. "Let go of her hand."

"I hardly think that you have the right to tell me—"

"Fox!" Maddie's face shone with a radiant smile.

"I'd watch my tongue if I were you, Mr. Scofield," Fox said in a low, menacing voice. "I have every right to threaten you at this moment. You're proposing to the woman I intend to marry this Saturday."

A series of gasps seemed to bounce around the parlor. Even Gramma Susan poked her snowy head in from the kitchen, her face bright with surprised pleasure. Stephen was trying to get out of bed, and Maddie had gone white, her mouth frozen in the shape of an O. Without another word, Scofield released her hand, twisted his derby, and marched toward the door.

"Don't hurry back," Fox called after him, unable to resist.

Scofield pivoted in the doorway. "No man humiliates a Boston Scofield and gets away with it. You have not heard the last of me, Mr. *Daniel Matthews*!"

Chapter Twenty-four

August 19, 1876

"I STILL CAN'T IMAGINE WHAT CAME OVER FOX," Maddie mused as she sat in a tin bathtub tucked into a curtained corner of the kitchen. "Are you sure he really means to turn up today, Gramma Susan?"

"Well, of course he does!" Susan O'Hara paused in the midst of spreading almond icing on the rich bride cake she had been laboring over for most of two days. Peeking around the curtain, she added, "I've spoken to Fox myself. He loves you, sweetheart. Don't you believe that?"

"Actually . . . yes." It was a mild day for August—a perfect day to spend in the Hills. Maddie drew her knees up in the small tub, tipped her head back over the rear lip, and leisurely soaped one slim arm. "In fact, I probably have more knowledge of his love for me than he does, but that doesn't mean I thought he'd *marry* me—especially on such short notice. Why, we've barely spoken since we got back to Deadwood! I mean, even after that crazy scene with Graham Scofield, he didn't take me off alone for a proper, tender proposal."

"No? I seem to recall that after Mr. Scofield's melodramatic exit, Fox turned to you and said something like, 'You and I are getting married Saturday, in front of your garden at one o'clock!' Do you mean *that* was the end of it?"

Maddie pointed a toe in the air, displaying an elegant leg, and gave Susan a winsome smile. "Pretty much so. He did ask me again, when he was hurrying off somewhere, did I really want to, and it was clear that he meant for me to say yes, and I did. The rest of the time, he's been building something over there on the other side of the pine trees, and we've been busy over here, and then there's been the whole situation with Sun Smile, and Saturday—today—came so quickly that I hardly have had time to think until right now.''

''I think this sudden wedding has been a happy distraction for us all,'' Susan admitted to her granddaughter. ''Even your father seems to be at a loss for a solution regarding Sun Smile. Have you noticed that Annie Sunday has been spending a good deal of time trying to draw her out of the wagon?''

''She's probably looking for a distraction of her own,'' Maddie remarked, with a touch of irony. ''If you want the honest truth, I think that Fox decided a wife in the house might keep his mother from taking charge of his household.'' She slid under the water to rinse her hair, emerging with a grin. ''Of the two of us, he doubtless believes I'm more manageable.''

Susan felt a pang of worry. ''Darling, I hope you are going into this marriage with a strong, full heart. I can understand that you might be nervous today, but not doubtful, I hope.''

''Oh, Gramma''—her voice broke with the emotion that swept over her body—''I've never been more certain of anything in my life than my love for Fox. I've missed him so much since we got home that I've just ached all the time. We were so close during those weeks away, and I was so happy . . . and I know he was, too.'' She stood, dripping and glorious, and reached for her towel. ''I can't deny that I find this wedding a bit peculiar, but there's nothing I want more than to become Mrs. Daniel Matthews. It's just my destiny, and I know it—to share his home and make a life with him.'' She paused in the midst of toweling her mass of hair to add, ''I just didn't expect it to happen so soon or so easily. Fox told me he couldn't marry me; that the sort of life I need wasn't possible for him.''

''Daniel Matthews *is* his real name,'' Susan said, as if attempting to make sense of it. ''I assume he was hiding something and then Annie Sunday appeared, spoke too freely, and liberated Fox from his secret.''

"I can't really talk about it, Gramma. Not yet, anyway."
Damp and glowing, Maddie drew on a loose muslin dressing
gown, pushed back the makeshift curtain, and approached
the impressive bride cake. "I just hope that Graham Scofield
can't find a way to use that knowledge against Fox. For a
fellow who professes to be a refined gentleman, he can get a
gleam in his eye that's positively *feral*."

"Well, I think Fox can take care of himself," Susan declared.

"Gramma, I must tell you that I find this cake simply
amazing! How can I thank you? If not for all your hard work,
we'd be forced to consume beans and jerky following the
ceremony!"

They laughed together, then Susan drew her granddaughter onto a chair and stood behind her, gently combing out
her wet hair. "I am delighted to do whatever I can to help
make your wedding day one you will recall fondly, my dear,"
she murmured.

"What comes after the icing? Can you put a little ribbon
on it made of icing, or a flower? I remember that you made
a birthday cake for me once when I was small, and there
were little candied violets clustered on the top."

Susan's soft voice was soothing. "Well, after this I spread
on the sugar frosting, and then I have to put all three layers
in a cool oven so that they have a chance to harden. Then,
after I take them out and assemble the cake, I'll color the
remaining icing with currant juice and squeeze it through a
pastry bag. Would you like pink icing ribbons that swirl down
from the edges of the layers in festoons?"

"Lovely." Maddie caught her grandmother's hand and
pressed it against her cheek. It felt fragile and cool and
smelled of almond paste. "Gramma Susan, you are very,
very dear to me. Isn't it wonderful that we won't be separated
by my marriage?"

"Indeed it is." She bent to kiss Maddie's hair, which was
drying quickly in the morning air. A breeze stirred the kitchen
curtains and a jay cried from the pine trees outside. "One

could almost imagine that Fox planned to make you his wife before be began building that house next to ours.''

"Oh, no. If anything, he meant to annoy me, not woo me!'' Maddie's radiant face grew dreamy as she recalled earlier encounters with Fox. Looking back, she knew that she had not begun truly to live until the day he'd ridden up to their door to bring Benjamin home from the badlands. Fox was the most stimulating person she had ever known. The prospect of sharing her life with him made her tingle with anticipation.

The mantel clock in the parlor chimed eleven, jolting her back to the present. "Goodness, I'd better begin to move! I'll look in on Father and see how he's faring. Do you want me to tell Benjamin to take his bath now?''

"Yes; that's a good idea, darling. Then I'll be up to dress myself, just as soon as I make some proper festoons on this cake.'' There was just a trace of weariness in Susan's voice. Maddie had risen and they stood looking at each other, each thinking the same thing. It was Susan who finally spoke. "Perhaps you should ask your father what he hopes to do about Sun Smile today.''

"Gramma . . .'' Maddie paused, biting her lip. "Would you think me terribly selfish and horrid if I said that I would rather not devote my thoughts and energies to Sun Smile today?''

With a reassuring nod, Susan wrapped an arm around her granddaughter's waist and walked with her to the kitchen doorway. "I understand completely, my dear. This is your wedding day! As for Sun Smile . . . perhaps we ought to just say, What will be will be and leave it at that. Hmm?''

A few minutes before one o'clock, the tiny group began to gather in front of the garden that Maddie had designed and tended with such care. The hollyhocks, canterbury bells, larkspur, blue cornflowers, cheerful zinnias, daisies, sweet william, and forget-me-nots were all in full, fragrant bloom, and even the pansies continued to turn their little faces up to the August sun. Behind the garden was the hillside that plunged down to the rag-tag streets of Deadwood, while beyond stretched the other rock-crowned walls of the gulch.

Preacher Smith had arrived early, conferring with Fox in his house before proceeding to the Avery property. Since arriving in Deadwood that spring, the Methodist minister had spent most of his time attempting to save souls in the badlands, and a proper wedding like this seemed almost to intimidate him. Fox had invited Colorado Charley Utter, since Preacher Smith seemed to feel more at ease with a familiar face at his side.

The first person to join them was Titus Pym. "We all look like we're fit to be laid out in our caskets," the Cornish miner observed, nodding to the minister in his Sunday best and ogling Charley in his rented black suit and paper collar. "I wouldn't get trussed up like this for anyone but me good lad Fox."

Charley Utter grinned. "Your own lad Fox owes me a mighty big favor when he comes up for air after this wedding. It took all my powers of persuasion to keep Calamity Jane, Garnet Loomis, and sweet Victoria from coming with us today."

Preacher Smith's eyes widened, but he pressed his Bible to the bosom of his shirt and refrained from comment. Titus, however, had less control over his tongue.

"God's foot, if Jane had come, and those others, we might just as well have held the wedding on stage at the Bella Union Theatre!" He pumped Charley's hand. "Fox'll be grateful to you, sir."

"I'm happy that he's found love. Not so long ago, I visited him during his . . . retreat—those days he spent holed up above the Gem. He was the picture of despair. Fox is a rare commodity in towns like this: an honorable man who helps his friends and enjoys a laugh. It's good to witness his happiness today, and I know Bill is looking on with a smile, too, from the great beyond." This poetic speech left Charley a trifle misty-eyed, but the moment was lightened by the appearance of young Benjamin Franklin Avery.

"You let them talk you into wearing all this stuff, too, Mr.

Pym?'' the boy exclaimed in disbelief, tugging at his small paper collar as if it were choking him. His wheat-colored hair had been parted in the center, oiled down, and coaxed into fashionable curls at the temples. The suit, which had traveled with the family from Philadelphia, bore witness to Benjamin's growing body, for it pulled across the shoulders and the pants gapped above his side-buttoned shoes. ''I *hate* this! When I grow up, I'm gonna be a pony express rider or a gambler an' I'm never gonna wear a paper collar!''

''Benjamin, dear, do try to remember that 'gonna' is not a word.'' Susan O'Hara spoke in tones of mild resignation as she walked up behind her grandson. ''Your mother would faint if she could hear what comes out of your mouth these days.''

Introductions were exchanged then, overseen by Titus Pym. Susan had dressed with care for this afternoon. She had brought one especially fine gown with her, just in case an occasion of this nature arose, and now she proudly wore a full-trained skirt and a basque made by the famous Parisian Worth. The dress was of sapphire blue silk, richly decorated with velvet and fringe, and its high ruched collar set off her timeless good looks. Sapphire combs adorned her neatly dressed white hair, and she carried a blue foulard parasol lined with white silk to protect herself against the midday heat.

Showered with compliments by the men, Susan felt herself flush with pleasure. ''How kind you are. I thank you. And, Reverend Smith, how good you were to come today and preside over this wedding.''

''It's a pleasure, ma'am, and a welcome change,'' Henry Weston Smith said. ''Are there any other guests we should wait for?''

''Only the mother of the groom,'' Susan said, with a telling glance toward Titus Pym. ''She ought to be here. I know that Madeleine and her father are ready to make their entrance from the house whenever Mrs. Matthews, and Fox, of course, are in place.''

''When I left Fox, he was tying his tie,'' Titus supplied.

"I'm to wave through the trees when we're ready for him."
He bent over just in time to catch hold of Benjamin, who was
preparing to kneel on the grass and seize a baby snake. When
he straightened up, he saw that the others were staring, silent
with shock, toward the pine trees that separated the houses.

Coming around the far side of the Avery house was Annie
Sunday Matthews, regal in a polonaise and skirt of rose taffeta silk trimmed in cream velvet. A pearl choker gleamed
at her throat, and her chestnut hair was carefully coiffed. Her
appearance was no surprise, of course, but her companion
was: walking beside Annie Sunday was Sun Smile.

"Good God," Gramma Susan pronounced, squinting
through her spectacles in disbelief. "Pardon me, Reverend,"
she hastened to add, still staring.

"Well, pickle me liver," Titus muttered, "will you look
at *her*."

"Who is she?" Charley Utter asked.

"My Injin sister," came Benjamin's dark reply. "She gives
me the willies."

Sun Smile was nearly unrecognizable. Somehow she had
endured a thorough bath, which included her hair, and was
now dressed up like a parody of a white woman in a simple
corseted gown of myrtle green silk, gathered in back over a
gingham underskirt. She walked slowly and awkwardly in a
pair of narrow slippers with one-inch heels, and her clean
hair shone in the sunlight, pinned into a coil at the nape of
her neck and decorated with a white felt princess hat, its
brim turned up on one side and trimmed with a green feather
and ribbon. Only her shadowed eyes, so mournfully gray,
and the downturned corners of her mouth, betrayed the farce
that she was enacting.

"I hope you will forgive us for being a few minutes late,"
Annie Sunday was saying as she drew Sun Smile into the
circle of guests. Fox's mother wore a proud smile. "I think
that our tardiness must be overlooked, however. Doesn't Sun
Smile look simply lovely? It took some doing, but I'm not
one to give up easily, and I knew that Sun Smile's presence

here today of all days would mean so very much, not only to Daniel and Madeleine, who brought her to Deadwood in the hope of giving her a more civilized life, but also to dear Stephen, who has agonized so over her welfare." Annie Sunday gave her charge a bracing squeeze that was meant to impart courage. "I'm so proud of her that I can scarcely contain myself!"

There was a pause, followed by a lot of nodding in response to Annie Sunday's speech. At last Susan took pity on the girl and gave her a warm smile. "We're happy to have you with us today, Sun Smile."

Fox appeared then, and the focus shifted from the young Lakota widow to the bridegroom. It seemed that everyone could feel his energy as he strode toward his wedding.

His formal attire—an immaculate gray cutaway coat and matching trousers, a starched white shirt and wing collar, a gray-and-white-striped four-in-hand tie, and dove gray vest—fit to perfection, as if he'd just come from London's Savile Row. His hair was burnished in the sunshine and as neatly trimmed as his beard, which followed the contours of his jaw. All in all, he was the picture of alert, carefully reined power.

"Finally!" He gave the guests a distracted smile and took Preacher Smith's hand. "Let's begin."

Benjamin was dispatched to signal the bride and her father, who came slowly out of the house's back door and crossed the yard toward the little group assembled in front of Maddie's garden.

Maddie and Gramma Susan had had less than three days to concoct a proper wedding dress, and they'd done their best. The gown, of white Victorian lawn trimmed in Belgian lace, featured a fitted bodice with a low, square neckline and a deeply flounced skirt overlain with side-pleated ruffles. She wore no jewelry beyond the locket with her parents' pictures, and under a gossamer veil, her face was radiant, her unswept curls undimmed.

Her heart drummed madly as they drew up next to Fox. Stephen gave her a loving kiss, patted her hand, and then placed it in the brown fingers of her bridegroom. Oddly enough, Maddie felt very close to Fox, even though he had yet to reassure her of his love and the reasons for this sudden marriage—even though they had scarcely spoken for days. She loved him so much that she would take him on any terms—and in her heart she believed that God would smile on their union.

Preacher Smith read a simple wedding ceremony, pausing only to interject one original touch: "Mr. Matthews has asked that I read a few lines written by a poet enjoyed by him and Miss Avery." Clearing his throat, he recited, " 'Camerado, I give you my hand! I give you my love more precious than money, I give you myself before preaching or law; Will you give me yourself? Will you come travel with me? Shall we stick by each other as long as we live?' " Preacher Smith seemed taken aback by what he had read, but forged onward. "Those lines were written by the poet Walt Whitman."

Wild and glorious emotions swelled Maddie's heart. Her eyes stung; her vision blurred. But still she saw Fox, so handsome that it made her giddy to look at him. For an instant his hand tightened around her own and she knew that everything would be just as she had dreamed between them.

Vows were murmured, followed by Preacher Smith's solemn intonation, "I now pronounce you man and wife. Whom God hath joined together let no man put asunder!"

Fox lifted Maddie's veil and gave her a secret smile. Then, tipping up her chin, he kissed her sweet, petal-soft lips and drew her body against his own with his free hand. When Susan began to clap, the others joined in.

Only Sun Smile stood apart. In the excitement, no one noticed the tear that slipped down her powdered cheek.

Chapter Twenty-five

August 19–20, 1876

AFTER THE BRIDE CAKE AND SEVERAL BOTTLES OF champagne were consumed, and the gifts were opened, and Susan O'Hara had told everyone the story of her parents' wedding—distinguished by the fact that George Washington had given away the bride—Fox managed to announce that he and the new Mrs. Matthews would have to be on their way. This led to another flurry of hugs and congratulations, then everyone began to move toward the kitchen doorway. Only Annie Sunday and Sun Smile were absent. Sun Smile had returned to the wagon after watching the others eat cake, and when Annie Sunday noticed her absence, she hurried out of the house.

"My mother loves a cause," Fox remarked to his new father-in-law. "Don't hesitate to speak up if you feel she's meddling where Sun Smile is concerned. I confess I have my doubts, but on the other hand, there was a great deal of room for improvement and maybe Sun Smile has needed a nudge back into the world." He shrugged, adding, "Ma's a great crusader. I predict that she'll soon go after the badlands."

This elicited a laugh from Charley Utter. "I'd like to see the look on Al Swearingen's face when your ma marches into the Gem Theatre!"

"For Pete's sake, can I take this durned collar off?" Benjamin asked for the dozenth time.

Susan shushed him, then whispered to Maddie, "Darling, you'll see my gift when you get to your new home. And don't

323

worry about supper. I'll set a tray outside the door at seven o'clock.'' She gave her granddaughter a wink.

"Thank you, Gramma." Maddie hugged her, then went into Stephen's arms.

"I don't know what I'm getting so choked up about," Avery muttered. "You're just going next door, for pity's sake!" He looked at Fox over his daughter's head. "I don't have to tell you that I couldn't wish for a better husband for my darling girl than you. I already think of you as my son."

"I appreciate that, sir." Fox extended his hand again to Preacher Smith. "And I appreciate your coming up here and giving my bride a proper wedding, Preacher. She's used to certain formalities being observed!"

"My pleasure, Mr. and Mrs. Matthews." Henry Weston Smith smiled behind his thick, dark beard. "I know that you will have a long and joyous life together."

"Amen," Fox said, then arched a brow and gave Maddie a wicked grin. "And I for one am ready to start this marriage in earnest!"

She blushed, clasped his arm, and they ran from the little house in a shower of rice. With her free hand, Maddie lifted her skirts and tried not to stumble. The little group behind them was cheering gaily, and Fox and Maddie laughed at the silliness of taking a wedding trip to the other side of the row of pine trees. As soon as they were out of sight, he swept her into his arms.

"At *last*." Before his breathless bride could reply, he covered her mouth with his own in a kiss so fiery that they both lost their bearings. When at last Fox lifted his head, he gazed into her eyes and said hoarsely, "I wanted to do that earlier, as soon as Preacher Smith pronounced us man and wife. Lord, how I wanted you then."

Another pretty flush stained her cheeks. "I don't think your mother would have approved, not to mention Preacher Smith."

Fox continued on toward the house, still holding Maddie lightly in his arms. "I can assure you, Mrs. Matthews, that my mother's approval is the farthest thing from my mind."

She snuggled against his chest and wrapped her arms around his neck, beaming. Then, a bothersome thought intruded. "Fox . . . we haven't spoken since you delivered that decidedly unorthodox proposal, and this wedding happened so quickly, that there are a lot of matters I'm not quite clear on—"

"There's only one matter that needs to be clear as far as I'm concerned," he interjected. "We're *married*, which means we are going to get in bed together and not come out until—"

"*Fox!* You'll scare me, talking like that!" Maddie struggled to look anxious, but frolicsome laughter bubbled up inside her and spilled forth. "Just tell me now what we're going to do about your mother. Is she going to live with us? I mean, I know that she *must* be going to, after tonight, that is, and I understand . . ."

Still carrying his new bride, Fox passed the front door of his log house and continued on around the corner. Maddie's eyes widened at the sight of a miniature version of his house situated just a few yards north. He gestured with his handsome head and explained, "Ma's going to live there. You're crazy if you think I'd have her in the same house with us!"

Maddie was agog. "I—For heaven's sake, when on earth did you build that cabin?"

"Titus and I built it, with some help from Charley and Wang Chee these past couple days. That's why you haven't seen me, Madness." He was smiling to himself now, pleased by the expression of shocked wonderment on her face. Carrying her back to the front door of his house, Fox said, "Now then, Mrs. Matthews, if you're satisfied that you won't have to share your home with the Dowager Queen, I'd like to go inside and set you down. It's not that my arms are getting tired, mind you, but I do have other plans for the afternoon." Eyes sparkling with devilment, he added, "Not to mention the evening, the night, and that pretty hour around dawn. . . ."

Maddie nestled her face in the starched edge of his collar and the warm, wonderful-smelling skin just below his ear.

"I'd be glad to go inside with you, Mr. Matthews." That name still sounded rather odd to her ears; it was odder still to realize that it was her name now, too.

Pausing with one hand on the knob, Fox kissed her ear, then whispered, "You may have noticed that I didn't give you a present yet. It's inside, along with the gift from your grandmother."

"Have you two been planning something behind my back?"

The corners of his eyes crinkled as he pushed open the door, lifted her over the threshold, and set her down on the pine floor. The sunshine outside had been dazzling and it took her a moment to adjust to the more shadowed interior of Fox's home.

For a few moments, Maddie was confused. Had she forgotten so much since her last visit here? Surely this house had been empty of real furnishings. But now, on one side of the open staircase, there was a pine table and four stick-back chairs in place of the assortment of planks and barrels. Near the stone fireplace stood a beautiful new stove and shelves stocked with some cooking implements, a few tin plates and cups, and some food staples.

Fox followed a few steps behind her as she wandered around. "I knew that you would want to choose your own dishes and linens, and things to make a parlor, but I wanted to have enough here to make us comfortable until you're ready to make other purchases. I even got us our own bathtub. It occurred to me that you might not want to go with me to the bathhouse," he added, with a wry smile.

Swallowing hard, Maddie struggled to find her voice as she turned to face him. The tentative, hopeful tone of his speech had touched her deeply. How much trouble he had gone to in three short days! "Oh, Fox, this is just *wonderful*. Perfect! There's just enough here so that I can feel as if we have our own little home, but it was excessively thoughtful of you to allow me to choose the rest." She brushed away a tear and gave a shaky laugh. "I must warn you that

I'm very tiresome these days. I cry at all the wrong moments.''

Wrapping her in his arms, Fox loosened the pins in her glorious hair and murmured, "And why is that, Madness?"

"Because I am so insanely *happy*." She whispered the confession into his shirtfront, discovering that her husband had stripped off his coat, vest, and tie while she'd been inspecting her new kitchen. "It's pointless for me to pretend to be above it all. I love you quite desperately. If you wanted to, you could break my heart."

"My foolish darling, why would I do that? You're safe with me, for the rest of your life."

His voice, low and incredibly intoxicating, set off another tide of emotion and more tears of joy. "Fox, why did you do this? Marry me, I mean. You told me—"

"Please, don't remind me of every stupid word I've spoken to you over the past weeks," he said, with a self-deprecating laugh, hugging her tighter. "From the moment we reached Deadwood and our separate and crowded houses, I've missed you so much that it became a pain inside me, gnawing at me night and day. Maybe it wouldn't have demanded such an immediate and radical solution if Ma hadn't been waiting here." He ran his fingers through her silky hair, smiling. "God, but she drove me mad. I couldn't be alone with you anywhere as long as she was here, and then she decided to make *me* her project. She had gone off to Star and Bullock's store to order furnishings for this house the same day I commanded you to marry me. I knew that I had to do something fast or she would have taken over and it would've been too late for this house, and maybe for us, too. Once Ma gets started, she's like a snowball that turns into an avalanche."

"I still cannot get over the fact that you built her her own cabin—and so quickly!"

He chuckled. "I started planning it the night we got home. Which reminds me . . . I started planning something else that night, too. Close your eyes and I'll show you my wedding present to you."

She squeezed her eyes shut while protesting, "But I didn't have a chance to get a present for you—"

"Madness, you're all the present I'll ever need," Fox replied in a voice rich with meaning. He took her hand then and led her under the back of the stairway to the other side of the house. "All right. You can look now."

Opening her eyes, she beheld a dreamlike four-poster bed reposing on the floor in front of them. A wide ray of sunlight streamed through the window and bathed the simple pencil-post creation in a golden haze. Attached to the posts was an unstained tester frame; yards of white lawn fabric were draped high and swirled down at the corners. The rope spring was covered with a deep, inviting feather bed and two puffy down pillows, and the crowning touch was an exquisitely stitched quilt in a multicolored wedding-ring pattern.

After a few moments, Fox produced a handkerchief and watched fondly as Maddie blotted a fresh shower of tears. "Do you like it?" he ventured at length, not without a trace of laughter. When she managed a mute nod, he wrapped his arms around her from behind and kissed the side of her neck. "I thought that you might. And of course, you've recognized your grandmother's gift to us. . . ."

"That quilt was a gift to Gramma Susan and Grandpa Patrick on their wedding day . . . sixty years ago. Gramma's mother, Meagan, made it for her at a quilting party with a lot of other senators' wives in Washington." Maddie shook her head, dazed with pleasure. "How wonderful of her to give it to *us* . . . and—Fox, did you make this *bed* as well as that little cottage for your mother?"

"In my spare time," he admitted laconically.

"And Gramma Susan knew all along what was afoot over here, didn't she?"

"Mmmm . . . yes." As his mouth brushed the nape of her neck, he murmured, "Christ, but you smell magical. Oh, Maddie . . ."

It came to her that his fingers had been unfastening the tiny buttons that marched down the back of her gown, opening them with such practiced skill that she hadn't even felt what was happening until the fabric separated and the heel of his palm touched the softness of her upper back. "This bed is the most beautiful present that anyone has ever given me," she said solemnly. "I just want to say that to you."

"Well, I have a confession to make." He drew the tops of her sleeves down and kissed each of her creamy shoulders in turn.

"A confession?" Little shivers of pleasure ran over her nerves.

"About the bed. As a present." Clasping her hips with strong hands, Fox drew her back against him so that she could feel his hardness even through their clothes. "My motives were not entirely sentimental. In truth, I may have even been thinking a little bit about *myself* when I built it."

She melted into him, cheeks flushed while a telltale tingling warmth blossomed under her skirts. "What were you thinking?" Her voice sounded drunk to her own ears.

"Shall I show you instead, Mrs. Matthews?"

"Please . . ."

The soaring within her reminded Maddie of the day she had stood naked under the waterfall, in broad daylight, and of the passion she had allowed to flourish when she and Fox made love outdoors, aglow in the prairie sunset. It was as if this magnificent being had lived always within her, and Fox had turned the key that liberated her. Thrilled with anticipation, Maddie smiled into his blue eyes as he undressed her slowly, slowly. Off came her muslin petticoat, and then her corset, unlaced by Fox in a way that tantalized her to the point of trembling. At last her breasts were bared, the nipples tightening in the air; but Fox chose to touch them only with his eyes.

Maddie had forgotten how weak she could become from craving Fox, how incredibly wanton he made her feel. He knelt before her, rolled her stockings down her legs and drew off her slippers, and she reached out to touch the ruffled hair on his head.

When he rose, Maddie stood before him wearing only her diamond wedding ring. "You are far too beautiful for words,'' he whispered. It made him smile and feel a rush of love to see how confident she was, her slim shoulders and back straight and her chin raised as she basked in the sunbeams and her husband's approving gaze. Her coppery-gold mane of hair spilled to her hips, more stunning than any piece of jewelry or expensive gown. It seemed ages since he'd taken in the sight of her shapely, milk-white limbs with their dusting of freckles, her full pink-crested breasts, her narrow waist, and dainty wedge of auburn curls that marked the apex of her thighs. His bride was so much more than a beautiful, desirable woman; her body was more perfect than any other because he loved her so.

"I like this," she said, with an irresistible smile.

"Oh?" How lucky he'd been to find this bright, enchanting woman.

Maddie stretched up her arms and rose on tiptoe. "This— this feeling that I've just found out I'm a butterfly, when all along I assumed I must be a wholly different species!" She bent her naked form into a graceful arabesque, eyes sparkling. "I wish I could explain—"

"You don't have to. I understand."

"Yes, I suppose you do." Her expression softened and she began to unbutton his starched white shirt. "You led me into this . . . metamorphosis." Her hands were small and pale against the muscled, nut-brown expanse of Fox's chest. She adored the sensation of his chest hair, crisp and soft at once, when she splayed her fingers and moved them up toward his shoulders.

Deftly Fox stripped off his own clothes and stood, bronzed and powerful, in the hazy shaft of sunlight. He lifted Maddie off the ground and covered her mouth with his own, aware in the midst of that endless, burning kiss of her exquisite fragility, of the swell of her breasts against his hard chest, the fineness of her bones when his hands caressed her. She smelled deliciously of herself; it was a scent he never could pinpoint. Wildflowers, vanilla, lavender . . . no, just Maddie.

His hands cupped her curved buttocks and she arched against him and brought her legs up, wrapping them around his waist. Both of them knew a sudden shock when her parted thighs afforded abrupt proof of her arousal. She was pink and dewy, like a rose opening at dawn—and it happened that she came flush against Fox's fully erect, throbbing manhood.

Their lips parted, their eyes met, widening, and then they shared a moment of delighted laughter. Fox murmured with exaggerated devilment, "Time for bed, my dear Mrs. Matthews. Don't be frightened . . ."

"My wifely duties," she whispered shyly, nodding. "I know that I must—"

"Yes, indeed!"

Their bantering was forgotten as he carried her the few steps to their marriage bed and settled her onto the sumptuous feather tick.

"It's like a cloud," she said in tones of wonderment.

"A welcoming bed is an important ingredient in a happy marriage," Fox told her.

"Who told you that?"

"Your grandmother. Now hush." He gazed down at her, starving yet wanting to make each blissful taste memorable for both of them. He lifted Maddie's foot and kissed her toes and the elegant curves of her leg. Then, as his mouth burned a similar path over the satiny flesh of her other leg, Maddie began to make little moaning sounds that betrayed her excitement.

Through her lashes, she watched as Fox kissed her inner thighs, and she ached, yearning for more. Then, like a dream, he was over her on the bed and their mouths fused, she was able to embrace him, touch him, soak up the texture of his warm, rugged body. They rolled together, thrashing, hungry, giving and taking. Then Maddie lay on Fox's chest and straddled him, her bottom up, rubbing against him insistently. With one hand he reached around while they kissed and stroked her bottom, then ventured farther between her legs. She flinched, then moved on his fingers and his shaft, rising up to brace herself on her hands so that he could kiss, knead, and suckle her breasts. He adored the sight of her above him, head thrown back in surprise and urgency as her climax built.

"Oh." Her eyes opened, then found his face. "Oh!" The contractions seemed to shake her entire body, and her nipples puckered in response. As she rode out the storm, Fox found his way into her, filling her to the hilt.

"This is . . . shameless," she managed to gasp at last, then lay down on him and forced a kiss on him.

Fox was curious to see what she'd do in this position of control, and she reveled in it, moving slowly, tantalizingly, over him. The pleasure was excruciating, and it came to Fox what joy lay ahead for them as they explored the possibilities of physical love.

"Sweet Madness, I love you," he murmured, then turned her into the snowy feather pillows without breaking the connection between their bodies.

"I love you!" Maddie cried, and found that she was weeping again as she met her husband's rhythmic thrusts.

He was filled with tenderness for her, as if they truly were part of each other, and bent his head to kiss away her sweet-salty tears. When his own climax came, it seemed to be torn from the deepest part of his soul, forging yet another bond between them.

Maddie cradled him against her, smoothed back his hair, glimpsed the telltale brilliance of his blue eyes. "Oh, Fox, we're very, very lucky, aren't we."

He could only nod.

Maddie awoke in the middle of the night and remembered again where she was and why. She liked awakening and remembering and then feeling the warm tide of joy that rushed over her. This was *their* bed, in *their* home, and tonight was only the beginning of decades of happiness beyond price.

It was a mild night in the Hills. The quilt Gramma Susan had given them lay folded neatly over a chair back. In the moonlight that spilled through the window, the fresh white sheets looked luminous, and Fox's body very dark in contrast. As her eyes adjusted to the darkness, Maddie saw the

dishes, with the remains of her grandmother's meal on them,
cluttering yet another chair Fox had dragged next to the bed.
The chairs had been pushed together to form a makeshift
table so that the couple could lounge in bed throughout the
evening.

And they had. They'd talked, shared more stories of their
childhoods, relived their separate memories of the early
weeks in their own relationship, and made plans for their
home. They'd eaten, sitting up naked against the headboard
and pillows, trading bites of berries or corn bread with honey
or succulent roast beef or acorn squash or peach cobbler.
And, every so often, they'd turned to each other with renewed hunger and rapture. Fox had brushed Maddie's hair
as the sun set, brushing and caressing until she'd begun to
doze off. She'd made him lie full-length on top of the sheets
and given him a head-to-toe massage by the flickering light
of an oil lamp. It was sheer pleasure for her to examine each
detail of the body she adored so. And, to her further delight,
she'd discovered that her big, strong husband was ticklish!

After midnight she'd come slowly awake to find that he
was touching her intimately with his mouth, and the realization was thrilling beyond reason. Each time they made love
seemed new and special and exciting in its own right.

When Maddie opened her eyes this time, however, she
sensed that dawn was approaching . . . perhaps in an hour
or two. Fox was awake again, but his mind had left their
marriage bed. Lying on his back, he was staring at the tester
frame he'd built. His hands were clasped behind his head and
every so often a muscle moved in his cheek.

"Fox?" Maddie spoke his name in a tiny voice. All night
they'd snuggled or at least held hands, but now she sensed
that he'd forgotten her. "Is—is something wrong?"

He didn't look over. "I'm worrying about a lot of things
I can't control," he replied, with cool irony. "It's a bad habit
men have—worrying that the worst will happen and there's
nothing to prevent it."

"I don't understand. What are you talking about?" Maddie propped herself on an elbow and tried to read his face in the shadows. Its chiseled lines only magnified her anxiety.

Fox sighed. "Well, if you care to ponder our current circumstances, you'll realize that nothing has changed since I told you at Bear Butte that I'd be doomed if I told the truth about my identity and my past here in Deadwood. Ma got here and spread my real name all over, though, so I thought what the hell and married you, too . . . for good measure." He continued to stare upward. "Fact is, though, I may have dragged you into this mess with me, if the worst happens. It could spell the end of this little dreamworld we've begun making here."

A strange sense of dread crept outward from Maddie's heart. "Fox, we can't think of all these things! I mean, we have other problems, real problems, but there's no use lying awake on our wedding night fretting about them—"

"Men don't fret, exactly," he interjected, with a trace of amusement.

"For example, what am I going to do about Sun Smile? Don't you think that I feel responsible for her, since we brought her back here and she's my half-sister? Don't you think I feel *guilty* for the way I've behaved toward her? I know that there must be something I could do to help draw her out and make her feel loved. Don't you think—"

"Ye gods!" Fox exclaimed, laughing. "Don't ask me if I think again, because obviously you've been doing enough thinking for both of us! It's clear that I'll have to give up my predawn brooding sessions now that we're married. How can I lie awake and brood if my wife won't be quiet?"

The cloud had lifted. They were both laughing now, huddling together under the sheet and kissing madly. Intoxicated with joy and relief, Maddie tried to tickle the secret places she'd discovered earlier, and Fox caught her wrists and pinned her beneath him on the bed.

"Never in my entire life has any female had the effrontery to tickle me!" he declared in a deep, commanding voice.

"Is that supposed to deter me?" Maddie countered, nuzzling his chest.

"I thought I ought to give it a try."

"Sorry."

Laughing, Fox released her and they began to kiss and caress each other with renewed desire.

Whatever the future brought to them, they could weather as long as they were together. . . . Maddie would have voiced the sentiment aloud, but her mouth was busy elsewhere. Besides, she figured Fox probably knew that as well as she did. . . .

Chapter Twenty-six

August 21, 1876

On Monday morning, Maddie and Gramma Susan went down to Main Street with Fox, who had a business meeting. He escorted the ladies into Bullock and Star's store, only to find that they were about to close up.

"Sorry, folks," said Sol Star. "We're goin' to the funeral."

Fox held his wife's arm. They glanced at each other, somehow sensing simultaneously that the clouds were rolling in again. "Funeral?"

"Oh, that's right; your family's been busy with a wedding! Congratulations, uh . . ." There was still a certain amount of confusion about Fox's surname, and Star was in no hurry to clear it up. "Well, I hate to be the bearer of bad tidings, but Preacher Smith's been killed."

Susan O'Hara gasped aloud, and Fox put his other arm around her for support. Maddie had gone stark white.

"Reverend Smith officiated at our wedding," she said weakly. "How could—I mean, less than two days ago he was eating bride cake in my father's parlor!"

In unison Star and Bullock intoned, *"Indians."*

"I hope you'll elaborate," said Fox.

Seth Bullock suggested that his partner go on ahead to the funeral, which was to be held at Preacher Smith's house. When the door had closed behind Sol Star, Bullock said, "I have just been composing a letter to a Reverend Chadwick in Louisville, Kentucky, informing him of the details of his friend's death. I discovered his name and address among Preacher Smith's things. It's a sad business."

"What *did* happen?" Fox pressed.

"Preacher Smith was attacked by a band of hostile Indians while returning from Crook City to Deadwood yesterday afternoon. He was shot through the heart, and we believe that death was instantaneous. Certainly there can be no doubt that he is with his Master now, in a far better world than this." Bullock removed his bowler and gazed sadly at the floor for a moment. "I'll be conducting the service at Reverend Smith's grave, and I plan to read part of a poem that he wrote. Have you heard it?"

"I didn't know that he was a poet," Maddie said. "I should love to hear the verses."

Seth Bullock took a piece of paper from his suit pocket, unfolded it, and read:

> This evening is the first of June,
>   And snow is falling fast.
> The tall pines sigh, howl, and moan,
>   Responsive to the blast.
> The shades of night are gathered 'round;
>   The fire is burning low,
> I sit and watch the dying coals,
>   And think of long ago.

Silence fell over the room, then Susan O'Hara spoke. "That was really very lovely."

Bullock nodded and put the paper back in his pocket. "Preacher Smith must've been among the first to come to Deadwood, if he was writing about a summer blizzard like that. He was a true man of God, living out here without any comforts, risking his life every day to bring some peace to the souls of others. I reckon he was a martyr."

Fox was thinking about Wild Bill. It was beginning to seem risky just living in Deadwood. "I wonder why Indians would kill Preacher Smith," he mused. "Did someone see them? Is there proof?"

"Well, sir, those that found the body told me it was Indians, so I guess there must've been some sign." He put his hat on again and started toward the door. "You're welcome to stay, ladies, and look through the sample books until I get back. Shouldn't take long." With one hand on the knob, he glanced at Fox. "Can't understand why you'd bring that squaw to a town like Deadwood. People around these parts will always look for someone to go after when they think they have a score to settle. I sure wouldn't feel safe in Deadwood these days if I was an Indian." Bullock's bushy dark brows rose as he added, "Nothing personal, of course. Just a word to the wise. I like you folks."

When they were alone, Maddie and Gramma Susan took chairs at the fabric table and began to leaf through Bullock's sample books, murmuring words of shock and sadness. Fox listened to them, his own heart tight with pain for the loss of one more good man. Bullock's "word to the wise" had started him off on a different trail of thought.

"Do you mind if I leave you two here for a while?" he asked. When Maddie encouraged him to pursue his own business so they could return home soon, he kissed her cheek, and Susan's, then strode to the front door.

"Aren't we all lucky," Susan said absently.

"Lucky just to be alive, it seems, in this town," Fox replied, and headed out onto Main Street.

In some ways, Deadwood looked just as it had that day he'd first ridden into town on Watson, and in other ways it was very different. The sides of the gulch were still barren and muddy, littered with burned trees that resembled black toothpicks from afar. There were still miners everywhere one looked, including in between and under the buildings lining Main Street and Sherman Street. There were still fancy girls leaning off balconies in the badlands, gamblers and rowdies flowing in and out of saloons, merchants throwing garbage into the streets, and Chinese still bustling about their northern section of Deadwood.

On the other hand, the narrow gulch was more crowded now than anyone could have imagined even a few short weeks ago. Fox thought back to the last walk he'd taken with Bill Hickok, when they'd remarked on the new establishments that were springing up like weeds. Jacob Goldberg had arrived from Montana while he and Maddie were away at Bear Butte, and now Goldberg ran the Big Horn Store in place of P. A. Gushurst, who had moved his business to Lead. There were new restaurants and hotels Fox hadn't noticed before, not to mention more saloons and hurdy-gurdy houses than ever. Jack Langrishe and his wife had established their theater, albeit out of canvas, and were now performing plays with the help of two other actresses. The other day Mrs. Langrishe had told Annie Sunday that a new school was going to begin serving the children of Deadwood, run by a teacher called William Commode.

Fox mulled over all these changes, realizing again that a prosperous future awaited those smart enough or crazy enough to stick it out. He and Maddie had decided to stay. He would start up his own sawmill, with Titus as the manager, and they'd begin by planting seedlings to replace the trees they took down. Progress would continue with or without them, and at least Fox and Maddie had some scruples.

Now, however, he was trying to get a feel for his town again. Preacher Smith's killing baffled him. He didn't want to think that any of the people he knew at Bear Butte could have done such a thing, but, remembering He Dog's words in the council tent, he knew it was possible. The Lakota Indians had a different point of view regarding whites arrogant enough to trespass like thieves in their sacred *Paha Sapa*. The citizens of Deadwood could never understand how the Indians felt; in truth, they had no interest in understanding or sympathizing with them at all. To do so would mean seeing them as fellow human beings, with rights and feelings, and that would complicate everything. The chasm between Indians and the whites was too great, it seemed, to ever be bridged.

Was Sun Smile in danger here?

Fox wandered into the badlands, listening and watching as he tried to get a sense of Deadwood's mood. It wasn't a difficult task. Within minutes Garnet Loomis blew out of the Gem Theatre like a frigate in full sail. Clad in a cheap gown of magenta silk trimmed in torn feathers, her debauched face painted in a way that seemed to accentuate each line and roll of fat, she was like a walking advertisement for the badlands.

"Wait justa minute, dearie!" She grabbed his shirtsleeve and held it fast. "What's your hurry? Come on in and I'll letcha buy me a drink!"

Her breath already stank of whiskey, but Fox tried not to make his revulsion too obvious. "It's kind of you to ask, Garnet, but in case you haven't heard, I'm a married man now. Newly married, in fact. I have to *try* to behave myself!"

She reached up with her other hand to touch the locks of hair that curled over his collar. "God was sure workin' hard when He made you! Doesn't seem right that one woman'd have you all t'herself! Well, at least our little Victoria don't hafta pine for you no more. A couple of days ago, a millionaire from Denver proposed to her. She went off with him this mornin'. Gonna live in a mansion and be a stepmama to three youngsters!"

"Is she indeed?" Fox's heart lightened at the thought. "I hope she is very happy. Victoria is one of the kindest women I've ever known. I might not be here if not for her."

"And what about *Lorna*?" Garnet hissed, wagging her head toward the red-haired girl seated forlornly at the bar inside. "Don't think we don't know how you broke her heart, and how you wanted her in the first place 'cause she looks like the snooty girl who thought she was too good to have me in her house!"

"You're referring to my wife," Fox replied coolly, "and I hardly think that Lorna is in a position to worry about having her heart broken. It seems to me that that would be an occupational hazard for upstairs girls. Now then, if you'll excuse me, I have other business—"

Suddenly Garnet's voice dropped to an evil-sounding whisper. "I knowed you was an Injin lover that first day I metcha! You think you're better'n the rest of us in your house

on the hill, but you can't make up your own rules and get
away with it!''

"What the devil are you talking about?" he demanded.

"That *squaw*. You think the people in this town'll stand
for that?''

"That's right, Garnet," called a familiar voice. "Our
friend here has set himself up as a sort of sultan in that house
that's tucked away from the rest of the town."

Fox whirled around to see who'd spoken. Graham Horatio
Scofield III, who had obviously been drinking, waggled his
fingers at Fox.

"*What* did you say?" Fox challenged in deadly tones.

"Just that you're like a sultan up there with your own little
kingdom and a white wife and an Indian wife. One shudders
to think what sort of goings-on—"

"Scofield, I suggest that you shut up before something
very painful happens to you," Fox cut in. "Sun Smile is my
wife's half-sister. She has come to live in the Avery household at the request of her father, Stephen Avery. Sun Smile
was widowed recently and is still in mourning for her husband, but we hope that she'll come to find happiness with
her other family, since the future for the Lakota Indians is so
bleak." He looked at Scofield, and then Garnet, who yawned
as if bored. "I have treated both of you with enough courtesy
to give you a truthful explanation of Sun Smile's presence in
Stephen Avery's home. I would hope that you would return
that favor by correcting any malicious gossip that you might
overhear." Fox pierced Garnet with a stare as sharp as splin-
ters of blue ice, and she dropped his sleeve and took a step
backward. "I bid you good morning."

Graham stepped in front of him, blocking his path.
"There's something about you that's just not right, Mr. *Matthews*. I'd bet my family fortune that you have a secret, and
I mean to discover what it is. Maybe it's common for men
around Deadwood to be known by just one name, and not
have a post—I mean a past—but why would an eastern gentleman like you, with an education and a fancy, well-bred
mother, do that unless you have a secret? You even dressed

up like a miner and acted like you were from the West, until your mama turned up to expose you! Simply inexplicable. I for one am proud as punch of each and every letter in *my* name, and—''

"Scofield, I don't mean to be rude, but you are a long-winded fool," Fox cut in, then turned and walked away. He hadn't proceeded more than a few steps when he heard Graham Scofield begin to speak again.

"Lorna! Loorrrna! . . . There you are! Just the beauty I've been searching for!" The rest of his speech was lost as the young man from Boston—with the extremely important name—staggered into the Gem and out of sight.

"Sun Smile would like to join us for tea, wouldn't you, dear?" Holding the hand of Maddie's half-sister, Annie Sunday drew Sun Smile into the kitchen of the Avery house. "Madeleine, Susan, would you think me overbearing if I asked that we take tea in the parlor today? I thought that it might be best for Sun Smile to experience this properly the first time." Annie Sunday's kindly voice brooked no argument from any of the parties concerned.

Maddie and her grandmother exchanged glances. "Actually I was thinking of inviting you to our home for tea. That's why I'd just come in—to ask Gramma if—''

"But you cannot mean it!" Annie Sunday laughed, although there was no humor in her demeanor. "In fact, I ought to apologize to you on behalf of my son. He wasn't raised to live like that, and I must tell you that I was shocked when I moved in over there and had a good look at that . . . *cabin*. I'm certain that he improved it to some extent before your wedding, but the place is no more fit for a proper tea than that tiny cottage where I now live." She paused. "Besides, it would be good for Stephen to join us. And while he may be much improved, he's still tired from the excitement of the wedding and should not be forced to leave the house."

Her reasoning was so sensible that they had to agree. While Maddie helped her grandmother prepare the tea and slice pieces of cake, she noticed that Annie Sunday had placed

Sun Smile on the settee and then brought Stephen out to sit beside his daughter. They made an oddly affecting picture: the earnest white man in his tailored trousers and stiff-bosomed shirt seated next to the neatly dressed yet spiritless young woman.

Maddie decided that Sun Smile seemed even more disturbing in her ladylike, white female's gown, because she still looked so much like an Indian, with her straight black hair and dark skin. Moreover, her eyes still burned with grief and pain, and another emotion that Maddie feared might be rage.

They all took seats in the parlor. Annie Sunday began to talk about the plans she had for Sun Smile: reading and writing and sewing and cooking, to name a few. Stephen voiced his approval and reached for his daughter's hand. Although Sun Smile did not resist, she continued to look straight ahead while he beamed at her.

Sipping her tea, Maddie tried to decide what she thought about her new mother-in-law. Annie Sunday had an annoying habit of taking charge of everything and everyone in sight, yet the fact was that she usually did have the best plan, and how could Maddie argue in the face of her sensible ideas? Now that she and Fox were truly married, she hoped that she would have an opportunity to become better acquainted with Annie Sunday. Perhaps they might even be friends, if the woman could back away just a bit from her efforts to control nearly everyone Maddie loved.

A good starting point might be a private conversation between herself and her mother-in-law, Maddie decided. Perhaps she could share what she had come to understand about the Lakota Indians, in the hope that Annie Sunday might not try so hard to force Sun Smile into the mold of a white woman. She was just about to invite the elder Mrs. Matthews to visit her when a rumbling noise reached her ears.

"What's that?" asked Stephen.

Annie Sunday went to the window and peeked through the ruffled curtains. "Why, . . . I believe that must be a—*mob* coming toward the house! Reminds me of some of the crowds that used to cause a ruckus in the streets of Washington before the Civil War broke out.'' She put on her spectacles, nodding. ''I believe they're angry about our dear Sun Smile.''

A torrent of emotions swept Maddie; she was surprised by the force of it. Jumping to her feet, she looked first at Sun Smile, whose eyes were as wide as a doe's, then at her father. Benjamin came clattering down the stairs, shouting, ''What'll we do? What'll we do? Where's Fox? Shall I get the gun?''

Maddie put a hand on his shoulder to stop him before he could scramble toward Stephen's room for the rifle her father kept propped against the windowsill. ''No. I'll get the gun.''

When she passed her father, she saw that he was squeezing Sun Smile's hand so hard that her fingers were white; his other hand was pressed to his chest. Clearly he was in pain. ''Madeleine . . . I can't let you go out there. I'm the man of the family—''

''Nonsense, Father,'' she replied briskly. ''You're ill. Do you think I'd allow you to risk your life over a foolish incident like this? I'll deal with those ignorant louts.'' When she returned with the rifle, she surprised herself with the wave of affection she felt toward Sun Smile. It caused her to reach out and caress the Lakota woman's cheek. ''Don't worry about a thing.''

Even Annie Sunday appeared to give in after considering what position to take. Although normally a dominating presence, she was not the sort to take charge when violence threatened. Now she stood aside and watched with a gleam of respect in her hazel eyes as her daughter-in-law threw open the front door and stepped onto the porch.

What appeared to be a sea of angry faces filled the open area in front of the house. Someone yelled, ''Injin lover! Bring out that Injin! She might be the one who killed Preacher Smith!''

There was a general rumbling of agreement; key words were repeated over and over. Deep in the crowd, a derby pulled down low on his head, was Graham Scofield. ''They're all animals!'' he was crying in an attempt to stir up the mob. ''Can't be trusted! We won't be safe until every Injin in Dakota Territory is dead!'' Each time he spoke, other voices rose in a chorus of repetition.

Finally Maddie pointed the rifle into the air and pulled the trigger. Again. And then again. When the mindless shouting died down, she turned the gun toward the mob and yelled, ''You all haven't the sense God gave a mule! My dear sister is no threat to any of you, or to anyone else! She is a member of my family and a peaceful person—with as much right to be in Deadwood as any of you. More, actually, since the Indians inhabited the Black Hills long before our silly white faces intruded. Now, unless you want me to shoot right into you, I suggest that you all turn tail and run as fast as you can off our property!''

With that, she cocked the hammer and watched as the people began to retreat. Gradually their grumbling ceased, and a few even offered her an apology in parting. When she went back into the house, she set down the rifle and walked to the settee. Her father was smiling, tears in his eyes. She hugged him, then turned to her sister and hugged her, too.

''Welcome to our family, Sun Smile,'' she whispered against her cheek. ''You'll be safe with us for as long as you care to stay.''

Maddie felt certain that she wasn't imagining the feeling that Sun Smile hugged her in return.

Chapter Twenty-seven

September 15, 1876

PARADISE ITSELF COULD NOT BE MORE SUBLIME than our life, Maddie thought. Her heart caressed each word as she formed them in her mind. In the first days of her marriage to Fox, she had waited for the joy to abate, yet the more she loved, the more it seemed her heart could hold. Both Maddie and Fox knew that what they were making together was a treasure beyond price, and they were wise enough to share a deep sense of gratitude.

Snuggling against Fox's tapering, tanned back, Maddie wrapped her arm around him and pressed kisses to the nape of his neck, to his shoulder blades and down his spine. Her hand felt the muscled ridges of his belly, then strayed lower to find Fox fully and invitingly erect. His body never ceased to amaze and intoxicate her.

"Madness," he mumbled, apparently still asleep, "I have a bite. A big one."

"You do?" Maddie propped herself up to peek at her husband's profile. His hair was tousled on his brow, and he looked engagingly boyish and worried. Maddie had learned that it was not uncommon for Fox to make sudden, clear statements in his sleep. Sometimes they were alarming, the product of nightmares, but more often when she heard his words she wanted to giggle. "What are you biting?"

Fox frowned. "I—what—?" Apparently unwilling to leave the dream, he burrowed facedown into his pillow.

Unable to restrain herself, Maddie nuzzled his shoulder

and ran her hand down the sculpted surface of his back and
buttocks. The morning sun drenched the bed with warmth,
so she swept back the covers. After a moment Fox turned his
head and opened one eye.

"I was fishing," he muttered accusingly.

"Oh!" Green eyes twinkling, she tried not to smile. "I
see!"

Fox pretended to begrudge her his embrace as she crawled
into his arms. In a voice husky with sleep, he complained,
"It was the biggest rainbow trout I've ever seen, and the
setting was magnificent—a secluded rushing stream high in
the Hills, a crisp morning, my wife perched on the bank,
watching in adoration as I reeled in the thrashing monster."
He sighed. "It must've weighed twenty pounds."

"Is that possible?" Maddie asked, her cheek against the
strength of his chest. "A twenty-pound rainbow trout, I
mean?"

"That's not the point! It was a *dream*, and I was enjoying
every moment." He saw by the sun that he had overslept,
yet still he lingered in the feather bed. Maddie was nibbling
at him, her hair like a soft stream of fire across his body.
They seemed to drink from the same well of joy these days,
and when his naturally more brooding nature rose up, Maddie surrounded him like an enchanting light, infecting him
with her own relentless high spirits. Gradually Fox was
learning that his sense of foreboding was pointless; all that
was real was the present moment. Marriage to Maddie made
each day so magical that he found himself worrying less and
less about tomorrow. "It's late," he said now without conviction.

Wearing only a wispy lawn chemise edged in lace, Maddie
straddled his hips and smiled with confident sensuality. She
tossed her head back so that her hair swept over Fox's thighs,
then drew the chemise over her head to reveal her narrow
waist and creamy, opulent breasts.

"You're insatiable," Fox declared, his voice a mixture of
amusement and arousal as he reached out to touch her.

"It's not my fault," Maddie replied, fairly purring under

the play of his fingers. "I'm insatiable because *you* are irre-sistible. Or maybe it's this bed. Did you put a spell on it when you built it?"

"I think we did that together, on our wedding night, dar-ling." With that, he drew her into his arms and they made love with sweet, feverish ardor.

It was nearly ten o'clock by the time Maddie and Fox were dressed, fed, and ready to begin the day. Sitting at the table as he finished a second cup of coffee, Fox gazed around the house that his wife had worked so lovingly to transform into a home these past weeks. Her touch was everywhere, from the flowers that brightened every tabletop, to the pictures on the walls, to the cozy, inviting settee and various other pieces of furniture that now filled the spacious rooms. Many things had been Colleen Avery's; Stephen had sent for many of the larger pieces in an attempt to cheer his daughter. Some—such as a ladder-back rocking chair with a woven rush seat, a decorated warming pan to use in their bed when winter struck, a set of silver candlesticks, and a beautiful hand-painted dower chest—had not been unpacked until now. The house was a happy mixture of family heirlooms and new pieces that Maddie and Fox had chosen together. Whenever Fox opened the door and stepped into this home, the sense of well-being and contentment that swept over him was pow-erful.

And in spite of the challenges of his new work, he also felt a tug when it was time for him to leave the house. It came now as he stood and set down his cup. Maddie was making a great effort to become a real cook, and she looked up from the pie crust she was mixing. "Are you sure you wouldn't like another egg?" she asked. "More ham?"

Fondly he shook his head. "I've no doubt that Titus is despairing of me. He's probably been at the sawmill, over-seeing construction, for hours while I lay abed."

"He understands," she said, smiling.

"For the moment. Now, give me a kiss, but don't try to take advantage of me again . . ."

Maddie cuffed his arm, wiped her hands on her apron, and

then stepped into his embrace. She walked him to the door, kissed him again, and then watched him walk out into the morning sunshine. It was a spectacular day: Indian summer with the promise of frost at night. As Fox left his wife and started off to fetch Watson, Annie Sunday's cottage door opened and she looked out.

"Daniel, you're lazier than you have a right to be, you know."

With an indulgent smile, he paused to kiss his mother's cheek. "Fortunately I have you to remind me of my short-comings."

"Don't be impudent." Annie Sunday wagged a finger at him, then asked, "How do you like the curtains?"

Fox thought for a moment before he realized that she was referring to the curtains she and Susan O'Hara had helped Maddie sew. The crisp, light panels of gathered muslin had gone up two days earlier. The triumph, as he saw it, was not the curtains, but the relationship that Maddie had worked so painstakingly to forge with his mother over the past weeks. As difficult as it was to believe, all three households now got along better than he would have ever dreamed possible.

"I like the curtains," he assured her, adding, "And I appreciate you, Ma. You're a good woman."

"I know it." She straightened her shoulders and gave him a bold smile. "Now be on your way. From the looks of things, you'll soon have children to feed, and you can't do it if you lie in bed with your wife all day, Daniel Matthews!"

Annie Sunday left the door to her cottage open after Fox had ridden off, and soon enough Maddie appeared. She stood for a moment in the doorway, gazing at her half-sister, who sat beside Annie Sunday in the window seat. A book was spread open on the older woman's lap and she pointed to pictures and said the words for each, which Sun Smile softly repeated.

"Good morning, you two," Maddie greeted them.

Sun Smile looked up and nodded, the corners of her mouth turned upward slightly. Maddie still had doubts about her mother-in-law's methods with Sun Smile, but she was so busy with her own life that she left them alone. At least Sun Smile appeared to be adjusting, and Maddie didn't know a better alternative than Annie Sunday's approach. What pleased her most was the tentative feeling that a bond of some sort was forming between herself and her half-sister . . . and that bond was even more evident between Sun Smile and Stephen Avery. Although they could not communicate in words, they had a relationship now that Maddie sometimes envied. Stephen seemed to be attached to Annie Sunday, too. Fox had discussed all these relationships with her and helped her to understand that Annie and Sun Smile were filling needs for Stephen that Maddie no longer had time to cater to. He helped her to feel grateful that life had shifted some of the characters around so that everyone was getting the love they needed.

"Daniel said that he likes our curtains," Annie Sunday said to her daughter-in-law. "Why don't you make yourself a cup of tea and sit down for a bit? The water in the kettle is still hot."

Maddie obeyed, listening to the English lesson until she took a chair near the window seat. "Actually I came over to copy down your recipe for wild plum pie."

"Where did you get wild plums?"

"Oh, one of Gramma Susan's friends brought her a bushel basket full from the lower hills. She says they're quite tart, but it'll be fun to see what we can make with them."

Annie Sunday removed her spectacles and tapped a fingertip against her chin in a gesture that reminded Maddie of Fox. "Wild plums are difficult to seed. Perhaps I should help Susan."

"I'm sure she'd appreciate it," Maddie replied. She could have sworn for an instant that Sun Smile gave her a knowing glance, but then her half-sister's gray eyes returned to the picture book.

At that moment, as if on cue, Susan O'Hara appeared in the doorway, holding a huge basket filled with oval, orange-red wild plums. "What a morning I've had! Today is Benjamin's first day of school here. Thank goodness for Wang

Chee, or he'd never have gotten there on time." She directed a faintly accusatory glance at her granddaughter, who had the grace to blush. "I understand that you are newly married, Madeleine, but I hope that you don't intend to leave me completely alone to care for your ailing father and rambunctious brother!"

Annie Sunday had taken the basket from the elderly woman and led her to a worn wing chair. Now she brought her a cup of tea. "Land sakes, why didn't someone tell *me* about young Benjamin's schedule? Sun Smile and I would have gotten him to school on time." She reached out to smooth back an errant white wisp from Susan's brow. "Now then, I want you to promise that if you need help, you won't give a second thought to calling on me. What else am I good for?"

"Oh, I—"

"I insist, Susan!"

The old woman sank back in the chair with a smile of surrender. Annie Sunday, it seemed, had grown on her. "Well, if you insist . . ."

"That's what family's for. We're all blessed to be here together, and we need to enjoy one another's company, just as we did while we were making those curtains for the children." Crossing the floor, she put on her spectacles again and took a plum from the basket, examining it with a critical eye. "These appear to be excellent wild plums. I was just telling my daughter-in-law that I know an easy way to seed these. Why don't we spend the afternoon making pies and jam?"

Susan smiled and nodded, adding that Annie Sunday's plan sounded like a wonderful way to pass an autumn day. Maddie glanced over to see Sun Smile nodding, too, her gray eyes wide with pleasure.

While Annie Sunday, Susan, Maddie, and Sun Smile were making wild plum pies in the cottage above Sherman Street, a very different drama was unfolding farther north on Deadwood's Main Street.

Graham Horatio Scofield III happened to be standing in

front of Nuttall & Mann's Number 10 Saloon when a group of what appeared to be half-dead soldiers came straggling down the hill into Chinatown. A few, including a man with a bushy, forked beard and an impressive uniform, rode horses; the rest were on foot. People began to stop and stare at them, pointing and chattering.

Scofield strolled over to a gambler who he knew had been living in this region for several months. The black-haired fellow sported a waxed and perfumed mustache and called himself Cheyenne Luke.

"Luke! What's this all about? Any idea?" Scofield had learned to adjust his manner to fit whomever he was with.

"Where you been, pilgrim? Didn't you hear that General Crook and his men was headed this way? They been starving all the way south from Little Bighorn, 'least that's what I was told. Those sneakin' red savages knew that Crook was hunting 'em down, so they burned all the grass and there wasn't food for the army's horses." Luke twirled his mustache thoughtfully. "I heard that Crook had revenge, though. Attacked a bunch of Sioux at Slim Buttes an' burned their village. Killed 'em all, I bet. They was those hostiles with Crazy Horse . . . I just hope Crook is gonna make a speech an' tell us he managed to blast a hole through that heathen Crazy Horse, too!" Cheyenne Luke paused to relight a cigar stub, then continued, "Anyways, by that time, a week or so ago, Crook's troops'd ate about all the horses, or so the story goes . . . an' from the look of 'em on foot, I guess it's true. Anyways, a relief force from Camp Crook, just a little ways north of here, took supplies up to the troops, an' now they've made it here."

"I hope that they mean to get reinforcements and go after every single Indian within a hundred miles of the Black Hills! The raids from that rabid Crazy Horse have got to stop! And, how can we allow Fox Matthews, or whatever his name really is, to keep that squaw in his home? He found her with Crazy Horse—For all we know, she is that evil savage's agent, planted among us by one of our own citizens!" Scofield raised his voice as he spoke, and it pleased him to hear rumbling agreement from the townspeople nearby.

Soon general pandemonium erupted as miners and upstairs girls alike surged into the street to welcome the mud-caked, emaciated troopers of Gen. George Crook's Third Cavalry. Graham Scofield had a feeling that something good was going to come his way as a result of these new developments. Even Calamity Jane, Capt. Jack Crawford, and Charley Utter were here today.

Wading through the crowds, he crossed Main Street and accosted a skeletal, ragged soldier in front of the Gem Theatre. Like his comrades, the fellow had broken ranks and was starting through the doorway in search of the pleasures within. Scofield caught his arm and felt the sharp bones of his elbow.

"My good man, I hope you will allow me to buy you a bottle. You look as if you could use one, along with a hot meal!" he cried in jovial tones.

The trooper blinked, then broke into a grin that revealed a stained front tooth broken in half. Before speaking, he sucked on it. "Well, sir, I'd be much obliged! Don't know which I need more, food or drink, but I kin tell you that I ain't had much to eat 'cept my horse for longer'n I kin remember."

Although horrified by this gruesome announcement, Scofield clapped the man on the back and led him into the dimly lit interior of the Gem. It was redolent of smoke, strong spirits, and cheap perfume. Scofield watched his new friend inhale with gusto. "Allow me to introduce myself. I'm Graham Horatio Scofield the Third, and it is my honor to be of service to a hero like yourself."

Stroking his straggly, tangled beard and sucking on his broken tooth, the trooper replied. "I'm Jeb Campbell. I nearly got killed at Little Bighorn, then I got sent off with General Crook and the Third Cavalry an' I thought I was gonna starve to death if I didn't get killed by more of that Crazy Horse's savage scum. This is been the worst summer of my life, sir, an' all I wanta do is get outta the army an' get rich.''

Scofield brought a bottle to their table, poured a generous drink for Jeb Campbell, and gave him a charming smile. ''I'd say that you deserve that and more, Jeb. And you've come to the right town. In Deadwood, a fellow can do just about anything he wants. . . .''

By the time Gen. George Crook emerged onto the balcony of the Grand Central Hotel to speak to the citizens of Deadwood, Jeb Campbell was pretty drunk and well into ogling Al Swearingen's soiled doves. Scofield had promised to buy one for him later, as he'd plied the man with more liquor in exchange for every detail of his life story.

''Crook's gettin' ready to make a speech!'' Garnet Loomis announced, waving at the boisterous crowd in the Gem to come join her outside.

''Let's go out and listen,'' Scofield suggested to Jeb. Nodding, the hapless trooper staggered to his feet and lurched out the door, with Graham Scofield a few paces behind him.

Main Street was as festive as if it were the Fourth of July. A brass band played a few patriotic tunes before General Crook appeared. It was difficult to hear what he was saying over all the noise and cheering, but Scofield did make out the general's promise that with his arrival, the threat of further Indian raids was over. The ovation that followed was deafening.

Jeb Campbell shrugged. ''Easy for him to say; he's leavin' tomorrow. Some of us'll stay behind, but I'm done with fightin'.'' He stared at Scofield for a moment with bleary eyes, then confessed, ''I almost ran before the battle at Slim Buttes. Plenty of others did.''

Through the crowd, Scofield glimpsed a face he now despised. Fox tried to blend in, to be inconspicuous, but his height, physique, and arresting profile drew eyes to him. Today, he was wearing the same brown slouch hat that had covered his head the day he'd first ridden into Deadwood, and a blue kerchief was tied around his neck, brushing the gold-and-chestnut whiskers of his close-trimmed beard. They helped to conceal his face, but Fox was a hard man to miss.

"See that man over there?" Scofield said in a voice that dripped venom. He poked Jeb Campbell in the side. "The one wearing the blue kerchief round his neck? There's a man who had had more luck than anyone deserves . . . in fact, he's had luck that should have come *my* way. He came here barely two months ago with nothing, and now he's rich, he has a home, a business, a beautiful wife who is the most glorious and desirable—"

"I *know* that feller!" Jeb cut in with a hiss, squinting at Fox. "Least I think so. He didn't have a beard, but . . . what's his name?"

"Well, he went by the name Fox when he first arrived, but I've recently learned that his name is Daniel Matthews. I have always suspected that he has a secret, and that if I could only learn it, it could spell his ruin!"

Jeb staggered drunkenly, grasped Scofield's arm for support, and leered into his face. "I know that secret, but I can't tell ya fer free."

After pushing the bony trooper up against the side of the Gem Theatre, Scofield looked around to make certain they were not being observed. "Listen to me, you stupid idiot! I'll pay you, if that's what you want, but if your information is truly valuable, we can use it against him and both become as rich as Croesus! We can ruin him and have all his possessions for ourselves!"

"Maybe, but I'd as soon see money *now*," Jeb slurred. Watching as Scofield dug through his pockets, the soldier mused, "Life sure is funny, ain't it? Who'da thought I'd see Cap'n Matthews again? Even when that squaw at Slim Buttes tipped me off that he was here, told me that he was ascared of bein' found out about Little Bighorn, I didn't think that she knew what she was talkin' about."

"What squaw? He has one here, too."

"Yeah, that's what this other one said. Her name was . . ." He scratched his head and a tiny black bug jumped downward. "Uh . . . somethin' like Runs Away. I didn't pay her much mind at the time, but prob'ly wouldn't of recognized him if that squaw hadn't reminded me.'' Belching, Jeb added, "Not a bad piece of tail fer a squaw, either. Had'ta burn her tipi anyways, even though I told her I wouldn't if she—''

Impatiently Scofield stuffed a number of bills and coins into the drunken man's grimy hand and said, "Now then, *tell* me! You called him Captain Matthews. What's that all about? Was he in the army?''

"How 'bout that pocket watch yer sportin' there on yer vest? Sure is purty.''

Scofield's eyes were glittering with rage and urgency as he unhooked the chain that extended from a buttonhole down to his watch pocket. Practically throwing the engraved heirloom, the property of generations of Boston Scofields, at the hideous Jeb Campbell, he cried, "Tell me, *now*!''

With a slow smile, the soldier beckoned him forward, then whispered, "Well, sir, the long and the short of it is that Cap'n Daniel Matthews deserted from the Seventh Cavalry just before the massacre at Little Bighorn. General Custer'd just divided the troops, an' Matthews was to go with Custer. I was with Reno . . . but I saw him leave, plain as day.'' Sucking on his tooth, he nodded. "Plain as day, I watched big, brave Cap'n Matthews ride his horse over the hill . . . an' he kept on goin'. He shoulda been with Custer, dead on that hill, but instead he ran—and now he's the luckiest man in Deadwood. Right?''

Scofield's heart pounded so that he feared it might explode. He didn't know whether to laugh or shout, but he felt more like fainting. Inch by inch, he turned his golden head and sought Fox's tanned, handsome face in the depths of the crowd. "Too lucky,'' Scofield murmured at last, and smiled. "But not for long.''

Chapter Twenty-eight

September 15–17, 1876

WHEN SHE SAW FOX AND WATSON APPEAR AT THE top of the drive leading to their little group of homes, Maddie lifted her skirts and rushed to meet him. The sight of her husband wearing a slouch hat with the brim turned down gave her pause. No sooner had Fox swung down from Watson's back and caught Maddie up in his arms, than she drew the hat from his head.

"I don't like the look of that!" she exclaimed. "Are you in disguise, my dear?"

"Disguise might be too strong a word . . . but not entirely inaccurate," Fox allowed, with a dry smile, leading Watson to the simple stable he'd built for himself and the Averys. After closing the horse in his stall with fresh water and food, he tucked Maddie's hand into the crook of his arm and they walked together toward their log house.

"I've been on pins and needles waiting for you to come home ever since we learned that General Crook and his troops were down on Main Street," she said. "What a bother it is to be a respectable female in this town. The *femmes de joie* have front-row seats for every event of importance while I languish in the hinterlands, practically expiring with curiosity because I have a reputation to maintain. Such a lot of nonsense!"

"You had your chance to take up with Garnet Loomis back in July and you wanted nothing to do with her, as I recall." It was a pleasure to banter with his wife after the tension of the afternoon, so much so that Fox wished they never had to

357

come to the point. "Where is everyone, by the way? Are you the only member of this family who wants to hear about General Crook?"

She waved a delicate hand dismissingly. "Your mother and Gramma Susan are up to their elbows in wild plum jam. I made us a pie and started pacing." Maddie pointed through the pine trees that divided the properties. "They're all at the main house, filling the kitchen. Even Father and Benjamin have been pressed into service by Annie. She's put an apron on Father!"

He chuckled at that image, then asked. "And Sun Smile?"

"Well . . . I believe that she may have taken her reading primer off somewhere for a bit of solitude, but I'm sure that she's not within earshot. Even if she were, she wouldn't understand what you're talking about." Maddie was growing agitated. "Do stop asking questions and enlighten me!"

"All right." Leaning against a tree, Fox told her about the campaign that was now being called General Crook's "starvation march." He described the ill and demoralized men who had survived to come to Deadwood, and what he had heard of Crook's speech promising an end to the Indian raids on the Black Hills.

"What else?" Maddie pressed. She wondered why every time she met Fox's crisp blue eyes he looked away.

"You're almost too smart. It's tiring," he complained, with mock weariness.

"Yes, yes. Go on!"

"Titus went into the Grand Central Hotel and hung around long enough to chat with some of General Crook's staff. I had heard that Crook had managed to stir up a fight near Slim Buttes, and I wanted to learn the truth of it rather than the drunken rumors that spread through the badlands." Untying the blue kerchief, Fox rubbed the back of his neck and sighed. "Someone even claimed that Crazy Horse had been killed, but that's not so . . . although others did die in the fighting a few days ago."

Maddie's eyes stung with hot tears. "Oh, Fox, there were

so few of the Lakota still free. Why couldn't they be left in peace?''

"We knew that it would come to this—that all of them must either go to the agency or be killed. And, of course, Crazy Horse incites the army by those raids into the Hills. You and I may understand why he does it, but his continued rebellion just drives men like Crook around the bend.''

"Tell me what happened.''

They began to walk slowly toward their house. "From what Titus was able to learn,'' he explained, "the saddest part of this story is that the village Crook attacked was made up of Indians who had left Crazy Horse's people the day before and were on their way south to the agency.''

"Good God!'' Maddie stopped, her expression one of horror and sadness. "How many—''

"I don't know. Titus heard that there were thirty-seven tipis burned. Apparently the soldiers that attacked were part of an expedition Crook had sent to the Hills for supplies— led by a Colonel Mills. The troops were near death from starvation, so after they drove the Lakota people out of the village and into the bluffs, they decided to have a feast on the meat they found there. Meanwhile, the Indians sent runners for Crazy Horse. He came with a couple hundred warriors and attacked, but there were more soldiers—and then Crook arrived with close to two thousand troops and Crazy Horse was forced to retreat.'' Fox's voice was raw. He squeezed Maddie's hand before continuing, "I can only imagine what Crazy Horse felt as he watched Crook's men burn the village. The only bright spot in all this is the report that Crazy Horse kept up a constant harrassing action directed at Crook's rear flank all through the next day, until the army was well into the Hills. These troops can't figure out how the Indians got ahold of so many rifles. . . .'' Fox's brow arched with bittersweet satisfaction. "Unfortunately, there just weren't quite enough.''

"Do they know how many Lakota people were killed?'' Maddie asked softly.

He shook his head. "The killed and wounded are always

borne from the battlefield, even when the other warriors place themselves at risk.'' Gently Fox caressed her cheek. ''Crook was said to have lost twenty men . . . and of course, his troops claim that Crazy Horse lost many times that number, but we shall pray that the outcome was different.''

As they opened the door to their house and entered, neither Maddie nor Fox saw Sun Smile. .She was pressed to the back side of one of the pine trees that stood between the log house and the steep hillside overlooking Deadwood. Her skirts gathered close about her so that she wouldn't be seen, Sun Smile wept silently for the ravaged remains of the Lakota nation. She understood far more than anyone knew, and her grief and determination remained undimmed despite the adjustments she had been forced to make to the white way of life.

These people cared for her, Sun Smile knew, especially her father, but they could never fully understand her. The grief she continued to suffer over the murder of her husband was deeper than any of them guessed. Her heart could not truly begin to heal until she could strike a blow for the pride of the Lakota people and the honor of her husband, who had been cut down by the greedy white soldiers. Now some of those same white soldiers had destroyed more of what little her people had left . . . and they had come here. At last Sun Smile felt that there was a worthwhile reason the Great Spirit had brought her to this place.

A full moon shone in the black sky over Deadwood Gulch, washing the rowdy settlement with iridescent white light. It was the kind of night that made animals restless and gave people nightmares.

Fox had kicked off most of the quilts that covered the feather bed he and Maddie shared, but he still held his wife's hand as he slept. Sometimes he dreamed that he was asleep, then awoke and wondered if the moonlight and the strangely warm night were a dream, too.

Then there was the sound of a crash, splintering glass, and a thud against the braided rug in the parlor area of the log house. For a moment Fox refused to open his eyes, so certain was he that everything was part of an endless, eerie dream. Then Maddie shook his bare shoulder and he sat straight up in bed, alert and aware.

"I—I think someone threw a rock through our window!" Maddie whispered in panicked tones.

"You stay right here." He pushed her back against the pillows and fixed her with a hard, gleaming stare. "Don't move." He reached for his trousers, which were slung over the back of a nearby chair, and pulled them on. Then he lit the oil lamp and, carrying it, went through the house until he found the broken window and the rock lying on the rug amid a shower of broken glass.

Beside his favorite chair were a pair of moccasins that Sun Smile had given him that very week. He slipped them on and went to retrieve the rock, around which was tied a piece of string and a crumpled sheet of paper. By the wavering light of the oil lamp, Fox opened the note and read:

Dear Captain Matthews:
Did you really think you could get away with deserting the Seventh Cavalry just before the Battle of Little Bighorn? It was a shameful sight, you riding away while the rest of us prepared to risk our lives. I'm afraid that the past has caught up with you, Captain, and you'll have to pay a price. If you don't want all of Deadwood to know your sordid secret, you'll bring five thousand dollars in gold to Wild Bill Hickok's grave on Boot Hill. I'll meet you there at five o'clock tomorrow afternoon, September 16. Until then, I remain,

A Former Comrade-in-Arms

After looking outside and assuring himself that no one was lurking nearby, Fox carried the note and the oil lamp back to bed.

"It seems I'm being blackmailed," he told his wife in an acid voice. "But then, I can't say I'm surprised."

"Let me see that." Maddie scrambled over to the edge of

the bed and scanned the letter while Fox held the oil lamp. When she had finished, she forced herself to remain calm. "Fox, do you have any idea who this person might be?"

He shrugged. "It could be almost anyone. I'm not surprised that someone from the Seventh who survived Little Bighorn would have gone on to link up with General Crook's forces. Crook was fighting the Cheyenne and Lakota up on the Rosebud in the middle of June, just before I arrived, and it was Crook who was assigned to chase Sitting Bull after Little Bighorn. Probably some of those who were looking to avenge what they saw as a massacre when Custer and his men were killed went with Crook." A note of wry pleasure crept into his voice. "Of course, Sitting Bull eventually escaped into Canada . . . and it seems that even Slim Buttes wasn't what the army would call a decisive victory, happily enough. Crazy Horse is still alive and unbowed . . . and Crook has yet to capture a single Sioux."

"Fox, I know that you men see threats like this in terms of a bigger canvas," Maddie interjected a trifle impatiently, "but aside from Crook and Crazy Horse, what are *we* going to do?"

He yanked off his pants and returned to bed, gathering her into his arms. "Nothing, my darling. Nothing at all."

"But—"

"What choice do we have? I certainly cannot consider meeting the demands of a person like this, not only because it defies my honor, but also because it would never end. There would be more threats, more demands. Only Custer could verify that I didn't desert, and I can't kill this blackmailer. Even if I believed that were an acceptable solution, again it wouldn't be permanent. There will always be someone crawling out from under a rock, threatening to expose my *secret*." Tenderly, Fox caressed her face and hair. "Secrets are poison. I'm done hiding my past . . . I'm only sorry if you're hurt by anything that happens from now on."

Maddie clung to him, tears in the kiss she pressed to his mouth. "Oh, Fox, I am so proud to be your wife! I love you with all my heart, and I will stand beside you and take whatever life has in store for us." They lay down together then, snuggling as if their bodies had been created to fit this way. Maddie basked in the glow of their love. "This may sound naive," she said, "but I truly believe that God intends this marriage to be productive and happy as long as we continue to live as we should. He knows what your motives have been all along, including that day at Little Bighorn, and I do not believe that He will make us suffer while someone evil reaps the rewards."

Fox wrapped his arms around her lithe body and kissed the curve of her neck. "In my heart, I believe that, too," he said softly, adding with a hint of irony, "I have to believe it."

Graham Scofield jumped when the first knock sounded at the door of his room in the Grand Central Hotel. There were shadows under his eyes and his clothing was uncustomarily disheveled as he threw open the door and pulled Jeb Campbell into the room.

"Where have you been?" he snarled. "It's eight o'clock!"

"Whatsa matter? You afraid I run with the money?" Campbell, although cleaner than he'd been upon arriving in Deadwood, still stank. The new clothes Scofield had given him were already stained with tobacco juice, and he scratched in a way that suggested his trip to the bathhouse might not have eliminated all the vermin living in his hair and beard. "You sure you wrote Boot Hill in that note?" he pressed Scofield, looking around for the whiskey.

"Of course I wrote Boot Hill! If you could read, you would have seen it for yourself, you twit!" The younger man was on the verge of hysteria. "What are you saying? Where's the money?"

"He didn't come." Campbell drank down half a glass of whiskey, then sucked on his broken tooth. "There ain't no money."

Scofield sank down on a rickety chair, ran his hands through his blond hair, and shook his head from side to side. "But, you said you saw Fox pick up the rock and the note last night!'' he wailed. "He must have read it! Even if he were foolish enough to ignore those threats, his wife wouldn't want to have her precious reputation destroyed! How could he just . . . not *act*?''

"I know. I'da thought he'd come and try to shoot me or somethin'." Jeb moved the plug of tobacco from in his mouth and refilled his glass. It was hard for him to look at Scofield without laughing, for the gentleman's hair was standing straight up from his head. "Maybe we oughta kidnap his wife—show him we're not to be reckoned with. I saw her lyin' in their bed." He licked his cracked lips at the memory. "I wouldn't mind dippin' into that one bit, I kin tell ya.''

"Oh, shut up! I don't care what you do to Fox to get that money, but don't touch his wife, is that clear?'' Scofield had already decided that both Fox *and* Jeb Campbell would have to be disposed of before this episode was ended. Jeb Campbell had stumbled into Deadwood at the ideal moment to take care of Fox for him, but *he* would have to deal with Jeb personally; no one must be left to link him to this affair. And when it was all over, he would deal with Maddie . . . and the fortune she'd inherit as Fox's widow. The plan was so juicy, so perfect, that his heart thundered each time he pondered it. The trick now was to get this ignorant, repulsive jackass lathered up enough to follow through to the bloody end.

"I'm hungry," Jeb complained.

"I'll send you downstairs with enough gold dust to indulge in one of Aunt Lou Marchbanks's most lavish feasts, my good fellow, but first we must decide on a course of action." Graham began to pace in front of the desk, now and then glancing at the early drafts of the blackmail letter still spread out there.

"Whatcha gonna do?''

"Well, Jeb, I think we ought to stick to our original plan. I've told you that I can get even more money from Mrs. Matthews later, but she mustn't suspect that I'm involved." He waited for Campbell to nod in the way that meant he was reasonably confused but didn't want to admit it. "I believe that the only course of action left to us now is for you to confront Matthews at his house. Doesn't it make your blood boil to think how he ran away from that battle and yet is revered in this town as a leading citizen? Is that fair to a *true* hero like yourself, a man who was forced to eat his own horse and march for days through the rain and mud to get here . . . while Dan Matthews lives in luxury, eating the best food and sleeping with that beautiful woman?''

"No. That ain't fair!" Campbell agreed.

"Of *course* it isn't! And what about that Sioux squaw he brought to live in his house? He went out to their village and rubbed shoulders with Crazy Horse himself before he brought that squaw back here and subjected Deadwood to her presence!" Scofield continued to rant on until Jeb Campbell was red-faced with outrage and jealousy. Then the blond gentleman from Boston paused before the trooper and said in a low voice, "Are we going to allow a man like that to *ignore* us? He thinks that he doesn't have to answer to anyone! Well, tomorrow morning you're going to teach Dan Matthews a lesson he won't forget . . . and after he's given you every dime he has and begged you for mercy, just like Custer's men begged the Indians for mercy, you'll finish him off. I'll meet you then, we'll divide the money in your favor and I'll give you a horse, and you can ride away a rich man. Nobody'll have any idea at all who killed Daniel Matthews. How could they? Not even his family know you or your name."

Campbell nodded, then spit tobacco juice into a pitcherful of water on the bureau. "Yeah. Y'know, that sounds like a lotta fun. Maybe I'll kill that stupid squaw while I'm at it." He paused. "I never did like him. I guessed he was an Injin lover back in Montana, and he always acted like he was better'n the rest of us."

Trying not to betray his elation, Scofield murmured, "So, it's settled, then?"

"Sure. I'll take care of him—just get me a real big gun."

When Jeb Campbell had gone downstairs to eat supper,

Graham did a little dance of joy round and round his hotel room.

Unable to convince Maddie to take the rest of the family and leave Deadwood until he could be certain all danger had passed, Fox decided to stay home and guard them all himself. It was a tricky situation, because neither he nor Maddie wanted any of the others to know that he had an enemy right here in Deadwood. So they told the family that he and Titus were waiting for a shipment of hardware to arrive before construction of the sawmill could proceed, which therefore left him a few days of leisure.

As it happened, Gramma Susan cooked a pot of potato soup flavored with bits of bacon, and they all gathered around the long trestle table in the Avery kitchen for the noon meal. Stephen was feeling better and better, and today he took his lunch with the rest of the family, sitting between Sun Smile and Annie Sunday. Annie urged him to eat and to drink the tea with honey that she'd fixed for him. Maddie could only look on with amazement when he obeyed, docilely, blushing with pleasure at her attention. From across the table, Gramma Susan waggled her eyebrows up and down at her granddaughter, who smiled broadly in response.

For his part, Fox laughed at Benjamin's antics and chatted with the rest as though he hadn't a care in the world. Mention was made of a treaty on the verge of being ratified that would formally give up the Black Hills to the whites, and Fox repeated the news that Captain Jack Crawford had signed on as a scout for Crook. Then, in a lighter moment, Fox reported that Watson seemed to have made friends with Titus's new mule. Susan was passing around pieces of wild plum pie when the boom of a gunshot brought everyone up short. Everyone froze, waiting to see what would happen next.

In a gesture of tender gallantry, Fox pressed Maddie's trembling fingers to his mouth, looking at her under his lashes. "My darling, have faith," he whispered, then said to the family, "I'll see what's happened. I suggest that the rest of you remain here until I return." Rising, he smiled into Maddie's anxious eyes, kissed the top of his mother's head, and left.

He went out the back door, walked around the house, then checked through the pine trees. There he discovered a deranged-looking man standing in front of his house, clutching a shiny new six-shooter.

"Can I do something for you?"

Jeb whirled around at the sound of Fox's voice, his face simultaneously registering rage, glee, and terror. "Well, well, if it ain't ol' Cap'n Matthews hisself! You been doin' pretty good for a yellow-livered coward, ain'tcha?"

"I'm not sure I'd put it quite that way," Fox remarked. As he stared at the man, his memory clicked and a grim smile touched his mouth. "Ah . . . It's Campbell, isn't it? How did you happen upon me here in Deadwood?"

Jeb shrugged. "Long story, and I ain't got a lotta time to waste with the likes of you. A squaw up at Slim Buttes told me about you bein' here. You musta done somethin' to make Miss Runs Away pretty durned mad, 'cause she's lookin' for yer hide, Cap'n! When she tole me yer name, I knowed who you was. I seen you ride away that day at Little Bighorn . . . but I didn't know where you went until that squaw told me." He cocked the gun and pointed it at Fox. "Now then, you git me the money I asked for before. I ain't too happy about waitin' fer you last night and you not comin'! These past few weeks've been pretty nasty, what with killing Injins all over Montana and Dakota, eatin' my horse to stay alive, and then havin' to walk all the way into the Black Hills in a rainstorm. I had better things t'do last night then sit around waitin' on you!" Jeb paused to suck on his tooth, then spit out a stream of tobacco juice through the gap.

"Who put you up to this?" Fox asked.

"Don't know what yer talkin' about."

"Well, you'll have to tell your friend, whoever he is, that there won't be any money. I will not be blackmailed, Private Campbell." Fox considered explaining that he *hadn't* deserted but realized that it would be a waste of breath.

Jeb turned redder and redder as he took in the refusal to

pay. Clutching the revolver with both hands, he snarled, "Oh, you won't, huh? Then I'll just kill you, the way you shoulda been killed alongside Custer, and I'll take yer money—and I'll take that squaw yer hidin' here, too!"

"Would you really shoot an unarmed man?" Fox asked quietly, knowing the answer and yet oddly unafraid.

"Damned right I would! Cowards like you deserve to die. I'm doin' this town a favor!" Squinting at Fox through bloodshot eyes, he pointed the gun and prepared to pull the trigger.

Boom! The rifle blast echoed through the canyon. Jeb Campbell dropped his gun, staring down as he watched blood gush from the place where his stomach had been.

Fox turned, expecting Stephen or even Maddie. Instead he saw Sun Smile holding Avery's rifle, her expression determined and satisfied as she surveyed the dead body sprawled across the yard. The others came rushing out of the house then, and when Maddie saw what had happened, she gave herself permission to weep with relief.

"At first we didn't even notice that she'd gone," she told Fox as he held her close. "We had gathered at the kitchen window, trying to see through the pine trees, and apparently Sun Smile slipped away, got the rifle from Father's bedroom, and went out the front door. We were horrified when we saw her at the edge of the trees, aiming the gun . . ."

"Sun Smile saved my life," Fox said, gazing at the Lakota woman. "Thank you."

"It was . . . justice, for my husband, for my people," she replied in careful English. It was the first time they had heard her speak a full sentence. "Now I can go home." She gave her father, Annie Sunday, and the others a bittersweet smile. "You have been good to me . . . but this is not home. I must be with my people."

Fox, meanwhile, was crouching next to the lifeless body of Jeb Campbell. He drew a gold pocket watch from the man's trousers and examined it carefully. The pieces were falling into place.

* * *

Everyone waited up for Fox that night, even though Maddie would have preferred to talk with him privately in their own home.

When he entered the Avery parlor, he found that a fire had been lit. Sun Smile, dressed in her soft, newly cleaned doeskin dress, with her hair plaited neatly into two long braids, wore a look of contentment. She appeared to be ready to depart immediately.

Benjamin, in his bathrobe, was jumping around the house like a monkey, excited by the drama yet furious that he had missed the actual spectacle of Sun Smile shooting the villain. However, when Fox came into the house, Susan collared her grandson and drew him down next to her on the settee.

Stephen greeted his son-in-law, while Annie Sunday restrained herself from rushing to him, and Maddie was glad when he took a wing chair and drew her down on his lap. The expression on his chiseled face told her that the danger was passed. More than anything else, she wanted to take him home to their bed.

"What happened?" They all seemed to speak at the same time, and Fox chuckled.

"I rousted out Seth Bullock, our new sheriff. He had a little trouble believing that Graham Horatio Scofield the Third could possibly have engineered all this, but he agreed to accompany me to Scofield's hotel room." He smiled as Maddie twined her arms around his neck and fussed with the curls that touched his collar. "I wish you all could have been there to see Mr. Scofield's face when he threw open the door and saw *me* standing there!"

"How did you prove that he was involved?" Stephen asked. "The pocket watch alone might be enough for us, but—"

"Well, I had showed Seth the blackmail note, pointing out that an illiterate weasel like Jeb Campbell could not possibly have composed such a letter. As it turned out, Scofield did the rest for us. The desk in the hotel room was littered with various versions of the note." Fox shrugged. "I'm sorry to report that the Boston Scofields now have a blight on their impeccable family tree. Graham is in jail as we speak, awaiting transport to Yankton, where he will be tried for various crimes.''

"When may I go?'' Sun Smile asked softly.

Everyone turned to look at her. Stephen's eyes were poignant with regret. "Someone will have to take you,'' he said. "Do you want to go to the agency? I'm not certain what conditions are now; we have heard that rations have been held back until your people agree to turn over the Black Hills. It's a terrible thing for our government to do, and I wouldn't want you to suffer, my dear. . . .''

"The paper will be signed,'' she said. "Winter is coming. My people will have to trade this sacred ground for food. What choice have the whites given us?'' Sun Smile was firm. "It is best that I go to the agency. I will be able to teach my people many white ways. Our lives are changed now . . . forever. It can never be again as it once was.''

Everyone was silent for a short while, then Annie Sunday said, "Stephen, I think that we ought to share our news.'' She sounded almost shy. "Perhaps we can take Sun Smile ourselves. . . .''

"Yes!'' he cried, brightening. "An excellent notion, my dear!'' Stephen rose, looked around the parlor, and said, "I want to announce to you all that Annie has done me the considerable honor of agreeing to become my wife. We intend to marry as soon as possible and then travel East for a wedding trip, remaining in Washington and Philadelphia through the winter.''

After the chorus of surprised questions and congratulations had died down, it was agreed that Stephen and Annie would escort Sun Smile through the Black Hills to the Indian agency in northwestern Nebraska. From there they would continue on their way via riverboat and railroad. More discussion led to an invitation to Susan and Benjamin to join the newlyweds on this journey, but their refusals were immediate. Benjamin had new friends and—as Maddie pointed out firmly—should not miss school now that Deadwood had a teacher, and Susan stated flatly that she was too old for another arduous trip across America so soon after the one she'd made to Deadwood.

Changes were occurring so suddenly that Maddie felt dizzy. First the shock of Deadwood, and the challenge of getting to know her father all over again. Then she'd had to adjust to her new identity as Fox's wife, to the home she shared with him, and to the presence of Annie Sunday and Sun Smile. Now it seemed that so much was going to be changing yet again! When she and Fox rose to leave, and she bent to kiss her grandmother good night, Susan patted her cheek with a crinkled hand.

"We'll be fine here this winter, you and Fox and Benjamin and I." The old woman winked almost imperceptibly. "To tell you the truth, I'm rather looking forward to a bit of peace and quiet . . . and when those two come back from their wedding trip next spring, *I'm* going to move into that sweet little cottage!"

Maddie looked over at her father, realizing that the true cause of her anxiety was the fear left over from her childhood that he might *not* come back. Stephen's eyes met hers, begging her to come to him, and she did. Sitting in the circle of his arm, it came to Maddie what a tumultuous, confusing few weeks they have lived through since July. So much had been transformed since that first glimpse of Deadwood. . . .

"Madeleine, your mother would be so proud of you if she were here," Stephen told her gently.

"I don't know—" Maddie flushed. "These days, I'm not very much like the lady she raised me to be, but I am much happier than I ever dreamed I could be before we left Philadelphia, and it's not just because I'm in love with Fox. I'm happy because I finally realized that doing things properly and having things *look* the way they ought doesn't have very much to do with heart-deep happiness. I had to come to Deadwood to find that out."

"My dear, do you remember what you used to call me when you were a very little girl?" Smiling ruefully, he added, "You learned to be quite dignified at an early age, I realize, but perhaps you haven't forgotten. . . ."

"Papa," she whispered thickly. "I used to call you Papa."

For a moment Stephen Avery's throat tightened so that he couldn't speak. "Yes, that's it exactly. How I loved to hear you calling 'Papa,' and to see that light in your eyes, Maddie dear. Would you consider calling me that again, after Annie and I come home in the spring and we all settle in here for the rest of our lives?"

Eyes stinging, Maddie nodded. She realized suddenly that this was all about recapturing the innocent trust she'd known as a little girl. "Yes . . . Papa."

A short time later Maddie and Fox strolled through the row of pine trees to their own home. When she inhaled deeply, the force of joy that welled up from her very soul was so powerful that she had to stop a moment and close her eyes. Overhead, above Deadwood Gulch, the moon was still round and luminous, the sky thick with glittering stars.

Fox wrapped his arms around her from behind and rested his cheek against her silky hair. "Someday, Fireblossom, I'm going to build you a wonderful house on this spot," he said in a low, compelling voice. "It will be a place where you can make dreams come true. We'll have a stone tower, and a music room, and polished paneled walls carved from exotic woods, and a bathtub painted with gold leaf that's big enough for both of us and has all the hot running water we want. You'll have a library all your own . . . and a big porch with a swing and wicker furniture . . ."

Caught up in the dreamy tone of his voice, Maddie leaned back against him. "Don't forget the gardens," she teased.

"We'll import trees and flowers from the Kew Gardens in London," Fox promised solemnly.

"Do you know the best part of all?" Turning in her husband's embrace, Maddie snuggled against the starched front of his favorite ticking-striped shirt.

"I'm waiting for you to tell me, love."

"The best part of all is that we'll be just as happy whether we have that house and garden and bathtub and porch swing or not. All we need is our feather bed and what we make together in moments like these."

''And we can go on making them forever,'' Fox finished. Under the stars, he lifted Maddie off the ground and held her thus for a full minute . . . before capturing her mouth in a kiss that seemed even sweeter than the one before.

Afterword

  REST ASSURED, DEAR READERS, THAT I STROVE FOR historical accuracy in this book, and I cross-checked the often dubious sources regarding the history of Deadwood and the Black Hills. I enjoyed reading personal accounts (often derived from oral histories) of life in 1876 Deadwood or Custer's last stand, or tales from those who knew Crazy Horse or Wild Bill Hickok, but of course one must take these with a grain of salt.

  It's important to me to make my characters live, but I regard the factual canvas of history as an exciting backdrop for my stories, and I feel it would be cheating to rearrange what actually happened. Besides, why tinker with a summer that included Custer at Little Bighorn, the arrival of Wild Bill Hickok and Calamity Jane in Deadwood, Hickok's murder, the August visit of Crazy Horse and his people to Bear Butte, the death of Preacher Smith, and the "starvation march" of General Crook's troops—which included the Battle of Slim Buttes and ended in (where else?) Deadwood!

  I've followed authentic dates as closely as I could make them match among sources. Word really did reach Deadwood on July 20 of the battle at Little Bighorn, Sol Star and Seth Bullock didn't get to town until August 1, the day before Hickok's death, General Crook made his speech from the balcony of the Grand Central Hotel on September 15, and so on.

  Most of us know that the Lakota people did not fare well in the months following the end of this book. The Black Hills were signed away to the whites in October, and the treaty was ratified in February 1877. That spring, Crazy Horse led into Camp Robinson, Nebraska, the last thousand Indians who had continued to hold out against agency life. He had run out of choices, for his people were starving and being hunted much like the buffalo that had once provided for all their needs.

Soon after his arrival at the white fort, Crazy Horse was stabbed to death in a scuffle with soldiers who tried to arrest him. The Lakota nation's age of glory on the Great Plains was at an end.

In the meantime, I am on to another book—the story of Fox and Maddie's daughter, Shelby Matthews, and her involvement in Buffalo Bill's own town of Cody, Wyoming. Our hero, Geoffrey Weston, the fifteenth earl of Sandhurst, is conned into going to Cody by Buffalo Bill himself during a tour of England with his Wild West Show. This book is just full of great fun and adventure, and I'm having a ball writing it!

Thank you all so much for your constant support and letters from all over the world! They mean more than you can ever know, and it's important for me to hear what you enjoy the most. Jim, Jenna, and I all send you our best regards!

Cynthia Wright Hunt
P.O. Box 862
Elk Point, South Dakota 57025